The Nick of Time

'*The Nick of Time* is a thoroughly engrossing and compulsively readable novel; an impressive achievement'
– Peter Burton, *Gay Times*

Praise for *Prodigies*:

'One of our great writers, of the calibre of Graham Greene and Nabokov'
– Beryl Bainbridge, BBC *Today* programme

'That rare phenomenon, a novel by a gnarled old literary presence that extends rather than consolidates his reputation. Very good
– D. J. Taylor, *Independent*

'A compelling work of fiction. It is often frightening (in its depictions of illness and savagery), often, in its exposure of colonialist assumptions, ruthless in its attack, and yet it is lit up by poetic and heartfelt tenderness'
– Paul Binding, *Independent on Sunday*

'A wonderfully rich and absorbing story, it surges with vitality . . . all the exuberance and moral seriousness of the great novels of the 19th century'
– Allan Massie, *Scotsman*

'Cool and elegant mastery of detail and description, but it is his venture into an area of human darkness that resonates with chilling and telling truth'
– Elizabeth Buchan, *Daily Mail*

'All the craftsmanship and descriptive richness of a Victorian classic'
– *The Times*

'I would recommend it to anyone between now and posterity who cares for adventurousness in writing as well as adventure'
– David Hughes, *Spectator*

'Defies all expectations in a thoroughly modern and audacious way . . . the author's prose is enriched by a poetic flair equal to his exotic locales'
– Richard Zimler, *The Literary Review*

'The world of European high society is evoked in vivid detail, a richness continued in the Egyptian and Sudanese chapters . . . an absorbing account of an almost obsessive personality and the consequences of her wilfulness'
– Graeme Woolaston, Glasgow *Herald*

'A pageant of a book from a master of his craft'
– David Hill, Auckland *Weekend Herald*

The Nick of Time

Francis King

A

ARCADIA BOOKS
LONDON

Arcadia Books Ltd
15–16 Nassau Street
London W1W 7AB
www.arcadiabooks.co.uk

First published in the United Kingdom 2003
Copyright © Francis King 2003

A catalogue record for this book is available from the British Library.

ISBN 1-900850-78-8

Typeset in Iowan Old Style by Northern Phototypesetting Co. Ltd, Bolton
Printed in Finland by WS Bookwell.

Arcadia Books distributors are as follows:

in the UK and elsewhere in Europe:
Turnaround Publishers Services
Unit 3, Olympia Trading Estate
Coburg Road
London N22 6TZ

in the USA and Canada:
Consortium Book Sales and Distribution, Inc.
1045 Westgate Drive
St Paul, MN 55114-1065

in Australia:
Tower Books
PO Box 213
Brookvale, NSW 2100

in New Zealand:
Addenda
Box 78224
Grey Lynn
Auckland

in South Africa:
Quartet Sales and Marketing
PO Box 1218
Northcliffe
Johannesburg 2115

Arcadia Books: *Sunday Times* Small Publisher of the Year 2002/03

To Laura Pope
for gallantry

Chapter I

'It was as though God had sent him to me,' Meg said to her sister Sylvia, about her first encounter with Mehmet. 'More like the Devil,' Sylvia had thought but not said.

Meg had been coming home from the Tesco at which her Nigerian neighbour Blossom worked with an irrepressible, smiling energy, her stubby fingers with their long, red-lacquered nails passing purchases speedily across and then no less speedily picking out the change from the till. 'Do you want any help with the chair?' Blossom had asked; and Meg had replied, as she always replied, 'No, that's all right, dear, I'll be fine.' She did not care, as she often complained to people, to be under an obligation. It was a matter of pride to manage on her own.

But that day the chair had suddenly given up the ghost as she was about to move out on to the pedestrian crossing. A car had halted for her, and the driver, a middle-aged man with grey, untidy, shoulder-length hair falling over his jacket collar, had waited, turning his head from side to side, an expression of exasperation on his face, as he had deliberately avoided looking at this wretched lump of a woman who did not seem to know how to get her wheelchair to work. Oh, for Christ's sake! Couldn't that biddy who had begun to cross the road herself give the poor creature a hand? These days there was no solidarity between people, it was a case of everyone for himself. He had begun to wonder if he should not get out of the car and give the chair a shove. It was then that a tall man, his muscular shoulders tensed back and his large head thrust forward as though into a buffeting wind, had come striding down the pavement, halted, said something. Perhaps he would help . . .

What Mehmet said, stooping down as though deafness were another of Meg's disabilities, was 'You have problem, madam?'

'Well, yes, I have.' Meg's crossness with the chair sounded like a crossness with him. 'This bloody chair's conked out again. It can't be the battery. It was charged only yesterday. No, I lie, the day before yesterday.'

'Not working?'

What a stupid question! Of course it wasn't working! Why else would she be stranded here, like a kipper on a fishmonger's counter, with that car and now another car behind it waiting for her? 'No, it's not bloody working.'

'I push then, madam. Yes?'

'Yes.' She all but added: 'Yes, bloody push!'

He pushed her up Kingsland Road and along Gordon Road and then into Melmount Terrace.

'Now right at Flatt Road.'

'Flatt Road?'

'Yes, it's an odd name for this road. It's not flat at all. First it goes up, then it goes down, then up again. Like life. Except that life ends by going down, down, down. So where do you live?'

'Nowhere.'

'Nowhere? Do you mean you're sleeping rough?' He certainly didn't look as if he'd been sleeping rough, with those well-polished shoes of his and those well-creased charcoal-grey trousers.

He laughed. 'Not yet. But maybe tonight. My landlord turn me out and so now I look.'

'Turned you out! You mean today? Without any warning? I don't know how it is in your country but a landlord can't do that here. You ought to take advice. The Citizens' Advice Bureau. Do you know of the Citizens' Advice Bureau? There's one – or there used to be one – in the high street, just next to that Ko-Hi-Noor tandoori place.'

She had twisted round in the chair to look up at him. He frowned, bit his lower lip, shook his head. 'Difficult, madam. Complicated.'

'How complicated? I can't see anything complicated about it. You're within your rights to demand proper notice. Perhaps as a foreigner you didn't realize that. But I'm telling you, as anyone else could tell you, being a tenant in this country, you have a right to proper notice.'

'Difficult, madam,' he repeated. 'Very difficult.'

She knew that he did not wish to discuss the matter, she would get nothing more out of him. Eventually she would learn to live with the resigned knowledge that he would never share more than a sliver of his life with her, whereas she would eventually come to share her whole life, such as it now was, with him.

'This it?'

'This is it. That porch needs repair and the whole shebang needs repainting but do the bloody Council care? Not on your life.'

Meg, still sitting, faced out onto the street, as he effortfully dragged her chair backwards up the nine steps to the front door of the block. The door of her flat was too narrow for the chair and so, as she explained to him, she had to leave it either in the old coalshed in the basement or in the hallway to the block. When left in the hallway it had more than once been vandalized. Even worse than finding the cushion ripped with what must have been a penknife or jackknife and the rubbish of plastic containers, a half-eaten sandwich and two beer cans placed on it, had been coming on that insulting message FUCKING CRIPLE, sprayed on to the back where the battery was housed. Whoever sprayed that didn't even know how to spell cripple properly. People of that sort were bloody ignorant.

In the hallway, she put out a hand. 'Give me a hoist, there's a dear. Once I'm on my feet I can manage.' She scrabbled in her large, worn handbag and pulled out a bunch of keys, most of them to suitcases long since jettisoned or to flats long since vacated. 'But open the door first. My crutches are just behind it – just by the spider, that thingummy where the coats and hats go.'

He opened the door; but instead of going in for the crutches, he said: 'I lift you, madam.'

'Oh, no, no!' She was appalled. 'No need for that. I can manage with the crutches. Mr Bagley usually gets them for me.

We have a porter here, you know, very grand, Mr Bagley he is. I warn him what time I'll be back and usually he hears me and comes up from his basement. I warned him today. I'm surprised he's not here. I can ring for him, he never minds – that bell over there.' She pointed.

'I lift you. Why worry Mr Bagley?'

He stooped and at once, before you knew it, she was up there, like a baby, in his arms. She let out a wail, then ordered 'Put me down, put me down!' If she had been able to do so, she would have kicked her legs in angry frustration.

'Through here?'

'Oh, very well. Yes, through there!'

It was a small room, crowded with the overlarge Victorian and Edwardian furniture that had come to her as her half share on the death of her mother, a German who had married an English soldier met, while he was part of the army of occupation, in the immediate aftermath of the war. The other half share had gone to her sister, Sylvia, who had promptly decided – or whose la-di-da husband had decided – that it was 'hideous' and had therefore at once sold it for a song to some totter who advertised in their local rag.

Mehmet wrinkled his nose. Meg knew why he did so. There was a sour smell in the room, as though milk had been spilled in it. Meg never noticed the smell, except for a few seconds after she had come into the flat following a period, however brief, out of it, but she knew from their expressions that other people did. 'Here?' he asked, indicating a vast armchair, with a soiled lace antimacassar draped over its back and a worn cushion, embroidered by Meg's mother with a now almost invisible bunch of poppies, placed over the broken springs of its seat. As those springs dug into her bottom, Meg would experience a perverse comfort, even pleasure, which she could not have explained.

'Yes, that's my perch.'

He lowered her gently.

'I'm quite a weight. As I daresay you discovered. I used to be a mere slip of a thing – if anorexia had been invented then, people would have said I was suffering from it – but as soon as this bloody MS hit me, I began to put on weight.' She wriggled, hunching up her shoulders and smoothing down her rucked-up skirt with her hands, as she settled herself. 'I never stop eating now. It's the boredom, not greed.' She pointed to a packet out of which chocolate biscuits had spilled across the low table beside the armchair. 'Look at those. I keep them there, a constant temptation. And then I munch and munch and munch.' Her usually cheerful face darkened. 'Well, what else is there for me to do? You wouldn't believe this now but I was once well known – well, at any rate known if not *well* known – as a formation dancer. I appeared oh, three times in *Come Dancing* on telly. Latin American – that was my speciality. Here – what about a cup of tea? Or coffee? Foreigners often prefer coffee. It's only Nes, I'm afraid, nothing fancy.'

'I must go look for a room. When I see you, I go to Greek agent in the high street.'

'Oh, keep away from a Greek!' she cried out. 'He'll be sure to diddle you.' Then, appalled, she asked: 'You're not by any chance Greek yourself, are you?'

'No, madam.' He laughed.

'No, I suppose not, not with that pale skin of yours. But that hair of yours makes you look a bit Mediterranean.' *Of Mediterranean appearance.* They often used that phrase on *Crime Watch* when describing someone with that kind of thick, black, tightly-curled hair.

He hesitated. 'I – I am Albanian, madam. Student from Kosovo.'

'Albanian! Well, fancy that! Mr Bagley and his wife went to Albania for a holiday only a few months ago. But they didn't really enjoy it. I don't like to tell you that, seeing that Albania's your country, but that's the truth. They thought they'd found a bargain – they're always looking for bargains, those two. Not much more than three hundred quid each for the week, all found. But the hotel was only half built, there was a main road just beneath their window, the lavvie was blocked, and both of them picked up some sort of tummy bug. Oh, and they said that their room smelt of sheep. Can you imagine?'

'Where was this?'

'Oh, I can't remember.' She paused, finger to lower lip, brows drawn together.' Let me think. Shkoddy something. Something like that,' she eventually got out.

'*Shkodra?*'

At first she was dubious, drawing her eyebrows together and pursing her mouth. Then she decided: 'Yes, yes, that was it! Do you know it?'

'I been there. My auntie live there. I am surprised your – your friends not happy there. Town very beautiful. Castle, Rozafat castle, very beautiful. One day I want to go back. See beautiful castle again.'

'Well, maybe they were unlucky,' she conceded. 'Or maybe they weren't interested in castles. You know how it is. When you go abroad, it's all a matter of luck. Well, for the matter of that, all life is a matter of luck. Isn't it?'

He nodded.

'Now come on – let's have that tea or coffee! Do you think you can make whatever you prefer? Then I won't have to struggle. Because it *is* a struggle – worse luck. I'm having one of my bad spells. It's strange, I'm nearly always worse in the autumn. I get these cramps all the time – it's either the cramps or the aches.'

As he got the tea, she shouted out directions to him, while at the same time peering at the television screen, on which an obese elderly man and an emaciated young one were exchanging camp insults as they flounced around in a demonstration of how to make *Boeuf Stroganoff*. She had pointed at the set and told him to 'be a dear and press that button over there' before he had gone into the stifling little kitchen, its sink brimming with the crockery and cutlery that would be washed the next day by Fiona, the cheerful home help.

'Let it stand a little. I don't like the gnat's pee that my sister and brother-in-law favour. You don't mind it strong, do you?'

He shook his head, smiling in bemused tolerance.

She took the teacup from him, when she had eventually decided that the tea had brewed long enough. She sipped and nodded: 'Fine. Just as I like it.' She reached out for a chocolate biscuit, replaced it and then picked it up again. 'I shouldn't but it's less harmful than a fag. That's my other addiction, cigarettes. D'you smoke?'

'Sorry. Yes.'

'You look too healthy to be a smoker. I sometimes wonder whether I caused my MS with too much smoking. But the doctor told me that's out of the question.' She munched at the biscuit. Then she said: 'Well, I suppose he must know. He's not an ordinary doctor, not my usual one, but this specialist, a Chinaman. I see him at University College Hospital every two months. He must get sick of seeing me. I certainly get sick of seeing him.'

'Another cup, madam?'

'Please.' Then, as he took the cup from her, she said: 'Oh, do stop all that madam business. You'd think I was running a knocking shop. Call me Meg. I'm Mrs Towling – if we have to be formal – but just call me Meg, as everyone does.'

'Thank you, Mrs Towling. Meg,' he corrected himself with a laugh.

'And you are?'

He pointed to himself. 'Me?'

'Your name. What do I call you?'

He hesitated. 'Mehmet.'

'Just Mehmet?'

Again he hesitated. 'Mehmet – Ahmeti.'

'Mehmet.' She savoured the word, as she had been savouring the chocolate biscuit. 'I like that. Somehow it suits you. Don't you think it suits you?'

He shrugged.

'*I* think it does. I don't know why.' She put down her teacup. She looked closely at him, taking in the elegant arch of the eyebrows above the long-lashed black eyes, the slightly hooked nose, and the fleshy, almost pouting lips. 'Are Albanians Christians then? Forgive my ignorance.'

'Some. Most Muslim.'

'And you?'

He again pointed at his chest. 'Me?' Then he nodded. 'As little boy, I am cut.' He made a gesture of manipulating scissors with his right hand and laughed.

'*Cut?*' She frowned for a second, then joined in his laughter. 'Oh, I see. Yes.'

'But I am not real Muslim. In my country people say "*Ku është shpata, është feja*". That mean "Where sword is, there religion is." Religion bad, bad.'

'Oh, not always! You can't say that.'

'In my country, yes. Always. Always bad. Make trouble. That is why leave.'

For a while she pondered, gazing at the worn kelim at her feet. Then she jerked up her head.

'Now what are we going to do about you?'

'Me? About *me*?'

'Where are you going to live?'

'I find something. I always find something.'

'You mean – you've had this problem before?'

'Sometimes. Two or three times. Landlords here . . .' He put his head on one side, smiled at her. She noticed for the first time that one of his eye teeth was broken. Pity. His smile was otherwise so attractive.

'Oh, I know, landlords can be villains. And the worst, I'm sorry to say, are the foreign ones. The Council gave a Kurdish refugee and his wife a flat upstairs – much nicer than this one, four rooms, a balcony, lavvie separate from bath. And now – believe me or not – they've become landlords themselves and there are seven, yes, *seven* other people living there, all Kurds of course. A complete ramp! Someone should tell the Council. But of course no one does. And if someone did, the Council wouldn't take a blind bit of notice.'

There was a silence, as she held another biscuit in a hand, now to suck and now to gnaw at it, like a child. 'I've been thinking,' she said at last.

He leaned forward. The light, which was necessary in the dark little room even on an afternoon of autumn sunshine, glinted on his hair. His hands were clasped together and she noticed, with satisfaction, that they were clean and uncallused, the nails well tended, and that on the fourth finger of the right he wore a large ring. One could see at once that his background was good.

'Yes. What you thinking, Meg?'

'Why don't you become *my* lodger?' When she had said that, wholly on an impulse, she was as astonished as he was.

He stared at her, with obvious pleasure. 'You think good idea?'

'Yes. Why not? It's not much of a room. You can have a look at it. The original idea was that my sister should have it and take care of me after – well, after the person who had been taking care of me upped and scarpered. But then she met this man – he's her second husband, her first died, cancer, poor chap – and he had a flat of his own, up in Highgate, really posh.' Mehmet was staring at her, saying nothing; but that pleasure was still there on his pale, handsome face, so that she felt suddenly joyful, as though she were about to set off, now, now, on some wonderful journey, of the kind that she no longer even contemplated, since getting over to Tesco or the newsagents had become more than enough of a journey for her. 'I'd not charge you much. My sister tells me that I could get as much as, oh, fifty, sixty quid a week for that room, but if you were prepared to give me a hand now and then, I'd, well, I'd charge you, say, thirty . . . Well, how about it?'

As though on an impulse, he jumped to his feet. 'Maybe I can see the room?'

'Of course you can! No one wants to buy a pig in a poke. It's over there, down the passage, first on the right. The room at the end is where I hang out. Go on! Have a dekko! It's rather dark, looking out on the well, and at present it's full of junk and there are things in the wardrobe . . .'

She did not say that the things in the wardrobe were clothes belonging to her husband, a purser on a cruise ship, who had gone off one day for work on a cruise of the Caribbean and had never returned. Her sister Sylvia had made enquiries of the firm, only to learn that, the cruise over, he had totally vanished, leaving with them an address which turned out to be false, so that inevitably his employment had come to an end. With a mixture of sentimentality and superstition she had hung on to the clothes, even from time to time dragging them out of the wardrobe and giving them a brush when she felt strong enough to do so, despite constant urgings from Sylvia to chuck them out. 'He's not going to come back, my girl. You'd better face up to that. And good riddance!'

'Well, what do you think of it?', she shouted out to him, at the moment when he had begun to weave his way through yellowing stacks of newspapers, a pile of cooking utensils, packing cases, and broken bits of furniture until he had at last reached the threadbare, brown velvet curtains, faded at the edges, which he then tugged back before throwing up the window to let in a sharply invigorating blast of cold air. This room also had a smell; but it was not that one of long since spilled milk but a strangely earthy one, as of rotting vegetation and damp soil under overgrown trees in a sunless corner of a garden. He leaned far out of the window, breathing in deeply, then closed it, tugged the curtains back, and re-emerged.

'Well, what do you think of it?' she repeated as he appeared in the doorway of the sitting room. 'You could give it a lick of paint. Did you see the washbasin? It's got its own washbasin and h and c. It's also got a radiator – though it began to leak the last time I put it on. We can tell Mr Bagley about that. He's supposed to see to things of that kind. The h and c and the heating are both provided by the Council. Well?'

He nodded, he smiled; and immediately she once again experienced a buffeting of joy, as though she were standing on a quayside, a salt wind blowing in her face, before embarking on that wonderful voyage that she would now never take.

'Do you really think you'd be happy here?'

'Why not? Much better room than room I leave. Why not?' he repeated and then he burst into laughter, as though he had caught the infection of her joy.

'As I said, it needs a lick of paint. But you could see to that, couldn't you? You look like the do-it-yourself kind. And it hasn't been hoovered for, oh, donkey's years. But if I give my Fiona – my home help – a little present, I'm sure she'd be only too happy to make it spick and span for you after having finished with looking after me. She's a nice soul, not all that bright but always willing to oblige. I know you and she'll hit it off.'

'I can hoover room myself.'

'I'd always heard that Muslim men thought housework was only for women.'

He smiled. 'I live for long time in England.'

'Well, if that's fixed, you'd better run along and get your things. Are they at your former place?'

He hesitated. 'No. I leave them with friend. Safer.'

'Is the – the friend far from here?' She wondered whether the friend was male or female, English or Albanian, but shrank from asking, in case he thought it nosey of her.

'Not far.'

'Can you carry them over?'

'Maybe.' He was dubious. 'Maybe I make two journeys. Or take taxi.'

If he was thinking of a taxi, then clearly he could not be skint.

As he was about to go out of the room, he turned back. 'Oh, Mrs, Mrs –'

'Meg.'

'Yes. Meg. I wonder – you – you want – want deposit?' He was embarrassed, poor love, she could see that at once.

She waved a hand in the air. 'That's not necessary. I have a feeling I can trust you.' She had said that to other people in the past, and her trust had been abused. But, as Sylvia often told her, she would never learn.

'But if you wish – '

'No, no! I trust you, I trust you!' She lunged out for the handbag on the table before her. 'Here! Take my keys. Then you can let yourself in. This – ' she held it up – 'is the Banham for the front door of the block. And this' – she held up another, smaller key – 'is the Yale for the door of this flat. Tomorrow I'll look out an extra pair of keys I've got put away somewhere. Or you can have another pair cut. Do you think you can manage?'

'Of course! No problem.'

When he had gone, Meg poured herself another cup of tea. By now it was not merely black and bitter but also lukewarm. But she did not mind. She sipped and sipped again, holding the breakfast cup up to her lips in both hands and then sipping greedily from it. Its design of large marigolds was a Clarice Cliff one, though she did not know that, having bought it long ago, soon after her marriage, in a Rainham junk shop. She had not experienced such joy for ages and ages – not since there had been that flash on the telly that Eric's ship was on fire, somewhere in the North Sea, and she had foolishly jumped to the conclusion that she was never going to see him again, and then, lo and behold, the Swedes had rescued everyone and in no time at all he had been flown back to Gatwick and there he was, safe and sound, and she was holding him in her arms, half crying and half laughing, while he kept saying 'Easy, girl! Easy!' That was before the MS had been diagnosed of course, although even then she was getting those weird pins and needles in her fingers and toes and that feeling that she was wearing a too-tight pair of stockings.

As Meg now waited for Mehmet to return, she began to go over in her mind everything that had happened before that last conversation that she and Eric had had together. Her reverie began with the visit that the two of them had paid to University College Hospital, where that specialist, the Chinaman, with the thick glasses and outsize trainers below trousers that were too long for his extremely short legs, just a boy he had seemed, had first told her and Eric 'I'm afraid the news isn't all that good' and then gone on to describe precisely what multiple sclerosis was. He had told her that, at present, no one could claim to have a cure for the disease, but that many people – and she was probably one of them – never suffered the more severe symptoms. In any case the progress was a slow one and there were usually remissions. He had had to explain that last word to her, as he usually had to explain it to the stunned, bewildered patients who sat across from his desk. He always hated this part of his job and often wished that he could merely hand them a sheet of paper and tell them 'Read this,' while he went out of the room.

At that period she was still able to walk. Eric suggested that they should take a taxi back to Dalston but she told him 'Don't be daft, I'm not *that* sick,' and so they took one crowded bus, in which they had to stand, and then another, less crowded. Neither of them spoke. Neither of them looked at the other. They stared either out of the windows beside them or else at the advertisements above the seats. Each had the same harassed, questioning expression, with pursed lips and downturned mouths.

When they had reached home, Eric announced: 'Well, let's have a cuppa.'

She sank into the armchair, its springs still intact, and bounced there, as though the up-and-down movement somehow appeased her, as such an up-and-down movement in the arms of its mother appeases a fractious child. 'Three spoonfuls!' she called out. Usually she took two.

'Righty ho!' Then he muttered, so softly that she did not hear: 'You've always been an extravagant one. Talk of beggars on horseback!'

She reached out a hand – odd, as the tips of her fingers met the saucer, they felt even more numb than when they had set off that morning for the hospital – and murmured: 'Lovely. Just what I needed. That tea in the hospital made me want to puke. You'd have thought they could have done better than that.'

He dragged an upright chair over to the table and then sat on it back to front. It maddened her when he did that, she could not have said why. But this time she let it pass without any comment. 'Poor old dear,' he said, genuinely compassionate. 'It's been a rough day.'

She stared into the teacup. The corners of her mouth sagged, she blinked two or three times rapidly in succession. He knew these as the signals that she was about to break down. But this time, to his amazement, no tears followed. 'It's a death sentence,' she said.

'Nonsense. Don't talk such rubbish!' His Essex accent became more pronounced, as it always did when she had managed to upset him. A hand went up and flicked away, with a finicky gesture, a lock of sparse, gingery hair that had fallen across his forehead. When she had first married him, there had been something girlish about him, as her mother had unkindly remarked; now there was something spinsterly. 'You heard what the doctor said. Yes, there's no cure – no cure *as such* – but there are these, these remission things, and in any case he doesn't think you have the severe kind of the disease. I don't

see it as a death sentence, not at all. Look on it as a life sentence.' He gave a nervous, hiccoughing little laugh.

She shook her head. She knew. She could even now view the
road ahead, constantly darkening, to its end.

Meg made an effort to stir herself out of this recollection –
the mental equivalent to the effort that she made every morning to clamber out of bed with the assistance of the hoists that
the Council people had installed for her. You're getting morbid,
my girl! Then she sank back again into the past, as she would
often sink back into her bed, incapable, at least for the time
being, of making any further effort.

At first Eric had been wonderful. He stopped going away on
the cruise ships and got a job as a night porter at a hotel in
Sussex Gardens. 'It's little better than a knocking shop,' he
would tell people. But the tips were good and he was able to
spend the days with Meg, the worsening of whose condition
had begun to accelerate. As Mehmet was to do later, Eric would
help her in and out of the bath, even dry her failing, constantly
fattening body. He would press her to have another cuppa, a
slice of cake, a fag – where was the harm in it? She might as well
enjoy herself while she could. In those days she did not have
the motorized wheelchair. Eric would push her out in the one
that maddened her with its creaking. He would oil the wheels
but somehow that doleful whine just went on and on. He
would push her to the cemetery – she would joke 'I'm not quite
ready to come here yet!' – to the shops and to that Italian café
in which a pretty little Italian girl with a scar down her right
cheek (what had caused it, they would wonder to each other
with an almost obsessive repetition) used to work. Eric would
joke with the girl, with a lot of innuendoes, which would make
Meg eventually protest: 'Oh, give over, do! Do you have to be
so vulgar? Can't you see that the poor dear is getting embarrassed?' But Meg didn't really mind. He had to have his fun.
There was little fun that she could now give him. The truth was
that fun, that sort of fun, was something she no longer enjoyed
or even wanted. She often planned to ask the specialist if that
was usual with MS but then, in the event, she was always too
embarrassed to do so. The times when Eric wanted that sort of

fun became rarer and rarer. Perhaps he was finding it somewhere else? Perhaps in that hotel which he so often described
as 'almost a knocking shop'? If so – well, good luck to him!

It had been a terrible jolt to her, almost as bad as when the
specialist had first told her what was wrong with her, when he
broke it to her that he had applied to go back on a cruise ship.
'But why, why?' she demanded. 'I know that hotel isn't perfect,
but you always say there's not all that much to do at night, that
for most of the time you can kip. And with the tips the money's
good. Isn't it?'

He did not answer, staring unhappily down at the thin, nico-
tine-stained hands that he was clasping in his lap.

'Isn't it?'

'It's not the money,' he said at last. 'The truth is – I get bored
there. The same routine, day after day – or, rather, night after
night. I want to get moving again, not sitting around on my
bum. That's the truth of it,' he added, a steely note of defiance
in his voice.

'And what about me? How am I going to manage?' But she
put these two questions merely to herself.

Ten days later, he had found a job. It was not ideal, he said –
a cut-price cruise on a small ship that was due to be scrapped,
to an area, the Caribbean, that he knew like the back of his
hand. But there it was, better that than nothing.

On the evening before his departure, they sat unhappily in
front of the television set, their eyes on *The Weakest Link* but
really taking in nothing, as he brooded and she fumed. Then
suddenly, as though, having long simmered, a kettle all at once
boiled over, she cried out: 'I don't understand it'.

He looked mournfully across at her with his bloodshot eyes.
'Don't understand what, love?'

'How can you do this to me?'

'Do what?'

'*Do what?*' Cruelly, she mimicked him. She had always been
a good mimic, sending the other people present into gales of
laughter in the days when she and he still went to parties and
the local. 'Oh, for Christ's sake! I never thought you'd give up
on me. No, I never thought that.'

There was a long silence. Then he nodded his long, narrow head, nodded it again. 'The problem is – the problem . . .'

'Yes, well what is the problem? What *is* the fucking problem?' He hated to hear her swear, it was different for a man but a woman shouldn't swear. He would often tell her that – which was why, in moments of anger with him, she made a point of swearing.

He got up slowly, one hand to the small of his back as so often when he was suffering from lumbago, and switched off the television. He groaned as he sat down again. He looked across at her. 'Oh, Meg!' There was both pity and reproach in the words, a bitter-sweet confection. Then he said the terrible words. 'I just can't cope any more.'

'What d'you mean?'

He stared at the blank television screen, one hand going up to scratch with the nail of a long, narrow forefinger at first his pointed chin and then at a nostril. 'I thought I could but I can't. It's the end of that road. I can't trudge along it any more. That's the truth, Meg.'

She stared at him, her face mottled with rage and desperation. 'So you can't cope! You can't bloody cope! Do you think that coping is more difficult for you than for me? I have to cope, I have to bloody cope. There's no alternative to coping, not for me!'

He hung his head. Then, with a grimace, he got up off his chair again, body once more bowed over and hand once more pressed to the small of his back, and went across to her. He knelt beside her, took her right hand in his right, and then with his left began to stroke it. 'You're the one who can always cope. You're the strong one, Meg. You know that.'

'But I don't *want* to be the strong one! Can't you see that?'

'Poor Meg!' He rested his head on her knee, the head turned sideways, the eyes shut. There was dandruff, she noticed, among the ginger-grey wisps of hair. She had bought him that treatment that she had seen advertised on the telly but would he use it regularly? Oh, no. He was too bloody lazy. In a sudden fury, she pushed him away, so that he sprawled across the carpet. 'Oh, you make me sick! Even sicker than I am with this bloody MS. I wouldn't be surprised if you didn't bring it on.'

From the floor he gazed up at her with a stricken expression which slowly, as he got first to his knees and then, putting out a hand to support himself with the table, to his feet, became adamantine, almost cruel. He walked slowly out of the room into the room that was eventually, four years later, to be let to someone else, so totally unlike him. Meg began to cry, first softly, as though practising something unfamiliar to herself, and then in gust after gust, each louder than the preceding one. She expected the noise would bring him back, but it did not do so. Instead, she heard the sound of the radio, the weather forecast for shipping. What interest could that have for him?

When the time came, eleven days later, for his departure, it was with a guilty awkwardness that, as he put his thin arms around her, he said: 'You'll be all right, old girl. And the money will come through, I fixed all that. And I'll telephone,' he added. 'However expensive it is, I'll telephone.'

She gently released herself from him. 'I'm sorry about all that carry on,' she said. He stared at her, sparse, gingery eyebrows drawn together, as though he did not understand to what she was referring, and so she went on: 'I can cope. Don't worry. I can always cope.'

He again took her in his arms, even though he sensed a resistance like an iron rod going right through her otherwise pliant being. 'Of course you can cope. You're strong. You're really strong. Nothing's going to get you down for long. Nothing. You know that.'

He never telephoned. Some money arrived, week by week, for almost two months. Then it stopped arriving.

'So much luggage!' Meg stared in amazement at the three large suitcases, the holdall and the innumerable carrier bags.

'Sorry. Too much?'

'Oh, no, dear! That's OK. If the worst comes to the worst, Mr Bagley can put what you don't want in the storeroom. But what have you got there?'

'Clothes. Mostly clothes.'

'Yes, I can see that you care about clothes. Like I did. Before this thing hit me.'

But she mustn't think about the MS. Or about Eric. It had been morbid to go over it all again in her mind, while waiting for Mehmet's return.

'You know what? Before you start your unpacking, I could do with another cup of tea. D'you think you could manage that for me?'

'Of course, Mrs – Mrs.' Again he gave that cheeky, friendly grin. 'Meg. Meg, Meg, Meg!'

'I'm glad you've got it right at last.'

Chapter II

Marilyn always differentiated between the shuffle of some of her patients on the narrow stairs and the thump of others. Those who shuffled were usually the elderly and it was they who most often wasted her time. Those who thumped were usually the impatient young, who would blurt out what was wrong with them even before they had sat down, and who would leap to their feet even while she was writing a prescription.

That day almost all the patients were elderly, some grimly stoical, some edgily jocular, some plaintive and fretful, as though she were somehow to blame for their nauseas, itchings, twitchings, tinnituses, giddinesses, cramps, throbbings, aches. The room was heated by nothing more efficient than a small electric fire scarred with rust, because something was again wrong with the boiler and the plumber, also one of her patients, was ill with flu and no colleague of his was free to come to fix it until the next day. As she touched the often misshapen, often wrinkled, often waxily yellow bodies before her, she would hear a gasp at the shock of her cold hands and would sometimes even catch, through a corner of her eye, a brief rictus, or sense, through her fingers, an involuntary shudder. About many of these ageing or even ancient bodies there was a terrible pathos, which usually filled her not merely with compassion but also with a remote, eerie grief. But today, mysteriously, she felt nothing but impatience, irritation, or even – when confronted by some of the most demanding – revulsion and something near to hatred.

Yet all through this day like any other day, she had known that eventually it would somehow be different. It would not be different like that terrible day, now more than a year past, when the happiness of driving through the Tuscan landscape had so abruptly been extinguished. This day would be different not because of a sudden plunging into darkness but because of a no less sudden soaring, as from the depths of an ocean, into a world of dazzle. Yes, she had been sure of that, it was what had buoyed her up when yet another flu patient, sneezing and coughing, soggy handkerchief pressed to inflamed nose, had asked her for the miracle – 'I wonder if antibiotics would be any help' – that so many of them imagined, even the most intelligent of them, that she withheld out of either caprice or a perverse desire to make them go on suffering. It was what had also buoyed her up when Jack, her senior partner, had come in to chide her for some deficiency in the latest entry, made by her in his absence also with flu, in the record of one of those elderly women who insisted that they must see not Marilyn but him and who showed their disgruntlement when this was not possible.

That emergence into the dazzle from the darkness occurred when, as she was tidying up her desk and shutting down the computer, she all at once heard Carmen racing up the stairs. There was a perfectly efficient intercom but Carmen would all too often prefer not to use it, just as, when warming up a pot of clammy noodles or a bowl of lumpy tinned soup for her snatched lunch, she preferred not to use the microwave. 'I suppose it's difficult for a girl from some Pyrenean hovel to get used to the gadgets of civilization,' Jack once remarked in his lordly way. But mingled with his condescension there was always a genuine, if surprised and even reluctant, affection for the Spanish girl.

'Dr Carter, Dr Carter!'

The voice often had that urgency to it, even when the problem, so far from being urgent, was utterly trivial.

'Yes, Carmen. What is it?'

Marilyn was tired, she wanted to get home, to have that first glass of vodka on ice, which so easily was followed by others, and then, stretched out on the sagging sofa, to pick up the latest murder mystery that Audrey, her sister-in-law, had brought from the library or scrupulously purchased, not appropriated, in the charity shop that she had started to manage after having been made redundant.

Carmen was pretty but wan. There were dark, shiny rings under her eyes and her face was so pale that her heavily-applied lipstick – she used no other make-up – had an arresting vibrancy. Although her legs and arms were sturdy, the rest of her body gave an immediate impression of fragility, even chronic ill health. Her energy was prodigious. 'She gets through more work than the rest of them put together,' Jack declared. When not on duty at the surgery, she was always rushing off to do some chore – have something photocopied, deliver a manuscript, register a letter, buy some toothpaste from Boots or fill in lottery numbers at Budgens – for the husband, Andy, at least twenty years older than herself, whom she proudly told everyone was a writer. But, apart from an occasional article or short story, Andy had published nothing. Jack said that he was even less likely to see a novel in print than to become a lottery millionaire.

'There is a man downstairs. Emergency! He is badly hurt. Please – come, come!'

Marilyn was used to Carmen's emergencies, which were never really emergencies but the case merely of an elderly asthmatic who was gasping for breath, a drunk who could not be aroused from a stupor, or a child who, out of boredom more than anything else, had vomited over the shoes of another, adult patient.

'One of ours?' Marilyn asked wearily, as she continued to tidy the papers on the desk.

'No, not ours. But he is bad, bad. Cut.' Despite half a dozen years in England, Carmen's English was surprisingly poor; and at moments of excitement, like the present one, it became even poorer.

'Well, in that case I can't see him. You know the rules. You must tell such people to go either to the doctors with whom they're registered or to casualty at Chelsea and Westminster.'

'He said he went to Cromwell but they sent him away.'

'Well, of course they did. There's no casualty department there. You know that. Tell him to go to Chelsea and Westminster.'

'He is bleeding, bleeding badly. Please Dr Carter!' After eleven years, Marilyn was immune to any concern, other than a professional one, for any of her patients except those few who were either personal friends or people for whom she had been caring ever since, eager, idealistic and still unmarried, she had first joined the practice. But concern constantly flowed through Carmen, a molten, irresistible stream, her dark eyes suddenly glistening and a hand going out impetuously to touch, stroke or support anyone, however unlikable, whom she thought to be suffering.

'Am I the only one still here?'

'Oh, yes. Yes!' Carmen came and stood close to Marilyn, as though more effectively to transmit her concern. 'Please see him! Otherwise – maybe he will die.'

'Oh, rubbish!'

Carmen would often decide that a patient was on the verge of death; but on the sole occasion when, soundlessly, without any fuss, an elderly man had indeed died while sitting alone, the last of the queue, in the waiting-room, she had been totally unaware of the occurrence, even though she had gone in to tidy the magazines and toys, as she always did at the close of a day. Subsequently, a fellow receptionist, the last to leave, had realized what had happened, after having first imagined that the shabby, urine-stinking, puce-faced old man, an alcoholic disliked by all of them because of his rudeness, was merely asleep.

On an impulse, Marilyn relented. Had she, she later wondered, relented because she had realized that this stranger whom Carmen claimed to be dying was the messenger who, all that long, tedious day, she had known, known by a strange fluttering of the nerves and a heightening of the senses, was on his way to her? 'Oh, very well, tell him to come up.'

'He is bleeding. Blood in waiting-room.'

'Well, give him a towel or something. I don't want him bleeding in here.' Unlike Jack, Marilyn was never rude or inconsiderate with the staff; but she was often abrupt with them. They had come to accept that. She was, they would say, a good sort, or at least not a bad sort; her heart was in the right place;

basically she was kind; after what had happened one had to make allowances. But for people to make allowances because of what they invariably called her 'tragedy', was something that only made that tragedy less bearable for her.

At first all that she could see of the man's face was the close-cut, black, wiry hair, coming down in a vee to his forehead, one eye under a thick, arched eyebrow, and his cleft chin. This was because one hand was pressing the multicoloured towel, here and there already blotched with blood, against the other eyebrow and his cheekbone. That silly girl had given him the roller towel from the loo only used by the staff, so that one end dangled down below his waist. Marilyn always noticed people's hands and so she noticed that the hand pressed against the towel was large and strong, with carefully tended nails and tufts of black hair sprouting at the base of each of the fingers. He peeled the towel away from his face and immediately drops of blood fell to the floor. Hurriedly he replaced the towel.

'Oh, don't mind about that,' she said as simultaneously he said 'Sorry.' She nodded to Carmen, who was standing behind him, her face puckered with solicitude. 'That's all right, Carmen. Thank you. I expect you want to be on your way.'

'Are you sure you don't want any help?'

'No, that's fine. I'll lock up.'

'Then I go. OK? If I don't hurry, then I am too late to buy Andy ticket.' No need to ask what ticket she meant. A moment later, Carmen was racing, thud, thud, thud, down the stairs. Was she ever not in a hurry? More than once Marilyn had seen her jogging away ahead of her, to or from the surgery or along the high street, as though – as Jack put it – the Furies were pursuing her.

'Nice girl.'

'Yes. A nice girl.' Marilyn sighed. 'Why don't you lie out on that?' She pointed to the couch. 'Then I can have a good look.'

He kicked off his expensive-looking moccasins, climbed up on to the couch, the towel still pressed to eyebrow and cheekbone, and then, eyes shut, wiggled his toes as she stooped above him. He was wearing grey cord trousers and a sweater with BRUNO MAGLIA embroidered on it. It had always struck her as vulgar of people to choose clothes that proclaimed to the world 'Look, this is a designer product, it was extremely expensive.' Suddenly she noticed that blood had congealed here and there on the fabric. 'Pity about your sweater. I hope that blood comes out.'

'My trousers too.'

As she examined his injuries, she asked: 'How did this happen?'

He screwed up his eyes. 'I trip. Crossing road. Maybe this car coming too fast, maybe I mistake. I jump to pavement, so not to be hit, and maybe judge wrong, I catch foot and bang! I fall, hitting edge.'

'Didn't the driver stop? He could have taken you to the Chelsea and Westminster.'

'Maybe no see me.' He winced as her rubber-gloved fingers felt the wound on his temple. 'Cromwell just round corner – I know Cromwell, two, three years ago my cousin patient there – but bastards there say, "No, no, go away". So I saw name outside house, doctor, and' – again he winced – 'here I come!'

'Yes, here you come.' She all but added: 'Making my day even longer and messing up my consulting room with your blood.'

Suddenly, for no apparent reason, he smiled at her. His front teeth were white, and regular except for one, an eye tooth, which was chipped. 'Did you break that tooth in your fall?'

'No. Long time ago. Some time I must have cap.'

She straightened, easing down the fingers of the rubber glove on her right hand with the rubber-covered fingers of the left. She could feel her palms sweating. She hated wearing the gloves but these days, with the prevalence of Aids, it was even more prudent than ever to do so. 'You know – I have to say this – these injuries don't fit in with what you've told me.'

'What you mean?'

'Well, if you'd really hit the edge of a pavement, there would be bruising. The wound would look quite different.'

His mouth, previously slack, straightened, his voice hardened. 'That is what happen. What I tell is truth.'

She shrugged. 'It's no concern of mine. But these are cuts made with, well, something sharp. A knife? No. My guess would be a bottle, a broken bottle.'

'You wrong. Truly, you wrong.'

She shook her head. 'No, I'm right, I'm pretty sure I'm right. Well, never mind. But that's why I must make sure there's no glass in the wounds before sewing them up.'

'Sewing them up?'

'I'm afraid so. But I'll give you a local. You won't feel anything – or, at least, not much.'

Stoically, eyes closed and teeth gritted, he endured what followed in silence. 'It's odd,' she said at one point, 'I was never any good at darning, in those days when people still darned things instead of throwing them away and replacing them, but when I do this kind of sewing it's always surprisingly neat.'

'It leave mark?'

'A scar? Not much. I hope not. If it does, a serious one, then we shall have to think of a plastic surgeon.'

'That cost lot of money?'

'Not on the National Health.'

He frowned. The answer did not seem to satisfy him.

She broke off from her work: 'Yes, I'd say that this was done with the jagged end of a bottle.'

He did not reply.

Later, she noticed the rent in his trousers, over the thigh, revealing purplish bruised flesh. 'Someone kicked you too.'

He turned his head aside, muttering something scarcely audible to her in what, she decided, must be some Eastern European language.

She had already begun to compare this youthful body, lying on the couch over which she was stooping, with those often misshapen ones – disfigured by operation scars, abdominal creases, flab, cellulite, varicose veins, eczema, psoriasis – that she had been obliged to examine throughout that long day. Removing his trousers before going to bed with her for the first time, Ed had said 'Lucky for me that women don't care much about how a man looks.' Nor had she indeed cared about how he had looked then, with his narrow, almost fleshless torso and his long, thin legs and arms. But it was a myth, comforting to someone physically so puny, that it was only to gay men and not also to most women that a man's physique mattered.

When she had finished the stitching and given him first an antibiotic and then an anti-tetanus injection – to her surprise he told her that he had never in his whole life been inoculated against tetanus – she said 'I'd better take a look at that too,' pointing to the rent in his trousers. He stared up at her. 'Slip them off.'

He got up off the couch, hesitated a moment, and then lowered the trousers to his ankles. 'Impossible wear these again,' he said, ruefully pulling down the corners of his mouth. 'New.'

'They look expensive.'

As he stood before her, he inserted his thumbs into the elastic of his Y-fronts. She read, embroidered black on the white, CALVIN KLEIN.

'You'd better get back on to the couch.' He swung himself back. The cheekbone and the flesh above the eyebrow were now slightly puckered, as they might have been after he had slept on them. Once again she stooped. 'My guess is that someone also kicked you.'

Again he made no reply.

'Were you in a fight?'

'I no fight, madam. Never.' He shook his head from side to side on the pillow. 'I man of peace.' She did not believe that, and she knew that he did not expect her to believe it.

When she had finally finished with him, he drew a wallet out of the back pocket of the trousers – so now she knew for sure that the reason for the attack had not been to rob him – and opened it. 'What I owe please?'

'Nothing. Forget it.' Why did she say that? she immediately asked herself. With those clothes and that expensive-looking watch, he could certainly afford to pay her for the half-hour that he had added to her working day.

So far from insisting or making any protest, he at once looked relieved, shutting the wallet and thrusting it back into the pocket. 'You very kind. I must really go hospital but . . .' He shrugged. 'Always long wait, and I bleeding, bleeding. When I see your name, doctor, like that, walking down street, I think maybe Allah show it to me.'

At the door she told him that he must come back to have her or one of the two practice nurses remove the stitches. She gave him a card. 'That's me, Dr Carter, Marilyn Carter, and that's my partner. You can ring up and make an appointment in ten days or so. All right?'

He slipped the card into the same back pocket in which he had pushed the wallet. He nodded. 'You very kind, Dr – Dr Marilyn. How I say thank you? It is late, I keep you.'

'Oh, I'm often as late as this.' She sighed. 'Too many patients, too little time.'

'Many patients, lot money.'

She was taken aback. She almost retorted: 'Not from patients like you.' But instead she replied with an assumed indifference: 'Well, like most doctors these days I manage to get by.'

He hesitated on the doorstep. There was no one at reception, the waiting room behind her was in darkness. Briefly, apprehension brushed against her, a damp and chill invisible presence. Jack always said that, when alone in the surgery, she should never see anyone whom she did not know. Only a few months before, he had pointed out, that Polish woman doctor in Kentish Town had been beaten up, in fact all but murdered, and robbed.

'You leaving now?'

'No. I've got some things to see to first. Among them – to get all your particulars on to the computer. We're great on records now. If I don't do it at once, I'll forget. You never told me your name.'

He hesitated. Why, she wondered, should he be reluctant to give it to her? Then he said: 'Mehmet.' Again he hesitated, screwing up his eyes and turning his head aside. 'Mehmet Ahmeti.'

She reached over to the reception desk for a piece of paper. 'Write it for me.'

Yet again he was reluctant. The script, when he finally took the biro from her and painstakingly inscribed the name, was curiously unformed, even childish, as though writing, at least in the Western alphabet, was not something that he was often called on to do.

She looked at the sheet of paper, holding it up to the light from above them. She said the name: 'Mehmet Ahmeti', her head lowered to it, then looked up at him.

'OK.'

'Is that an Arab name?'

'No.'

'Where are you from then?'

'Albania.'

'Albania! You're the first Albanian I've ever spoken to.'

'Many Albanians in London.'

'Yes, I know. But somehow . . . Have you been here some time?'

'Some time. Yes.'

Suddenly she sensed an unease even more acute than when she had asked for his name. He raised a hand first to the wounded cheek and then to the temple and rocked back and forth in those expensive, highly-polished brown moccasins of his with the floppy, tooled-leather tongues. 'I go now. Late for you. Thank you. You very kind. Very good with needle.' He made a gesture of sewing and laughed. 'I feel nothing.'

'That wasn't because of any skill. That was because of the local.'

He stepped out into the street and began to move off with a strangely dragging gait. She stood in the doorway, watching him. His leg must be painful after the kicking – yes, it must have been a kicking – she thought, as she called out: 'Don't forget to take those antibiotics!'

He turned. 'No forget!'

'And it might be a good idea to take a couple of paracetamols or aspirins before you go to bed.'

'No need! I always sleep like – what you say? – rock. No. Top.' He waved. Then, no longer limping but moving with what struck her as an extraordinary grace despite the injury to the thigh, he hurried off at a speed accelerating with each stride.

'And telephone for that appointment!' she called after him. But probably he did not hear that, since he did not turn.

Suddenly she felt exhausted. Why had that stupid girl not sent him on to the Chelsea and Westminster and so saved her an extra half-hour of work? But she was not really angry with Carmen. What had exhausted her was not that extra half-hour but those – what? – six, seven hours of all the other people who, at ten or fifteen minute intervals, had demanded her attention. With this – this – she struggled to remember the name, her brain confused and numb – this Mehmet whatever-it-was, she had felt increasingly exhilarated, even though stitching a wound late in the evening after a day of dull, depressing work was not normally something that would have caused her any exhilaration at all. Would she see him again? Presumably he would telephone to make that appointment to have his stitches removed. Well, one of the two practice nurses, one young and frivolous and one middle-aged and grim, could deal with him. But she knew that she did not really want either of them to do that. She wanted to deal with him herself.

She picked the towel up off the back of the chair where he had thrown it. In some places it was stiff with dry blood, in others still damp. She stooped and used it to wipe some drops of blood off the floor and a corner of her desk. But, whereas it was easy to remove the blood from the tiled floor, she could not remove it from the desk even with rubbing. She went over to the washbasin and ran some water over a corner of the towel. She was about to rub once again at the desk, then gave up. Mrs Flynn, the Irish cleaner, could deal with it. If she noticed it, that was. Mrs Flynn had a way of not noticing even the most obvious things. Perhaps she should leave a note for her? But in the end she could not be bothered even to do that.

The pollution was getting worse and worse, she thought, as she strode up Gloucester Road and tasted the air, damp and metallic, on her lips when she licked them and in her mouth each time that she opened it. No wonder so many of her older patients suffered from bronchitis and asthma. Instead of pre-scribing Pulmicort and Bricalyn, she ought to tell them, Move, get out of this city of dreadful smog, go to the Mediterranean or Switzerland or South Africa, or, if you can't afford that, try Bournemouth or even Brighton. What was his name? Mehmet – Mehmet – yes! – Mehmet Ahmeti. From Albania. From time to time she'd thought she'd like to go there. Now she had a reason. She smiled to herself.

It was then, as she strode, on the other side of the road, up past the Underground station, that all at once she saw him. He was standing in the station entrance, leaning against a wall, with one leg crossed over the other just above the ankle and the palm of his right hand resting against the cheek that she had stitched. He was looking away from her, into the station. Was he expecting someone? But, unless he had a mobile phone, how could he have made the rendezvous? Unless, of course, he had made it before the 'accident' and he had got away from the surgery just in time to keep it. But all through the time that he had been with her, he had never looked at his watch; and he had been in no hurry to go. In fact, when he had asked 'You leaving now?', she had assumed that he was about to ask her to walk with him. Strange. She was almost tempted to wait, here, just here, outside Harts, so that, if he saw her, she could pretend that she was about to go in to do some shopping or had just emerged after having done some. But then she told herself 'This is ridiculous!' Why should she be interested in whom a complete stranger, fortuitously encountered, was waiting to meet?

She hurried on, then looked back over her shoulder. He was still there, in that same posture. The light from the interior of the station shone on the polished leather of the moccasin resting above the other, on the close-cut, wiry hair, which came to a peak above his forehead and on the pale, high cheekbones. There was something at once negligent and wary about the way that he stood there, motionless, relaxed and yet, she imagined, with every sense alert. That was how her cat Monkey, now dead, used to wait in her small garden for a bird. Monkey seldom failed to catch one.

Chapter III

People so often complained of being disturbed by neighbours who were quarrelling. Meg was disturbed by neighbours who were happy. The shouts from Blossom and her husband, a medical student and also Nigerian, were not shouts of recrimination or rage but of two people who each shouted to the other because that struck them as the most powerful way to convey a constant, delirious joy. When they were not shouting – 'Hi, there, girl!' as he threw open the front-door, 'Chow's up!', as she summoned him to the kitchen table – they were laughing, seemingly at nothing, or, late into the night, they were making love with what Meg called their 'jungle noises' – screeches, wails, yelps, groans – which, as she lay rigid and sleepless on the narrow, hard bed so close to their wide, sagging one, would fill her with amazement, admiration, envy and exasperation all at one and the same time.

'You must speak to them,' Mehmet would tell her, when, staggering and lurching to the breakfast table on her crutches, she would sigh 'Another ghastly night!'

She would shake her head. 'No, I couldn't do that. Oh, no. They have a right to be happy.'

'You no have right too?'

She drew an even deeper sigh. 'I sometimes wonder.'

Now, at this late hour, long after eleven, the couple seemed to be chasing each other round their little flat, with whoops from him, screeches from her and a lot of maniacal laughter from both of them. Those jerry-built walls were made of paper. 'Don't you dare, don't you dare!' Meg heard Blossom shout at one point. Then the thudding of their feet was suddenly silent and all Meg could hear was a cooing sound, as of some distant pigeon. She smiled to herself as she nestled down deeper into the chair from which she was watching television. They were really such a sweet couple, though for some reason or other Mehmet couldn't abide them. You'd have thought that, being coloured like them, he'd have been better disposed. How could that man be a medical student? Mehmet often asked. He was ignorant, both he and she were ignorant, little better than savages. 'Oh, Mehmet, why do you have to be intolerant of others? It takes all sorts, you know.' To which he replied: 'Mamma – better world if there are fewer sorts.'

Meg looked again at her watch. What had happened to the boy? It was as a boy that she always thought of him, even though he was now thirty-one and so only twelve years younger than she was. One never really knew what he was up to. Mysterious. He liked to lead another life, parallel to the life that he led with her, and she accepted that, since she was not in a position, seated in her wheelchair or staggering and lurching around on her crutches, to venture out with him on his jaunts to the betting shop or the park or the pubs or who could say where else.

He had now been living in her council flat in Dalston for almost nine months – for four of them as her lodger and for three of them as a combination of lodger and what she would call, without any rancour, non-paying guest. 'You're too good-hearted,' Sylvia would tell her. 'There you are, finding it far from easy to manage, and you could let that room, that nice room, for at least, oh, fifty or sixty pounds a week. Twenty is a farce. And if he has so much difficulty in finding even that amount, then that's an even stronger reason for giving him the old heave-ho.' Meg would then point out how useful Mehmet was to her – getting the electric buggy out onto the road and helping her into it, running out to buy her a packet of cigarettes at the pub when she had smoked more than her ritual twenty each day, lowering her into the bath or hauling her out of it, putting out the dustbin. How had she ever managed without him? If she told him to go, who would ever take his place? At that, Sylvia would purse her lips and draw in her pointed chin. If he went, she replied, then the social services people would have to pull their fingers out and do more for her, much more.

Meg started up from a sleep at the sound of the front door opening and shutting. A thread of saliva descended from one corner of her half-open mouth, down her chin and on to one lapel of her dressing gown. She raised a hand and brushed it away. Then finding that it was now stuck to her hand, she wiped the hand on a side of the battered armchair. 'Is that you?' she called. 'Mehmet!'

'Hello, Meg!' His voice was strong and cheerful, not wispy and weary as Eric's used to be when he returned home, early in the morning, from the hotel.

She looked at the man's watch, once Eric's spare and found in one of his drawers after his departure, which she wore even when sleeping. It was old and cumbersome, with a dial that glowed in the night, in a way that modern watches no longer did. Her first action on waking each morning was to wind it. 'Gracious! It's almost midnight. What have you been doing?' She shouted the last question, since, instead of coming into the sitting-room, he had at once gone down the corridor without even looking in on her. Probably he was desperate for a pee, she decided. She waited for a while and then, when he did not return and there was no sound of the lavvie being flushed, she called out: 'Mehmet! Hey! What are you up to?'

'Just putting some things away,' he called back. 'I be with you in a minute.'

The minute struck her as an extremely long one. When he did at last appear, a gasp of astonishment puffed out of her. 'What have you done to yourself?' There was sticking plaster above his left eye and over his left cheekbone, and his face was paler than she had ever seen it before, even when he had had that tummy bug that had laid him low for a whole weekend.

'Nothing to worry. I leave work and I decide take tube to Manor House and then bus, because so late. Then – then I trip on escalator and – and . . .' He shrugged. 'I cut face, tear new trousers.' He looked down. 'I just change. Others – throw away.'

'Oh, you poor love!' He had approached the chair and was looking down at her. When he looked down at her like that, with a mixture of tenderness and amusement, she would feel a sudden easing of the spirit, sometimes even a joy. 'Did someone see to the cuts for you?'

He nodded. 'I go Chelsea and Westminster. Wait, wait long time. Many drunks, many peoples with nothing wrong. You know how hospitals are. But it is good there, very good. This old doctor, old man, good. He fix cuts. No expect old man good at sewing! Very good. No pain. A local. Now a little pain, because local wearing off. Maybe I take paracetamol.'

'Oh, yes, yes! You must do that. Otherwise you won't get a good night's sleep. There's a packet of them in the bathroom cupboard. But make sure you take the right packet. I don't want you to take my senna pills by mistake! They look so alike.'

'Yes, I want sleep well. Lot of work tomorrow.'

'Oh, your friend wants you tomorrow too! Oh, good!'

He made no response.

Mehmet's work was never regular, and she was never sure what precisely it involved. From time to time, having gathered her courage, she would ask him, sometimes directly but more often obliquely, but always he was vague. Clearly he did not like people knowing too much about his business, and she understood that. She herself always clammed up when solicitous neighbours – like that ever so grand Lady Muck at no. 14 who was perpetually on at her about claiming all her *entitlements* (that was Lady Muck's word) from the Social Security people – became too nosey about her affairs. All that Meg knew about his work was that it was something to do with export and import and that he worked no fixed hours but would go when asked to do so, even sometimes in the evenings, to help a friend of his, also an Albanian, who had an office somewhere in Chelsea. Pay was as irregular as the hours, with the result that, with many apologies and with embarrassment as much on her side as on his, he would often either fail to pay the rent altogether when it was due or offer her no more than a small instalment.

Now, once again, she could not resist the impulse to probe. If you really cared about someone and cared *for* someone, then it was natural to want to know everything about them, wasn't it? It was not like that one upstairs who asked all her questions about those *entitlements* not because she wanted to help but only because she could never keep her nose out of anyone else's business. 'Was it a busy day then?' she asked. 'You went out so early.'

He nodded. 'Busy.'

'I suppose in your line of business it's more a case of mental tiredness than the physical kind.'

'Yes. Only physical kind is opening drawer, taking file, working computer. And going to toilet.' He laughed. Then he pointed at her. 'Like me to give you hand?'

No, she would never get him to talk. He always changed the subject.

'Well, just the crutches, dear.'

He stooped, picked them up and then placed them on the table beside her. As he did so, one of them dislodged some of the cards of the patience that she had been doing when she had dropped off. 'I never used to have the patience for patience, but I now have all the patience in the world,' she had once told him, as she often told others.

'Oops! Sorry!'

'Doesn't matter. I'll start again tomorrow. It was a devil, that one. That's why I gave up on it and had a kip instead. I only hope I haven't ruined my night's sleep.'

He put out one of his hands – how strong the fingers were, not at all like Eric's spidery ones, and how cool the palm – and she took it in hers. She could still exert a grip but she knew, each time that that Chinaman held out his hand and ordered her 'Now grip my hand as hard as you can – hard, please, hard, hard!' that that grip was weakening. One day she would not be able to grip at all, she knew that.

'There we are!' He had learned that phrase from her, since she often used it – 'There we are!' as he set down a cup for her, as he appeared in the doorway, as he helped her out of the bath, as he switched on the television set or the lamp beside her chair.

'You are good to me!' she said, as she so often said. 'What would I do without you?'

'And what I do without my Mamma?'

She did not really care for him to call her that. But then, having suffered a momentary exasperation at the words, she would tell herself that it was sweet really, it showed how fond he was of her and how close they were.

'Eric and I saw a film once, called *The Odd Couple*. I sometimes think – that's what we are. The Odd Couple.'

'Nothing odd if two people care each other, help each other. Yes?'

She smiled up at him. 'No, of course not, love. Of course not!'

Chapter IV

Audrey's father, Laurence, would often describe her, with a mixture of grudging admiration and guilty derision, as a good woman. When he was exasperated with her, he would exclaim, sometimes to her but more frequently to himself 'God save me from a good woman!'; but when he was reluctantly grateful to her for something that she had done for him, he would often tell her, with one of his quizzical smiles, what a good woman she was. To that she once responded: 'Is it a compliment to be called a good woman? Sometimes I rather wish that someone would call me a bad one.' But no one would ever do that.

It was goodness that had propelled her out early that morning, the pavements spiderwebbed with frost, even before her sister-in-law Marilyn had left for the surgery, to sell flags 'for my children' – as she referred to the charity, set up to help children orphaned in Rwanda, for which she worked voluntarily, as she also did for Oxfam. Later, it was goodness that, as she was making her way from her beat outside Kensington High Street station to the Oxfam shop, made her pause and then turn back to where, in the doorway of an empty block of offices, a young man with a ponytail and blond stubble pricking through the slack, grey skin over his jaws, had positioned himself with an elderly, rheumy-eyed mongrel bitch and a shoebox containing some twenty, ten and five p pieces and a single pound. Propped against the shoebox was a ragged piece of cardboard on which he had scrawled in capital letters: STARVING. PLEASE HELP. Fearful of being late at the shop, Audrey had just hurriedly bought herself two packets of sandwiches, tuna-and-salad and tandoori chicken, in Marks and Spencer. She hesitated, dipping her hand into the plastic bag containing them, jerking it out as though it had encountered scalding water, and then thrusting it in again. Finally, she stooped and held out the sandwiches. The dog gazed up at her with its vague, constantly blinking eyes and then extended its greying muzzle to sniff at the offering. 'Perhaps you might like these?' Audrey said. That STARVING had moved her; but since she was always in control of herself, her matter-of-fact tone did not betray that.

The young man stared up at her. Then he squinted down at the two packets of sandwiches. Having appraised them, he tugged at the piece of rope around the bitch's neck, jerking her inquisitive muzzle away, while pulling a face expressing his affront. In a parody of her well-bred voice, he said: 'How very kind of you, madam! But no, I don't think that I'd really like them.' Then all at once the voice dropped its mocking gentility and became nasal and brutal: 'Oh, fuck off! Just fuck off, you stupid cow! What d'you think I am – a pigeon or a pig, to be fed on your scraps?'

'Oh, I'm sorry. I just thought . . .'

Audrey hurried off, with thumping heart and a sensation of everything – passersby, traffic, the portly newspaper vendor under his flapping canvas awning at the corner – deliquescing into a murky torrent before her eyes. Then slowly she recovered. Well, yes, she supposed that it was only natural that he should resent that kind of charity, the modern equivalent of a Lady Bountiful arriving at some labourer's fetid cottage, where the children were all pale and emaciated and ailing with a variety of sicknesses, carrying with her a basket containing a nourishing broth and some religious tracts. It was clumsy of her and, yes, insulting to hold out those sandwiches, among the cheapest on offer, when what she should have given him was some money, preferably a five or even ten pound note. But I'm not *that* rich, she protested to herself, and then gave the answer: But you're far richer than that poor boy.

Later Audrey was to demonstrate her goodness by telling the woman who was on duty with her in the shop and who, eyes blurred and lips parched, was suffering another of her frequent migraines, to go home and go to bed. No, no, she could

manage perfectly well on her own, Thursday was always a
slack day.

Later still, she was again to demonstrate that goodness when
she glimpsed out of the corner of her eye – she was serving
another customer, the Brazilian cleaner from the next-door
house – that an elderly, well-spoken man, who shuffled almost
daily into the shop with a grave, sometimes even sepulchral
'Good day to you, ladies,' before going over to the bookshelf
where he would browse for as long as twenty minutes on end,
was surreptitiously slipping into a pocket of his worn, dark-
blue, overlong Crombie overcoat not one but two paperbacks
off the shelves. 'Excuse me,' she said to the Brazilian woman,
preparatory to tackling the perpetrator of this blatant act of
shoplifting. But then she changed her mind. What was the
point of humiliating the poor old chap for the sake of two battered paperbacks, priced at 50p each? At that, she turned back
to the Brazilian. But as though he had somehow mysteriously
intuited that she had seen him, the old man was already hurrying at a sideways shuffle out of the shop, his head lowered,
without his usual 'Well, goodbye then,' or his frequent 'That
was really quite a rewarding little visit.'

After the Brazilian had at last gone, bearing with her three
Pyrex dishes for which she had tried to knock down the price
('No, I'm sorry, the prices on all items are fixed'), Audrey went
over to the till, took a pound coin out of her handbag, which
was hidden under the counter below it, and then dropped the
coin into the till. Oxfam was not going to lose the price of those
paperbacks.

Her long day at last over, Audrey arrived back home, breathless and her lips blue from the walk through the autumn chill.
But it was once again her goodness, the automatic pilot on
which she always travelled through life, that immediately sent
her up the stairs, to make sure that everything was in order in
Marilyn's room before she returned. Audrey not merely
accepted Marilyn's untidiness – the papers piled higgledy-pig-
gledy on the desk by the window and even on a corner of her
dressing table, the clothes all over the place, the unmade bed
with the half-drunk glass of whisky and water on the floor

beside it – but even welcomed it, albeit unconsciously, since it gave her goodness free rein.

She began on the bed and then, since the effort of that had made her once more breathless, she sat down at the desk and began to work at sorting the papers, placing bills in one heap, opened letters in another, unopened envelopes in yet another. From time to time a foreign stamp would catch her eye. Later she would have to remind Marilyn to save those stamps for her – something Marilyn usually forgot. The constantly ailing, eight-year-old son of that nice Indian couple, the Patels, who ran the paper shop, was already a collector of stamps. It was touching to see how proud his parents were of his hobby. It was chiefly that pride that had impelled her to give him a stamp album, eliciting from his mother: 'But Miss Carter, it is not even his birthday today!'

Having finished her tidying, Audrey began on her preparations for supper. A vegetarian, she overcame her scruples, as she habitually did, and prepared for Marilyn, though not for herself, some shepherd's pie, since Marilyn always expected meat or fish for what she regarded as her chief meal of the day.

After that, she once again looked at her watch. What could have happened? If Marilyn had been planning to go out for the evening, she surely would have said so? In the immediate aftermath of the tragedy, when only she, Audrey, had fully realized how sick the poor dear was, totally destroyed as it seemed, Marilyn would often fail to appear until long after Audrey had expected her. When asked what she had been doing or where she had been, she would either make no answer, turning her head aside with a sharp intake of breath and an impatient grimace, or else reply with something like 'Oh, walking, just walking,' 'I wanted a breath of fresh air,' 'I needed to be alone to try to sort things out,' or, even more alarmingly, on one occasion merely 'I can't remember. I honestly can't remember.' Often, after one of these fugues, she would for a brief time display a febrile gaiety, talking and laughing too much and too loudly in the little kitchen, until Audrey felt that she would drown in the cascade of din. Then, as though an invisible hand had suddenly switched off a glaring light, Marilyn would abruptly retreat back into the shadows in which so much of her life was passing.

It was in the immediate aftermath of the tragedy that Audrey had come to share the house, now far too large for a single occupant. As though a train had been derailed twice in succession, the lease of her own flat in Dulwich had come to an end only shortly after she had been made redundant, at the age of fifty-four, from the publishing firm in which she had worked for twenty-two years. Her father, who had at first tried to dissuade her from taking so drastic a step, warning her that the most effective way to ruin a friendship was to share either a holiday or a house, had eventually stumped up the money to have the basement turned from a labyrinth of small, interlocking rooms, empty but for the often forgotten things haphazardly stored in them, into a large, low-ceilinged bedroom overlooking the narrow garden, an even larger sitting-room overlooking the street, and a combined lavatory and shower room. In effect, Audrey had her own flat. 'That way you two are less likely to get on each other's nerves,' he told the two women, to which Marilyn replied 'But Audrey has no nerves.' Audrey did not know whether that was intended as a compliment or not. Since her father laughed at the remark, probably not.

In fact, they had never got on each other's nerves, chiefly because their lives touched each other so little. On the rare occasions when they did so, however, those totally different lives would suddenly and briefly intermesh, so that Audrey, who as an adult had always lived for others but rarely with others, would feel that here was an intimacy, created even more by shared grief and guilt than by physical proximity, such as she had never known before. Whether she liked such intimacy, she could not be sure. It was like suddenly shooting up in a funicular to the top of a mountain, and then feeling simultaneously excited by the magnificent panorama all at once revealed to one and terrified that one would be overcome by a crazy, irresistible impulse to hurl oneself down into the abyss below.

Again Audrey looked at her watch. Usually so calm, she felt a rising panic, of a kind that, of all the people whom she knew, only Marilyn was able to induce in her. It was three or four months since the last time that Marilyn had been so late without any explanation. Audrey opened the oven door, saw that the crust of the shepherd's pie had begun to blacken, and turned down the gas. Then she went over to the refrigerator and jerked out the ice tray, which had got stuck to the base of the freezer. Marilyn would constantly fill the tray too full and so inevitably spill part of the water when replacing it. Audrey was surprised that someone so impractical should be so good a doctor. She herself was wonderfully efficient at doing all the things – mending fuses, testing the smoke alarms, videoing television programmes, changing clocks from winter to summer time and back again – at which Marilyn was such a duffer. But, good heavens, she could not conceive of ever having been a doctor.

Audrey seated herself at the kitchen table and, pushing to one side the setting which she had laid for herself, placed her elbows on the worn formica and then rested her chin in her palms. No one had ever thought her pretty but in recent years people had often thought her handsome. Her hair, blonde streaked with grey, curling up at the edges on either side of the square, strong-jawed face, had not thinned with the years but was still as vigorous as when she had worn it loose to the shoulders. Her eyebrows were also thick – more than once her father had asked why she did not pluck them or at least trim them – and beneath them the gaze of her widely-spaced grey eyes was calm, assured and reassuring. Her colleagues had been amazed when the conglomerate that had taken over the small publishing firm had made her, of all people, redundant. It could only have been because of her age, they decided. She was intelligent, totally reliable and, of course, such a good woman.

Although so many others now thought of her as handsome, that was never how she had thought of herself. The problem for her had always been her adored and envied older brother, Ed. As a young boy, with his impish, triangular face, spattered with freckles, and skinny, gawky frame, he was physically unimpressive, and so he had remained into his late forties when, after a dissolved marriage to an Indonesian girl met when he was working on an assignment in East Timor, he had married Marilyn. But although Marilyn was then almost twenty years younger, no one, despite his appearance, was impelled to ask what she saw in him. Everyone knew. From his earliest years, he had had charm, and, as his and Audrey's father Laurence, also a man of irresistible charm, would often remark: Blessed are the charmers, for theirs is the kingdom of heaven. Audrey, wishing for that charm for herself, would often try to analyze what was its source. Eventually she decided that it derived from a ready wit and the even readier interest and sympathy that Ed gave the impression of bringing, with an undiscriminating eagerness, to every encounter. Were the interest and sympathy genuine? Audrey would often ask herself that question and she once, while he was still alive, also put it to Marilyn – who was affronted by it, answering emphatically, even indignantly: 'Of course they're genuine! What an idea!'

Ed's charm had, all through their childhood, done her the disservice of throwing her charmlessness into even bolder relief. She was too stiff, too much lacking in any sense of fun and, above all, too honest in everything she said, however discouraging or depressing, for anyone to feel an instant attraction to her, as they did to Ed. People said that it took a long time to get to know her. It also took a long time to understand her and even longer to appreciate her.

Because of the cruelty of the contrast between the plain, emotionally gauche girl and the attractive, emotionally agile boy, there were often times when she hated her brother. But far deeper than that hatred was her love for him. He was the person that she most wanted to be with – and to be. All through the years when he zigzagged about the world seeking out danger and disaster, she would keep scrapbook after scrapbook of the journalism that he, along with everyone else, regarded as admirable but ephemeral. Now that he was dead, she would take up one of those scrapbooks at random and peer down, often with eyes made misty and unfocused with the imminence of tears never shed, at some photograph of him – in boots, parka and jaunty fur hat, in khaki shorts and open-necked, short-sleeved shirt, in ill-fitting dinner-jacket to accept an award for distinguished services to journalism. She would even read the account of some long-forgotten campaign in some remote corner of Africa, or of some insurrection, smashed with cold-hearted despatch, in some no less remote corner of the Soviet Union, with total, aching absorption.

It was their love for Ed, so different in every way, that had brought Marilyn and Audrey so closely together after the tragedy and had finally determined that, once so remote from each other both emotionally and geographically, they should share the same roof. But, as Audrey was the first to acknowledge, Marilyn's furious, hysterical grief was on a scale totally different from her own restrained, fatalistic one. Audrey had for so long expected to read of Ed's sudden death – by bomb, by bullet, by execution, by infection – that when it had finally occurred, it came as no surprise. But to Marilyn it was as astonishing as if a meteorite had fallen out of the sky to obliterate him.

Ah, there she was! Audrey could hear the key in the lock of the front door and then that abrupt, nervous cough – almost a way of saying 'Here I am' – that had intermittently afflicted her ever since Ed's death.

'Is that you?' Audrey called out, not knowing that that question, like so many other things said by her, always irritated Marilyn. After all, since no one else lived in the house and the cleaning woman always came on Tuesday and Friday mornings, who else could it be?

'Yes, it's me.'

'What happened to you?'

Marilyn came into the kitchen, slinging her large bag off her shoulder and pushing her pronged fringe of dark-brown hair off her pale forehead. 'Oh, I had an emergency. That silly girl Carmen should have told him to go to casualty at the Chelsea and Westminster – he wasn't even on our list – but as always she let her good nature get the better of her.'

'Yes, it is a good nature.'

'Oh, yes! But sometimes I wish it were a little less so. Instead of getting home on time from a particularly unrewarding day, I spent half an hour doing needlework.'

'Needlework?'

'On the man's wounds. He said he'd fallen, but it was obvious to me that he'd been in what the papers call an affray. *Affray*

- that's a word that no one ever actually uses in conversation, do they?'

As Audrey stooped to place the plates in the oven, Marilyn rose from the chair into which she had so recently collapsed and said tersely: 'I must get a drink.'

Audrey wanted to protest 'Oh, must you?', since she rarely drank herself and never liked to see Marilyn do so. But she had trained herself to stop putting that question, since it made Marilyn angry.

When Marilyn returned, already sipping from the tumbler half full, as always, with vodka, Audrey asked: 'Would you like some ice?'

'Why not?'

Audrey began to move towards the refrigerator, but Marilyn forestalled her, putting down the tumbler and hurrying over. 'I'll get it. You're tired.'

'Well, so are you – after such a long day.'

But the strange thing to Audrey was that, though Marilyn had looked so pale when she had first come into the kitchen and though her eyes had had that disturbingly unfocused look that always indicated that she had suffered too long a day of too much work, she did not seem to be truly tired, not as she so often was, even at the weekends when an agency took over from the practice.

After Audrey had served her sister-in-law with the shepherd's pie and some runner beans and then set down for herself a small, crumpled tomato-and-asparagus quiche (she had unwisely packed it at the bottom of her shopping bag, where it had rested all day), she surreptitiously glanced across the table between each mouthful of food. The two women often ate in a comfortable silence, each following her own train of reverie; but for Audrey there was no comfort in the silence now. Something had happened. Audrey sensed it; but she did not know why she sensed it or what it was. It emanated from Marilyn, so close across the table from her, like a cobwebby ectoplasm, a scent still faintly lingering in a room long shut, or a trilling of so high a frequency that the human ear could barely catch it. But what, what?

'How was your day otherwise – apart from the needlework?' Audrey so much wanted to discover what that something was.

'Oh, like all my days.' Marilyn reached out for another slice of wholemeal bread (she preferred white but it was wholemeal that Audrey always bought) and began to butter it. 'Tiring, boring. It's not a good combination – patient and impatient doctor. If I were capable of doing anything else for the same financial return, I'd do it.'

Marilyn had often said the same thing or approximately the same thing in the past and Audrey had never had any reason to disbelieve her. But she disbelieved her now.

Yes, something had happened.

In the days that followed, that something did not disperse and grow mute for Audrey but, instead, became more and more insistent. She was exasperated both by her inability to define it and her reluctance to ask Marilyn to do so.

Chapter V

Marilyn had woken early, a few minutes after five, and had then been totally unable to go to sleep again. After having listened to an irritatingly mechanical Bach fugue on her bedside wireless for a time, she scrambled out of bed, had a protracted soak in the bathroom off her bedroom, and then dressed and tiptoed down to breakfast. Careful to make as little noise as possible, she prepared herself toast and coffee and sat down at the table which, as always, Audrey had laid. She wanted to hear the news, since the papers, *The Times* for her and the *Guardian* for Audrey, had still not arrived, but decided not to do so. Poor Audrey was such a light sleeper and the previous morning she had once again sallied out early in order to sell flags to the first commuters to enter the Underground station.

Suddenly, however, the door creaked open and there Audrey was, a red crease running like a scar down one side of her face where she had slept on it, and her hands thrust into the pockets of an ancient camel-hair dressing gown, appropriated from her father, who, always dapper, had been about to throw it away.

'You're very early.'

Audrey had what amounted to a genius for stating the obvious, Marilyn thought, annoyed at the interruption. But she looked up and smiled. 'And so are you. I hope I didn't wake you.'

'Oh, no. I heard the paper boy. He often wakes me. Why does he have to come so early and make so much noise? Usually I go to sleep again. But this time . . .' Audrey went over to the percolator. 'Are you going to drink all this coffee?'

Although she had intended to do so, Marilyn replied: 'Oh, no. Do take as much as you want. Shall I make you some toast?'

'I'll see to it. Thanks.'

Marilyn did not demur. Audrey usually saw to all the household chores.

'The days keep closing in.'

'Yes, they certainly do.' It was another statement of the obvious.

'Christmas will soon be on us.'

Oh, God! With difficulty, Marilyn concealed her mounting irritation. 'Yes. Christmas! I don't think I'll send any cards this year.'

Soon after that, Marilyn gulped at what was left of her coffee and, wishing that Audrey had not deprived her of her third cup, rose to her feet.

'Off so soon?'

'In a few minutes. There are – things I want to see to on my desk before the patients start arriving. I have so little time for all the paperwork.'

'I thought that that Bessie or Tessie or whatever she is called saw to all that for you.'

'Not all. There are certain things she can't see to. Unfortunately.' Marilyn pulled open the door. 'Have a good day,' she said. 'As they keep telling each other in America.'

'And you do the same.'

It was far too early for there to be anyone other than the cleaner at the surgery. Mrs Flynn, having changed from shoes into slippers, as she always did for her work – it made her feel more comfy, she would explain – was strenuously thrusting the Hoover back and forth in the waiting-room, banging it against table and chairs as she did so. From the reception area Marilyn could already hear her singing above its growl. What she was singing, she could not recognize, but the full-throated, not always accurate contralto expressed a surprisingly vivid melancholy, as Marilyn caught the words 'Somewhere, somehow, some time', and then 'Return, return, return!' in wailing crescendo.

Marilyn put her head round the door. 'Good morning, Mrs Flynn.' She had once, coming down the stairs, overheard Mrs Flynn complaining to one of Carmen's colleagues that 'That One' (i.e., herself) was so unlike Dr Lawson, not at all friendly, not even ready to give a soul a civil good morning. Since then she had guiltily tried to give that civil good morning and to be as amiable as possible to a woman whom she had never really liked, considering her to be not merely slack in her cleaning but also insincere in her constant addressing of everyone, doctors, nurses, receptionists and even patients, as 'dahling'. So much did Mrs Flynn resemble some amateur actress, long over the hill, in a Sean O'Casey play, that Marilyn would often wonder whether her sole claim to Irishness might not be her marriage to Mr Flynn, who had died prematurely after fathering a huge brood of children. Of these children, constantly sick, out of work or, as Mrs Flynn would put it, 'in a pickle', there was a lot of talk – bewildering because it was difficult to distinguish between so many of them – over the Hoover, the mop or the sink.

'Ah, good morning, dahling!' Mrs Flynn kicked at the switch of the battered machine with a misshapen, slippered foot in order to gag it. 'You're an early one this morning.'

'Yes. I have things to see to before the patients arrive.'

'Always busy!'

'Yes, always – or almost always – busy. There's never any recession in the medical business.'

'Well, don't overdo it, dahling, that's my advice. You can't look after the patients if you don't look after your good self.'

'Well, I suppose that's true enough.'

As Marilyn climbed the stairs up to her room, she felt an increasing ache in her calves. It might have been the end of the day, instead of its beginning. She lowered herself into the metal chair, functionally perfect but made so hideous by a seat covered in a jazzy red-and-black synthetic fabric that she kept telling herself that she must exchange it for one from the waiting-room, and then switched on the computer, preparatory to writing the first of a number of letters of referral. She stared at the screen. It was eleven days now since she had stitched up that Albanian's face and he was long overdue to have the stitches removed. Or could he have got someone else to remove them? She had already inquired twice if he had been in, each time to be told that he hadn't. Unbidden, even unwelcome, he kept coming into her mind, like some nagging infection, ebbing away and then flooding back.

That morning, soaking in the bath, she had, as so often in the months since Ed's death, made a half-hearted effort to pleasure herself. It was like smoking, she often thought: it brought no lasting relief, merely within a short space of time an arid craving for more. On this last occasion, the cold tap dripping (Audrey had promised to change the washer but must have forgotten) with a persistent lisping sound on to instep of her foot and then transmitting a chill through it outward to the farthest extremities of her body, she had begun by fantasizing, as always, about Ed making his gleeful, energetic, often inconsiderate love to her (a lot of laughter, a lot of throwing himself about, a lot of almost suffocating her as he squeezed and squeezed her body as though it were a bolster). But then, suddenly, it was not Ed but the young Albanian who was clutching her. Astonished, she had sat up in the bath, so violently that water splashed out on to the worn linoleum. Then, slowly, she had lowered herself into it again and resumed what she had been doing – welcoming back the previously intrusive but now wholly desired guest with a sudden, frenzied enthusiasm.

There was a thud, thud, thud on the stairs. It could only be Carmen.

'Oh, Dr Carter. Wonderful news! I must tell you!' She was laughing with joy.

'Yes?'

'An agent is interested in Andy's novel. He will take him on. He has read two, three chapters and he thinks them *striking*.' Carmen was clearly using the adjective that the agent had used. 'He says he has high hopes.' Again she must be quoting. 'Isn't that wonderful, Dr Carter?'

'Yes, that's wonderful, Carmen. But you do realize, don't you, that that's just a first step? I mean – many are chosen by agents but few are called by publishers.'

Carmen stared at Marilyn, bewildered.

'I mean, it's terrific to be taken on by an agent. Many people try and try but never achieve it. But after that, there's the next hurdle. Problem,' she amended, since Carmen was frowning, as though she did not understand what 'hurdle' meant. 'It's awfully difficult, from what I've heard from writer friends, to get a publisher actually to take a first book.'

Carmen was crestfallen. In a small, troubled voice she said: 'Andy is so happy.'

'Well, of course. Of course! He has every reason to be happy. I'm sure that soon he'll have some more good news and be even more happy. Let's keep our fingers crossed.'

Carmen nodded and then gave a reluctant smile.

'Tell Andy how pleased I am for him.' Marilyn had never met Andy, but she imagined someone both physically and psychologically ungainly, awkward and grubby, whose belief in his talent, perhaps even genius, made him regard poor little Carmen merely as his handmaiden.

'Thank you, Dr Carter.' Then Carmen added: 'He wishes one day to meet you.'

'Yes, we must try to arrange that,' Marilyn murmured, having no wish that they should ever do any such thing.

'I think you know many writers.'

'Did, did. When my husband was alive. But he was the one they were interested in,' she added with some bitterness. Over the months, Ed's friends, initially so sympathetic and supportive, had remorselessly fallen away.

'I must go down. Patients will be arriving.'

As Carmen left the room, still disconsolate – oh, heavens, why had she crushed the poor girl like that? – Marilyn called out after her: 'That man hasn't come back to have his stitches removed, has he?'

Carmen turned. 'Which man, Dr Carter?' At least half a dozen patients had had stitches removed in the course of the last few days.

'Oh, you know . . .' Marilyn put on an act of being vague about the details. 'The one – the foreigner – Albanian was he? – who arrived just as we were shutting up shop. With those – those cuts. You remember, don't you?'

'Oh, yes, yes!' Carmen's previously glum face was once again irradiated with pleasure. 'He telephone, just telephone. Five, ten minutes ago. Just before I come up.'

'Oh, good. He was overdue. I was wondering what had happened to him.' Marilyn made an effort not to show the joy that had suddenly surged up within her. 'Did he make an appointment?'

Carmen nodded. 'I put him down for Ellen.' This was the old and grim practice nurse, not the young and frivolous one. 'You have such a busy day today.'

Marilyn frowned and pursed her lips. 'Oh, I don't know . . . I'd really like to see him myself. I want to make sure his face isn't going to be too scarred. Otherwise I must send him to see a plastic surgeon.'

'Yes, he is so handsome,' Carmen said seriously. 'A pity if he has scars.'

'What time is his appointment?'

'I think eleven – eleven twenty?'

'Well, show him up here, don't send him to Ellen. Fit him in somehow.'

'OK, Dr Carter.'

Carmen began to race down the stairs. Marilyn returned to her desk.

The morning chugged along, like some branch-line train that stops at every station and is even from time to time marooned out in the deserted countryside, where no station exists. She was brusque with some of the more tiresome patients and rude to one, an overdressed, actressy, middle-aged woman, with a piercingly high-pitched voice that suggested that she was being auditioned for a part at the Olivier and feared that, with that dud acoustic, she might not be heard. Perhaps she really was an actress? She was always full of complaints – about the 'attitude' (a favourite word of hers) of the nurses or the reception staff, about her treatment when referred to Chelsea and Westminster, about the side effects caused by the most innocuous of drugs. On this occasion she was indignant that neither Marilyn nor Jack had been prepared to come and see her when she had been in bed with flu.

Eleven came and then half-past eleven and there was still no sign of Mehmet. Marilyn was tempted to check whether, by some error, he had been sent to see Ellen, as first arranged. But she restrained herself.

Then, at long last, shortly before noon, when she rang down for the next patient, she heard a strong, regular footfall on the stairs and at once she knew, knew with a blazing certainty, she could not have said how, that it was he. She half rose from the chair in eager anticipation, then subsided again. She turned away from the door to the computer, so that her face was averted when, after the brisk rat-tat-tat of his knock and the assumed weariness of her 'Yes! Come in!', he entered the room.

'Dr Carter! Good morning. Or is it afternoon?'

It's almost afternoon and you're late. But she merely replied in an off-hand voice: 'Good morning.' She turned back to the computer, put a hand out to the mouse, moved it at random, clicked it. Head still averted, she said: 'Sit down. I'll be with you in a moment.' Her heart seemed to be beating somewhere high in her throat. She swallowed hard. Then she turned back to him. 'What can I do for you?'

'You remember me? Stitches?' He raised a hand and touched the red corrugation of first one scar and then the other.

'Oh, yes, of course! You want them taken out.' She got up from the desk. 'Why don't you sit over there? With luck it won't hurt.'

They were both silent as she made her preparations – getting out the scissors and the kidney dish, pulling on the rubber gloves that she so much hated but knew to be necessary. All the time she was conscious that he was watching her with a faintly smiling intentness, as though he found what she was doing not merely interesting but also amusing. 'You should try not to be late for doctor's appointments, you know.' The reproof was friendly.

'Yes. Sorry. Not easy get away.' He did not explain what it was that he had had to get away from.

'We work to such a tight schedule here. All NHS doctors do. From what I hear, my patients constantly complain that I give them too little time. But the truth is that, except in an emergency, I have to ration them to ten minutes each.'

'Last time my ration more than that.'

'Well, you were an emergency, weren't you?'

He laughed.

As she leaned over him, one of her thighs briefly touched one of his. She had long been anaesthetized to any contact with her patients; such contact was now no different from the ones that she regularly made with her chair, her desk, her computer or her prescription pad. But on this occasion, with a hyperaesthesia both thrilling and shocking, she was aware, within that second or so of contact, of the warmth and resilience of his flesh through his jeans and her tights.

'Let's see.' She examined the scars. 'Yes, I'm pleased with that. It's not often I'm pleased with my sewing.' At home, it was always Audrey who did any sewing for her. Marilyn's stitching of the wounds, so neat as to be all but invisible, was worthy of her sister-in-law. 'Yes! That's good. With time hardly anything will show.'

'One friend say scar on man's face make him more attractive.'

'That must be a woman friend.'

He nodded and then winced as she snipped at the first of the stitches above the eyebrow. She was wondering who was this woman friend who had said that to him. Was he married? Living with someone? She felt an urgent craving to know. She had already looked up the address that he had given her in the *A to Z*. Dalston. She had never been to Dalston.

'So. That's done. It wasn't too painful, was it?'

'Not at all. You expert, I see.' He got to his feet and, head tilted forward at an angle, smiled up at her. 'Thank you. *Merci beaucoup.*' Did he add that to show off to her? If so, why not use some French phrase not known to everyone in the civilized world? But the accent was certainly good. 'Now – Dr Carter – please – not angry what I say.' He put out a hand and placed it on her arm, in a gesture that was confidential, even intimate. 'I not your NHS patient. Not – how you say? – on your list. I must pay you.'

She shook her head. 'No, no! That's not necessary.'

'Please. *Please.*' As on the previous occasion, he reached into the back pocket of his jeans and pulled out his wallet.

As he opened it, she said sharply: 'Put that away! We decided all this the last time. Remember?'

He looked at her, grateful, quizzical, rueful. Then he gave a small shrug.

'Now I must see my next patient. I'm terribly behindhand.' She reached for the door handle and pulled it open, so clumsily that it banged against her foot.

'You very kind.' He passed through the door and then abruptly turned. 'I think some way to make return to you.'

'No return is necessary.'

He began to race down the stairs, calling out 'Goodbye, thank you, thank you,' as he disappeared from sight.

Marilyn shut the door and walked slowly back to her desk. Although there were still three patients waiting to see her, she did not at once ring down. She gripped the edge of the desk before her with both hands, as though preparatory to pushing it away from her or even overturning it. She craned past it to look out of the window. But she could see nothing of him, among the people hurrying along, many of them under umbrellas. He must have gone the other way.

She rang down for the next of her impatient patients.

Two days later it was Saturday. Although it was already past eleven, Marilyn still lay in bed, listening to the Mahler Fifth on a CD. Audrey had brought her up her breakfast (tea, toast and a warmed croissant as a special treat) and a copy of *The Times* soggy from having been thrown on to the doorstep in the rain instead of pushed through the letter box. She had eaten the breakfast, not really wanting the croissant but not daring to leave it, since each Saturday it had become a ritual for Audrey to present one to her. She had then skimmed through the paper, irritated by the difficulty of turning and folding the pages. After that, she had lain back, shut her eyes, and begun to doze.

The front-door bell aroused her. Hell! Was Audrey in or had she already gone out to Sainsbury or Tesco – her patronage shuttled between the two – for the weekend shopping? Oh, thank God. She was about to swing her legs out of the bed, when she heard the firm, unhurried tread on the stairs up from the basement. Then, amazingly, all at once, even before Audrey had opened the door, she had known – as she had previously known when waiting for the next patient in her consulting room – that it was he and no one else. But why should he come to the house? And how did he know where it was?

Now she did swing her legs out of the bed, her nightdress rucked up to her knees. God, she must look a fright! And at this hour too! Frantically, she smoothed down her hair with both hands and then stooped for her slippers.

She could hear his deep, vibrant voice: 'I look for Dr Carter. Excuse me – she live here?'

'Oh, yes, she lives here, this is our house. But whether . . . I'm not sure if she's gone out or not,' Audrey lied. 'Or she may be busy. If so, she'll be upstairs.'

'It does not matter. I brought her present. She know why. A return for – for something kind.'

Marilyn jumped off the bed, grabbed her dressing gown and frantically thrust her arms into it. Then, still tying the cord, she hurried down the stairs.

Audrey turned at the sound of her descent. Her eyes widened and her mouth opened in astonishment that Marilyn should appear dishevelled and in a dressing gown for someone who must be hardly known to her. 'Oh, Marilyn, this – this gentleman has brought you some flowers.'

Beyond Audrey, Marilyn could now see Mehmet. His pale face was upturned to her, not vulnerable and bewildered like Audrey's, but totally self-assured. *Luminous*, that was the word for it she thought. 'Good morning, Dr Carter. I am sorry I wake you.' Even before she had reached the bottom step he was holding out the flowers. It was a vast bunch, a variety of flowers in various shades of pink. She had never liked pink flowers.

'Oh, no, no. I wasn't asleep. But on Saturday we have an agency to look after the practice and so I take it easy. I was reading,' she added. 'I get so little time for reading.'

He pushed the bunch of flowers towards her. 'For you.'

'For me? But what a lot of flowers! They must have cost a fortune.'

'Too little for all you do for me.'

'But that was nothing.'

Audrey continued to stand, arms folded, a little apart from them. As they talked, she looked at each of them in turn, with a bewildered, almost frightened look on her face. Marilyn had seen that look on the faces of patients who were about to undergo some strange and therefore dreaded procedure – a prostate examination, an endoscopy, even a simple drawing of a specimen of blood.

'It was very much.'

Again he held out the bunch, with a pleading, placating look, almost as though he were coaxing a nervous animal. This time she took it. The smell of the hothouse blooms was languorous and sweet. She wondered if the florist had sprayed them. Florists sometimes did that, she had heard. She looked down at them. 'Lovely. How very kind of you. We seldom buy flowers for the house, because I'm too lazy and Audrey has an allergy.'

As though to confirm this last statement, Audrey suddenly sneezed and sneezed again, raising a forefinger to her nose and then pressing the side of it up against its tip.

'I'll put them in my study. Or bedroom. At this time of year, it's lovely to have flowers to look at. The garden is so bleak.'

He smiled and nodded, clearly delighted.

'How did you find me?'

'First to the surgery. No one there, just – just Spanish lady.'

'Carmen,' Audrey said, like a teacher correcting a pupil.

'She tell me you not come today. But she give me this address and tell me how I walk here. Not far!'

Marilyn had repeatedly told Carmen on no account to reveal her home address to anyone. She would have to have a word with her on Monday.

'I look in directory – telephone directory. Many Carters – no Dr Marilyn Carter.'

So he had remembered her Christian name. 'We're ex-directory. In some ways it's a boon, in some ways a nuisance. My – my husband wanted it that way and I've never done anything about changing it. If there's an emergency, the agency has this number.'

'You are married?'

She resented the question; but then she reminded herself that probably in the culture from which he came to be inquisitive was not impolite but merely an indication of concern.

'Was. My husband is dead. I'm a widow.'

'I am sorry.'

Audrey intervened: 'You know, Marilyn, you shouldn't be standing around in this draughty hall in your nightdress and dressing gown. Particularly when there are all these colds and flu about.'

'No, I suppose not.' Marilyn restrained herself from snapping back that colds and flu were caused by viruses, not by standing around in draughty places. She had been wanting to offer him a cup of coffee. But that was out of the question with Audrey present, even though at this hour Audrey and she would be thinking of their elevenses. Indeed, the coffee might already be percolating.

'I go now.' He turned towards the door, then turned back. 'Maybe I see you again?' He put the question hesitantly, with a note of pleading in his voice.

'Yes. Maybe.' Because of Audrey, she showed none of the pleasure that she felt at the suggestion. Why on earth did she have to go on standing there, arms crossed, with that vaguely puzzled, vaguely disapproving look on her face?

'I give address and telephone number?'

She already had his address and telephone number on the computer. Had he forgotten that or did he want to ensure that she had them here, in her home, instead of at her place of work? 'Well, yes. If you'd like to. Yes. Thanks.'

He drew a piece of paper out of the breast pocket of his tweed jacket, which he was wearing with an open, blue-and-white check shirt. Wasn't he cold, dressed like that, with no tie or scarf, no overcoat and no sweater under the jacket? 'Please.' He held it out.

Amazed, she realized that he had already prepared the piece of paper. There was the name 'Mehmet Ahmeti' and under it an address and an outer London telephone number. Did he really imagine that she was going to take the initiative of getting in touch with him? She put out a hand, took the piece of paper, and thrust it into the pocket of her dressing gown. All at once she knew that, despite the seeming triviality of a piece of paper having been passed from one of them to the other, something fateful had happened.

On an impulse, she said: 'I'd better give you my number. You have the surgery number of course. I mean the number at this house.'

'Oh, please!' He was eager.

As he said this, Audrey turned and began to retreat to the back of the hall. Then she was descending the stairs to her basement.

Marilyn found a pad and biro in their usual place by the telephone. Audrey saw to it that both were always there, as she also, each morning, made it her task to tear off from the pad any out-of-date jottings. Marilyn wrote 'Dr Carter', crossed that out, and then wrote 'Marilyn Carter'. Below the name she wrote the number.

He stared down at the paper when she handed it to him. 'Marilyn Carter,' he said. 'I like name Marilyn. Marilyn Monroe,' he added and laughed.

'I'm afraid I'm nothing like her.'

'She no good doctor.'

'And I'd be no good as a sex symbol.'

They both laughed, then shifted awkwardly, their eyes lowered. Marilyn stepped past him and opened the front door. An icy blast stung her bare legs. He gazed momentarily at her with eyes that seemed to have lost their dangerous glitter and become soft and gentle. Then he gave a little shrug and walked past her and out.

'Thank you again for the lovely flowers. I'll get Audrey – my sister-in-law – to arrange them for me. Even if they do make her sneeze! I'm no good at arranging flowers. Thank you, thank you so much.' She was really thanking him not merely for the flowers but for having made the effort of finding out where she lived and coming so far, and, even more crucially, for having redeemed yet another weekend with too little to do and too much to think about.

Standing on the bottom of the cracked steps, he turned to acknowledge her thanks. '*Il n'y a pas de quoi.*' He raised a hand in farewell, the fingers oddly curved, almost as though they were trying to snatch at something invisible. '*Au revoir!*'

'*Au revoir!*'

As, having reluctantly closed the door, she prepared to go upstairs again, she saw Audrey emerging from the basement. Audrey walked towards her, her expression a mixture of anxiety and disapproval. She held out her large, capable hands – a man's hands, her father would describe them.

'Let me have the flowers. I'll arrange them. Even if they do make me sneeze.'

Chapter VI

When Jacek got the job at the car wash, Mehmet had already been working there for several weeks. He was the first person that Jacek noticed, apart from Mr Klingsman. This was partly because Mehmet was so much at his ease, partly because he was so handsome and strong, and partly because he looked so smart in his white overalls and trainers. But chiefly it was because, alone of all the workers, Mr Klingsman treated him as if he were both an equal and a friend.

On that first day, stooped beside a ramshackle Escort in a hangar-like building full of cars, vans and weary workers, Jacek from time to time twisted round his head to peer, with grudging envy, through a wide, low plate-glass window into Mr Klingsman's untidy office, littered with files, opened and unopened letters, ancient girlie magazines, overfull ashtrays and heavy-duty cups containing the dregs of cups of coffee days old. He was fascinated by the sight of the two men, the owner and his favourite employee, chatting together. Each was smoking a cigarette. Mehmet was sitting upright, one leg crossed high over the other, in the revolving chair beside Mr Klingsman's desk. Mr Klingsman was lolling back in a dilapidated sofa, his huge stomach stuck out in front of him and the buttons of his shirt all but bursting from the fabric strained tight across his prodigious embonpoint. Mehmet was doing most of the talking, Mr Klingsman most of the laughing.

When Mehmet at last returned to work, Mr Klingsman followed him out of the office. 'I don't give you a chance with that one,' Jacek heard Mr Klingsman tell Mehmet in that accent which Jacek took to be German, to which Mehmet replied

'Want to bet?' Both men laughed and then Mr Klingsman shouted out 'Oh, get on with it, you stupid bugger!'

When Mehmet did get on with it, there was no doubt that he was one of the most efficient of the workers. But he took many such breaks. He would also spend a lot of time chatting to the customers. When other workers did this, Mr Klingsman would soon nip out of his office to ask of the customer 'Is there any problem?' or to tell the worker 'You won't be long over that, will you? We've got a real rush ahead of us,' or something of that kind. But he never interrupted Mehmet.

That first morning, soon after eleven, a middle-aged blonde in dark glasses drove up in a long Mercedes coupé of a kind that Jacek, who had had little experience of luxury cars in his native Poland, had never seen before. All the workers stopped what they were doing to stare first at the car and then at her. Mr Klingsman did not send Roberto, a tiny, grubby, unshaven Italian, who was free, to deal with this new arrival, but summoned Mehmet from another job. She and Mehmet at once began a long conversation. She leaned negligently against the car, in her black-and-white check trouser suit, her tongue moving constantly round her lips when she was not talking or smiling. He stood opposite to her, his hands encased in the pink rubber gloves that, along with the constantly laundered white overalls, made Jacek think of a surgeon. Mehmet smiled, nodded, smiled again, then burst into laughter. The woman was talking in so low a voice, her head close to Mehmet's, that maddeningly Jacek could hear only a word here and there.

After the woman had gone, Mr Klingsman emerged from his office, scratching at his crotch. 'She's loaded that one,' he told Mehmet, who had already opened the door of the car preparatory to cleaning the interior. 'English but married to a Greek. He's too busy running his restaurants to give her what she wants, if you ask me.'

'What you suggest? I give it to her?'

Both men laughed, Mehmet briefly, no more than a chuckle, and Mr Klingsman in an explosion of mirth hardly merited by the remark. Jacek wondered if he and Mr Klingsman would ever come to laugh together like that. Forlornly he doubted it.

Tips were important to all the men, since the pay, £3.50 per hour, was so niggardly. All tips were meant to go into a tronc, kept in the office, but when a tip was unusually large, then most of the men – Roberto was one of the few exceptions – would surreptitiously keep back a quarter or even a half of it. Jacek soon learned that often the largest cars brought the smallest tips. On his first day, a diminutive man with a button nose and sticking out ears, in a baseball cap worn back to front, had arrived in what was clearly a new BMW. Jacek, who was the only worker who was doing nothing and who was therefore summoned over by Mr Klingsman to deal with this customer, at once assumed that he must be the chauffeur of the car. But most of the other workers at once recognized him for one of the most popular and durable of television comedians and as a consequence kept pausing in their work to stare at him.

To Jacek the man was curt in his instructions, gesticulating with white, pudgy hands laden with rings. It was only after he had strutted off that one of the other workers, an elderly Indian called Selim, called out to Jacek 'Did you recognize him? That cap and those glasses don't fool nobody', and then, amazed by the Pole's ignorance, told him the comedian's name and the title of the sitcom in which he was appearing.

Jacek worked harder at that BMW than he had ever worked before. But, returning, the man barely glanced at it. Having gone into the office to pay Mr Klingsman, he clambered on to the two cushions placed on the driving seat and started the engine. Then, with a grimace, he wriggled round, plunged one of those pudgy, heavily beringed hands into his trouser pocket and eventually, after a lot of fiddling and more grimacing, came up with a fifty p piece. He lowered the electric window to pass this to Jacek. 'Thank you, sir,' Jacek said. The man did not look at him at any time during this transaction.

'How much? How much?' Selim called across, and the other workers were soon halting at their tasks to ask the same. Jacek held up the coin, with a rueful smile. Few of them believed that that was the total sum. They assumed that, by some brilliant feat of legerdemain, Jacek had contrived to magic away the major part of the tip.

Jacek, who in childhood had acquired a latent anti-Semitism from his prematurely widowed mother, was surprised to discover that the taxi drivers, many of whom were Jewish, were the most lavish tippers. Were not Jews supposed to be stingy? This lavishness was most apparent during the night shift, when they would bring in their cabs because a drunk had either vomited or, less frequently, urinated in them. 'Sorry about that,' they would say to whichever worker had the unenviable task of mopping up and scrubbing, before they went off to the Cypriot greasy spoon, open for twenty-four hours of each day, up an alley behind the car wash. The stink would often make Jacek's empty stomach heave. But he did not mind that. The tip in those instances would often be as much as five or ten pounds.

Jacek did not like to leave his English girlfriend, Polly, for the night shift, since, as an assistant in a branch of Next, she inevitably worked days. But the overtime and the tips made it vital for him to do so, if he was to fulfil the task that he had set himself in coming to England. He had imagined that it would not take him long to complete that task. He had not reckoned on the smallness of the wages paid to illegal workers and the much higher cost of living. If his accommodation had not been free in Polly's little flat, it would hardly have been worth his while to stay in Britain.

Mehmet also preferred to work night shifts, presumably for the same reason. He was on the best of terms with the taxi drivers, greeting many of them by name, joking with them, and telling them 'No problem, no problem!' when they apologized for the disgusting state of a cab. Late one night, when both men were on duty, Jacek was so tired that he could hardly lift his short, bow legs, let alone a pail of water or a vacuum cleaner. All at once he was roused from his stupor by Mehmet shouting out gleefully to a departing taxi driver: 'Now what this, what this?' He was waving something, held between thumb and forefinger, in the air.

The taxi driver, a pear-shaped, totally bald man who, like Mehmet and Jacek, liked to work nights because that way there was more money and less hassle, turned, peered and then threw up his hands as he burst into laughter. 'Nothing to do with me, mate! Must have been one of the clients.' He put the last word into derisive inverted commas. 'Why not wash it out and use it yourself? Waste not, want not.'

Mehmet raised his arm and threw the object at the driver. It fell short of him and sploshed on to the concrete. Jacek then saw that it was a condom. Would Mehmet retrieve it and put it in the rubbish bin? He never did. Later Mr Klingsman picked on Roberto – he was always picking on Roberto – to do so.

That was the night when, for the first time, Mehmet and Jacek had a conversation, as distinct from a few hurried words. By three o'clock business was so slack that Mr Klingsman told the two men that they could knock off for half an hour.

'Hungry?' Mehmet asked Jacek, when they accidentally coincided while the former was hanging up a hose and the latter squeezing out a sponge.

Jacek was hungry, but he shook his head. He made it a rule never to spend money in the café where the other men and their taxi driver customers congregated. If he spent money there, then his period of exile and servitude would become even longer. From time to time Polly would tease him for what she saw as his stinginess. It irritated her that he did not even help out with the rent. Her teasing sometimes had an acrid taste to it – 'What do you do with all that money you make? I'm beginning to think you've got another girlfriend.' Since, fortunately, he had never told her of his wife and daughter in Katowice, he would merely reply to that often asked question: 'You know, Polly darling, I want make enough money to buy little flat or maybe a little house.' 'And you expect me to go to Poland to live in it?' No, he did not expect that, he did not even want that. But he never told her so.

'Well, cup of coffee then,' Mehmet insisted.

Jacek was undecided. On the one hand, he wanted to get to know Mehmet, on the other hand he did not want to put down the money even for a cup of coffee. When he worked days, he always brought with him a packet of sandwiches wrapped in a page of Polly's *Mail* or *Standard*. Ashamed of the thick slices clumsily crammed with hard-boiled egg, cheese or pork luncheon meat, he would eat them surreptitiously behind one of the

cars or hunkered down in one of the two malodorous lavator-
ies, the bowls of which were all too often choked with paper
and cigarette ends.

As though he had at once intuited the cause of Jacek's inde-
cision, Mehmet put a hand on his shoulder and said: 'My treat.'
When Jacek, not understanding the phrase, peered up anx-
iously at him with his pale blue eyes, the skin around them grey
and shiny with fatigue, Mehmet said: 'I pay.'

Jacek was still dubious. He hated to, in effect, live off Polly.
He hated even more to accept what he saw as charity from this
fellow worker. But his determination to finish his task in each
case eventually overcame his reluctance. He nodded. 'OK.'

The café was empty. Was it his tiredness that made the light
seem dimmer than usual, Jacek wondered, or had it been
dimmed as an economy measure so late at night, when so few
people, and those mostly prostitutes, came in?

The large, sleepy Cypriot woman – it was she who always
worked nights, her husband days – yawned as she stretched out
a monumental arm for the coffee kept perpetually warm in its
Pyrex glass jug on a low flame. She smiled. 'How's things,
Mehmet?' Everyone knew Mehmet by name. She ignored Jacek,
as everyone tended to do. In his too short, grease-stained grey
cotton trousers, his clumsy shoes with their thick plastic soles,
and his open-necked check shirt under a worn leather jacket, he
stood less than five and a half feet high. Insignificant: that was
how, resignedly, he thought of himself and of how other people
thought of him.

'Not so bad, mamma,' Mehmet said. 'All this night I been
thinking of mamma's coffee. And doughnut,' he added, pointing. 'For you doughnut?' he asked Jacek.

Jacek shook his head and again lied: 'Not hungry. Thank
you.'

'Yes, for you too doughnut. Two doughnut, mamma.'

Jacek was now certain that Mehmet had, through some mysterious insight, known at once why he had pretended not to be
hungry. Perhaps, through that same insight, he was also now
discovering what Jacek had told to no one in England, not
even to Polly: that he had undertaken this journey because it

was only in that way that he could get himself, his wife Ewa and their ailing daughter Anna (she was now seven but looked four) away both from Ewa's parents' house, where the three of them felt constantly oppressed in the low-ceilinged attic room that constituted their whole accommodation, and from Katowice itself, with its miniature volcanoes of factory chimneys vomiting flame and smoke into a sky that, low and leaden, resembled dead flesh raked here and there with lurid orange and red scars.

The two men sat down at a table so shaky that they soon moved to another. Next to this second table sat two women, each with a plate of spaghetti Bolognese before her. The women ate in silence, coiling the spaghetti expertly round their forks and then sucking it in through their brightly-painted mouths. The lipstick on the mouth of one of these women had been smeared up along her cheek by the clumsy passage of a strand of spaghetti.

Mehmet nudged Jacek under the table with one of his trainers and tipped his head in their direction. He leaned forward: 'You know what they are?'

Jacek was afraid that the women would hear. He shook his head.

Again Mehmet leaned forward. He mouthed the word: 'Tarts.' Then, because Jacek clearly had not understood, he mouthed: 'Prostitutes.'

Jacek glanced across at the two women. He felt both disgusted and fascinated. His widowed mother had told him of women like that. It was wicked, she had repeatedly said, to go with them. It could also be dangerous, since they might rob one or give one some terrible disease. But these women looked just like any other women. Polly looked no different from them. In Katowice one could at once recognize such women – they wore brighter and better clothes, painted their faces more vividly, talked and laughed more loudly, puffed at cigarettes more blatantly in the street. How did Mehmet know that these women were what he said they were?

Suddenly, to Jacek's amazement, Mehmet was leaning across to address the women. 'How's business?' he asked, in the same conversational tone of voice that he used when asking the same question of some taxi driver.

One of the two women turned and pulled a face, drawing her mouth together so that small, cobwebby lines radiated out from around it. She was both older than the other one and older than she liked people to think. 'Poor.'

'You don't get so many punters on the run-up to Christmas,' the other said. 'Saving up for toys for the kiddies.' She laughed and then raised the cigarette that she was holding between middle finger and ring finger and dragged on it, eyes half closed.

'How about you two?' the other asked. 'Ready for a bit of fun?'

'Sorry. I wish possible. But we must go back work.'

'Work! What you doing then?'

'Car wash.'

'Oh, that place! We get the occasional cabbie from there. While their cabs are being done – so it has to be a quickie.'

'You look too good for that kind of job,' her companion said. 'They employ a real ragtag and bobtail in that place. All foreigners by the look of it. Pity! We could have enjoyed ourselves.'

People never tipped in the café, since it was self-service. But, as he got up to go, Mehmet took some loose change out of his pocket and placed it by his empty coffee cup, neatly stacking the coins on top of each other. Jacek was to learn that Mehmet was always both generous and meticulous.

'So – goodnight, ladies. I hope business go well.'

'Goodnight, love.'

When he had shut the café door behind them, Mehmet laughed: 'Terrible! So ugly! And one with black hair – so old, hair dyed! Terrible! Of course business bad for them. What they expect?'

Jacek was amazed. So far from thinking them ugly, he had been overcome by their allure. All through the encounter he had been aware of the scent, heavy and musky, that had wafted over from the other table. It had made his head swim and his heart accelerate.

The two men were due to knock off at six o'clock. Selim, not for the first time, had failed to turn up at that hour and so Mr Klingsman asked if either of them would like to stay on – 'night rate, of course' – until some of the other workers had turned up at nine. Mehmet shook his head decisively. 'Sorry, Fritz. I must get home. I'm finished.' He did not look finished. He looked as fresh as his overalls.

'What about you, Jack?' Mr Klingsman had a way of converting foreign names into more manageable English ones.

Jacek's exhaustion was making him feel as if he were stumbling through a sea of viscous, clinging mud; but he thought of his task and all the months that it was taking to fulfil it and he nodded: 'OK.'

'Good man!'

When, bleary-eyed, Mr Klingsman had returned to his office – unusually, he had been on duty that night because his night manager was ill – Mehmet said to Jacek: 'You crazy? Let him do work himself!'

Was he crazy? Sometimes Jacek thought that, in setting himself his task and then pursuing it so single-mindedly, he was. 'I need money,' he said. 'Good money.'

'You must sometimes think other things than money.'

Jacek sighed and then turned at the sound of a taxi being driven in.

Mehmet put a hand on Jacek's shoulder and squeezed it. It was the first time, since Jacek's arrival in England seven months before, that anyone in England, apart from Polly, had shown him any affection. He wished that he could respond in some way, but from a combination of awkwardness and exhaustion he found that he could not do so. An essential part of himself – that part that in Katowice made his fellow workers in the factory regard him as a good sport and good fun – had mysteriously drifted off and no effort, however frantic, availed to summon it back.

Jacek now thought of Mehmet as his mate. From time to time, he would experience a sharp pinch of jealousy when he would see him chatting to one of the other workers. He would even occasionally break his rule of never entering a restaurant,

café or bar, and instead would follow Mehmet to the greasy
spoon, where he would insist: 'No, this time I pay, I pay!' Carefully he would count out the coins in a palm and then hand
them over to the Cypriot woman. 'Thank you, madam.' Unlike
Mehmet, he never tipped.

To Mehmet he began to reveal all the things that were secret
even from Polly: that his wife's parents had been furious when
she had announced that she would marry him and had
attempted to make her change her mind – he wasn't good
enough for the daughter of a master baker, they said, he was so
squat and ugly, half-educated, grubby, smelly; that Anna had
been born with a malformation of the spine, eventually corrected by a drastic operation for which the parents, blaming
Jacek's 'heredity', had reluctantly paid; that they constantly
threw in his face his inability properly to support his own
people, so that even his mother, now nearing seventy, was
working in a laundry.

Mehmet at first listened to these confessions with sympathetic interest; but when Jacek went over them again and again
in conversation, just as he also did in his feverish, disjointed
reveries while working on a car, Jacek would notice, with
dismay, that his attention was straying. His eyes would follow
some woman passing their table, stare moonily out of the
window beside them, or suddenly shout out something to the
Cypriot or his wife behind the counter, or to some other worker
also taking a break in the café.

One day Jacek revealed the circumstance of his admission to
the United Kingdom. A cousin of a cousin, who had once
worked illegally as a builder's labourer in Brighton, had told
him what to do. He should register at a school of English run
by a Pakistani in Clapham. The school was cheaper than most,
the Pakistani did not care whether those who registered at the
school attended classes or not. The Pakistani would give Jacek
a letter, and with this he would, with luck, get a temporary
permit to stay in the country. Jacek had that luck. He had then
found work with a builder, a Pole married to an Englishwoman
and therefore possessing both residence and work permits.
The Pole paid his illegal workers far less than his legal ones,

just as Mr Klingsman did. The advantage of working for him was that over his workshop, under a roof covered with corrugated iron, was a long, narrow attic, a single window at one end, where he let his foreign workers, most of them Poles like himself, live for nothing. In the summer, when Jacek arrived, the heat and stench there was ghastly. But at least he was earning a regular wage, had virtually no expenses, and was surrounded by people who, for the most part, could speak his own language.

One day, early in the morning, while the men, a few of them in pyjamas and the rest of them in their underwear, were still sleeping, uncovered because of the heat, in the two congested rows of mattresses supplied by the boss, the police burst in. Jacek's place was the most coveted, under the window, and at once, without any thought, he first leapt up and perched on its ledge – 'Watch out for that one!' he heard one of the intruders shout – and then launched himself from it, down on to some bushes below. He felt an agonizing jolt to his spine, and at the same time a pain that shot, like a surge of molten metal, up one side of his leg. Somehow, barely able to run, he managed to escape, first crossing the next-door garden, then stumbling down a ginnel, and then miraculously managing almost at once to thumb a lift in a small white van driven by a sturdy woman with close-cropped hair, wearing jeans. Later, when, with extreme caution, he returned in the late afternoon to the workroom, the Pole, so far from welcoming him, told him to make himself scarce. What had happened to the other men? Jacek asked. The Pole shrugged. They would be detained and then deported. He himself would probably face prosecution for employing them. That was what happened when you tried to do other human beings a good turn. His face was stony and haggard; he had been through all this once before, though Jacek did not know that.

Having collected his few pitiful belongings from the attic, Jacek slept rough that night. Then he trailed from place to place in search of work. Limping, dirty and unshaven, he made the worst possible impression. One or two people were at first prepared to take him on but then, inevitably, there was the question of whether he possessed a work permit or not. He would have to admit that he didn't and that was the end of it.

Briefly, he got a job as a part-time cleaner with a firm that was short of staff. An old drunk, encountered on a bench in Battersea Park, had suggested it to him. The job was a night-time one, as part of a gang, many of its members from Africa, who swept up the rubbish on empty and eerily echoing Underground platforms and passages.

Eventually, he heard, again from someone met by chance, this time a Romanian in a café, about the car wash. Once he had persuaded Mr Klingsman to take him on, things continued to improve for him. After only a few days in his new lodging, a Brixton dormitory which he shared with five other men, all of them black, he had been travelling to work on an empty night bus and had found himself sitting opposite two chattering, giggling girls, both of them pleasantly tipsy, who were clearly returning from a party or a disco. When the older and plainer of the girls – she eventually turned out to be Polly – jumped off the bus, she was so absorbed in talking to her companion that she forgot the bag that she had set down on the seat between them. Jacek at once saw it, snatched it up and jumped off the platform of the by now accelerating bus in pursuit. 'Hey! Hey!' he shouted at the girls, who halted and, arms linked, stared back at him in alarm, their mouths open. Then Polly saw that he was waving her bag at her and at once ran forward. 'Oh, thank you, thank you. What an idiot I am! That's what comes of drinking too much.' He handed it to her. She was breathing heavily, and her square, stolid face, with its shiny, bulging forehead over small eyes behind granny glasses, was flushed with relief.

'And now you'll have to take another bus,' the other girl said. 'It may be an age.'

'Let me give you the fare for a taxi,' Polly suggested, opening the bag.

Jacek frowned, then slowly realized what she was offering. He shook his head. 'I walk. Not far. OK.' But the jump from the bus had made his leg, damaged in the frantic leap from the workroom attic, throb again.

'Are you sure?'

He nodded. 'Sure.'

Polly would often say later that, if she hadn't been so pissed that night, she might not have gone on talking to him, and then where would they have been? 'You're foreign, aren't you?' she said. That he was foreign must have been obvious even to someone as pissed as she was.

He nodded. 'Pole.'

'Oh, I used to work with a Polish girl. She was a cashier. I don't know what's happened to her now. She left to have a baby and never came back.'

He nodded, smiled, not understanding.

Still chattering, the girls accompanied him back to the bus stop and stood there waiting with him. Jacek took his worn pocket dictionary out of the plastic bag in which he carried it along with his work clothes, his sandwiches and Thermos. With its assistance – in turn, they held it up to the light from a lamp post and leafed through its pages – the two girls and he somehow managed to communicate. Eventually, Polly said 'We should get together some time.' She had had rather a dismal time at the disco, she was later to tell Jacek after he had moved into her flat, with the boys clearly interested only in her companion, so that she was soon made to feel that she was merely tagging along. When she had seen Jacek opposite her on the bus, looking so sleepy and awkward, she had therefore been in the mood to think him really sweet and to take to him at once.

Jacek nodded eagerly. 'Meet,' he said. 'Yes, yes!' Then he held out the dictionary, which he had opened at its flyleaf and said: 'Telephone, telephone.' The girls searched for a pen or pencil in their bags, until the younger one eventually, with a screech of triumph, jerked a biro out from the bottom of hers. Polly wrote down her name and her telephone number. The younger one made no move to do so, and Jacek, having already decided that she was far too attractive and self-assured for him ever to get anywhere with her, did not urge her to.

Having repeatedly confided in Mehmet, Jacek eventually made an effort to get Mehmet to reciprocate. The return seemed essential if they were truly to be mates. But Mehmet remained evasive.

'Was it difficult for you to come?' Jacek asked.

'To come? To England?' Mehmet shrugged, raised his coffee cup, sipped from it, sipped again. '*Comme ci, comme ça.*' He shrugged again. Jacek knew no French.

'You have permit – work, stay?'

Mehmet waved a hand back and forth as though to dissipate cigarette smoke or some unpleasant smell. 'All OK.' He nodded: 'Yes. Mehmet OK.' Jacek had noticed that he often spoke of himself in the third person.

There were to be other clumsy attempts. All were equally fruitless. All that Jacek ever learned about Mehmet was that he was from Albania, that he was not married, and that he lodged somewhere in North London. None of the other people at the car wash, not even Mr Klingsman, knew more.

One evening, Jacek stood eating some cereal, the bowl held under his chin, in the tiny kitchen, and Polly, who was obsessively tidy, was rearranging some cutlery in a drawer. It was then that he suddenly found the courage to tell her of the plan that had been forming in his mind over the past few days. She knew that chap he had told her about, that Mehmet, the one that was always so friendly to him? Polly nodded and muttered, head bent over the drawer, 'H'm, h'm.' She had never met Mehmet, never even seen him, but she had confided in Renée that she did not at all care for the *idea* of him. Jacek would go on and on so about him, he thought that the light shone out of his arse. But she got this feeling, she could not say why, that he wasn't right for Jacek, that he could only be bad news. In a peculiar way, she was jealous of him, she told Renée, and that worried her. Why on earth should she be jealous of a bloke?

'Well, I'm thinking, Polly, maybe we ask him round one evening.'

Polly was astounded. 'Ask him *here*?' She turned from the drawer, two spoons gripped in her right hand, to face him. 'Are you crazy?'

He had expected some such response and had dreaded it. But he persisted. 'He kind, kind to me, very kind. He my – my

– only mate. You like him, Polly. Truly. Good man. Nice. Yes, you like him. Promise.' He continued to cajole her and she continued to protest that it was all too much trouble, they were both too busy, Jacek hardly knew Mehmet and she did not know him at all. Jacek eventually put his arms around her sturdy body and hugged her to him. She tried to push him away – 'Oh, do give over!' – but he hugged her even harder and, as they struggled, she began to giggle. 'Just some beer,' he said. 'I buy beer. And maybe sausage rolls, sandwich. Maybe cake? Yes?'

'Oh, very well? But I don't want too much drinking. And I don't want him to stay too late.'

'All as you wish. As you wish, Polly darling.' He kissed her on the forehead and, then holding her chin in his hand, on her mouth, first gently and then attempting to insert his tongue. Polly abruptly turned her head aside. 'Oh, do let me get on with what I'm doing.' Polly had confided to Renée that she had never really known what sex could be like until Jacek had come into her life. But there was a time and place for sex, and seven o'clock in the evening in the kitchen was not it.

When they both knocked off on the evening planned for the visit, Jacek imagined that he and Mehmet would travel together to Polly's Barnsbury flat. But Mehmet said that he had something to see to first, it wouldn't take him long, he would be with them in, oh, half an hour, maybe three-quarters. He did not specify what it was that he had to see to first, and Jacek, by now used to his reticence, did not press him.

'Where is he?' Polly demanded as soon as she saw that Jacek had entered the flat unaccompanied.

'Something to do.' Jacek shrugged and pulled face. 'Say nothing. But he come soon, half-hour, little more.'

'Oh, really!' Polly had made the excuse of a fictitious dental appointment to get away early from work. 'I hope he's not planning to let us down. I've baked a cake.'

'Did you buy sausage rolls?' Jacek had given her some money to do so.

'No, I certainly did not. I made some sandwiches. Look!' He followed her into the kitchen and inspected the sandwiches laid out on two plates. The bread thinly cut and its crusts removed, these sandwiches were totally different from the thick, clumsy ones that he made for himself. They were even garnished with parsley and tomato rosettes. Admiringly Jacek picked up one of the rosettes in fingers stained ineradicably with engine oil. 'Don't touch!' Polly screamed. But by then Jacek had bitten into it. When Jacek attempted to place the half-eaten rosette back on the plate, Polly screamed again: 'No! No!'

Jacek began to set out the beer cans and the glasses on the table. One of the glasses was smeared. He held it up to the light, then breathed on it and wiped it with a dishcloth hanging beside the sink. 'Fine,' he said. 'Very fine.' He picked up an edge of another dishcloth covering the chocolate cake, squinted under it and then let it fall back. 'Good.'

'I didn't want the flies to get at the icing.'

'Very good.'

When Mehmet arrived, Jacek at once realized why he had said that he had something to see to first. No longer in his work clothes, he was wearing a charcoal-grey suit, all three buttons fastened, a grey and white striped shirt, and a brilliant tie, red arabesques on dark blue. Jacek felt embarrassed that he himself possessed nothing of that kind into which to change. But at least Polly had made up her usually sallow face, and put on her best dress and an elaborate filigree silver necklace that a previous boyfriend had brought her back after a holiday in Goa.

Mehmet was totally at his ease, and totally charming. So much prejudiced against him before his arrival, Polly was captivated. As he talked to her about incidents, some dramatic but mostly comic, at the car wash, she squealed with laughter. When Jacek had recounted many of the same incidents to her, she had merely put up a perfunctory show of interest.

Mehmet ate only two of the many sandwiches – could it be that he had already eaten when changing his clothes, Jacek wondered? – and he declined any beer, saying that all that he really wanted was a glass of water. 'I'm afraid we haven't any mineral water,' Polly told him. 'We ran out yesterday and somehow I forgot to buy any more.' In fact, they never bought mineral water – 'a total waste of money,' Polly would say. 'OK, OK, don't worry,' Mehmet told her. 'Tap water fine.' 'With ice?' He nodded. 'Please.' Then he added: 'You spoil me. I hope you also spoil Jacek.'

'Of course.' Again she giggled. 'Provided he behaves himself.'

'He sometimes not behave himself?'

'Sometimes. He can be quite a naughty boy, you know.'

Mehmet was full of praise for the cake. 'You make this cake? I cannot believe! In my country we have Albanian sweets, wonderful sweets, my sister and mother make. But nothing similar this.' He raised his slice of cake in his fingers, although Polly had given him a fork, and again bit into it. 'Beautiful.'

'I'll make you some coffee,' Polly volunteered, suddenly having thought of it.

'Is trouble?'

'No, of course not.' Polly leapt up from her chair and began to fill the kettle at the sink. 'It's only Nes,' she said. 'Does that matter?'

'Nescafé fine.'

'Well, actually it's not Nescafé,' Polly admitted, holding up the jar. 'But it's just the same. Safeway.'

Jacek would have liked to have had a cup of coffee too. But Polly did not offer him one and he did not like to ask, in case it caused trouble. Nor did she offer him a second slice of cake, although she cut one for Mehmet and another for herself. As the two of them chatted, he felt increasingly excluded. It might have been Polly and Mehmet who were the partners, and he merely the guest. He felt both a joy that two people so close to him should be getting on so well, and also a reluctant annoyance that, in getting on so well, they paid him so little attention. If only he could understand more of what they were saying! If only he could say more himself!

Jacek caught Mehmet looking surreptitiously at his watch. His method of doing so was to place his wrist on his knee, under the table, out of sight as he thought, and then with two fingers of his other hand to ease back his shirt cuff and glance down. A few minutes later he again looked at the watch in the same manner. 'Sorry. I must go.' He pushed back his upright bentwood chair, rose, smiled first at Polly and then at Jacek. 'Sorry.'

'But it's still so early!' Polly protested. 'Little after nine.' Desperately, she went on: 'Why don't you have another sandwich – or another slice of cake – and I'll make you some more coffee.'

'Sorry. Long way to Dalston. And so much work today – many cars, many trucks, many taxis. I little tired. I sure Jacek also tired.'

'No, no!' Jacek shook his head vigorously.

Mehmet put a hand on Jacek's shoulder, patted it, then squeezed, in that way that had now become a habit. 'Yes, Jacek. You tired. You must go sleep early. Yes.' It was like a father talking to a young son who had protested about being sent up to bed.

As Polly began to wash and Jacek to dry the things, Polly broke the silence: 'Well, he's certainly a charmer!'

Jacek said nothing. He had been wondering whether the visit had been a success. On the one hand Mehmet had got on so well with Polly; on the other hand he had stayed for less than an hour.

'He's dishy,' Polly remarked in a low, soft voice, unlike her usual piercing one. To Jacek she seemed to be talking more to herself than to him. 'I don't usually like that kind of beaky nose but on his face . . .'

'What I do with sandwiches?' Jacek picked up one of the two plates, its sandwiches almost untouched.

Polly stared down at them, her previously cheerful face suddenly growing sombre, even sad. After a while she said: 'Well, you could take them with you to work. Tomorrow. Why not?'

Now Jacek also stared down at the uneaten sandwiches. 'OK,' he said resignedly, without any pleasure.

'You could also take a can or two of beer and some of the cake.'

'OK!'

Then a thought suddenly struck Polly. She slapped a hand to her forehead. 'Oh, what a fool. I should have given him the rest of the cake to take away with him. He said how much he liked it.'

That night Jacek knew that Polly, snuggling up against him, wanted him to make love to her. But for once, he had no desire to do so and, despite all her efforts, his penis would not harden.

'Oh, shit!' She turned away from him and jerked one of the pillows under her cheek. Soon she was snoring.

Jacek stared up the ceiling, a grey space bisected by an arrow of yellow light through the chink in the curtains from the street lamp outside.

It was a few days later that Selim got the sack.

From time to time he and Jacek had worked together. From time to time, too, when Jacek had wished only to be away from everyone to eat his sandwich lunch, Selim had unaccountably sought him out, and in his near-falsetto voice had then ranted about some grievance or other: that Mr Klingsman was picking on him in assigning to him too many, not enough or the least attractive jobs; that someone or other, on a bus, in a shop or in the street, had treated him like shit; that his tips were smaller than those of the other workers because the clients did not respect him, considering all Indians to be no-good people.

Jacek understood little of all this and, stolidly chewing away at his sandwiches, would wish only that this dishevelled figure with a ponytail of lank hair, black streaked with grey, dangling almost to his waist, pan-stained teeth and prominent eyes in a face in which muscles seemed to be constantly writhing under the taut, tawny skin, would go away. Why did he have to pick on him? There were two other Indians, a Bangladeshi and a Pakistani all working in the place; but, so far from seeking them out, Selim avoided them.

To everyone else Selim was a joke. When he was at his most agitated or angry, they would even bait him, as one might a fierce dog safely tethered to a chain, until he bared his teeth, his eyes blazing, and shouted at them not in English but in Hindi. This would cause even more derision. But to Jacek he was a figure at once weird and frightening, never an object of fun. He always dreaded his approach and felt an intense relief when he either wandered off of his own account or was summoned back to work by Mr Klingsman.

Selim alternated between working frantically or at so lethargic a pace, dragging his feet in their worn plimsoles and muttering inaudibly to himself as he circled some car or van as though undecided how to set about it, that a job took him twice as long as it did anyone else. Sometimes, like Jacek, if there were a lot of work on hand, he would volunteer to follow one shift with another, working on and on with no sign of the intensifying exhaustion felt by the Pole. But on many days or nights he would drift in late, with some excuse (the bus on which he had been travelling had been involved in an accident, there had been no Central line trains, he had had to help an old woman who had suffered a fall just on the other side of the street from the car wash) so bogus that Mr Klingsman would shout in fury that he didn't fucking want to hear that sort of crap, would Selim just shut up and get on with it.

For all of that last week Selim drifted in late, sometimes, head down, tonelessly whistling to himself, and sometimes greeting the other workers with what struck Jacek as an ironically jolly 'Good morning, good morning!' Surprisingly, once so fertile in excuses, however absurd, he now offered none, even when Mr Klingsman challenged him 'Where the hell have you been?' or 'D'you realize that you're more than an hour late?' Nor did he ever utter an apology.

On Selim's last day, Mr Klingsman rushed out of his office as soon as he wandered in. 'Right! That's it! I warned you! Don't say I didn't warn you.' He raised his left hand and jabbed with the forefinger of his right at the watch on his wrist. 'Look at that! Ten past ten! D'you realize that you're fucking meant to be here at nine?'

Selim, often so vehement and even violent in his responses, remained totally calm. He walked over to Mr Klingsman, bent over and, head tilted to one side, hitched up the sleeve of Mr Kingsman's shirt and inspected the watch for himself. Then he straightened up again, gave a little bow like the one that he would often give to his fellow workers, and said in his high, sing-song, nasal voice, almost a chant: 'Good morning, Mr Boss. How is Mr Boss today?'

Paradoxically the Indian's calmness maddened Mr Klingsman far more than any indignation or rudeness would have done. He stood over him, his whole body shaking. 'Right! Right! Now I'll tell you what! I give you ten minutes to pack up all your gear and get yourself out of here. D'you get me? Out of here. In ten minutes sharp. And I don't want to see your black face round here again or to smell your fucking curry smell. Got it?'

'You wish me to go, Mr Boss?'

'That's it. Well done! You've got it. You've got it exactly. Out! Now! Now!'

Selim shook his head, as though in disbelief. The eyes that were often so dull in the narrow, emaciated face now glinted. 'OK, Mr Boss. But I want notice. You give me two weeks notice or you pay me two weeks.'

'Are you crazy? For days and days you've been farting in here late and then drifting around, just drifting around, no fucking use at all. You're going to get your money for the past week and that's it. That's it!' he shouted. There was saliva glistening in either corner of his mouth, his chin was jutting out pugnaciously.

'I want notice. Or three weeks pay – one week gone, two weeks coming.'

'Well, you're not going to get it.'

By now all the men had stopped working. They were gathered in a narrowing circle around the couple, most of them grinning. Jacek stood a little apart from them. Mehmet was on the next shift and was therefore not there.

Mr Klingsman went into his office, unlocked a cash box and began to count out some notes. Still totally unperturbed, Selim squatted on his hunkers outside the office, from time to time grinning at several of his workmates. Catching Jacek's eye at one moment, he put his hands together and gave him an ironic salaam.

Mr Klingsman emerged with some notes in a fist. He thrust them out. 'That's more than you're due and far more than you deserve.'

Calmly Selim got to his feet, took them and began to count them out. Then he said: 'Not enough, Mr Boss. I say –'

'I don't care a fuck what you say!'

Selim tucked the notes into a pocket of his worn jeans. 'You foolish, Mr Boss.' His voice had suddenly deepened, it had totally lost its frail, metallic quality. 'I make trouble, big trouble.'

'Out! Out!' Mr Klingsman bellowed. 'I never want to see your face here again! Go on! Beat it!'

Selim gathered the saliva in his mouth and spat, so accurately that the gob landed on one of Mr Klingsman's shoes. Pan had streaked the saliva with a vivid red. Jacek, seeing it, recoiled in momentary panic, having imagined the streaks to be blood. His dying father had coughed up phlegm streaked like that, when Jacek was only a small child. Then, swinging the plastic bag which he had brought with him in his right hand, while he kept rhythmically clicking the fingers of his left, Selim walked jauntily through the circle of workers and out towards the exit. Just before the exit, he swung round.

'Take care. Something bad! Something bad!'

He raised a long, admonitory finger.

Then he hunched his bony shoulders and loped off.

Near the end of the following week, business was so slack one morning that, soon after eleven, Mr Klingsman told Mehmet and Jacek to take their lunch break then instead of waiting for another hour. 'D'you mind?' he asked, and both of them, though they thought it far too early, said that they didn't. Mr Klingsman then said: 'You don't have to race back. Take your time.'

'Coming?' Mehmet asked Jacek.

'Where?'

'To pub. Or caff. Where you like.'

'I have lunch. Sandwich.'

'Oh, forget about them! Come on!' He made a beckoning gesture with his head. Then, seeing that Jacek was still reluctant, he said: 'My treat. I pay.'

'No, no! You pay too much, pay always.'

'Come!'

'OK, I come, I come!' Jacek had balanced the cost against the pleasure of talking alone to Mehmet. He would have a cup of coffee and a doughnut or a bag of crisps and then, later, he would eat the sandwiches.

It was a fateful decision.

Jacek had wanted to go to the café, since a cup of coffee there cost less than half a pint at the pub and he was in any case nervous of alcohol, remembering how his mortally ill father would fly into terrifying rages after draining glass after glass of vodka kept in a bottle under his sickbed. But Mehmet had insisted, repeating 'My treat, my treat!' Jacek had then attempted, as he had so often done in the past, to pay at least for himself; but again, as so often in the past, he had not been successful. There was, to Jacek, something aristocratic about the way in which Mehmet thought nothing of spending money. Jacek found that both attractive and alarming, having been brought up by his mother always to be thrifty. To leave change on the counter of a bar, as Mehmet always did, was to him not merely a waste but a moral lapse.

As they munched their way through the ploughman's lunches for which Mehmet had also insisted on paying, they talked of Selim. Mehmet, imitating the nasal, near-falsetto voice with remarkable accuracy, repeated that final 'Something bad! Something bad!' What could the idiot do? He laughed. Put a spell on them? Jacek wondered aloud what had happened to Selim. No one knew anything about him, he had never made any friends. 'He not find it easy get other job,' Mehmet said. He shook his head and pursed his lips. 'And he illegal – so – no social security.' He drew a forefinger across his neck. Then he laughed again.

Unaccountably, Jacek all at once felt sorry for the Indian. Selim had so often exasperated him beyond endurance, attaching himself to him unasked and then vomiting out the molten lava of his fury against the whole world. But now, without knowing why, Jacek had started to miss him. They seemed to be closer in Selim's absence than they had ever been when Selim was a constant, importunate, irritating presence.

Eventually Mehmet looked at his watch and said: 'Well, we return? Yes?' He got to his feet, picking up the copy of the *Sun* that he had been carrying around with him. At one point he had opened it and looked at the horses, prompting Jacek to ask: 'Do you – do you . . .?', a forefinger indicating the page, since he did not know the word 'bet'. Mehmet had nodded. 'Sometimes.

And often lucky. Last week, I place ten pounds – thirty-two to one. I win!'

Jacek had only half understood. He had known that something good had befallen Mehmet but he could not have said precisely what.

When they entered the hangar-like garage, it was eerily silent and empty. Outside it, Roberto was smoking a cigarette, leaning against the wall in a patch of fragile sunlight. He did not greet them or even smile at them when they passed him; his usual cheerful face was pensive, even glum, as he sucked on the Gauloise pinched between grimy finger and thumb. Two men, both English, were working together on a taxi at the far end. They looked up when Mehmet and Jacek entered and then at once looked down. Jacek sensed something dark and treacherous, like a plague about to erupt.

Suddenly Mr Klingsman emerged from his office, his plump, round face pale and puckered. He drew a handkerchief from his trouser pocket and held it to his lips, as he might have done if someone had punched him in the mouth and it was bleeding. When he was near them, he lowered the handkerchief. His bottom lip was twitching. 'You two had better beat it as quick as you can.' The urgency with which he spoke at once communicated itself to Jacek, he knew at once that something bad had happened. But Mehmet was totally unaffected. 'What up, Fritz?' he asked in the sort of voice in which he might have asked what needed to be done to a vehicle just brought in.

'It must be that little shit Selim. You heard him threaten me when I gave him the shove. They were here, the police and immigration people. Half an hour ago. Took everyone – except those with permits. I've lost the whole bloody lot. You'd better scarper before they return. *If* they return.'

'What going to happen to them?' Mehmet asked, in the same calm, relaxed tone.

'To who?'

'To others.'

'How do I know?' The tone was peevish. 'Deportation most likely. That's what usually happens. Except for those fly buggers who manage to claim asylum. Then – who knows? There's such a state of bloody chaos at that place in Croydon that they can often spin it out for years and years. As often as not the papers just get lost. The other day in the *Sun* there was something about the rats having been at work on some of them.'

Jacek was now desperate to get away as quickly as possible. He had not understood all that Mr Klingsman had said but he had grasped the reason for the men's disappearance and had guessed that he, too, might suffer the same disaster. 'We go,' he whispered urgently to Mehmet. 'Quick!'

But Mehmet paid no attention. 'What about our money, Fritz?'

'Your money?'

'Five days.'

'All right, all right! Yes. I'll get it for you. But after that you'd better make yourselves scarce.'

Mr Klingsman rushed into the office. Mehmet pointed to the shed in which the staff left their belongings and, during their breaks, could perch uncomfortably on one or other of two long wooden benches. 'You have things in there?'

Jacek nodded.

'Me too. We better fetch them.'

Mehmet took his time collecting his belongings, while Jacek waited on the threshold of the hut in mounting dread. Finally Mehmet was ready. He smiled cheerfully. 'Let's go.'

Mr Klingsman padded over. He pushed across the notes to Mehmet. 'There you are! You can split that. Fifty-fifty. I've added something for the tips. Mehmet – I'm sorry about this. You were a bloody good worker. And you're a bloody good chap. All these fucking regulations!' He was genuinely upset to see Mehmet go. He paid no attention to Jacek.

Mehmet threw his arms around Mr Klingsman and kissed him ceremonially first on one flushed cheek and then the other. 'This how we say goodbye in my country,' he said. Once Mehmet released him, Mr Klingsman edged away, more embarrassed than pleased.

Outside, as they began to walk towards the Underground station, Mehmet said: 'Well, *c'est fini*. Too bad.'

'Difficult to find job.'

'It get more and more difficult as more and more refugee come.'

Jacek tried to quicken their progress, for fear of being caught if the immigration people and the police were to return. But Mehmet refused to respond.

'Maybe I must go back to Poland,' Jacek said bleakly.

'No, don't do that. Something good come. Sure.'

Jacek was far from certain of that. 'So you are also illegal.' It was something about which he had never been sure. Now he was.

Mehmet did not answer. He merely smiled, more to himself than to Jacek.

At the Underground station, Mehmet said that he had some things to do, he would not be taking his train yet.

Jacek, who was desperate for them to get even farther away from the car wash, pleaded with him: 'No, no! No here, no more here! Come, come.' But Mehmet repeated: 'I have some things to do. Someone to see. Sorry.'

'Then . . .?' There was a note of both pleading and interrogation in Jacek's voice.

'Then – we say goodbye!' Mehmet's laugh rang out.

Jacek pointed at Mehmet's chest. 'You.' He pointed at his own chest. 'Me. See again?'

'Maybe. Yes. Why not?' Again Mehmet laughed.

'But . . .' Jacek frowned, like a child brought close to tears by something he cannot grasp despite all his efforts. At last he said, again pointing at Mehmet's chest: 'Address? You – address?'

Mehmet pulled out a pack of cigarettes and held it out to Jacek. Had he not remembered that Jacek had given up smoking in order not to spend money on a habit so expensive? When Jacek shook his head, Mehmet drew out a cigarette for himself, in slow motion as it seemed to the Pole in his increasing agitation to be off, and carefully lit it. He puffed, once, twice, three times. Then screwing up his eyes as a gust of sulphur-laden wind blew smoke into them, he said: 'Soon I move. So – ' he shrugged – 'no use give you my address now. But' – he put out a hand, placed it on Jacek's shoulder and then squeezed it, as he had so often done in the past – 'I have your address. And telephone number. So – we keep touch.' Jacek was looking up at him with a distracted, frightened expression. It was almost as if those palest of blue eyes would all at once fill with tears. 'So – we – keep – touch.' Mehmet isolated each of the words as he repeated them more loudly. He might have been talking to someone deaf.

Jacek nodded gratefully. 'Please. Telephone. *Please!*' The voice became desperate. He stared up at Mehmet, he choked as he struggled for words. Then again he pointed. 'You. You my. Only. Friend.' He nodded. 'Friend. Brother. I dream of such a brother. Then you come. Dream become true.'

Mehmet smiled at him, head on one side. There was indulgence in the smile, also a vague fondness. 'So, Jacek.' Now he put both hands on Jacek's shoulder, he drew him to him. 'So. We say goodbye. And in my country . . .' He kissed Jacek first on one cheek and then on the other, as he had kissed Mr Klingsman. There was little emotion in the kiss and Jacek was cruelly aware of that.

A moment later Mehmet was gone. He swung round on a heel and then, even as Jacek was looking after him, he disappeared into a crowd of people who, a train having just arrived, were pouring up out of the station.

For a few moments Jacek's gaze fluttered hither and thither. Then he knew that it was no good. He began his descent.

'Jacek! What's the matter?'

Polly, who had not gone to work because of one of her bad periods, knew at once that something was wrong.

'Oh, Polly, Polly!' Like a child seeking his mother's arms, Jacek rushed at her, as she stood staring at him from beside the sink. Water dripped off her hands and then they were moist through his grubby shirt, as she enfolded him to her, squeezed him.

'Something terrible happen. Terrible. Terrible.'

'What is it?' He did not answer, his cheek now laid against her left breast and his hand on her right. 'What is it?'

'Terrible. I no see. No see. Mehmet again.'

It was only later that he told her about the loss of his job, and even later of his decision to go back to Poland.

Chapter VII

In a mood of uncharacteristic gloom, Meg had leaned against the frame of the sitting-room window, her crutches resting beside her, and stared out into a street in which everyone seemed to be rushing to work. She would now never rush to anything, she had bitterly mused. It would be enough if she could crawl there. After several minutes, she had then turned back to Eric, who was sitting in an armchair behind her, checking a telephone bill received that morning. From time to time he had been addressing her back with some remark like: 'Who the hell telephoned Godalming for eleven minutes? I don't know a soul in Godalming. Do you know anyone in Godalming?' or 'Here's a call to Edinburgh, I don't believe it, I just don't believe it.' Meg had made no answer, indeed had hardly heard him, so absorbed had she been in the reverie that was sweeping her along on its black, rushing, subterranean stream.

Eventually she had swung herself round. 'What the hell are these remissions that people keep talking about?' she had demanded, the bitterness that had been fermenting in her suddenly exploding in anger. 'That's what I'd like to know. I've had no remissions, not a single one. I'm no more likely to have a remission than to fly in Concorde or win the lottery. They tell one these things to keep one's spirits up. That's all, that's bloody all.'

Eric had looked up from the bill. 'It'll come,' he had said, making one of those efforts, which were becoming increasingly difficult for him, to be reasonable and calm when she raged against her condition. 'You wait and see. It'll come.'

Now, so many years after Eric had upped and left her, the remission had indeed come, just as he and that Chinaman had predicted. Less and less did she need to summon Mehmet's assistance, shouting out to him 'Mehmet, could you come and lend a hand?' or, more peremptory, 'Mehmet, Mehmet, I need you. Yes, at once!' She was able to take a few faltering steps without the crutches, and to hold a full kettle in one hand instead of needing both. 'It's odd,' she told Mehmet in a peevish, complaining voice that might have been expected if her condition had deteriorated instead of improved, 'last night I never had a single one of those spasms and all day yesterday there were no pins and needles. What d'you make of that?'

'You getting better.'

She frowned at him: 'That'll be the day.'

Soon, she no longer needed him to stand over her, ready to pass her soap, facecloth and scrubbing brush when she took one of her rare baths. He would merely help her into the tub and then leave her to soak on and on there, from time to time running in some more scalding water, until she called out to him to help her out. Once she was out of the bath, there was no longer any need for him to hand her the towel or even to rub her down.

Then the day came when, having managed to get up from the armchair unaided, she suddenly appeared, hanging on to the jamb of the half-open door of his bedroom, to ask if he felt like a breath of air.

'Oh, Meg, this marvellous!', he cried, his pleasure an amplified echo of hers. 'A miracle!'

What tosh! A miracle was something that lasted. This was a *remission*. But nonetheless, as he helped her on with her overcoat and then firmly took her arm, she felt a sudden excitement. This excitement intensified when, for the first time for so long, she was seeing everything and everyone in the street from a totally different perspective from that provided by the chair. 'Hold me tight!' she told him. 'Don't let me fall!'

'What an idea!'

'Yes, you're strong,' she told him appreciatively. For so long she had been unable to grip anything. Now she could actually squeeze his arm. 'Unlike my poor Eric. When I started to be ill, before they gave me the chair, it was always a problem for him to help me around. He was always frightened of his back, that was the thing. "I'm going to put out my back again," he'd tell me. He'd always had this trouble with it. No, he was not strong like you. Always something wrong with him.'

That first walk was a brief one, up slowly to the Methodist church at the end of the road, then a rest on the bench outside it, fortunately for once not occupied by what Meg called vagabonds, and then even more slowly back again. 'Oh, I feel quite done in!' she sighed, as she flopped back into her arm-chair on their return. But there was colour in her cheeks and her eyes shone. 'Be an angel and make me a cuppa.' She knew that Mehmet shared in her joy at her recovery of the powers that had for so long seemed to have been lost forever, and she was touched that he should do so. It made her feel even closer to him and even fonder of him.

'You're a good sort, Mehmet. Do you know that?'

'Am I? Am I really?'

'Yes. You're a good sort. I'm telling you that.'

Mehmet was late. He was often late, never giving her a reason. Perhaps he had a girlfriend? she pondered for the umpteenth time. Or perhaps he met up with other Albanians in some caff or bar? She never asked about his whereabouts, because she had learned that he did not like her to do so and would politely evade any answer if she did. Today, she was impatient for his return, because she wanted to tell him that, no longer with the crutches but merely with a stick, she had ventured out on her own and had even been able to make her way, unaided, to the tobacconist's. As both a trophy and a proof to him that she had been there, she had even bought him a packet of the Superkings Light that she knew that he smoked – not when with her in the sitting room, unless she was smoking herself, but in his bedroom, the window wide open even on the coldest day, so that the smell should not bother her, even though she repeatedly told him that of course it never did, she was such a heavy smoker herself.

At last she heard the sound of his key in the door.

'Is that you, Mehmet pet?'

'Yes, Mamma. Just one moment. I must go toilet.'

His voice usually sounded so cheerful and vigorous when he returned from the car wash, it always gave her a lift after she had spent a long day on her own. But now it had a weary, discouraged sound to it. She knew that something had gone wrong.

When he eventually appeared, she said: 'Well, what sort of day did we have?'

He shrugged, pulling down the corners of his mouth, and then picked up her copy of the *Radio Times* and flicked over the pages.

'Busy?'

'So-so.' He threw down the magazine on to a worn leather pouffe, brought back by Eric from a Middle East cruise, and said: 'Bad news.'

'Bad news?' She was meant to be the one who had bad news, he the one for whom the news was always good. She stared at him, a hand going up to a cheek and stroking at a coffee-coloured mole on it. 'What's happened, dear?'

'I have lost job.'

'*What?* How?'

He perched on an arm of the sofa opposite to hers and began to tell her the story of his departure from the car wash.

At the end, she said: 'You never told me. I never knew.' It was more sorrowful than accusatory.

'Never told what? Never knew what? What you talking about, Mamma?'

She was now embarrassed. The secret was, she had decided, a shameful one, and to reveal it was like revealing that one had Aids or had been in the nick. She turned her head aside and, biting her lips, said nothing.

'What you mean?'

'Well – I had no idea that – that you were – well – an *illegal*.'

'I did not wish worry you, Mamma. You have too many worries already.'

That touched her; he was always thinking about what was best for her. 'Yes, and that was sweet of you, Mehmet. But your worries are my worries. Surely you know that by now.'

About his illegal presence in the country he was clearly not prepared to tell her more. But, consumed by both anxiety and inquisitiveness, she persisted. 'Why didn't you come into the country regular like? Wasn't that possible for you?'

'Difficult,' he said. He frowned, tugging viciously with one hand at the leather fringe of the moccasin that, legs crossed one over the other, was resting on his knee.

'Don't do that, dear,' she chided him, as she might have chided a child for picking its nose or scratching at a scab. 'You'll pull it off.' Then, when he had let go of the leather fringe, she said: 'How did you get in then? Were you one of those smuggled in a lorry or in one of those small boats?'

He shook his head. Then reluctantly he said: 'I come as tourist. From Paris by Eurotunnel. Easy. Then – I just stay. I like it here, I stay.'

'And you found that job – that car wash job – easily, did you?'

'Oh, I have other jobs before. You know that, Mamma.' He laughed. 'Some good, some bad, some very bad. But car wash was good. Good pay, good tips. Regular. Better than when I work for my friend in Chelsea. You remember? One day work, two days nothing. I have trouble with rent then. Bad for me, bad for poor Mamma.'

'Oh, it's such a shame you've lost that car wash job.'

He nodded ruefully. 'Jobs now not easy for illegals. There is new law, did you know that, Mamma? Now not only illegal gets punished, employer also. So – employers are frightened.'

'Do you think you'll be able to find another job?'

He shrugged and again tugged at the fringe of the moccasin. Suddenly she noticed that that morning he must have gone out without shaving. He was always so particular about looking just so. There was a dark shadow of stubble on the lower half of his face. In a weird way, it made him look even more handsome, she thought. But it was odd that he hadn't shaved. Perhaps he had had some premonition.

'Do you?' she persisted. 'D'you think you can find something else?'

'I must try.'

'Perhaps I can ask Mr Jarrett – the chappy who runs the Rat and Parrot. He was a chum of Eric's. Sometimes I had a real job keeping Eric away from that place.'

'Yes, a pub good. I like that. Please, Mamma. Yes, ask him.'

'He's quite a hard taskmaster. I remember that one of the girls there told me that. Always fussing and chivvying them around.'

Mehmet laughed. 'I deal with that.'

Meg glanced over to him, her eyes brimming with love. 'Yes, you can deal with anything.'

For the rest of that evening, he did not watch television, as he usually did when he had not decided to go out, he never told her where, but instead sat perched on the edge of an armchair in a corner of the sitting room, head bowed over one of the puzzles that from time to time he brought back to the flat. Familiar to her from her Pakistani dentist's waiting room, she had long since decided that these puzzles had become an obsession with him. In this one, there were eight balls that, skidding erratically, like bubbles of mercury, hither and thither, had to be coaxed one by one through an elaborate maze into eight holes. Usually, frowning in concentration and sometimes biting his lower lip, he eventually succeeded. But on this occasion, though he stuck at the task all through *Who Wants to be a Millionaire?* and some minutes of an old Astaire and Rogers film, he never did so.

'No luck?' she looked across to ask him when she yet again heard a muffled grunt of rage.

Without answering he threw the puzzle across the room on to a chair opposite to him.

'Fuck!'

He had never before used that word in her presence. 'Mehmet! Please!'

Without even a word of apology, he jumped to his feet and ran out, leaving the door open behind him. Soon she heard, far, far louder than usual, the sound of Albanian music blaring from his room.

Next day, soon after noon, Meg dragged herself up to the Rat and Parrot and then sat on and on, a glass of Guinness on the table before her, while waiting for Mr Jarrett to come back from the betting shop.

'Hello, sweetheart!' he greeted her, with obvious pleasure, on his return. 'Long time, no see.' He appraised her and then looked briefly at the heavy stick with the rubber ferrule resting across the chair opposite to her. 'You look a lot better.'

'I am better,' she said. 'I'm having what they call a *remission*.' As always she brought out the word as though it were a foreign one.

'Well, long may it last.'

Since the bar was virtually empty, he went and fetched himself a gin and tonic and then, having moved the stick to another chair, placed himself opposite to her. Again he appraised her. He had always thought that she was a handsome woman and, after Eric's disappearance, had even wondered whether there might not be something doing there. But then she had fallen so ill, and illness always put him off, he could not do with it.

They began to talk of general things. Mr Jarrett produced a series of frisky innuendoes, and Meg alternated between looking shocked by them and throwing back her head and laughing so hard that the tears welled out of her eyes. Then, at last, she broached the subject of a job behind the bar or in the kitchen for Mehmet.

'Yes, I know who you mean,' Mr Jarrett said, surprising Meg, who had had no idea that Mehmet had ever entered the Rat and Parrot. 'That Albanian, yes? He comes in here from time to time – usually for a game of pool.' The game of pool was also a surprise for Meg. 'Nice bloke. Always quick to buy his rounds – unlike a lot of those foreign ones. But' – regretfully he shook his head – 'I just daren't take him on. It's different now, you see. Last year I had that Hungarian girl. Lili. You may remember her. That was OK, no one was any the wiser, cash in the hand. But now . . . They've become strict, *very strict*. Oh, yes. I could get the brewery a hefty fine. And then – well, I might be out on my ear.'

When Meg told Mehmet of Mr Jarrett's response, he was less crestfallen than she had feared. 'Yes, I told you,' he said. 'Not easy now. But . . . I must continue to try.'

She admired the way in which he refused to be worried by the setback. She herself was worried sick.

Some ten days later, Mehmet came home after an absence of many hours to announce that he had got a job – not a good job but a job – as a kitchen porter in an Arab restaurant off the Edgware Road. He did not really like Arabs. But he could not be choosy, he must take what was offered.

'But a kitchen porter!' Meg exclaimed. 'You're too good for that, dear. You're an educated man. You can't do a job like that.'

'I must. Nothing else.'

'Oh, you poor thing! It's terrible.'

He put a hand on her shoulder and squeezed it. 'Not too terrible, Mamma. Mehmet will survive.'

'Well, no doubt Mehmet will. But Meg feels terribly sorry for him.' When he spoke of himself in that way in the third person, it always for some reason made her feel uneasy.

Mehmet would leave for work in the restaurant in the early afternoon and then return long after midnight. Meg would lie awake listening for him. But when she at last heard the key in the door and then the creak of the loose floorboards as he tiptoed to his room, followed by the banshee wailing of the hot-water system, she restrained herself from calling out to him, since she had guessed that he did not like it. Instead, at last at peace, she would curl her body into a foetal position, put a hand under her cheek, and at once fall asleep. When she awoke in the morning, long before he had, she would sniff as, leaning on her stick, she heaved herself along the passage to the bathroom. There was still a residual smell of rotting food in the air, and by now she knew that he brought it in with him. No doubt one of the poor lamb's jobs was to haul away the rubbish from bins crammed to overflowing with leftovers, and their stink then got on to his clothes.

One day, almost a month later, Mehmet was clearly brooding on something when he came into the kitchen, long after eleven, to have his usual breakfast of cereal, toast and honey, and Nescafé made in the mug which he himself always washed out and which, he had made clear, was for his use alone. He had once told Meg he'd been given the mug, which had

Shakespeare's face printed on it, as a souvenir by an American tourist met by chance on a visit to Stratford.

Mehmet was silent once he had greeted Meg with a wan good morning and a peck on the cheek. Meg, who had also made herself a cup of coffee when making his, sat opposite to him, with an expectant look on her face. Something was up. Surely he would tell her?

Finally, her patience exhausted, she said: 'What is it, dear?'

He raised the coffee cup and stared down into it. If Nescafé left any dregs, he might have been seeking an answer about his future from them. Then he said: 'That job finished.'

'Oh, Mehmet!' She clasped her hands together, as though to implore him to confess to her that it was not true, he was only pulling her leg. 'How did that happen? Did the – did the police make a problem?'

'No. I made problem.'

'How on earth –?'

'I was idiot.'

He began to tell her what had happened; and, as he did so, she suddenly thought that his English seemed suddenly to have become even less fluent. Could the shock of losing his job have done that to him?

It transpired that that 'bloody Syrian' (as Meg would always now refer to him) had been paying Mehmet only two pounds an hour – 'Can you imagine, *two pounds an hour?*' – even though he was working halfway through the night. There was another illegal who was getting the same pittance. But the regular workers were getting three pounds fifty, even though they were always leaving the heaviest jobs to the two illegals. Eventually, Mehmet had decided that it wasn't good enough, and before leaving the restaurant for home had told the proprietor that he must have a raise. What sum did he have in mind? The proprietor, who was young and graceful, with full, soft lips, soft hands and a soft, silky moustache, looked up at him with an oddly yearning expression as he put the question. He sounded amenable, even eager to do what Mehmet asked. But when Mehmet said 'Three pounds fifty,' the proprietor gave a high-pitched, jeering laugh. Out of the question. He couldn't possibly pay as much as that. Didn't Mehmet realize – it was possible to get an illegal Indian or Pakistani to work, not for two pounds, but for one pound fifty an hour?

Mehmet had said nothing more. He had collected his belongings and, still silent, had walked out of the restaurant, never to return.

'Are you very worried?'

He nodded. 'Not very worried but, yes, worried. And angry.' He sipped from the by now cold coffee left in the mug. Then he said: 'What worries most is how Mehmet pay Mamma.'

'Pay me? Pay me for what?' Obtusely, at first she did not understand.

'For room. Rent. Now I have a little money, but very little. I leave restaurant and do not ask for my money. One week.'

'Oh, Mehmet, how silly of you! Why did you do that?'

'I am Albanian,' he said in a cross voice, as though that explained it.

'Yes, the Albanians are a proud people,' Meg said, having read or heard that somewhere. 'But how are you going to manage now?'

'I can always manage. But . . .' He raised both hands and then dropped them to his knees. 'Maybe it take long time to find other job. And then – what about rent?'

'Oh, that's the last thing to worry about! Forget it! What does worry me is what you're going to live on.'

'But I must pay rent. You need rent. Yes, Mamma?'

'Well, the rent is certainly useful. I won't say it isn't. But there it is. When you have a job, then you can start paying me back by instalments.' But she knew already that she would never keep him to that. She felt an extraordinary secret happiness at the thought of his living on in the flat for nothing. 'In any case, you do so much for me. So to let you off the rent for the time being is only a small return.'

'Mehmet does not do so much for Mamma now. You are much better, no need.'

'You do a lot for me just by being here.'

Impulsively she put a hand on his knee, and slowly he then covered it with his own.

Meg never liked it when Sylvia arrived unexpectedly.

This time they had hardly greeted each other when Meg said in an irritable, aggrieved voice: 'I do wish you'd give me some sort of warning. Then I could get things nice and ready for you.'

'Oh, don't be so silly. I am your sister, aren't I?' Sylvia pulled off her gloves and then her navy-blue, military-looking overcoat with its wide collar, heavily-padded shoulders and large brass buttons. 'You don't have to make any preparations for me, for God's sake. I happened to be driving up Kingsland Road after one of my committee meetings and I suddenly thought, Hey, I haven't seen Meg for an age, why don't I look in on her?'

'Well, anyway, it's nice to see you,' Meg conceded grudgingly. 'Would you like a cup of coffee?'

Sylvia pulled a face. 'Oh, Meg, haven't you learned after all these years? Coffee never agrees with me. But' – she looked at the watch on her wrist – 'is it too early for a drink?'

'In my view, it's never too early for a drink.' Meg began to scramble out of her armchair, hands pushing down on its arms and slippered feet pressing on the floor.

'Oh, don't get up! Don't get up!'

But by then Meg had succeeded in raising herself. 'You can see that I'm much better than when last you saw me.'

'Yes, it's wonderful. A miracle.'

'It's only a *remission*, mind. Who knows how long it will last?'

'Well, some remissions last for ages – even for a lifetime. There's this colleague at the school, cancer, a mastectomy. The poor dear was told, oh, ten, fifteen years ago that the cancer had already spread all over the place. But there she still is, bright as a button, busy as ever, seemingly cured.'

'What d'you fancy?'

'Have you got some sherry?'

'You know I can't abide the stuff. I've got – let me see – vodka, gin, Scotch. Oh, yes, and some liqueur of some sort, I can't remember what. Eric brought it back from that last cruise of his. He didn't like it and I didn't like it.'

'What about some tonic water?'

'Yes, I can manage that. But can you really drink it?' Meg pulled a face. 'Like drinking quinine.'

'Well, it does have quinine in it, you know.' Sylvia began to ease down the cuticles on the fingers of one hand with the fingers of another.

'Lucky I asked Mehmet to bring me in two bottles yesterday when he went up to Safeway for some fags. It's a scandal the way that tobacconist on the corner charges twenty p more than Safeway for a packet of Superkings Light.'

'You're not smoking, are you?' Sylvia said, as she took the tonic, in its smeary tumbler, from her sister.

'Oh, lordy, no!' Meg lied. 'Well, just one now and again. But Mehmet smokes them.'

Sylvia sipped daintily; then burped behind a raised hand as the bubbles exploded in her throat. 'You must have read about the dangers of passive smoking.'

'Oh, who cares! I'm far more likely to die of this MS thing than of breathing in other people's smoke.'

'I didn't know that he was still with you. I thought . . . Now why did I think that? He lost his job, didn't he?'

Meg was pouring herself some gin. She splashed in a finger and then, after a moment's thought, head tilted to one side as though she were listening for something, splashed in another. She would often say that Sylvia was enough to drive one to drink. 'He lost two jobs. His problem is not having a work permit.'

'Does he have a residence permit?'

Mehmet had repeatedly told Meg not to reveal the details of his situation to anyone. She wished now that she had not said anything to Sylvia. 'I'm not sure,' she said evasively, hiding her face in her tumbler.

'I bet he hasn't!' Sylvia took another dainty sip. 'It's a disgrace that so many of these people have managed to hang on in this country without either work permits or residence permits.'

'I feel sorry for them.'

'What about feeling sorry for the English people they keep out of jobs?'

Meg decided not to answer.

'What about his rent?'

'What about it?'

'Well, is he paying it?'

Meg, the younger of the two sisters, had learned as a child that it was useless to tell a lie to Sylvia since, uncannily, she would always sniff it out. 'From time to time.'

'What does that mean?'

'Well, sometimes he gets a temporary job and then, well, he tries to pay me something. He's good about that. Once he gets a permanent job, then I'm sure I'll get the whole caboodle.'

'You certainly won't! I'll take a bet on that.'

Over the years there had been innumerable unsettled bets between Meg and Sylvia; they were constantly telling each other 'I'll take a bet on that', only to lose all subsequent interest in the outcome.

'He's honest,' Meg said firmly. 'Absolutely honest. He's been here months and I've never missed a thing. I leave my bag around, he could easily pinch something. No, in due course, he'll pay me everything he owes me. I'm dead sure of that.'

'Well – we'll see. But don't say I didn't warn you.' Over the years the two sisters had warned each other of innumerable disasters, few of which had ever occurred.

'Are you sure you wouldn't like some vodka or gin?'

'Yes, I'm quite sure. Thank you.' Sylvia looked around her, with that half-pitying, half-contemptuous expression to which Meg had long since become habituated. The Highgate house was always spotless and neat. Sylvia was constantly saying that, if there was one thing that she hated, it was mess. Mess was something to be excluded as strenuously from her life as from her house. 'That cover could do with a clean,' she said, indicating the sagging sofa, piled high with magazines and newspapers and with three of Mehmet's puzzles in one corner.

'A lot of things here could do with a clean. Fiona is a dear, I've become very fond of her, but . . .'

'You should complain about her to the social security people.'

'Oh, I wouldn't dream of doing that! She's become a real friend. Fortunately Mehmet does his share. Muslims aren't domesticated, one just has to face that, but if there's something really urgent to be done, I can always rely on him.'

'You always make him sound like an angel,' Sylvia said derisively.

Meg wanted to retort: *Well, he's the nearest to one that you're ever likely to come across.* But she merely sighed and said: 'He's a good sort.'

Sylvia began to speak about her family. Had she told Meg about Dennis? After the handover in Hong Kong, she and Paul had been so afraid that the business might be affected and that he would have to come home. But things seemed to be getting better and better. Oh, it had been such a relief! And Mo was now pregnant and the two of them, she and Dennis, were just praying for a girl. Francine was still up at Somerville. She had got over that anorexic phase, thank goodness, largely due to this wonderful man she had been seeing at the Maudsley, yes, all that was now far behind her, and it really looked as if she were on her way to a First. PEP, they called it – Philosophy, Economics and something or other. Politics, was it? She was also tipped as a future president of the Union, they had women presidents from time to time now, oh, and she had just been cast as Perdita in a college production of that Shakespeare play, she could not for the life of her remember the title for the moment, her memory was getting so bad . . .

Meg eventually ceased to listen, merely grunting or nodding her head from time to time.

At last Sylvia looked at her watch. 'Well, Meg dear, it's been lovely to hear all your news and to see you so much better. But I really must be making tracks if I'm to get my Paul his lunch on time. You know how obsessive he is about punctuality.'

Meg knew only too well. She had more than once sent him into a rage when she had failed to be ready when he had called for her in the car. 'He's been made redundant now, hasn't he?'

Sylvia did not care to be reminded of this bad news among so much that was good. 'Well, he'd half decided to go anyway. There are so many things he wants to do. On his own, not as part of a large organization. He's always been so independent-minded.'

Bloody-minded, Meg thought. 'Give him my love,' she said. 'It's an age since I saw him.'

'It was a pity you decided not to come to us for Christmas. It was one of our best. Goose instead of turkey was a brilliant idea.'

'Well, I was so poorly then. But maybe next year . . . If this *remission* continues.'

'One day Paul and I want to come in the car and drive you to somewhere like Kew. At Kew they have these chairs you can borrow, and we could push you around in one. You ought to get out more. It must be awful being cooped up in this tiny little flat day after day.'

'I do manage to get out from time to time now that I'm so much better.' By now Meg was fuming. The condescension of it!

'Well, just up the road to Safeway is hardly getting out.' Sylvia struggled into her overcoat and began to do up the vast brass buttons. Meg looked enviously at her sister's small, narrow feet. She always wore good shoes and she was wearing good shoes now, low-heeled, their leather supple and glossy.

When Sylvia swung open the front door – she had stooped before doing that to pick up some letters, saying 'I'm afraid these all look like bills' – there, on the doorstep was Mehmet in a tracksuit, breathless and with beads of sweat on his forehead, nose and high cheekbones. He had been out jogging.

Meg greeted him with delight. 'Hello, Mehmet. You must have been running very fast to get back so quickly. Or did you cut your usual route short?'

'No, Mamma. Just the same.' He was looking at Sylvia, his mouth open and his chest heaving, and Sylvia was looking at him.

'Sylvia, this is Mehmet. My lodger,' Meg added needlessly. 'Mehmet, this is Sylvia – my sister. You two have never met each other.'

'Delighted to meet you, Mehmet.' Sylvia put out a gloved hand. She was taking in the still heaving chest – how muscular it was! – the slightly hooked nose, the mat of close-cropped, black hair. Despite the striking alabaster of the skin, there was something negroid about his looks, she decided, no doubt of that. But it only added to his attraction. 'Meg's been telling me how kind you've been to her.'

'Mamma very kind to me.'

Sylvia was not sure if she liked all this Mamma business. 'She's also told me of your job problems. I'll keep an eye out. My husband might well hear of something. You're not too particular, are you?'

Mehmet shook his head. 'Not at all. I take anything, anything.'

'Perhaps at my husband's club . . . I know they have a lot of foreign waiters there.'

'Thank you.'

'You wouldn't mind a job as a waiter?'

Again he shook his head. 'Any job. I been waiter.'

Meg was glad that he had said that and not kitchen porter.

'Oh, good!'

Mehmet accompanied Sylvia down the steps to her car and then the two of them began to talk together, looking each other up and down and smiling away at each other, as though Meg were invisible. Finally Sylvia got into the driving seat and Mehmet, with a lot of shouting and beckoning, saw her out from the narrow space in which the car had been hemmed in by some inconsiderate van driver. Meg felt twinge after twinge of jealousy. She might not have been there. It was only to Mehmet that Sylvia waved when the car had finally been extricated and began to move off.

'Your little sister very attractive,' Mehmet said, as he walked back into the sitting room.

'She is *not* my little sister. She's three years older than I am.'

'She looks – ' he began with uncharacteristic tactlessness.

'Yes, I know, I know. She looks like a hundred dollars and I'm just a mess. But she's always had it easy. And, yes, I'll admit, she took all her chances, while I just . . . Oh, well. No use crying over spilled milk.'

When she collapsed into a chair, a look of intense disgruntlement on her face, he came and perched himself on its arm. He leaned over, placed his cheek against hers, and hugged her. She could smell the sweat from the exertion of his run and the aftershave from that bottle that he kept, one of many ranged tidily one beside the other, on 'his' shelf in the bathroom. She had felt exasperated with him for paying that rubbishy Sylvia so much attention and all but ignoring her. But there was no doubt that in the end he could always make things right.

Chapter VIII

There was still a nip of winter in the air, but now that the days were rapidly lengthening Marilyn had begun to feel less depressed. In December it had been like going into a long, eerily dripping tunnel, unsure whether one would ever emerge. And now she had emerged. She began to hum to herself – what was it? Something trite and perky. Oh, yes, 'The Sun Has Got His Hat On', that was it. Not long before That had happened, she and Ed had gone to that old musical, *Mr Cinders*, at the King's Head. She had thought the show awfully silly but he had loved it. Strange that a man so serious should have had such an appetite for silly things.

'Hey! Hey!' She heard the voice and, though she could not see from whom it was coming, she recognized at once, from something thrillingly distinctive about its resonant timbre, that it could only be Mehmet. At that moment she was passing Gloucester Road Station and, as she looked across the road, she saw him standing precisely where he had been standing, at the entrance, only a few weeks before. Was it just a coincidence that, living so far away in Dalston, he should twice have been standing at precisely that place? Or could it be that he regularly met someone there?

Weaving perilously between the rushing cars, he raced across the road to join her. 'Dr Carter! You remember?'

'Of course.' *How could I forget you?* She peered at his face. 'That's healed well. I'm proud of my needlework. You can hardly see the scars.'

'How long? Three, four weeks? I want to telephone, but . . .'

I wanted to telephone too, often, often. 'But what?'

'Maybe you too busy. Maybe you do not want to see me again. Which way you walking?'

Surely he must know? He must have seen the direction in which she had been going. 'Home. It's been a long day. Most of my days are long,' she added.

'Mine too. Which worse – too little work, too much work?'

'You've got too much work?'

'Too little.' He pointed ahead of them. 'I walk with you?'

'If you like.' She at once wished that she had shown more enthusiasm. She certainly felt it, but an uneasy caution had restrained her. 'But weren't you – weren't you waiting for someone?'

'Me?' He frowned, pulled down the corners of his mouth, shook his head. 'No one. No.'

Then why was he standing alone outside the Underground station, just as she had seen him standing alone outside it on that previous occasion?

'I never thought that we would meet by chance here. Now, if I had had some reason to go to Dalston . . .'

'You remember I live there!'

'Yes, I remember. I've never been there,' she added.

'No reason to go. Ugly. Slum.'

'You say you have too little work. Why's that?' They had begun to walk, he remaining so close to her in the crowded street that she had the choice of either brushing against the shop windows or brushing against him. She zigzagged between the two.

'I did not tell truth. I do not have too little work. I have no work.'

'Oh, I'm sorry. Why's that? Is it that –?'

He merely shrugged and then, obviously eager to change the subject, said: 'Wonderful. Almost seven o'clock and not yet darkness.'

'Yes, I have this glorious sense of relief when the days begin to lengthen.' She also had a glorious sense of relief because, after so many days of thinking about him, she was walking so close at his side. At one moment their hands brushed against each other, at another his left shoulder brushed against her right. Probably, with any other companion, she would not even have been aware of the fugitive touch and go of these contacts. But a sharp, almost painful hyperaesthesia gave them all the significance of an embrace or a caress.

Ever since he had called at the house with the flowers, she had been intermittently wondering in what sort of conditions he lived in that district of northern London of which she must have vaguely heard the name but of which she knew nothing.

'What brings you all the way from Dalston to Kensington?'

'A job. *Hope* of a job. But – no good. No vacancy.'

'Have you been looking for a job for some time?'

'From time to time, yes, I look for job.' *From time to time*. The answer struck her as odd: either one was looking for a job or one was not looking for one.

'Has it been difficult?'

'Yes. Difficult. For East European – jobs not easy here. People think East Europeans dishonest, lazy, no good.'

'Oh, I don't think so.'

'Yes. English are racist people. Very racist.' His mood had suddenly darkened, and his face, when she looked up at it, had darkened with it. *Livid* – that was the word that came to her mind; but livid not merely with rage but also with indignation and resentment.

'Do you have a family over here?'

'No. No family.' He was peremptory. Did that mean that he possessed no family or that the whole family was in Albania?

'So you live alone?' she persisted. She felt ashamed of this inquisitiveness – she was not naturally an inquisitive person – but she had to find out everything she could about him.

'No. Not alone.'

'With other Albanians?'

'No.' He hesitated, clearly reluctant to tell her anything more. Then he said grudgingly: 'I am lodger. With English lady.'

'And that's OK?'

'OK?'

'I mean – you're happy there, it suits you?'

'I must be happy there. I have not enough money for my own flat. But – she is good woman. Kind.' Once again she turned her head and looked up at his face. It was no longer angry, indignant or resentful; but she could see, from the slightly compressed lips and the frown, that he did not like to be asked all these questions. He went on: 'She is sick. Illness called MS.'

'Well, yes, I know about MS. Two of my patients suffer from it.'

'Of course you know about it. You are doctor.'

'Poor woman. Is she seriously ill?'

'Once. Now – she has remission. She is brave,' he added. 'Very brave.' There was no doubt of the sincerity of the tribute. Marilyn at once wondered: How old was this woman? Was his relationship with her merely one of lodger and landlady?

They were nearing the Regency house, a tall, narrow building, one of a row, which was covered in ivy, damp in winter and dusty in summer. Audrey and she were always saying that they must get someone to cut back the ivy but neither did so. 'Would you like to come in for a drink?'

Without any hesitation – as though the whole object of accompanying her had been eventually to secure that invitation – he said 'Why not? I am free. No more interviews for jobs, nothing.'

Marilyn could see the light on in the basement window; she could even hear the distant rumble of the television news. She hoped that Audrey would be too absorbed in it – 'I must know what's going on' she would constantly say, even if what was going on was merely some arid debate in the Commons or an account of Bush's most recent speech – to rush upstairs.

But, as soon as she and Mehmet had entered the hall, even before Marilyn had taken off her coat, Audrey was calling out: 'Hello! Late again!' and was hurrying up. When she saw Mehmet, as she crested the last step, she froze, a hand going up to her mouth as though to stifle something that she knew she must not say.

'You remember Mr – Mr –' At first, only his first name, Mehmet, came to her. That was how, in her reveries, she always thought of him. 'Mr – Mr Ahmati.'

'Ahmeti,' Mehmet corrected. Smiling, in no way disconcerted by Audrey's sudden emergence, he went towards her, holding out his hand.

'You are Dr Carter's sister, yes?'

'Sister-in-law. She was married to my brother. I'm Miss Carter – Audrey Carter.'

'We met each other when I bring flowers.'

'That's right.' Audrey was staring at him in a way – wary, almost hostile – that both irritated Marilyn and made her feel uneasy.

'We ran into each other by the station. So I asked Mr Ahmati – Mr Ahmeti – in for a drink. I certainly need one after all that work. Why don't you join us?'

There was a momentary hesitation. Then Audrey said: 'You know I rarely drink before supper. And there's some news from Afghanistan. I don't want to miss anything. It's ghastly, what's going on there.'

'It's ghastly what's going on all over the world,' Marilyn said. Unlike Audrey, always so quick to feel for the misfortunes of others, she could not work herself up into a state of anger or even compassion over unknown people suffering in some far-distant country.

'Well . . .' Audrey gave Mehmet a nod and then turned back to Marilyn: 'What time would you like to eat?'

'Oh, about the usual time. Eight. Eight-thirty. Whenever suits you.'

'All right. Let's say eight-thirty.'

At that, Audrey was gone.

'Do sit down.' Marilyn pointed to a Queen Anne chair, inherited, along with some other antique furniture, from an aunt. 'That's more comfortable than it looks.'

He shifted uneasily in it. Then he laid his head back: 'Very comfortable.'

'Yes, I like it. And it looks so good. Even though it's due for reupholstery.'

When asked what he wanted to drink, he said some beer. She then had to tell him that there was none, she and Audrey never drank it. 'Never mind. I drink what you drink.'

'I drink vodka. Too much of it, I'm afraid. I thought that Muslims didn't drink alcohol.'

He laughed. 'They are not allowed to drink alcohol. But that is something different. What you say? – when in Rome, do what Romans do.' Again he laughed.

'You have a good grasp of proverbs.'

'Please?'

She did not explain. 'Most people pay lip-service to one set of rules and live by a totally different set.' But not Audrey, she thought; and not Ed. It was that that had differentiated the two siblings from her and why she had always felt morally inferior to them. As she and Audrey sat watching the news on the television, Marilyn would sigh and then exclaim angrily or despairingly 'How can people do such things to each other?' But it was Audrey who, often watching in silence, would later write the cheque, join the demonstration, or sell the flags on some windy, noisy corner of a street.

He frowned at her remark, making little or nothing of it. 'In my country many people drink. They are Muslim, they think good Muslims, but they drink.' He raised his glass of vodka and tonic. '*Santé!*' Then he sipped from it. 'Bitter!' He sipped again. 'When I drink vodka, I drink with orange juice. Bitter, bitter!' He pulled a theatrical expression of disgust.

She laughed. 'That's the point about tonic. It's bitter.'

As though to avoid any more questions about his life, he now began to question her about hers. Had she been born in London? Where did she train to become a doctor? Had she found it difficult? How much had it cost? Were her parents opposed to such a career? She began to weary of the inquisition, wondering what possible interest her answers could have for him.

Then the questions became more insidious. It was like a police interrogation, she thought: first the innocuous questions about name, address, profession and so on; and then the questions which lead to a conviction of the person being interrogated.

'You are married, Dr Carter?'

'Was.'

'You are divorced?'

She shook her head. 'No. My husband died.' She jumped off the sofa in which she had been sitting and splashed some more vodka into her half-full glass. She wondered what he, a Muslim, would make of a woman drinking so much alcohol. She gulped, then gasped as the fire caught hold first in her throat and then in her stomach. Whatever happened, she was not going to talk to him about That. She never talked to anyone about That, except to Audrey or to her friend Vicky at extreme moments of guilt or despair.

'And you have no children?' Suddenly his voice was soft, gentle, soothing. It was as though he had intuited the horror and anguish that she was determined to hide from him.

She shook her head. After all, it was not a lie. She had no children now. Carol was also dead. 'None.'

He looked across at her, his body leaning forward in the chair, the tumbler clasped in both his hands. Irrelevantly, she once again noticed how beautifully manicured they were. Did he pay someone to manicure them for him, as her father-in-law, in his vanity, did every week? 'It is pity,' he said slowly.

'What is a pity?' She became suddenly fearful. What was he going to come out with next?

'That you have no children. You must have children. You will be good mother. Yes, I think so.' He nodded at her.

'Oh, I'm far too busy to start to have children! And anyway at my age . . .'

'What you say? You not old! Thirty – thirty-five – yes?'

'Thirty-seven.'

'You do not seem so.'

'I feel so. Sometimes much more than thirty-seven.' She gave a small, abrupt laugh. 'A hundred even.'

Suddenly he had jumped up from his chair and, glass in hand, had placed himself beside her on the sofa. It was so narrow that it was usually only when the room was full of party guests that two people ever occupied it at the same time.

'Why you say such nonsense?'

She made no answer, merely staring down into her glass. She felt vaguely light-headed, with an insistent throbbing between her eyes, and wondered whether the cause was such a strong drink on an empty stomach or the shock of the way in which he was talking to her. She might have been someone known to him for years.

'I think your work not good for you.' It was something that she had herself often thought after That. Some people, Audrey among them, had even tried to persuade to give up her job, at least for a year or so. After all, the insurance had brought in enough for her to survive on it for a time, and her father-in-law had told her 'You can always call on me if you're in any need.' 'It is – how you say? – depressing work. You are always with those who are sick, old. Very depressing.'

'If I didn't have something to occupy me, then things might be even worse.'

'Then find something else to occupy you. You are so – so sad. I must say this. *Sad.*' SAD. That was what nowadays one called her sort of depression. Seasonal affective disorder. But there was never really a close season for her depression. It merely waned for a while as the daylight waxed.

'I'm not sad at all.'

'You must learn smile. Please.' Suddenly he put out a hand and took her chin in it. She tried to jerk her head away but he held it firmly. 'Smile for me! *Smile!*'

Again, panicky, she tried to jerk her head away. 'I can't.'

'Yes!'

Then his head was approaching hers, with an extraordinary, inevitable slowness. She looked into his eyes, still struggling to turn her head aside. He put his lips to hers. She could feel his tongue against them, then pushing between them. All at once, with a sense both of relief and abasement, she gave way.

'You will call me?'

They stood together in the hall. He said it in a whisper.

She nodded. 'Yes. Yes!' She, too, whispered. Then she wondered: Why are we whispering? So little had happened, a few kisses, some hurried caresses. All the time she had been conscious that Audrey must already be in the basement kitchen, preparing the supper. Should she invite him? No, she did not want Audrey to be any part of this.

'Or I call you.'

'But not at the surgery, please. One never knows who's listening in there. Ring me here, if you want to. But remember, if

it's – she made a downward pointing gesture to indicate the
basement flat and Audrey in it – 'then be very careful what you
say. Just say that you want to talk to Dr Carter. Or leave a message for Dr Carter.'

'I understand.'

'How are you going home? I don't – don't drive now or I'd
offer you a lift. Audrey drives me if an emergency crops up – or
I have a minicab. A minicab is inconvenient and expensive for
a doctor, but there it is. Thank goodness the surgery is so close.'

'I will take Underground train and then bus. But first – I have
some things to do here.'

She wondered about the nature of these 'things'. Once again
the suspicion slithered into her mind that somewhere in this
district he had a girlfriend. It would be odd if a man of his age,
and one so handsome, didn't have one.

'Goodbye.'

She put her face forward, knowing that he would kiss her.
But this time, instead of putting his lips to her mouth, he
merely brushed them, a faint, fleeting touch, against first one
cheek and then the other. 'Goodbye, Marilyn.' He pronounced
her name as though it were Mary-Lynne. Like that, it sounded
odd, even faintly ludicrous to her.

'Goodbye, Mehmet.'

As she was about to go back into the sitting room, having
quietly shut the front door, she heard Audrey's clear, loud
voice: 'Marilyn! *Marilyn!* He's gone, has he?'

'Yes, he's gone.'

'Then I'll dish up.'

'I'll be down in a moment.'

Standing before the cheval glass that had also been inherited
from her aunt, Marilyn nervously smoothed down her hair,
straightened her skirt, and did up the top button of her blouse.
When lovely woman stoops to folly . . . Except that the folly had
been so brief and trivial, no more than what she and Ed had
committed when, teenage neighbours, they had snogged
together (she had always hated the ugliness of that word) on a
sofa before the television set in the absence of the parents of
one or other of the households.

The table was carefully laid, as always. Nothing would have to be fetched as an afterthought, as on those rare occasions when Marilyn had laid it. The clean napkins were there in their silver rings, each with its engraved initials; the mats were the ones, reproductions of Monet water-lily paintings, that a grateful patient had presented to Marilyn after she had spent the best part of a night by her bedside, nursing her through an agonizing bout of biliary colic; the glasses for the wine were highly polished, after having been washed by hand by Audrey, who said that they were too good to trust to the dishwasher.

'This soup is terrific,' Marilyn said.

'I'm glad it's all right. I made it out of some odds and ends in the fridge. I wasn't sure how it would work out.'

Their conversation was stilted, as it rarely was, except after one of their infrequent and transient rows.

Marilyn was conscious that Audrey was surreptitiously examining her as, with one of those large, capable hands of hers, the nails cut short and unpainted, she raised spoonful after spoonful of soup to her lips. What was she looking for? What did she suspect?

'He seems a nice enough man,' Audrey said all at once as, her soup finished, she laid down her spoon with a decisive click. 'And he has such an attractive smile. I'm always affected by smiles.'

'Yes, it *is* an attractive smile. Smiles depend so much on teeth.'

'He has good teeth, yes. Except for that broken one.'

'Like yours. I wish mine were better.'

To Marilyn the conversation was becoming more and more absurd.

'What does he do exactly?'

'Well, at present – nothing.'

'Then how does he keep himself?'

'I've no idea. We're not on the sort of terms that would allow me to ask him.'

'He looks prosperous. Nicely dressed. Expensively dressed.'

'Perhaps he is prosperous.'

'Yes, that's not impossible.'

That was the end of the conversation about Mehmet, at least for that evening. But the unease that it created in Marilyn, a kind of repeatedly surging and then ebbing discomfort, remained with her until, long after she had gone to bed and turned off the light, she at last rocked off, as on some lethargic tide, into a sleep constantly interrupted by terrifying dreams of That.

Chapter IX

Laurence shaved with even more care that morning and spent even longer than usual on deciding what he would wear. Whether he wore the brown suit with the Liberty tie or the more formal, dark blue pinstripe one with the Pierre Balmain tie, was something that Marilyn would not notice. Hers was now only a perfunctory interest in him. Whereas Audrey would trek out to Wimbledon at least once each week, bringing with her a home-made cake or jar of marmalade or some book that she had enjoyed and that he himself would certainly not enjoy, Marilyn came seldom and brought nothing. But he was, as always on these occasions, still dressing for Marilyn and not for his daughter.

These mornings he would emerge from sleep early but slowly and reluctantly, as though he were some moribund fish being dragged by an unseen angler from the sludge at the bottom of a river. The bed was narrow, the room – one of two assigned to him by an ancient and extremely rich charity – was small. As he swung his long, purple-veined legs out from under the bed-clothes, he would stare down despondently at them, wriggling the toes, and then ask himself: 'What's wrong with you today?' But this morning, as on every morning when Marilyn was due to pay one of her rare visits to the Grange, he instead told himself with joy: 'She's coming.' So happy did he feel that, for once, he did not brood over the mystery of why, yet again, he had enjoyed – or was it suffered? – the marathon dream.

Careful not to nick himself, as he so often did, he moved the cut-throat razor down his left cheek and peered with blood-hound eyes at his dim reflection in the steamed-up bathroom mirror. As he did so, his joy became even more intense. But then he thought: Steady old boy. She doesn't care a damn about an old fart like you. Never has, never will. It will never get you anywhere. But, for all that, there had been times when he had managed to fool himself that it might get him somewhere – or even all the way.

He had become Marilyn's patient eleven years ago, when, eager and fresh, she had just joined the practice, and he was still living in the Brompton Square house, spacious and crammed with objects (almost all now sold!) picked up on his various postings abroad. He had been going to Lawson for years, ever since he had decided that, on his pension, he could no longer afford a private doctor. But Lawson had been on holiday and so, instead, Laurence had found himself faced by this incredibly sweet and attractive girl, her thick, curly brown hair parted in the middle and fastened on either side with large amber clips and her smile at once shy and welcoming. She did not seem to be in any hurry, as Lawson always was, his initial expression of assumed sympathy changing first to abstraction, while he fidgeted with papers on his desk – no doubt he was already thinking of the next patient to come – and then to irritation (Oh, get on with it, get on with it! that expression said). Laurence, his stick between his legs and his hands resting, one on top of the other, over it, for once took his time with this newcomer. He did not want to hurry, and she did not seem to expect or want him to.

'It's made me feel better just to talk to you,' he said at the end. It was no empty compliment; he did feel better.

Marilyn got up and opened the door for him. It was something she rarely did for a patient. Then she once again gave him that singularly sweet smile of hers, the full lips turning up at the ends and small wrinkles, like fine cobwebs, appearing under her eyes. As he smiled back at her, he was suddenly reminded of an adored Norland nurse of more than sixty years previously. After three or four weeks, this nurse had mysteriously disappeared, overnight, without any goodbye to him, to be replaced by another, far older nurse, to whom his mother would refer behind her back, partly in mockery but chiefly in respect, as 'The Dragon'. When he asked what had become of the Dragon's predecessor, his mother had told him, in the tone, which she used only when administering a reprimand: 'She had other things to do.' What other things, he had asked; to which his mother had replied 'Oh, things, things,' and his father had added 'Forget about her.' But he had never been able to forget about her.

After that first, fortuitous meeting, Laurence had always asked to see Marilyn and not Lawson; with the result that, when he ran across Lawson in the bridge club to which they both belonged, there was a shifty embarrassment on his own side and a cold hurt on Lawson's. 'The good thing is that she's prepared to *listen*,' he told both Audrey, then living with him in the overlarge house, and many of his friends. But if that was the good thing, the wonderful thing was that, for the first time since his wife had died (a little whimper, a hand stretched out as though in appeal, and then a clattering lunge across the dining-room table, so that a glass of wine went flying, its contents looking like arterial blood on the white damask), he felt actually excited by a woman. Paradoxically, when his wife had been alive, many women – shop assistants, bus conductresses, bank clerks, figures glimpsed only momentarily as they hurried down a street towards him or boarded an Underground train – would each day fill him with a heaving, giddying excitement at often no more than a glimpse of the light on a cheekbone, the tautness of a calf, the swell of a breast, the arch of an eyebrow. But when she had died, that appetite had also died, until, totally unaware of what she was doing, Marilyn had arrived to revive it.

It was obvious to him, during those first days, that Marilyn had taken to him. When he entered the consulting room, her vaguely worried frown would relax and she would jump up from her chair and greet him with something like: 'Hello, Sir Laurence! You're looking very natty today,' or 'I can see that those pills bucked you up.' To the last of these his reply, with a roguish toss of the head and a smile under the neatly-cropped moustache, was 'It's *you* who buck me up, not those blasted pills. Those pills give me the most god-awful indigestion.'

One day, after the protracted consultation had at last juddered to its close, he said to her, as he drew on a chamois glove of the same old ivory shade as his professionally manicured fingernails: 'There was something a little embarrassing that I wanted to ask you, my dear.'

She had become used to that preamble from elderly men. It usually meant that they were worried about their sexual shortcomings – or, all too often, no comings at all.

'Nothing embarrasses me,' she said. She gave the giggle which, overnight it seemed, she lost forever after That had happened. 'I've heard it all. What is it?'

'Well, it's not really all that embarrassing. The thing is that I've had an invitation to a Royal Garden Party and it's for both myself and, yes, my poor dead wife. Odd that they should have got that wrong, but there it is. Anyway, I wonder if you would like to come with me? I've asked my daughter but she's far too much of a republican to be tempted. And I can't really think of anyone else. How about it?' He looked across, head tilted to one side, with a coaxing smile.

'Do you want me to impersonate your wife?'

His long, narrow, still handsome face, bisected by the clipped white moustache that made many people assume that he must have retired from the army, not the Foreign Service, began to redden. 'Oh, good God, no. I'll tell the gang at Buck House that I'd like to bring you as, well, my companion, and ask if that's all right. I know one or two people in the office there – one is a former colleague, in fact I was his boss in Vienna. So I don't think there should be any problem.'

Marilyn hesitated, as she tapped on her lips with the biro with which she had just written him a prescription. Then impetuously she said: 'Well, it might be fun! What do I have to wear?'

At that time, she dressed carelessly and informally. Because of that, he had for a while hesitated whether to issue the invitation or not. It would be embarrassing if she turned up without a hat or in unpolished shoes or in the sort of rough, serviceable coat and skirt that she was wearing now. 'Well, it is a *party*,' he said. 'And a royal one. So I suppose . . .'

'I've got it. I'll dress as though I were going to some posh wedding.'

'Yes. Yes, that ought to be fine. Good, good.' He was relieved.

He told her the date and the time at which he would pick her up. 'I don't think I'll take my old banger. It won't look too good. I think I'll hire a car with a driver.'

'It all sounds tremendously grand.'

Her playful irony was lost on him. 'Oh, there's nothing to be nervous about.'

'And terribly expensive.'

'One likes to make a splash from time to time. And why not? I'm a widower now and both my children are earning well.'

Having arrived home from the garden party – he had first dropped Marilyn off at the surgery, since she had said that there were some things she had to see to – Laurence told Audrey that his companion had 'really turned up trumps'. She had been elegantly but unshowily dressed, he said, and her cartwheel hat had been *a triumph*. 'If she had really been my wife, I'd have felt tremendously proud of her,' he concluded.

Without looking up from the table, which she had started to lay for supper, Audrey said: 'I've seen her only once or twice – when Dr Lawson couldn't see me. She never struck me as anything special. But then,' she added in a small, carefully enunciated voice, 'of course I'm not a man.'

'She certainly looked special this afternoon.'

That was the beginning of the friendship between Laurence and Marilyn. He was fond of good food and, having soon learned that she was also fond of it, he would invite her to meetings of the Wine and Food Society, to his club ('I think that, as clubs go, it probably has one of the finest kitchens and cellars in London'), or to one of the half-dozen or so restaurants that he had frequented often enough to be sure of a good table, a fulsome greeting and assiduous service. It was a wonderful moment for him when Marilyn leaned across the table at Incognico and said: 'I love eating out with you. Everyone treats you like royalty.'

Their meetings became more frequent and more intimate. Now he would ask her round to the house for a drink before they had eaten or back for one after they had done so. Half-heartedly he would from time to time suggest that Audrey might like to come along too, but she rarely accepted. Tactful of her, he would decide approvingly. But then the thought would come to him: Perhaps the old girl doesn't like Marilyn? Children were often resentful when a widowed parent suddenly took up with someone else.

Once, as they entered the house, he and Marilyn were both laughing at something he had just said, and on an impulse, in an upsurge of happiness, he put his arm around her and hugged her to him. Immediately, he became aware that Audrey, emerging from the basement with his hot-water bottle, had seen them. She was curt in her greeting to Marilyn and she paid no attention whatever to him. Hugs of this kind, an occasional grasping of her hand or a fugitive patting of her cheek, were as far as he ever allowed himself to go. He did not want to make a fool of himself; he did not want to shock her and so lose her. So far from being annoyed or disconcerted by these contacts, Marilyn seemed to welcome them – but not, he despondently acknowledged, as indications of his love for her, of which she had clearly guessed nothing, but merely as tokens of friendship.

One evening, emboldened by sharing a bottle of Chablis and then one of claret with her at his club, he had said: 'Wouldn't it be rather fun to go to Paris? I haven't been there since my wife died. I know this delightful little hotel by the Palais Royal. Nothing grand, but well run, very well run, and comfortable. Why not take a weekend off and let me – let me treat you? I was once *en poste* in Paris, you know, in the days of Duff and Diana. I could show you a lot of things you won't have seen before, and I've bags of friends there – French friends, not English – who would be certain to push out the boat for us.'

He broke off when he took in the look of stricken embarrassment on her face.

'I'm so busy at present. I mean, even at the weekends. I often have to go into the surgery on a Saturday or Sunday in order to see to the backlog of paperwork.'

'Oh, dear.' The sigh and the two monosyllables did not do justice to the depth of his disappointment and dread. Had he spoiled it all between them? He had an impulse to assure her: 'I'm not suggesting a dirty weekend, you know. I just thought it would be fun for us to be there together as friends.' But that, he knew, would only have made it worse.

A few weeks after that the calamity happened: Ed returned from Africa, yellow and emaciated but in surprisingly jaunty spirits, for treatment for some sort of persistently malevolent tummy bug that he had picked up in Senegal. When away on one of his already perilous assignments, he was reckless about what he ate, neglected to have the prescribed inoculations and to swallow the prescribed pills, and would as often as not drink water from the tap. After his release from the Hospital for Tropical Diseases, it was to Marilyn that he inevitably went for his weekly check-ups. Soon, she was visiting the house more as his guest than as Laurence's.

Now it was three of them – and sometimes four, if Ed had succeeded in persuading Audrey, his closest friend, as he would often declare, to come along too – who went to dine at Laurence's club, or at Rules, the Ivy or L'Etoile. Laurence mused with increasing bitterness that the old intimacy and comradeship between him and Marilyn was inexorably being eroded. It was to Ed that she now usually addressed her conversation; and it was his jokes that provoked her loudest laughter. Laurence had always thought that laugh of hers, so joyous and free, one of the most attractive things about her. But when he heard it now, it scraped on his nerves, in the same way that the inane laughter from some unseen television comedy, reverberating up from Audrey's room, scraped on them.

Then came the evening when Ed, dressed with unusual elegance in a charcoal-grey suit and black brogues, his hair carefully brushed, had put his head round the door of the sitting-room and announced to Laurence and Audrey 'Well, I'm off now.'

Audrey looked up from her needlework, surprised. 'Where are you going?'

'Oh, gosh, I thought I'd told you. I won't be in to dinner. I'm taking Marilyn to this awards party. You know, the one for the trade. At the Dorchester.'

'Are you getting an award?'

'Doubt it. Apparently I'm shortlisted.'

'Why on earth didn't you tell us?' Leonard demanded.

'I thought I had. Anyway – it's no big deal.'

When he had gone, Audrey said: 'I needn't have bought that second steak.' Laurence could see that she was upset. In the days before Marilyn had entered their lives, it was she whom Ed would have taken to the dinner.

'Fancy not telling us. He really is extraordinary.'

'Oh, you know how vague and forgetful he is. It amazes me that he ever gets to any war on time to cover it.'

Laurence could not sleep that night. He lay awake waiting to hear the crisp click of Ed's key in the door and his firm tread up the stairs. It was long after two o'clock when he did so. That sort of dinner could not have ended so late. What had he and Marilyn been doing in the meantime? He felt jealousy rising up in him like an acid vomit. Intermittently, it was always to be there now, a poisonous, viscous mass usually just below his diaphragm, to surge up unexpectedly into his throat and even into his mouth and behind his eyes. That he and Marilyn had never exchanged anything more than the most conventional of kisses, at the start of one of their evenings together and at its end, had never mattered until then; but the thought that she and his son might have made love was disgusting and devastating.

It was from that time of raging jealousy and abject despair that he had begun to have the marathon dream. A good shot and an even better horseman, he had never been any bloody use when forced to run at Eton. But now he would often dream that he was taking part in a marathon and, racing ahead, the wind in his face and the asphalt like rubber under the soles of his old-fashioned gym shoes, he would soon leave the rest of the field far, far behind him, until at last triumphantly, the crowds roaring around him, he breasted the tape. What did the dream mean, he would wonder each time that he had it? In all the races for which he had entered, he had never been up there among the leaders. At Magdalene, he had been thought lucky to get a 2.1; he would never have been accepted for the Foreign

Service if repeated vacations in his maternal grandmother's house in the Auvergne had not enabled him to acquire near-perfect French; he had married not the woman whom he had really loved but, as a compensation for her perfunctory rejection of him, her sister; and, despite all his and his family's friendships with influential people, he had never progressed beyond the rank of counsellor before his premature retirement. Did he dream the marathon dream precisely because in every marathon for which he had entered in life he had so ignominiously brought up the rear?

Now Laurence began to wish that Ed would be sent off on another assignment, as far away as possible. There were even times, in the early hours of the morning when, still sleepless, his mouth rancid, his silk pyjamas drenched in sweat, he would wish that on that next assignment some stray bullet or some lethal bug would get his son, finish him off, eradicate him.

It was bloody stupid that in the high-ceilinged dining room, its three long tables gleaming under the neon lighting necessary even for a summer morning, everyone should always be obliged to occupy the same place at every meal. Laurence's was between a wizened former chartered accountant, so deaf that, despite his two hearing aids, he had given up on any attempt at conversation, other than a muttered good morning and from time to time a querulous request to be passed something out of his reach, and a former Foreign Service colleague, Mervyn.

'Good morning, Mervyn.' Because he was so soon to see Marilyn, Laurence's greeting was cheerier than usual.

'Good morning.' Mervyn looked up from his bowl of prunes. 'And how is Sir Laurence Bart this morning?'

Laurence always detected a sly mockery in that 'Bart' – a reminder that, unlike his colleague, who had ended his career as Head of Protocol and therefore with a knighthood, he had merely inherited his 'Sir' and had done no better through his own efforts than a CBE.

'Not too bad, not too bad, thank you.'

'We're very *endimanché* this morning? Do we have visitors or are we planning a trip to the smoke?'

'Am I dressed any differently from usual?' But Laurence had certainly dressed with more care. At least, he thought, I haven't let myself go as you have – no tie, collar frayed, scuffed shoes, sagging pullover, dandruff on the shoulders of a suit that would certainly be rejected by Oxfam.

Mervyn put out a hand and tweaked towards him one of the two newspapers that Laurence had placed on the table beside him. 'You don't mind, old chap?' he said, as he said every morning. Usually, Laurence responded to this request merely with a grunt. But today he said: 'It beats me why you don't order a paper like everyone else.'

'What would be the point?' Mervyn replied amiably, opening *The Times*. 'I'm in no hurry, and between us all here we must buy dozens and dozens of papers. Why waste the money?' Mervyn had always been obsessed with lineage, treating every social occasion as though it were a launch party for the latest edition of *Debrett*. Now he was no less obsessed with spending as little as possible.

'You have far more money to waste than I have.' It exasperated Laurence that this silly little man should not merely have earned a bigger pension but should also have handled his investments so much more astutely.

'Waste not, want not.'

How could this double first and triple blue have shrivelled up into someone so pitiful and ludicrous? In his exasperation, Laurence totally forgot to retrieve *The Times* when leaving the table.

Later, in the lavatory, right hand holding his trousers at half mast just above his knees, Laurence examined the five small Turner watercolours hanging there – three of Venice under an azure sky, two of the Alps under a livid one – as he did every morning. He drew constant solace both from their perfection and from his canniness in having saved them from the rapacious demands of Lloyds. He was absolutely broke, he'd tell people, those sharks had stripped every ounce of flesh off his body. But eventually, he would comfort himself, Marilyn would discover the value of the three Venice views, and Audrey of the two Alpine ones.

Having flicked through the *Telegraph* with mounting disgust – there was now something irredeemably middle class about it, he thought – he lumbered to his feet and decided that he had better set off for the village to buy the cakes for Audrey's and Marilyn's tea, or, at least, for Audrey's, since Marilyn had a way of departing soon after lunch on some flimsy pretext or another.

That day of late spring, the gardens looked particularly beautiful. They, along with the two sturdy girls who tended them, were for him the chief solace for being incarcerated in this luxurious boneyard.

'Bart! Bart!'

Blast! Mervyn, having lowered the copy of *The Times*, was calling to him from a bench under a weeping willow beside the artificial stream that bisected the lower part of the garden.

Laurence was going to ignore him and hurry on, despite an impulse to march up and snatch away the paper. But Mervyn persisted, his plummy voice cracking as he raised it. 'Sir Laurence Bart! Where are you off to in such a hurry?'

'To the shops.'

'Oh, in that case, I wonder if you'd . . .' Mervyn got to his feet. Laurence guessed what would follow. Would Laurence be a dear fellow and buy him some shaving cream (stamps, shoelaces, sherry)? Unfortunately, Mervyn would continue, he had no cash on him, he'd left his wallet in yesterday's jacket, but he'd settle just as soon as Laurence got back. This settlement was never in fact achieved before a lot of reminders. But this time Mervyn changed his mind before making his request. 'On second thoughts – I might as well walk there with you. Internal affairs are not progressing as smoothly as they should – despite a more liberal helping than usual of prunes over brekkies. So perhaps a leisurely walk – not to say, your always stimulating conversation – might hasten them along.'

Oh, hell. The problem of living in an institution where you were obliged to see the same people, willy-nilly, day after day was that you could not be rude to them. Laurence, who wanted to say 'Frankly, I'd prefer to go alone,' instead said nothing.

Once they had reached the village, Laurence decided to shake Mervyn off. He pointed at his bank: 'I've got to go in there to have a word with the manager about something. We'd better go our separate ways.'

'Oh, all right.' Mervyn looked despondent. 'Well, I'll see you at luncheon.'

'Not today. I have my daughter and daughter-in-law coming.' Host and guests were accorded a table to themselves in a corner of the hall so dark that it seemed as if the management of this all-male foundation wished deliberately to conceal them.

Mervyn pulled a face. 'It's at least a month since any of my three daughters deigned to visit me. I often feel like King Lear.'

Over lunch, Marilyn struck Laurence as being more than usually distracted and distant. She ate a few mouthfuls of food and then gave up. Admittedly the school dinner provided by the college – toad-in-the-hole, lumpy mashed potato, what were not so much spring greens as autumn ones, a steamed treacle pudding – fell far below the standards set by the restaurants to which he had taken her in that now long-ago, paradisal past, or even set by Audrey; but Marilyn had never before rejected it quite so decisively. Repeatedly Laurence attempted to drag her into the conversation and no less repeatedly she resisted his efforts, replying merely with a Yes, No or I suppose so. When the pudding arrived, she pushed it aside and, to his amazement, took out a packet of untipped Camels.

'I've never seen you smoke before.'

'Oh, I do from time to time.'

'I'm afraid smoking's not allowed in hall. Don't you remember? So many of these old gents suffer from asthma, emphysema or heart trouble that I suppose there's some sense in the prohibition. Not that *I* mind smoking in the least,' he added, as she irritably pushed the packet back into her bag.

The three of them adjourned to his tiny sitting-room, made to seem even tinier by the jumbo pieces imported into it from the Brompton Square house. 'Isn't this room just a wee bit over-furnished?' Mervyn had commented mockingly on his first visit there. Marilyn puffed at first one cigarette and then another. Laurence had said that he did not in the least mind smoking, but that was because she was the one who was wishing to smoke. In fact, he thought it a disgusting occupation.

'Why don't you have one?'

'Oh, I'm far too old to start acquiring new habits. My old ones are quite bad enough. But thank you all the same.'

One of Marilyn's legs swung with metronome regularity above the other. He stared at them with melancholy concupiscence, as Audrey began to narrate one of her boring stories about doings at the charity shop. He had always noticed women's legs, and been conscious that his wife's were unattractively bowed – no doubt as a result of a regime of constant riding from childhood.

It was only a few minutes after two when Marilyn, without any warning, jumped to her feet. 'Well, it's been lovely seeing you, Laurence. And looking so well.'

'Do I look well? I wish that I felt it. *Anni ruunt, Postume, Postume, The years that pass are lost to me, lost to me . . .*' Then he realized the fatuity of quoting Horace to these two women. That ass Mervyn might have given an appreciative chuckle.

Having told Audrey 'I'll just accompany Marilyn to the gate, I shan't be a moment,' Laurence walked with her down through the garden. The spring flowers under trees just putting forth vividly green shoots, seemed extraordinarily bright, even dazzling, so that, looking at the daffodils on a bank, he put up a hand to shield his eyes.

All at once Marilyn slipped an arm through his. Surprised, he patted her hand. The contact, he was convinced, was not merely a physical one. After a long period, when her life seemed to have swerved away from his, he felt that once more, however briefly, it had touched it.

'In many ways you're lucky to be here. Aren't you?'

'Lucky? No, my dear. I see now that coming here was the greatest mistake of my life.'

'But you had to sell the house. There was no other way. Or that's what Ed and Audrey told me.'

'Oh, yes I had to sell it.' He spoke as though he were savouring something extremely bitter on his tongue. 'Those buggers who ran the syndicate saw to that. But it would have been better to have rented a basement room than to have landed up here. I could even have slotted myself in with Audrey in that little flat in Barons Court.' After Audrey had moved, to his amazement, into the Kensington house with Marilyn, he had even thought of deserting the Grange and asking them if he might join them – after all, he had put up some of the money, out of his dwindling resources, to help Audrey to redeem the basement for her use; but then he had decided not to risk the humiliation of what he thought would be, all too probably, a refusal.

'But everything always strikes me as so pleasant here. I know that your rooms are rather cramped, but you don't have to bother about anything, do you?'

'The worst thing about old age is not having to bother about anything. If one is bothering about things, then one is still alive. And not already embarked on the process of dying,' he added.

'Oh, poor Laurence!' She squeezed his arm, genuinely concerned and sad for him, as she had not been for a long time.

'Sorry,' he said. (Now come on, pull yourself together, stop all this self-pity!) 'I think I must be more depressed than usual today. Perhaps that perfectly ghastly lunch depressed me. They spend so much money on having resident nurses, resident gardeners, even a resident seamstress for God's sake, but they can't get hold of a half-decent cook, resident or not.'

'You must come and see us soon. Then Audrey can cook you something you really like – or we can take you out to one of the neighbourhood restaurants.'

'Yes, I'd like that. I'd like that a lot.' The two women now invited him less and less often to the house.

At the high, elaborate wrought-iron gates, he said: 'Maybe I'll walk you to the station.' It had been like old times, he was thinking, their leisurely walk down through the spring flowers and then under the trees by the stream, with her arm always in his and her still lithe body always so close.

'Oh, no, don't bother about that. Thank you.' Why, oh why, did she now have to spoil it all? 'You've got Audrey waiting for you. And it's such a dreary trek, all up and down hill past such ugly little houses.'

'Well, if you really think . . .' he mumbled despondently.

Then, suddenly, she made it all all right again. 'Dear Laurence.' She was putting up her face to his, so far above hers that she had to strain on tiptoe. 'Forgive me if I've seemed to be, well, not entirely with you today. But it was nothing to do with you. I've – I've had something on my mind.'

'Something serious?'

She laughed. 'I hope not. Who knows?'

'Something you can tell me?'

'Well, I *could* tell you. But there wouldn't be any point. You couldn't do anything about it – though I know that you'd try.' She reached up an arm and pulled his head down towards her, tipping off his old, perpetually serviceable Lock's brown trilby as she did so.

Neither of them paid any attention to the hat, as she kissed him lightly first on one cheek and then on the other. He felt an excruciating longing and a no less excruciating regret. The two things remained with him not merely in the moment when she released him, but also as he waved goodbye to her, stooped, breathing heavily, to pick up the hat, and then, with quickening strides (now no Mervyn by his side, to slow him down with his snail's pace, as he had done that morning) and made his way back to his set.

Audrey had kicked off her shoes and was reclining on the sofa, her eyes shut. At the sound of his entry, she opened her eyes, swung her legs down from the sofa and tugged at her skirt.

'I was taking a nap. It must have been that excellent Fleurie you gave us.'

'The last time I opened a bottle of that, my friend – friend in inverted commas – Mervyn drank most of it. On that occasion I had been hoping to make it last for dinner as well. He's the sort of man who, on the rare occasions when he invites you to a restaurant, always chooses the second cheapest wine on the list. But he recognizes a good wine when someone else has bought it.'

'Pity that Marilyn had to rush off like that. I don't know what's eating her. This morning she told me she had nothing to do all day.'

'She wasn't herself.'

'When some people aren't themselves, it's a good thing. But that can't be said of her.'

'What do you think is up?'

'Well, it could be this toy boy.'

'Toy boy?'

'I'm only joking. But she's palled up with an Albanian, and from time to time he comes to the house.'

Laurence plonked himself down into a chair. He felt breathless, giddy and vaguely sick, as he did when he had hurried at a near-run, instead of slowly walked, up the stairs at an Underground station. In each case it was his heart that was the cause: the heart that had a defective valve and the heart that constantly ached with his yearning for his former daughter-in-law. 'Who is this Albanian?'

'Search me! Apparently she sewed up his face after he was involved in what sounds like a brawl, and he then brought round what must have been an extremely expensive bunch of flowers.'

'And she sees this – this creature regularly?'

'Regularly? I don't know. I'm so often out. But she certainly sees him often. Well, fairly often.'

'And you've met him?'

Audrey nodded. 'From time to time.'

Laurence picked at the William Morris fabric over the arm of his chair, with those beautifully manicured, long nails of his. He was making a successful effort to appear to be only vaguely interested. In the poker game of diplomatic negotiations he had always been regarded as a master. 'What's he like?'

'Oh, handsome. In a lush way. Full of charm. Well-mannered. What else can I say about him?'

'You don't like him.' It was a statement, not a question. He knew her so well, the dislike was obvious to him.

'No, I don't like him. But I can't really say why. He's never done – or said – anything objectionable in front of me. But somehow . . . Oh, I'm probably doing him an injustice! I try to see as little of him as possible,' she went on.

'But, as you say, Marilyn sees a lot?'

'Quite a lot.'

'Well, I suppose it's good that at last she's emerging from her shell.'

'If a snail emerges from its shell, then there's all the more likelihood that a bird will gobble it up.'

He considered that, bloodhound eyes fixed intently on their own reflection in the Regency mirror above her head. She turned her head, wondering what he was staring at. 'Well, I suppose no harm will come of it.'

'With luck – no.' She paused, gave a crooked smile. 'She once described him to me as a dream. That's what he is for her, I think. A dream that became reality. But when that happens, the dream can also become a nightmare.'

'Oh, no, no! Don't be so pessimistic.'

After tea, Audrey said: 'What about your toenails? I've brought the scissors. Those strong ones, you know the ones I mean.'

'Oh, don't let's bother with that. We can do it on your next visit.'

'But I haven't done them for yonks. Or have you found someone here to do them for you?'

'Good God no!'

'Well, then . . .' She knelt down before him and began to untie the laces of his left shoe and then to ease it off.

He pulled a face, as though the removal of the shoe had been as painful as the pulling away of a sticking plaster.

'Put your foot up here,' she ordered, pointing to a low stool, on which he had piled magazines and newspapers. One of these newspapers, a *Times* with its crossword half-done, she unfolded and draped over the others.

He did as she had told him. Then, with disgust, he looked down at his misshapen toes, the yellow nails curled round them like horn. If these little piggies went to market, no one would want to buy them. 'Why does one have to become so revolting when one grows old?'

'Oh, don't be so silly!' With difficulty, gritting her teeth and pressing down hard on the scissors, she began to cut the thick, obstinately resistant nail on his big toe.

He thought: 'Thank God Marilyn can't see this', forgetting that daily, as a doctor, she saw far worse.

When she had finished, Audrey's face was red and glistening from the exertion. She was a good woman, he thought with grudging admiration and gratitude, doing something so disgusting for him of her own free will.

He had hoped that, after that, she would leave. But, instead, having folded up the copy of *The Times* with the clippings and stuffed it into the wastepaper basket, she once again settled herself. Wearily he let his head loll back against the cushion behind it and closed his eyes. But, failing to take the hint, she went on talking, at first once again about her work in the Oxfam shop and then about a group of Somali refugees whom she had befriended. At long last, she said: 'Well, I think I really must be going. I'm sorry to cut things so short, but I promised the vicar to do something about the bazaar for him.'

He chuckled. 'I like that – cut things so short.' But she had intended no pun.

He did not walk down to the gates with her, as he had done with Marilyn. Instead, as she kissed him on the cheek in the doorway to his set of rooms, something odd and alarming happened. She was saying: 'Well, goodbye, Father. Take care of yourself. I'll come to see you again soon'; and then he heard the voice of a ghostly presence somewhere close to him reply: 'I've seen enough of you,' and realized, with a start, that the ghostly presence had spoken in his voice and could only be himself. What – or who – had possessed him?

Fortunately – and amazingly – she had either failed to hear what he had said or, having heard it, had failed to take it in, occupied as she was with doing up the buttons of her overcoat. That task completed, she looked at him with a vaguely sad, affectionate smile and murmured 'Dear Father'.

Once she had gone, striding purposefully down the garden, on to which a filmy evening mist was settling, he asked himself: What on earth made me say that? Had he intended the words or had some slip of the tongue changed 'I've not seen enough of you' into 'I've seen enough of you'? He was intelligent enough to know that it is often through slips of the tongue that people come nearest to telling the truth.

Chapter X

Vicky carefully spread butter on a slice of ciabatta and then bit into it. She chewed for a while, gazing at Marilyn. Then she said: 'You know – you're somehow different.'

That was shrewd of her, Marilyn thought; but she had always been shrewd. That was why she had been so successful a psychiatrist before her marriage to an even more successful dermatologist and her retirement to produce a brood of virtually indistinguishable female children, all with gypsy-black hair, wide foreheads and small, turned-up noses, who constantly raced about the ancient Spitalfields house like dementedly hyperactive mice. After That had happened, Marilyn had, in effect, undergone therapy with Vicky, even though Vicky had already retired and even though, close friends as they were from student days, there was never any question of money changing hands.

'Am I?'

Again Vicky scrutinised her. 'Yep. Definitely. You're happy. At last – after so long – you're happy again.'

'Maybe.' Marilyn considered it, head on one side. Then she said: 'Yes, I think you're right. But one has to differentiate between contented and happy.'

'How d'you mean?'

'Well, so many people – people like my father-in-law for example – tell one that the happiest period of their lives was during the war. But few people were *contented* then. They didn't have enough food, there was so little to buy, they had to put up with the discomfort of sleeping in shelters or Nissen huts, they were constantly afraid that they might get killed or that people close to them might get killed. That wasn't contentment, of course it wasn't. But for many people that was happiness. Why?'

'Because life had a purpose?'

'Yes. And because at long last they were fully, willy-nilly, engaged in it. Well, that's how I feel now. I'm not contented for most of the time. But, yes, I am happy.'

The tables were so close to each other in this new and unaccountably fashionable restaurant, and the low ceiling so reverberant that Marilyn was suddenly aware that she was shouting all this across the table. Briefly she felt as embarrassed as she would have been if, on a crazy impulse, she had stripped at a party. Then she realized that everyone else was also shouting and therefore no one could overhear her.

'I'm so glad, Marilyn. You were always a naturally happy person, weren't you? I mean I never knew you to be depressed, not even for a moment, however badly things were going. And then – then of course it all changed, when that ghastly thing happened. It's wonderful that you've got back your zest for life. I always knew you would in the end. I always said so. Remember?'

Marilyn nodded. Then she was overcome by the need to confide in Vicky, as she had so often done in the past and, as on this particular matter, she knew that she could never confide in Audrey, close though they were. 'Someone has come into my life and totally changed it. Or totally changed me. Just like that. Almost overnight.'

'Someone? Be more specific.' There were times, in the course of her sturdy, steady marriage to a man so busy that in a single day she often saw him for little more than an hour altogether, when Vicky briefly and guiltily wished for a similar someone.

'He's totally unsuitable for me. Albanian. Eleven years younger than I am. With none of my interests. Loves football and even from time to time plays it with cronies in Finsbury Park. Hates classical music. Reads the *Sun*. Constantly gambles on horses and the lottery. We have nothing in common. It's – mysterious. Audrey even thinks he's sinister,' she added. '*Sinister?*'

'Oh, of course, he isn't really. But she's got that into her head. And that can make things even more difficult than they might have been. He's sharp and he's twigged that she doesn't like him – even though she tries not to show it. He says she's a racist. But that's nonsense. If she were a racist, she would hardly spend so much time on her Kurds and Somalis and all her other lame dogs.'

'You're in love with him?'

Marilyn chewed on a piece of her steak for a while, then swallowed. She put her head on one side, considering. She felt as though she were back in Vicky's sitting-room, during that grey, chill, seemingly endless winter, when she would face up to question after question and probe deeper and deeper into her inmost being for an answer. It was like an agonizing and agonized scrabbling about in one's own bleeding guts, she had once told Vicky, hitting on a simile that she now found totally disgusting. Meanwhile, outside the sitting-room or over it, there would be the sounds – laughter, thudding feet, shouts, screams – of 'the girls' (that was how Vicky always referred to them) racing about in the state of happiness that she herself felt that she would never again inhabit.

'You're in love with him?' Vicky repeated, more insistently. It was important for her, she did not know why, to establish this.

'Am I? Oh, I don't know. But I'm infatuated with him. Absolutely.' Marilyn looked at her watch. 'In two hours and nine minutes he is going to come to the house. Unlike most East Europeans – certainly my East European patients – he is always punctual. Well, almost always. And – and though I love being here with you, eating this delicious lunch at your expense and confiding once again in you, I want even more to be with him. I want the time to fly. I just can't wait.'

Vicky smiled. 'What is it you're waiting for. Sex?' It was years since she herself had had sex in the afternoon.

Marilyn nodded. 'Yes. Sex. Wonderful sex. The most wonderful sex I've ever had. More wonderful than I'd ever imagined it could be. I'd often heard that phrase multiple orgasms, but until he came along I'd absolutely no conception of what it really meant. With Ed there were even times – as you know – when there was no orgasm at all.' She looked around her. Was anyone listening? Could anyone hear? She giggled. 'Yes, the earth constantly moves for me – and him – in 11 Standish Grove.'

'Lucky you.'

'Yes, lucky, lucky me. I can't believe my luck. So much so, that I keep asking myself if it can possibly hold.'

'Why shouldn't it?'

'Well, my luck ran into the sand once before. It might do so again. Yes?'

'Don't think about that. Just enjoy yourself. Oh, I do envy you! I'd love to have a lover.' Vicky laughed. Then she said: 'A pudding? Or shall we think of our figures and just settle for coffee.'

'I ought really to have a pudding – the sweetest and stickiest on offer. Mehmet says I'm far too thin. But I won't.'

Walking home, Marilyn began to regret having confided in Vicky. Never try to tell your love . . . It had been as though she had passed over to her some extremely valuable and also extremely fragile possession – a Shang dynasty vase, a Roman gold-glass ewer – for her inspection. There was no possibility that she would steal it but she could so easily, through a single clumsy move, destroy it.

As she entered the house, Marilyn at once heard the sound of music from the basement. Hell! Either she had miscalculated and this was not the Saturday on which, in a change of schedule to accommodate a colleague, Audrey was to have been at the shop, or else the schedule had suffered a last minute change.

Whatever she was doing – dressing, cooking, cleaning, reading, writing, sometimes even sleeping – Audrey had to do it to noise. It was as though silence terrified her, as solitude terrified other people. 'Oh, do turn that off!' Laurence would often bawl out to her in exasperation in the days when she was living in the Brompton Square house. Marilyn was often tempted to shout out the same. But today she was glad of the noise. If Audrey were in the basement, with her wireless blasting away, then she was the less likely to hear what was going on above her. But just to know that she was down there was in itself inhibiting and embarrassing.

Mehmet always brought some present. Sometimes it was a bottle of wine or of sherry, sometimes a box of chocolates, sometimes – as this afternoon – a bunch of flowers. He held out the flowers to her, as she opened the door; but, taking no notice of them, she threw herself at him, her arms going round him and gripping him to her, as though she were drowning. 'It seems so long!'

'Is that my fault?' He put out a hand behind him and pushed the front door closed.

'No, mine, mine. I wish I could see you every hour of every day. But my work keeps me . . .' She broke off. 'And yesterday there was my father-in-law to visit, far, far away in Wimbledon.' It was not really far, but Mehmet would not know that, she thought. 'Oh, it's lovely to see you.' Again she kissed him. 'You smell so *good*.'

'For you.' Again he held out the flowers.

'Oh, but Mehmet . . .' She pressed the huge bunch against her chest, and then looked up at him in both gratitude and reproach. 'They're so beautiful. But I don't need these presents, and certainly not presents so expensive. You didn't have to buy me all these roses. Just a small bunch of daffodils would have been fine.'

He shook his head. 'That is not Albanian way. I told you. Many times.'

'I wish it were. Couldn't you adopt the English way now that you live in England? No presents or small presents.'

She went into the sitting-room, laying the flowers down on a chair, and he followed her. Coming up close behind her, he put his arms tightly around her waist and hugged her. With a giddying surge of excitement, she felt the hardness of his erection against her. She turned. 'Oh, Mehmet!' She picked up the flowers. 'Let me just put these in water.'

'Leave them. Later.'

'But . . .'

'Later.'

'When you have so much difficulty in finding regular work, please, please don't spend money on me. *Please*. It's so sweet of you but you really mustn't do it.'

'It is Albanian way,' he repeated. Then he grabbed her arm roughly, so that she was to find a mark on it, deepening from red, through purple, to yellow in the days ahead. 'Upstairs.'

'But don't you want a drink first?'

She wanted him to say No and that was what he did. Then he repeated: 'Upstairs.'

Later, in the fine rain that had started to fall, they went out together to the cinema. By now she knew the sort of films that he liked: gangster films, noisy with the firing of guns and the crashings of cars; science-fiction films, lurid with visitors from other planets, animals, insects and even humans grotesquely mutated, and voyages into far-distant galaxies; soft-porn films, heaving with naked bodies. These were the sort of films that she herself had always hated. He would sit through all this rubbish so much absorbed that he would be unaware that, repeatedly, she was turning her head to watch him, in thrall to the beauty of his high cheekbones, his broad forehead and his thick, black hair, all intermittently revealed in the flickering illumination of the wide screen.

Later still they went to the Italian restaurant that, she had now learned, was his favourite. When they had first gone there, he had whispered to her that he was sure that their pallid, lethargic waitress was Albanian. She had then asked him 'Why don't you talk to her in Albanian?' He had answered angrily, with a vigorous shaking of his head: 'No, no! I no want her know I am Albanian.' Foolishly, she had pursued the subject: 'Why not?', for him to retort even more angrily: 'You know I am illegal!' What did he imagine? That discovering that he was an Albanian illegally in the country, the young, awkward, constantly yawning waitress, perhaps herself without a work permit, would at once go to a telephone and report him? It was absurd. But she decided that it was better to say nothing further.

As always, he ate vast amounts. She herself hardly touched her pasta, happy to transfer most of it from her plate to his; and later, when her lamb cutlets arrived, she began to do the same thing. 'Why you no eat?' he asked in an accusatory voice, as he so often did on such occasions.

'Because I have such a small appetite. You know that, darling. And because I had a huge lunch with my girlfriend.' She always said 'girlfriend', not merely 'friend', because by now she had experienced his jealousy.

'Who this friend?' He was clearly suspicious.

'Vicky. You've heard me speak of Vicky. She and I were students together. She used to be a psychiatrist.'

He shook his head. 'I no hear of her.'

'Of course you have.'

Fortunately his moods quickly changed. He began to talk about the people met that afternoon at the betting shop to which, she had long since come to realize, he went almost every day. 'Is it a good idea to waste money on horses?' she had once asked him. 'I do not *waste* money,' he had retorted. 'Small bet, often I win.' Then he had added: 'I do not go for bet. I have friends there. Talk, laugh, smoke together. Good.' It was, she thought, the downmarket equivalent of Laurence's club.

Listening to him now, she thought once again how well he talked – provided he was not in one of those moods when he began to spit out his fury at having no work or residence permits, at some slight or insult (often, she suspected, imagined) from someone encountered in a shop, on a bus or in the street, or at the general racism, as he blackly and bleakly saw it, of the British. He was so observant of the oddities of the people around him; and despite the recurrent inadequacies of his English, he constantly had the ability to come out with some arresting simile or observation.

Arm in arm they left the restaurant at shortly after eleven.

Suddenly he said: 'I come back with you?'

Oh, God! she thought. We've been through all this before.

'Better not. Sorry.'

'You have guest room – two guest room.'

'True. But – well – my sister-in-law . . .'

'Does she own house?'

'No. We both do.'

They were repeating virtually verbatim an increasingly acrimonious conversation of only a few days before.

'Why she tell you I cannot sleep in house?'

'She hasn't told me. The subject has never come up between us. But somehow I feel . . . Another time.'

'I think she is racist, very racist.'

'Not at all. She does a lot of work with – and for – foreign people. Rwandans, Kurds, Somalis. Please, Mehmet. We've had a lovely evening.'

'I am your lover. I cannot sleep in your house. Strange.' He frowned, brooding on it. He had released her arm from his and now he moved away from her, so that a passerby walking towards them on the narrow pavement opted to walk not round them but between them.

'Try to understand.'

But she knew, with a sudden feeling of hopelessness, that he would never try, and that, if he did try, he would almost certainly not succeed.

The rain had ceased. Suddenly he looked up into the sky, halted, put out a hand to grab her wrist and jerk her to him, and then pointed upwards. 'Look! Moon! A new moon! A beautiful new moon! For us a beautiful new life!'

There was something disturbing about these abrupt changes of mood. But she was too much moved, as he now put his cheek against hers, both of them looking upwards at the brilliant shaving of light in a sky now vast in its total emptiness, to dwell on that.

As they approached the Underground station, he once again halted and turned to her. 'Marilyn.' (He still pronounced it, as he was always to pronounce it, 'Mary-Lynne'.) 'Something I must say.'

'Yes?' He was hesitating. 'What is it?' she prompted.

'You will not be angry?'

'Why should I be angry? Of course not.'

'Marilyn – I ask something of you.'

'Yes?'

Embarrassed, he bit on his lower lip, eyes lowered. Then he looked up: 'Please – lend me some money. Twenty, thirty pounds,' he went on. 'I have problem. My landlady – I owe money, money for rent. If I do not pay soon, then I must go.'

'Have you had no work at all?' He had always told her that he lived by taking casual work in restaurants, sometimes as a waiter, more often as a kitchen hand.

Gloomily he shook his head. 'Nothing. Not for seven, eight days. I am sorry, Marilyn. What can I do? You are my only friend in England. And my family . . .' He shrugged. 'Poor. Father dead. Brother in army.' It was the first time that he had ever mentioned his family to her.

'I'm not sure what I've got on me. I'd like to help you, of course I would.' She put up a hand and rubbed at her forehead. The she lowered the hand to the clasp of her bag. 'How much is it that you want?'

'Twenty, thirty?'

'I'd better give you fifty.'

His face lit up. 'You are friend, true friend! I promise soon, maybe next week, when I find more work . . .'

'Don't worry about it.'

She was embarrassed as, at the entrance of the station, she began to count out the notes. What would the passersby think? Then she told herself that they were in far too much of hurry to get home and to bed to think anything.

To her amazement, he himself began to count the notes after she had given them to him. Then he pushed them into the back pocket of his trousers, not into the wallet that he usually carried in the breast pocket of his jacket. He smiled at her. 'You are very kind to me, Marilyn. Always very kind.'

'You are very kind to me. Always very kind.'

He took her in his arms and kissed her on the mouth. Then, still holding her with one arm, he put up a hand and, with extreme tenderness, stroked her hair.

'You're a wonderful lover,' she whispered. 'The best.'

'Only a lover?'

'No, no! Much, much more.'

At first she had been disconcerted to be asked for the money. But as she walked home – he had offered to accompany her but she had said no, it was such a long journey to Dalston, he might miss his connections – she realized that that act of handing over the notes had brought with it its own odd, even shameful but also wonderfully exhilarating thrill. What did fifty pounds matter? Last week she had spent more than that on having her hair done by that man recommended by Vicky.

Chapter XI

Meg was thinking, as so often now, about the past. Going back into it was like sailing up a river, leaving behind a landscape shrouded in mist and gradually moving into one gleaming with sunshine.

That must have been the happiest day of her life, that Easter Monday, oh, ages ago, when she and Eric had been marooned in that gondola high up above the Bank Holiday crowds at Alexandra Palace. It was he who had persuaded her to go on the Ferris wheel – 'Oh, come on, Meg! You can't chicken out. It's perfectly safe.' Peering down, with a mounting nausea, and then throwing an arm around him and pressing her face against his bony shoulder, she had thought: This is it. What a way to go! But, eventually, after some minutes had crawled past, she had released him, sat up, pulled down her rucked-up skirt, and even managed a nervous giggle. 'What a lark!'

He patted her knee in comfort. 'That's my girl. No problem. They'll get us down in a jiffy. There are some kids down there' – he pointed but she did not dare to look – 'and they're taking it all as a joke. And an old granny. Look!' Still she did not look. 'It's lucky you had that wee before we came up.' He was always taking the mickey over her inability to last out as long as he could. 'Your bladder must be made of rubber,' she would tell him.

Suddenly he turned to her. 'Since we've been stuck up here together for so long, how's about our getting stuck together forever?' He said it in a conversational tone of voice, as though he were asking her: How's about us going down to the Kingsland Road for a Kentucky Fried Chicken? The result was that at first she was bewildered, not taking in his drift. Even with Eric for company, she could think of nothing more awful than a lifetime stuck up here on the Ferris wheel.

'Eh?'

'I'm asking if you'll let me make an honest woman of you.'

She stared at him for a second, then let out a squeal. It was something totally unexpected. When they came to the end of an evening together, he had always given her the chastest of kisses, no more than a brushing of a cheek with his lips except on the one occasion when, tipsy after Sylvia's wedding reception, he had caught her coming out of the bathroom, had pushed her back into it and had then started smacking his lips all over her face while at the same time grabbing at a breast. Despite that single onslaught, Meg had sometimes moodily and even despairingly wondered whether Sylvia might not have been right when she had told her airily: 'Oh, do put him out of your mind. It should be obvious to anyone that he's not the marrying kind.' Well, now with this apology for a proposal, high in the air above London, he had shown that Sylvia was wrong. He was the marrying kind. He was going to marry her.

Yes, that had been the happiest day of her life, no doubt about it. But, once her long reverie had ended, she suddenly felt down, really down again, almost as though she had fallen off that bloody Ferris wheel. Early that morning, waking her, Fiona had telephoned to say that one of her kids was sick, she had to take her to the doctor and so she would have to come another day, she could not now say when. Meg looked forward to these visits, Fiona always cheered her up. Then the post had brought a devastating telephone bill, which had shown two calls to Mantua, one to Lyons, and one to Barcelona. All had gone on for several minutes. At first she was furious that such mistakes could be made. But then she had thought: Might not Mehmet have made the calls? If so, he was a naughty boy not to have asked her first and not to have settled with her. Except that, with a lot of rent now being overdue ('You're an utter idiot to put up with it' Sylvia had told her), how could he have settled a telephone bill when he could not pay her even a promised instalment?

But worse than either of these two shocks had been her fear that the remission might be over. All the previous night she had suffered cramps and spasms, and that, she remembered, was how she had first known, long before the diagnosis of MS, that something was going wrong with the bodily machinery in which she had always had such faith. At breakfast, she had said to Mehmet: 'Do you remember that Sandie Shaw number 'Puppet on a String'? No, of course you wouldn't, being Albanian and so young. But that's how I felt all through the bleeding night. Jerked one way, jerked the other – as though this invisible giant was jerking me. Diabolical.' Then she realized that, checking his lottery numbers in the *Sun* that he went out each morning to buy, for some reason insisting that no, he did not want it delivered along with her *Mail*, he wasn't really listening to her. People didn't like to hear about other people's illnesses, they only liked to talk about their own. She had learned that in the course of innumerable visits to Dr Karapiet and to the hospital.

Now, as so often, she waited for Mehmet to return, looking repeatedly at that old-fashioned, oversize watch, its large figures phosphorus green, that Eric had left behind. When Mehmet had departed that morning, first bending over her, as he always did, to give her a kiss on the forehead, then saying 'I'm off then, Mamma,' and finally, newspaper under arm, striding to the door, she had called out after him: 'Hey!' She did not really know why she had done that. She guessed that it might have been her way of saying to him 'Help me!' 'Yes, Mamma?' He came back into the room. He spoke considerately, his face was serene, he seemed not to be in a hurry or flurry; but she could glimpse in his eyes a look of impatience. She had to think of something to say. 'You haven't told me where you're going and what time you'll be back.' The look of impatience did not leave the eyes, it merely intensified, accentuated by a small frown. Then in the same amiable, calm voice, he answered: 'I have people to see. Maybe job. Other things too.' He was always vague like that. 'I come back evening. As usual,' he added. *But what time in the evening?* she had wanted to pursue. But by now she knew that that would only annoy him. 'OK, love,' she said.

What could have happened to him? But the truth was, she told herself, that he was often late like this and nothing had happened to him – or, at least nothing that he would tell her. She managed to get to her feet with difficulty and then all but toppled over, putting out a hand to the back of a chair only in the nick of time. As she tottered to the kitchen – should she get the crutches that had stood, unused, beside the hatstand for so long? – she savoured that phrase, the nick of time. Why nick? Then she thought: Nick means a little cut. And that is what time does to one, it gives one these endless little cuts, until sooner or later one of them finishes one off. Another thought came to her: Nick means a prison. Time was the prison from which there was never an escape – until, well, something like this bloody MS at last prised open the door of one's cell.

She stretched up for the teapot on its shelf and again almost toppled over. Then with clumsy hands – I'm all thumbs today, she thought, and these thumbs had the added disadvantage of being numb at their tips – she filled the kettle. It was at that moment that she heard his key in the door.

'Mehmet! Come and join me for a cup of tea or coffee.'

He looked pale and worried, poor dear, with grey, glistening rings under his eyes. He had been looking like that for some days now. But his smile was cheerful. 'Let me get it, Mamma, you go and sit down. Yes? You had that bad night.' So she had done him an injustice. While checking his lottery numbers, he had clearly taken in what she had been telling him.

He placed the tray on the table, pushing to one side some of the old magazines and newspapers, and then he began to pour out the tea. 'Mine first,' he said. He liked his tea without milk and weak. 'Milk in first for Mamma.'

They sipped their tea in silence. Then he asked: 'What sort of day did Mamma have?'

'Oh, a day like any other day. I didn't feel up to going out. And Fiona let me down. That girl of hers has something wrong with her again. She's never really well, poor little thing.' She sighed and added: 'It's a boring life, and it's boring to talk about it.' Then she hated herself for the self-pity of it. When she sat with other MS patients at the hospital, she always avoided those who were self-pitying. 'And what about your day?'

He shook his head. 'I hear of one job, only one job. No good. I met Indian from car wash. Crazy man. He was sacked from car wash, now works as office cleaner. He tells me about it. Terrible pay, start work at five, sometimes four.'

'But it would be *something*, wouldn't it?'

'No, no. Too little money.' It was no use arguing with him, he always knew his own mind.

Then suddenly he brightened. He put down his cup and leaned towards her. 'I have idea, beautiful idea. Paper say that tomorrow hot, sunny. We go to Brighton.'

'To *Brighton*?' She had not been there since, as a child, she had paid a weekend visit during the school summer holidays to a cousin of her mother. She did not even know if the cousin were still alive or not. After her marriage to Eric, she had lost touch with so many of her relations, because of her resentment of the sniffy way in which they would treat him. 'Are you crazy? What would we be doing in Brighton?'

'What everyone else does in Brighton. Enjoying ourselves. Come on, Mamma!' He put out a hand and gripped hers in entreaty. 'Fun. Let us have some fun.'

Suddenly, forgetting the aches, the cramps, the unsteadiness and, worst of all, that terrible puppet-on-a-string feeling, she smiled at him in radiant acceptance. 'OK! Why not?'

All through the day, he was an absolute angel to her, even though, admittedly, it had been a shock when, at Victoria, he had first placed her on a chair outside a café, then brought her a cup of coffee and, then going down on his hunkers beside her, had said: 'Now I will buy tickets, please wait for me. But, Mamma – forgive me – Mehmet has no money. Money all gone.' He laughed but the laugh was an embarrassed one and she at once felt a pang of compassion for him.

'Of course, love.' She scrabbled in her bag and eventually produced a twenty-pound note. 'Will that be enough?'

'Maybe another ten. I do not know.'

'No problem.' Then, as she handed over the second note, she said: 'I suppose there's one of those cash dispenser things at Brighton?'

He laughed. 'Yes, many, many. Do not worry!'

He continued to be assiduous in his attentions to her, supporting her with one hand as they walked to platform 19, while the other hand gripped the straps of her handbag; asking her whether she wanted to face the engine or have her back to it; offering her a choice of newspaper, even though he knew that the *Mail* was her favourite. Having read his *Sun* for a while, he put it down and now stared out of the window and now looked, smiling, over to her. Each time that he smiled at her, she smiled back. Yes, he was a dear, a real dear, so considerate, with such beautiful manners. One could see, she told herself as she now often did, that in his own country he must have come from a posh family.

He found the right bus at Brighton station, and he and a foreign-looking, elderly man in an open-necked aertex shirt and a Panama hat, helped her up the steep steps on to it. 'I'm quite a weight,' she told the elderly man, who was out of breath when he and Mehmet had finally got her to a seat. 'No, no, madam. No!' the old man gallantly protested between puffs for air.

When they reached the front, she and Mehmet strolled, arm in arm, along it. Like two lovers, she thought. Then, because she was getting an ache in her calves and had increasing difficulty in picking up her feet, they sat in one of the shelters. 'I like just sitting here – watching the world go by,' she told Mehmet. And what a world! There was an almost nude, elderly man (no more than a rag of a thing to cover his parts), who was pierced with rings everywhere, nipples, nostrils, navel, earlobes, even *there*. The Lord of the Rings, she told Mehmet; but of course he didn't get her little joke. There was a young couple, she extremely fat and he extremely thin, who were so much all over each other, hands everywhere, mouths glued together, that one wondered how they were able to walk. A real exhibition! There were also innumerable old people, hardly able to totter along, with their little, yapping dogs. There were also a lot of people – the young were the saddest – who were being pushed along in wheelchairs by minders whose faces almost all had identical expressions of combined dutifulness and boredom. She pointed to one of these wheelchairs, containing an ancient, bearded man, his shrivelled legs bare beneath exiguous shorts, with a tall, erect woman, like a grenadier, pushing him. 'That's how I'll end up,' she told Mehmet. 'Nonsense, Mamma. You are getting better and better.' When he said it with that conviction, she almost believed that the troubles of the night before had been no more than a nasty nightmare.

Before they went for fish-and-chips at a café down on the beach, she told him that they must find that cashpoint. It had to be a Woolwich one, she said, but after examining the card he said No, she could use that card anywhere, though that way it might cost her a little extra. Would she like him to go to get the money – he was sure that there'd be a bank somewhere near – while she waited for him in the shelter? She suffered a brief dread (once she had told him her pin number, might he not draw out what he could and vanish?) and then a deep shame at having entertained such an idea. Anyone could see that he was honest, one hundred per cent – which was more than could be said for Eric, who was constantly returning from his cruises with things that by rights were the property of his employers.

The fish-and-chips were delicious, much better than those from that chippy in Kingsland Road, and she enjoyed her glass of Guinness with them. Mehmet had opted for a glass of wine, from which, at his urging, she sipped, wrinkling her nose. 'I've not really got the taste for wine. Now my Eric – with him it was a different matter. He was quite the connoisseur.'

It was a long walk, with many stops to rest on a succession of benches, to the pier. There were some really gorgeous girls about and you'd have expected him to look at them. But not a bit of it. 'That girl's giving you the eye' she told him at one point; but he laughed and shrugged, totally uninterested. 'Well, it's only to be expected,' she said. 'You're much the most handsome man to be seen.'

'Nonsense, Mamma!'

On the pier they played the machines with money that she recklessly dug out of her bag. From time to time they were laughing together and even hugging each other at some small win; but more often they were groaning when, just as the grabber seemed about to bring them some treasure, it suddenly dropped it, or when a ball just failed to enter a hole.

The most wonderful moment of the day occurred at the shooting gallery, where, after a number of tries, he at last won her a huge pale-blue teddy bear. At once he handed it to her. 'For you, Mamma.'

'For *me*?'

'Sure.'

'But haven't you a girlfriend to whom you'd like to give it?'

'I have no girlfriend.'

Could she believe that? She found it hard to do so. She held the teddy bear up before her, inspecting it, and then she cuddled it against her face. It had an odd smell, like that of the cellophane wrapping taken off a packet of fish fingers. But she loved its soft fur and its small, expressionless, night-dark eyes. 'You'll have to carry him,' she told Mehmet.

'That's all right, Mamma.'

On the journey home, the train was crowded; but they had been early enough to get two seats. 'I think I'll take a little nap,' she told him. 'I feel quite done in. But in the nicest way,' she added. She put a hand on the head of the teddy bear, which was seated in her lap.

'Maybe I go along to the bar.'

'Yes, do that, love. It's boring for you to sit here listening to me snoring.'

'I bring you something?'

'Oh, no. Thank you. I've eaten and drunk far too much already.'

'Sure?'

'Sure.' She looked up at him, with a sudden access of gratitude and love.

When she opened her eyes, the train was entering Victoria and he was walking down the aisle towards her. She yawned and then, putting a hand up to her mouth, yawned again. 'I had a lovely snooze.'

'I saw you.'

'I don't feel tired at all now. Quite my old self.'

'Quite your young self,' he corrected her.

As they were passing out through the automatic gates – these days there never seemed to be anyone to inspect the tickets, there must be an awful lot of cheating going on – an odd thing happened. There were three girls behind them, and one of them jostled her rudely in her eagerness to hurry through. Meg turned to say something, but before she could open her mouth another member of the trio addressed Mehmet. 'So we meet again!' She laughed. 'A bad penny,' said the third girl. They all laughed. Then they all pushed through and the girl who had jostled Meg turned her head and shouted at Mehmet: 'See you!'

'See you,' he repeated in an unenthusiastic, embarrassed voice.

'Who were those?' Meg asked. A shaft of jealousy had pierced her, taking her by surprise, since jealousy was something almost unknown to her.

'Oh, they were in bar. One spoke to me. Asked for cigarette,' he added.

Meg felt like saying 'Pull the other one!', seeing that there was no smoking on the train. The jealousy lingered.

Back home, Mehmet sat her down in her armchair and said that he would make the supper for them.

'There's not much in the fridge,' she said.

'Never mind. I make pasta.' He went into the kitchen and soon began whistling as he went about his task.

Meg cared for pasta even less than for pizza. It was odd that he never remembered that. But she would not tell him that she would much rather have two poached eggs, or even sardines, on toast. Suddenly Mehmet reappeared with a glass of Guinness for her. 'Oh, I mustn't! You want to make me squiffy!'

'I want to make you happy.'

'But I am happy. Very happy.'

There was a lot of this kind of affectionate banter between them as they ate the spaghetti, which he had prepared with some tinned tomato sauce found in her store cupboard.

'I know it's wrong to cut up spaghetti, but I just can't manage it otherwise.'

'I'll show you.'

They both laughed as his lesson all too often ended in a strand of spaghetti falling either on the length of tissue that she had tucked under her chin or on to the floor.

'I'll never get it,' she sighed, her eyes moist with tears of laughter.

'Mamma will, Mamma will!' It was as much an order as a prophecy.

She watched the telly, the teddy bear once again in her lap, while he washed up. Then he returned. 'All done,' he said. He rubbed his hands together, as though on that warm day he was feeling cold. He gave a little shudder. She wondered if perhaps he was sickening for something. Once again his face, so healthily flushed in Brighton, was looking alarmingly pale.

'Are you all right, dear?'

'All right? Of course, Mamma. What is wrong with me?'

He sat down in an upright chair just behind her, as though he were planning to watch the television programme over her shoulder. She heard the chair creak and creak again, as he shifted in it. Then he said: 'Mamma, there is something I want ask you. Something important.'

'Yes, love? Anything, anything.' But already she felt uneasy. He had never before addressed her in that sombre, official tone. It was like being spoken to by that young man at the Social Security, the one who always wore a tie-pin and glasses attached to a silver chain which dangled round the back of his neck, to swing from side to side when he was being emphatic about something.

'I am in trouble, Mamma. No residence permit, no work permit. You know so. Any work for me without work permit is bad, long hours, little money.' He sighed.

She had half-turned her head but she could not see him properly, seated there behind her. Why couldn't he come and sit in the sofa, where she could see him? 'Do turn that off,' she said. She pointed at the set. 'I haven't got the thingummy.' He jumped up. Somehow she had sensed already that what he was going to tell her was too important for her to listen to while she was also watching *Eastenders*.

Reseated, still behind her, he resumed. 'I need you do some-thing. You my only friend in England. Others – a lot of talk, a lot of "Hello, Mehmet, how is Mehmet, let me buy Mehmet a drink", but when I need help, real help . . .'

'What is it you want?' Her anxiety was mounting.

Suddenly he rose, lifted up his chair and placed it in front of her. He sat down on it, leaned forward.

'Two days ago, in bar, I am talking to man. From Ukraine. Before he is illegal. Illegal like me. Now he has residence permit, work permit. How?' He put the question that he had clearly been expecting her, sitting dazed before him, her mouth open, to put. 'He marry English girl. Not real marriage,' he went on. 'English girl is – what you say? – likes other women.'

'Lesbian,' Meg murmured. She had had a schoolmistress who had been like that. She was always trying to persuade Meg and one or two of the other girls to go bird watching with her. Not that she ever laid a finger on any of them or even said any-thing, but one always knew, didn't one?

'He give her thousand pounds and she marries him. Easy. For six months he lives in flat with her and her friend, girlfriend. After – free!'

'So?' But she already knew what would follow.

'I want you marry me.' He leaned forward in the chair. His eyes pleaded with her. She had never been able to resist the beauty of those eyes, glittering like mica when tiredness had not dulled them. 'You have done so much for Mehmet, Mamma. Please! It is not real marriage,' he added, as though she had not already taken that in. 'Easy. And so important for me. Of course,' he hurried on, 'I cannot give you thousand now. But when I have work permit, I have job, and when I have job, I have pay, good pay.'

She felt one of those puppet-on-a-string spasms jerk her whole body to the right and then upwards, almost as though she were about to levitate. She had a momentary difficulty in getting out the words that she wanted. Then she said: 'But Mehmet – I'm married already!'

'If husband leave wife – vanish – you cannot get divorce?' He was incredulous.

'But I don't know that I *want* a divorce. I mean – he might come back. Any day.' But since more than four years had passed, she knew that that was now highly unlikely.

Again his eyes pleaded with her, searching her face and, as it seemed to her, her inmost being for what he wanted. *'Please!'*

She gazed at the unlit television screen, seeing on it a multi-coloured blob, the reflection of herself, and, obscuring that blob, another, uniformly dark one, of him. 'I don't know,' she said, knowing already that she had, in effect, to choose between him and Eric. Then, surprising herself as much as she surprised Mehmet, she suddenly found herself sobbing. 'Why does life have to be so bloody difficult?'

'What is so difficult, Mamma? This is not difficult. First divorce. Then marry. Then live together, as we live together now. Easy!' He got off his chair and knelt on the floor beside her. That was how men were supposed to propose to their sweethearts in the old days, but there was nothing romantic about this proposal. 'Mamma, Mehmet beg this of you. For him it is – it is life or death. Ukraine man told me – '

She cut in on that. She had no desire to hear anything more about that bugger from the Ukraine. 'I must think about all this. I feel confused. It's been so – so unexpected. My poor head's in a whirl, aching.' She was struggling to get out of the armchair. Suddenly she thought, as she pressed down on the arms of the chair with her hands and down on the carpet with her feet, all to no purpose: Yes, this is the end of that remission. I knew the bloody thing was coming back and now here it is.

As in the past, when he saw her struggling to rise, he jumped to his feet and put out a hand, which she then gripped. Automatically, as she got to her feet, she said 'There we are!', as she had always said. And then: 'Thanks.'

'Lean on me,' he said.

But for some reason, having done that so often in the past, she now had an aversion to doing it. 'I'm all right. Just give me the crutches, there's a love.'

He fetched them for her, handing them to her one after the other. She settled them in her armpits, wriggling her body. 'Feels quite like old times.' She smiled but it was not really a joke. 'I'm going to turn in,' she announced. 'It's been a long day.' And such a happy day, she thought, until he had had to spoil it. 'I'll be thinking – thinking about that – that' – she all but said 'proposal' and then went on – 'that idea of yours. I can't give an immediate Yes or No. You can see that, can't you?'

'Of course, Mamma.' But she could see that she had upset him, from the way in which, instead of looking at her, he kept looking either in the direction of the television set or down to the floor. 'I get you something before you go bed?'

'Nothing, thank you, love.'

'Some tea?'

'Oh, no. That'll only keep me awake.'

But she was kept awake anyway, as she struggled with her dilemma. She loved that boy, there was no doubt about it, she had to face the fact. He was always being so good to her, cooking her that blasted pasta he so much liked or warming her up a pizza, fetching her cups of Nes or tea, helping her to make her bed, and even insisting on doing the ironing if Fiona hadn't had enough time. He was always so affectionate, holding her hand, putting an arm round her, or kissing her to say good morning or goodnight. He called her mamma and she really did believe that that was how he thought of her – she was now his mother in place of the mother so far away in Albania. Oh, she so much wanted to help him, and Sylvia had told her that, now that Eric had been gone so long without ever giving any sign, a divorce would be as easy as pie. But, but, but . . .

The truth was that she still believed, she still *knew*, that some day, suddenly, without any warning, she would hear a ring at the door and there would be Eric, the two battered Revelation suitcases, fastened with straps, beside him and his brown trilby jauntily tilted to one side of his head, smiling at her, as in the old days when he returned from a cruise. How could she divorce him when, sure as eggs is eggs, eventually that would happen? How could she then face him and say: 'Sorry, sweetheart. I'm married to another bloke'? She could never do that to him. But, but, but . . .

When she was not telling herself that she had to think of Eric, she was telling herself: 'You have to think of yourself, old girl.' That had been shitty behaviour of his, saying that he just couldn't cope any more, and then skedaddling like that, without a word of warning. Who could forgive something like that? But she knew the answer to that: she could. When she searched her heart, she knew that Eric was not merely the first but also the one and only. Yes, she had to admit it, Sylvia was right when she had told her 'I do believe that you still love that little rat.'

Eventually, shortly after four, Meg tottered out of bed and in doing so swerved against the chest of drawers in the overcrowded little bedroom and knocked off it the bulky Argos catalogue balanced on its edge. There was a loud thump, and then Mehmet was calling out: 'Everything all right, Mamma?'

'Yes, everything all right. I'm just on my way to have a wee.' She had not really been on her way to have a wee, but now she felt obliged to make her perilous, painful way down the corridor to the bathroom.

'Want any help?'

'No, love. Thank you.' Perhaps he, too, had been too worried to sleep.

Back in the bedroom, she took from a drawer the bottle of sleeping pills prescribed for her by Dr Karapiet. He had told her never to take more than one but now she recklessly swallowed three. The glass of water that Mehmet placed each night by her bedside was already almost empty but she managed somehow to get them down.

When, next morning, she entered the kitchen, Mehmet was sitting in his usual chair, his back to her, and eating his usual breakfast of a bowl of cereal and three slices of toast. Strangely, he did not turn round at the sound of her approach.

'Good morning, Mehmet. How are we this morning?'

She hoped that her assumed cheeriness would conceal her feeling of dread.

Slowly he turned, without his usual smile. 'Good morning, Mamma. You sleep well?'

'No. Hardly a wink until at, oh, it must have been past four, I took a sleeping pill. Three sleeping pills, to be exact.'

'Why you do that?'

'Because I couldn't sleep.' She limped over to her place and sat herself down. Her left leg was tingling. 'I feel a wreck. I don't know why I take those sleeping pills. Talk about that morning after feeling! They give me a real hangover.'

Usually he would have said something sympathetic, even patted her hand. Now, lifting a spoon of cornflakes to his mouth, he merely nodded his head.

'Would you be a dear and pour me a cup? I'm afraid of lifting up the pot. I'd probably drop it in my present state.'

His mouth and eyes sulky, he carefully poured out the tea. Then he held out the cup: 'OK?'

'Lovely. Just what I need.' She sipped and, though the tea burned her tongue, sipped again. Then she set down the cup. 'Mehmet,' she began.

'Yes, Mamma?' She could see that her tension had transmitted itself to him.

How was she to begin? She had rehearsed her lines but now, an actress drying with stage fright, she had forgotten them. 'I was thinking about your – your suggestion.'

'My suggestion, Mamma?'

She wished that he would drop that irritating Mamma. 'Yes. You know – you know the one.' She shrank from saying the word marriage, since it would be so humiliating.

'Yes, Mamma?' Deliberately he placed his spoon in the empty cereal bowl and then reached out to the toast rack. Clearly, like her, he was determined to pretend that this was a breakfast like any other breakfast.

'It wouldn't be right, love,' she said abruptly. Then putting a hand over her eyes, as though the early sunshine through the window were too much for her, she added: 'I couldn't do it.'

There was a long silence, during which he merely stared at her with unblinking hostility. Then in a hissing voice, he said: 'I thought you my friend.'

For the first time Meg felt that he was not a friend but a stranger and enemy. Then that horrible moment passed and she began tentatively: 'No, Mehmet – don't you see? – it wouldn't be right. Not for me it wouldn't.'

'You mean – illegal?'

'Oh, no! Of course not! I don't care whether it's illegal or not. It's just – just Eric.'

'*Eric!*'

She knew why the name exploded out of him like that. She had so often complained to him of Eric's sudden desertion – like a rat leaving a sinking ship, she had said on more than one occasion. He must be thinking: Why take a rat into consideration now? 'What you have to understand, love, is that, though he behaved so bad to me at the end, we did have our good times. Yes, many of them. We were together for – what? – almost twelve years and there was never a cross word between us. Well, not really a cross word.' She was speaking in a tenderly reminiscent, beseeching tone; but so far from reconciling him to her decision, she could see that it was only making him even more indignant. 'You can't live like that, with a man, with your husband, for all that time and not – not – well, feel he's part of you. For better or worse. That's what you say, isn't it? I mean, when you marry.'

'*I* say? I say nothing!' His fury suddenly gushed out of him in a scalding, malodorous stream. 'I thought you my friend, my only friend. But you like all English. Racists. Hypocrites. You pretend you like me but when I ask something, something easy, something simple, then it is other matter.' He gave a contemptuous, snorting laugh. 'Yes, it is always other matter.'

She quailed under this onslaught. She wanted to flee the kitchen but she wondered if her legs would be up to it. The pins and needles were no longer pricking at them; instead, they were twitching with spasm after spasm. 'You must try to understand, Mehmet. I'd do anything for you. But any day – perhaps even now – Eric might return. That happens, you know. When I was a small girl, there was this neighbour, a council gardener he was. His wife suddenly vanished, just like that, he came home, tea laid, no sign of her. She was away, oh, it must have been for quite as long as Eric. And then, one day, cool as a cucumber, she was back. What had she been doing? He never learned. Never. Perhaps he didn't want to know. My guess is that she went off with another bloke and eventually thought better of it. But there you are!'

As she gave this account, his face showed an increasing derision. 'And you think Eric gone off with another woman?'

'Oh, no! I'm sure not. Well, I don't think so. No. I think it was
just that he was worn out, poor soul. He just couldn't shoulder
the burden of looking after me any longer. Well, I understood
that – not at first, of course, but after I'd had time to think about
it. Some people have a gift for looking after others, it comes natural to them. You have that gift,' she added tentatively, looking
across at him with woebegone eyes. 'But my poor old Eric
didn't. Not his fault. That was how he was made.'

With an exclamation of disgust – as though he could not bear
to listen to all this nonsense any longer – Mehmet jumped to
his feet. 'OK, OK! You do not wish to help me. Thank you,
Mamma, thank you!' The sarcasm was brutal. 'Never mind.
Mehmet will think of something else – someone else. Yes!
Never mind!'

He strode out of the kitchen and into his room. Meg laid her
crossed arms on the table and rested her head on them. Her
head was pounding and she felt a stabbing sensation in her left
eye. Then she heard his feet hurrying down the corridor and the
front door first opening and then being slammed shut.

That was that. It was all over. He would come back, of
course, for his bits and pieces, but he wouldn't stay now, not
after she'd behaved so badly to him. It was terrible when you
could only stick by one person if you chucked the other over-
board. Arms still crossed, she sat up erect in the chair and then,
involuntarily, let out a single, jerky sob.

That afternoon, cool as a cucumber, as though all that
rumpus had never taken place, Mehmet entered the flat. He
was whistling tonelessly as he walked down to the bathroom,
and Meg could still hear the whistling, shrill and slightly off
key, along with the noise of his peeing. The walls were as thin
as paper, she would often complain.

Her heart began to accelerate, as though there were a fist
inside her chest which kept hammering there. Would he come
in to the sitting-room to confront her or would he go straight
to his room?

Pulling a comb through his wiry, close-cropped black hair –
at moments of affection she loved to run her finger through it
– he stood on the threshold.

'How's Mamma?'

He smiled, he walked towards her. She tried not to shrink
away from him. Then he stooped, put a hand on her shoulder,
and kissed her.

It was a return just like any other of his returns.

Chapter XII

'Oh, it's you.' Involuntarily, having opened the front door, Audrey pushed it towards him, as though to bar his entry, instead of drawing it farther back. The sun, low in the early evening sky, was just behind him and all she could make out, having come from the gloom of the basement, was a dark silhouette. But she knew at once who it was.

'Good afternoon, Miss Carter.'

'Good afternoon, Mr Ahmeti.'

They always addressed each other with this formality. 'Why don't you use his Christian name?' Marilyn had once asked Audrey, who had replied: 'Because he hasn't got one. He isn't a Christian.' 'His first name, I mean,' Marilyn had then countered irritably.

'Is Dr Carter in?'

'I'm afraid not. She had to go out urgently to see a patient.'

'She away long time?'

'I've no idea. One never knows. Someone has had a fall.' Her voice sounded as though she were clipping at the words with a pair of scissors. She was still holding the front door almost closed, after having resisted the temptation to put it on the latch. He might have been some bedraggled stranger who, having rung the bell, had then held out the permit dangling round his neck, before asking her if she wanted to buy some sponges, dishcloths or mops at a price far higher than she would have had to pay at any supermarket.

'Maybe I wait.'

'Well . . .' She did not at all like to admit him to the house. But if she sent him away, she knew that Marilyn would be furious with her. 'Oh, all right. Come in!' At last she pulled the door wide open, but she still remained where she had been standing, so that he had to edge in sideways past her. 'You'd better wait in the sitting-room,' she told him, and then at once wished that she had said the library. With its few bookcases, most of them paperbacks, its seldom used television set and its ironing board and iron, the room hardly merited that description and was seldom used. What now recommended it to her was the absence in it of any small objects of value. The sitting-room, on the other hand, was full of them – including some Chinese snuff bottles, Laurence's property on long-term loan, which, set out on a shelf, would be all too easy to rifle. To date, she had had no proof of Mehmet's dishonesty, but she was sure that one day, sooner rather than later, it would reveal itself.

Mehmet entered the sitting room. She remained in the doorway, reluctant to let him out of her sight but not in the least wanting to sit there with him, a wary guardian. With anyone else in similar circumstances – Carmen on some errand, a patient out of surgery hours, even the window cleaner – she would have had no qualms about immediately quitting the room. To Carmen she might even have first offered something to drink. Ah, well! She had better to get back to those shop accounts. 'I'll leave you then,' she said.

As she turned away, she heard his resonant voice: 'Miss Carter!' She hated that voice, because it was so often audible to her from this room or even from Marilyn's bedroom, when she had left doors open in her basement.

'Yes?' There was a sharp upward inflection, which said: Please don't bother me.

'I have question to ask you.'

'Oh. Yes? And what is your question?'

He smiled at her in that spuriously winning way of his. Then his soft gaze suddenly hardened and his mouth hardened with it. 'Why you dislike me, Miss Carter?'

She was so much taken aback by this sudden verbal blow that she recoiled, as though at a physical one. 'I don't dislike you.' But there was no conviction in it. He was right, of course. From the first she had disliked him. 'There's something chilly and chilling about him, like a snake,' she had once confided to Laurence, and he had then laughed, shaken his head and said: 'That sounds awfully melodramatic and not in the least like sweet, tolerant you.'

Once again smiling – apart from that chipped, discoloured eyetooth, she had always had to acknowledge that his smile had singular charm – he nodded his head. 'Yes, Miss Carter, you dislike me. But what I done? Nothing. I am polite to you, nothing bad. I am friend of Dr Carter. Is that wrong? Yes?'

She did not know what to say. She could not say: 'I don't trust you. You're up to something. I'm afraid of what you might do to my sister-in-law.'

Stubbornly she repeated: 'I don't dislike you. You've got it all wrong.'

But of course, as he obviously knew, he had got it all right.

'I'll leave you then,' she said, wishing that her voice did not quaver.

He turned away from her and reached for the copy of the local paper that had been pushed through the door that morning.

Audrey had often wished that her hearing were not so acute; she had also often wished that the house, jerry-built at a time when a Napoleonic invasion had appeared to be imminent, were not so flimsy. One began to hammer a nail into the wall and at once one heard a patter, as of small rodents scattering behind the elegant wallpaper. One began to settle to reading a book and, as though one were a sudden victim of tinnitus, one would hear Marilyn dropping her shoes to the floor of her sitting-room and then, barefoot, pouring out one of her over-large measures of vodka before causing the sofa to creak as she collapsed into it.

When at last Marilyn returned from the visit to her patient, Audrey had no wish to listen to what she said to Mehmet or Mehmet to her. But snatches of conversation, disconnected but vaguely disturbing, kept drifting down – 'God what a day!' 'You're looking terrific,' 'Let's go out, let's try that Tunisian restaurant,' from Marilyn, and from him: 'Nothing, nothing,

nothing. I walk, walk, walk. Nothing,' 'Truly I am depressed, broken down,' and then, far more loudly, 'Yes, yes, yes! Now, *now!*'

Audrey knew what it was that he wanted Now, *now*. She always knew. There was a long silence – she imagined him holding Marilyn and kissing her, and then her pushing him away with a whisper or a sigh – and, after that, the regular, slow heartbeat of feet ascending the stairs. They couldn't have enough of it, she thought. Well, he was probably a terrific lover. People said that East Europeans were. There was that crude, jolly Australian, an actress out of work, who used to help out in the shop. She had a lover from – where? – Bosnia or somewhere like that – and she was constantly arriving late, yawning and exclaiming 'God, I'm worn out', before embarking on a detailed account, continued even when customers were in the shop, of all that she and her lover had been doing all through the night. 'He never wants to stop. I say "Enough is enough" but, bloody hell and thanks be to God, enough is never enough for that one.'

Now the thumping and thudding started, soon followed by the groans (she never knew whether they came from Marilyn, from him or from both of them) and the moans, hers much higher than his. Then, inevitably, there was his 'Yes, yes, yes!' on a crescendo. It was not, she told herself, that she was in the least bit puritanical. For eleven years she had carried on an affair with the chief accountant at the publishers where she worked, so discreetly that no one, she was sure, had even guessed at it. Often both of them would stay late in the office, on the pretext of having an accumulation of work to finish. Often he would take her to a little Sussex Gardens hotel, spartan but clean, with a cramped en suite bathroom containing a sitz-bath and a bidet, for a few hours. Sometimes he would come to the Brompton Square house, if Laurence were away. Secretive by nature, she never spoke to Laurence about the affair and she was sure that, like her office colleagues, he was totally unaware of it. In fact, his antennae were so sensitive that he had soon guessed, from her unexplained or inadequately explained absences, her sudden high spirits and her no less sudden lapses into depression, that *something* was going on; but he was unable to define precisely what that something was and even wondered whether Audrey might not be having what he called a ding-dong with another woman. Either way, he did not care. He was only telling the truth when he boasted: 'Nothing shocks me.'

The reason why Audrey's colleague would not marry her was that he was already married to a woman, a lecturer at Imperial College, who suffered from manic depression. He couldn't possibly leave her, he would tell Audrey, it would be too cruel in her fragile mental state, it might finish her off; and Audrey would then be filled with both sadness and admiration for his decency. In the end, he did leave her, but not for Audrey but for someone far younger, a tiny, babyish, doll-like creature, with bubbles of pinkish-blonde hair falling round her face, who had recently come, straight from university, to work as a secretary in the firm. When, in a turmoil of grief and anger, she had confided in Laurence – he had found her crying alone at the kitchen table and had asked what was the matter – he had patted her shoulder and said, inadvertently cruel but intending to comfort her: 'A banal tragedy. I'm so sorry.' After a brief rage against him, she had later thought forgivingly: Didn't Hannah Arendt write of the banality of evil? Well, her father was right, tragedy was all too often also banal.

The noises from upstairs had become far louder than they had ever been in the past. Audrey gritted her teeth, threw down her book, and then leapt up and turned off the television. Arms crossed and head cocked, she stood in the centre of the room, avidly listening and yet disgusted with herself for doing so. Had Marilyn lost her reason? No one would expect a woman in her late thirties to remain faithful to the memory of a husband now dead for more than three years. But when she knew so many men eligible as lovers or even husbands, why pick on someone so *ghastly*? Of course he was attractive, in his gigolo way, with those wide shoulders and those narrow hips and that pale, clear skin and those eyes that could within a few seconds turn from being soft and lambent with sympathy into glittering with a dangerous allure. But he and she belonged to totally different worlds, with nothing in common but their greed for sex. One might as well have an affair because of a shared passion for lobster or caviar!

Oh, it was too squalid to stand here deliberately listening. She hurried to the kitchen, switched on the portable wireless, and then, when the noise from above still penetrated through that, turned up the volume to maximum. After that, she sat down at the kitchen table and began to polish some silver. This was not a task that Marilyn would ever undertake. Laurence would often refer to his daughter and daughter-in-law as Martha and Mary. She was bitterly aware that it was the Mary whom, like Christ, he preferred to the Martha.

Eventually, after the 'Das Lied von Der Erde' had drawn to its close and the clapping and occasional 'Bravo!' emerged, disagreeably distorted, from the old wireless, she heard Marilyn and Mehmet coming down the stairs. On a shameful impulse, she put out a hand, switched off the set and then stood motionless, listening once more.

'What about trying that Turkish place?' she heard Marilyn asking.

There was a silence. Probably he was shaking his head or looking unenthusiastic.

'Or we could go to Momo. You like Momo. Though it is rather expensive,' Marilyn added.

'Yes, Momo!' He was eager. Of course he wouldn't care a damn if it was expensive or not, Audrey thought.

'Where have I put my bag? . . . Oh, yes, here it is! Are my keys in it? Yes.'

Another silence, briefer then the previous one. Then: 'Marilyn, do not be cross with Mehmet. Please! I have something to ask you.'

Money, money! Audrey thought, with a mixture of fury and triumph.

'Yes?'

'Can you lend me some money? I am – sorry – I am broke again.'

'Oh.' Audrey imagined the look of consternation on Marilyn's face. Women never felt humiliation when asked by women for a loan, but they usually did when asked by men. 'Oh, Mehmet! It was only last Tuesday that I –'

'Yes, I know, I know. But – my landlady . . . Again she say I must pay her money, some money, or I must go. I have nowhere to go. You say I cannot stay here. Sorry, Marilyn. Sorry.'

Silence. Then, wearily: 'How much do you need?'

'Fifty pounds?'

'*Fifty*! I gave you fifty –'

'What I do? I have no work. I try, try. No use. No permit, no work.'

'Poor Mehmet. It's awful for you. But you know, I'm not . . .' She broke off. What was she going to say? 'I'm not rich,' Audrey guessed. 'Oh, well, let's see what I've got. We can always go to the cashpoint. . . . Yes. Here it is. Fifty.' She was obviously counting out the notes.

'How do I thank you? How? It is terrible for me . . .'

'Yes, borrowing money is always humiliating.' (So, all too often, is lending it, Audrey thought). 'I do wish that there was some solution for you.'

'Only solution is go home.' He said it bitterly.

'Oh, no! We can't think of that. No, no!'

'You are very kind to me.'

A long silence followed. Audrey imagined that they were embracing up there in the draughty hall above her. Then she heard Marilyn give a brief, high-pitched, girlish laugh, not at all like her usual one.

The front door opened, the front door closed.

Audrey returned for a few minutes to the silver. But she could not concentrate on it. The smell of the polish was beginning to nauseate her, and her head was throbbing. She got up and wandered out into the corridor. Then, after a brief struggle with herself, she began to mount the stairs at a rapidly increasing speed. She threw open the door of Marilyn's room, put a hand to the light switch, and stood on the threshold looking in. She might have been a passerby staring at a traffic accident. Her mouth was open and a hand was pressed to her chest. Her face was greenish in the light from the landing.

A tangle of sheet and blankets seemed to be on the verge of

slipping off the wide double bed to the floor. When they had first moved into the house together, Audrey had wondered why, since the room was so small, Marilyn had insisted on a bed so large. Now she knew. There was a rank smell of sweat and sex, and mingling with it the scent, sweetly dizzying, which she had come always to associate with his presence, so that, entering the house, she would at once know that he either was there or had recently been there.

Again she looked at the bed. It was there that, after That had happened, Marilyn would so often retreat, like a wounded animal to its lair, either to sob quietly or to lie on her back, absolutely silent and motionless, and stare up at the ceiling. Audrey would go into her and would sit on the edge of the bed and try, sometimes with some small success and sometimes with no success at all, to comfort her. She would put a hand to her forehead or to her hair, stroking them while she murmured the usual trite things – there, there, you've got to try to put it behind you, you have to make a fresh start, you can't go on like this forever. Marilyn had accepted her in this role of comforter, as she had refused to accept Laurence, who had once been so much closer to her. That had always puzzled Audrey and not merely puzzled but also lacerated him. 'I sometimes think that she hates me now,' he once told Audrey. 'What on earth have I done?' 'She's not herself,' Audrey said. 'You have to understand.' But she, like Laurence, could not understand the sudden aversion.

Audrey looked around the room, at the undrawn curtains, the comb thrown down on the desk instead of on the dressing table, the soiled tights dangling over a chair. Then she looked at the floor and saw the screwed-up balls of tissue.

She pulled a face of disgust and retreated on to the landing, tugging the door shut behind her, as on some suddenly discovered fire. She began to run down the stairs.

Soon after that, Audrey realized that Mehmet's visits had come to follow a timetable. There was the Wednesday visit, when he would arrive late, after Marilyn's return from the surgery, would have a quick drink with her, retire with her to the bedroom, and would then go out with her for the evening, not to return. There was the weekend visit, when he would arrive soon after lunch, he and Marilyn would follow no regular pro-gramme, and he would not leave until Sunday evening or even Monday morning. The Wednesday visit was bad enough; but the weekend visit was the one that she really dreaded and hated. Each time, she told Laurence, she felt as though the house were being violated, and so – though she did not tell him this – in some subtle, dreadful way, was she.

The first time that he stayed for the weekend, Marilyn amaz-ingly gave no warning to Audrey. But, propped up in bed with the latest Ruth Rendell, Audrey knew that he was there from the vague sounds that lapped around her. She kept thinking Now he will go, but he never did. The vague sounds died away and eventually she fell into an uneasy sleep, half-expecting that they might flood back to awake her.

Audrey was, as usual on a Sunday morning, the first to start on breakfast. She had all but finished when Marilyn joined her, in dressing gown and slippers. Stretching indolently, yawning and then rubbing with the back of a hand at an eye, she made Audrey think: You're the cat that's been at the cream.

'How are things today?'

'I didn't sleep so well,' Audrey replied in what she had intended to be an amiable tone but which emerged with a veiled hostility.

'Oh, poor you!'

Marilyn went to the kitchen cupboard and began to fetch down cereal bowl, plate, cup and saucer.

'What are you doing? I've laid for you.' But Audrey knew per-fectly well what she was doing.

Marilyn turned, cereal bowl in hand, and gave an awkward smile. 'We have an overnight visitor.' Audrey stared at her. 'Mehmet.' Still Audrey stared. 'It was too late for him to trek back to Dalston, with all those changes. So I made him stay the night.'

I bet that didn't require much making, Audrey thought. But she restrained herself. 'Is he still asleep?'

'Yes. He was snoring his head off when I left him.' Marilyn, having finished laying the place for Mehmet, now set about making toast and more coffee for herself. She sat down, composed, clearly at ease with the world and herself. Audrey, her breakfast finished, picked up the *Observer*.

'You don't like him.'

'I hardly know him.'

'I think he'd like to get to know you better.'

Audrey went on reading.

'Do try. It would make it all so much easier for me.'

The calm, sweet reasonableness of the appeal briefly touched Audrey. But still she said nothing. She got up and began to stack her used breakfast things in the dishwasher. 'Are you in to lunch?'

Marilyn considered. 'No. No, I don't think so. It might be better if we took ourselves out. I thought I might show him Greenwich. He's never been there. We could take the Light Railway one way and come back by boat.' On an impulse she added: 'Why don't you join us?'

'Thank you. But I want to go to church and then I want to pay a visit to that Rwandan family . . .'

Marilyn bit into a piece of toast. Then she looked up at Audrey: 'I'd so much like you and Mehmet to be friends. Do try!'

Audrey had no intention of trying.

When, late in evening, Mehmet had left, Marilyn and Audrey, both about to go to bed, coincided on the stairs to the basement, Marilyn coming up from them with a glass of hot milk and Audrey going down them with the newspaper she had fetched from the sitting-room.

'You're late going to bed,' Marilyn said.

'So are you.' Audrey began to retreat backwards up the stairs, to enable Marilyn to pass.

'I hope Mehmet won't miss his last connections. I tried to get him to stay but he wouldn't. He feels so responsible for his landlady – I can't think why, since she's constantly demanding the rent.'

'That doesn't seem unreasonable of her,' Audrey said dryly.

Marilyn decided to treat that as a joke. She laughed. 'No, I suppose not.'

The two women were now together in the hall. Audrey picked up an ashtray, in which Mehmet had stubbed out one of his Kingsize Lights. She stared down into it. 'Did he sleep in Laurence's room?' It was really their guestroom, and Laurence rarely used it; but they kept up the fiction that it was his, since clearly that gave him pleasure.

'Yes. I can't take the snoring. It keeps me awake. So that seemed to be better. In any case, he likes to sleep late and I don't – or, rather, can't.'

Audrey was about to go down the stairs, when Marilyn said: 'Oh, by the way – there's something I wanted to ask you.'

'Yes?'

'Would you mind awfully if he used the basement shower? I mean – just for a shower. He'll take care not to use it when you want it.'

'Why can't he use your bathroom?' Audrey had always regarded the bathroom in the basement as hers, even though Laurence or an occasional guest might use it when Marilyn was occupying the upstairs one.

'Well, of course, he can. For washing his hands, shaving, other things. But he much prefers a shower to a bath. He thinks that baths never leave one really clean, since one lies around in water full of one's washed-off dirt. It's logical, I suppose.'

'I'd really rather –'

'Oh, come on, Audrey! What harm can it do? I'll tell him to leave everything as he finds it.' She laughed. 'He's totally house-trained, you know.'

Audrey began to make her way down the stairs. She said nothing more, not even goodnight. She was aware of Marilyn standing motionless above her, mug of milk in hand, looking down.

The next Sunday morning Audrey got up deliberately early, long before the paperboy had arrived. She did not wish to coincide with Marilyn, much less with Mehmet, for breakfast. She carefully laid places for herself and Marilyn, as she had always done in the past. But she laid no place for Mehmet. He – or Marilyn, if she was determined to continue to make a fool of herself – could do that.

Chapter XIII

'Where is Marilyn?'

Laurence, standing under the porch to the quadrangle where he had his rooms, said the words even before he had greeted Audrey, who was trudging, plastic bag in hand, up the drive towards him. Then, realizing that she might be offended, he quickly said: 'Hello, my dear. Lovely to see you.' He extended his cheek for her to kiss, making no attempt to kiss her back.

'Hello, Father.' Her voice was listless. 'I had those shoes repaired for you.' She held out the bag. 'Rather a lot of money.'

'Well, Lobbs always were expensive. But one has to have their shoes repaired by them.' Then, unable to contain himself, he repeated, as he took the plastic bag from her: 'Where is Marilyn?'

'She couldn't come. She sent her love.'

Audrey began to walk ahead of him towards the quadrangle. He noticed with a pang, as he followed her, that she was not carrying herself as she usually did, but bowed as though under some invisible burden. 'Couldn't come? But she sent that message last time that she would certainly be here this time.'

'Well, you know how things are now.'

'That rascal?'

Audrey did not answer.

'I'd like to meet him. I'd soon tell him to go about his business.'

'He hasn't got a business. That's the problem. Unless being a rent boy is a business.'

Laurence pondered on that; but it was not until he had hung up her overcoat that he summoned up the courage to pursue it. 'Does Marilyn – does she support this Mehmet?'

Audrey nodded. 'To all intents and purposes.'

'H'm.' He was digesting that, in disgust. 'A glass of sherry wine?' He was constantly railing against the sloppiness of young people, otherwise well-bred and well-educated, who spoke of 'a sherry', used the word 'gay' instead of 'queer', and were incapable of differentiating between 'uninterested' and 'disinterested.'

'I'd rather have some vodka and tonic.'

'Then vodka and tonic it shall be. For you and, yes, also I think for me.'

After a few mouthfuls of his drink, he could not resist returning to the subject of Marilyn and Mehmet, just as, sleepless during the long nights, he had not been able to resist scratching at the patch of senile eczema on his right elbow, until it had acquired the bluish-red colour of an uncooked steak. 'So you think that that chap is bleeding Marilyn white?'

Audrey laughed. 'Oh, I wouldn't put it as strongly as that. But she seems to be his chief – perhaps his only – financial support. He dresses extremely well, you know. I can't think how he manages that. And whenever he comes to the house, he comes with some present. Bought with the money she has given him, I imagine.'

As though to denigrate Mehmet was a conspiracy on which, by tacit agreement, both of them had now entered, Audrey began to tell her father about a discovery that she had made in the guestroom. Last Saturday Marilyn had gone out to meet Mehmet, instead of waiting for him to come to the house. The two of them were 'apparently' – in fact, Audrey had overheard Marilyn reveal this on the telephone – going to an early cinema. 'I had to go upstairs to your room – the room that he now takes over – for something or other, and there, on the dressing table, I saw these notes laid out. Five twenties.'

'A hundred, you mean?'

'A hundred. She had obviously left them there for him.'

'So she makes him an allowance?'

'You could call it that.'

He shook his head. 'Poor Marilyn.' He stared down into his glass. He felt a rage not only against this bloody Albanian but also, bewilderingly, against his daughter. A case of wanting to shoot the messenger? Then that rage was obliterated by his sorrow for Marilyn. How could she have got herself into such a humiliating and potentially dangerous situation?

Audrey had miraculously tuned into his thoughts. 'I can't understand it. Marilyn has always struck me as being so level-headed. Sensible. Yes, I know she has that drink problem but after all she went through . . .' She sighed. 'Poor dear.'

'I never see her now.'

'I hardly ever see her. She's so busy with her patients during the week and so busy with him at every weekend.'

Eventually Laurence looked at his watch and decided that they had better toddle along to lunch. He was not going to inflict another ghastly meal in hall on her but instead was going to take her into the village to a recently-opened Japanese restaurant. Did she feel adventurous enough to try Japanese food? Audrey had already tried it as the guest of the Australian woman who worked at the shop, and she hated it. But she said Yes, of course, that sounded fun.

Laurence was in a fretful, uncommunicative mood as, his arm linked in hers, they made their way down through the gardens to the road below. At one point, he halted and pointed with his stick. 'Look at those wretched camellias. There was hardly a single blossom on them this year. Or last year. Every year I tell those girls who look after the garden that camellias don't blossom if one cuts them right back, and then each year they do precisely that. I can't think why they call this place a College when no one is capable of learning anything at it.'

Soon after they had begun on their sushi, he threw down his chopsticks and said: 'This place was a mistake!'

'Oh, I rather like it,' Audrey said, though she agreed with him.

'And it's bloody expensive!'

If Marilyn had been his guest, he reminded himself, he would

not have worried about its being expensive. At that, he felt a
brief stab of guilt. Why couldn't he be nicer to this only surviv-
ing child of his? He brooded on that question, hardly aware of
what she was saying, as she started on some wearisome
account of an old man who tottered into the shop almost every
day to filch the cheapest of paperbacks.

He had been jealous – yes, he had long since acknowledged
that to himself – of Audrey during those days when Marilyn
hadn't wanted even to see him, let alone talk to him, but would
nonetheless welcome Audrey. Sometimes during those terrible
days he would stand outside Marilyn's bedroom and, unknown
to the two women inside it, would listen to the stronger comforting the weaker. He had then so much wanted to be the one
who was saying the soothing, strengthening things that Audrey
was saying.

He roused himself from this bitter reverie to hear Audrey
concluding: '. . . I never do anything about the poor old chap.
He looks so lonely and frail. What does it matter if we lose one
or two paperbacks at fifty p each? I just put what's owed into
the till, out of my own pocket.'

He stared at her, with his vacant, bloodhound eyes. 'Fifty p?'
he repeated automatically, just to demonstrate that he was still
a party to the conversation. 'And you say Marilyn is dishing out
eighty pounds each week to him?'

'Worse. A hundred.'

He knew that she was thinking: How vague he's getting, can
this be the beginning of Alzheimer's?

'I must tell you something. Rather amusing. Old Mervyn –
you know whom I mean, once Head of Protocol? – had this
guest to lunch the other day and asked me to join them. The
guest – Sir Somebody or Other – is an eminent – all these con-
sultants are eminent, have you noticed? – an eminent geron-
tologist. You know what that means? Of course you do – you're
an educated woman, Roedean, St Anne's and all that. Well, he
was talking about some mutual friend of theirs and he said "I'm
afraid he's suffering from Alzheimer's." So – as a joke, of course
– I said to him, I said, Oh, Sir Somebody or Other, do tell me,
I can never remember, I can never remember, what *is*

Alzheimer's? And, do you know, quite serious, he began to explain to me – patiently, as though to a child – at absolutely *enormous* length.'

He looked up at her and laughed, but his eyes were stricken and sorrowful.

Dutifully, she managed to laugh back.

After the pretty, sulky waitress, whom Laurence had declared to be Chinese not Japanese, had taken away their half-emptied plates of soy-saturated food and their half-drunk cups of pale-yellow tea, Laurence called for the bill. 'Yes, pretty steep, pretty steep,' he sighed. It was so much easier to be lavish to someone with whom you were in love. He threw down some notes and said: 'They don't deserve a tip as large as that, but I can't be bothered to wait for the change. It'll be an age in coming, the service is so slow. I'll walk you to the station.'

He could see from the hurt expression on Audrey's face that she had been expecting to return, as she usually did, to the college for tea, but he was feeling tired and depressed and his neck was worrying him again.

'I can find my own way there,' she said in a vaguely offended tone.

'No, I'd like to go with you,' he assured her, now guiltily eager to make amends.

They walked in silence through streets that were surprisingly – and to him in his sombre mood, eerily – empty. Then all at once, apropos of nothing, he exclaimed: 'What a rum do!'

She looked at him interrogatively.

'This business of Marilyn and her rent boy.'

Audrey sighed. She wanted, he knew, always to be fair to everyone – as though that were ever possible in a life made up of illogical likes and dislikes and preferences and prejudices. 'Well, I suppose that men constantly pay women for sex – with presents if not with money. So why shouldn't a woman do the same with a man?'

'You're very emancipated.' He said it tartly.

Although she begged him not to, he insisted on using his OAP pass to descend with her to the platform. After a few seconds there, he put his hand into his pocket, pulled out two pound coins, and hurried over to a slot machine. He returned with two chocolate bars. He held out one. 'For you.'

'For me? Oh, I don't think I can eat it. Why not keep both for yourself?'

Unlike him, she had never had a sweet tooth. His sweet tooth was strongest when, as now, he felt unhappy.

'Are you sure?'

'Quite sure.'

The trivial refusal intensified his dejection.

Walking up through the garden, Laurence swivelled his head from side to side. Each turn brought with it a spasm of pain, but he went on with the swivelling. The physical pain obliterated the emotional one of longing and loss. Who would have supposed that a seventy-nine year old man would be capable of an intensity of passion such as had always eluded him in his philandering youth?

Suddenly breathless, he sank on to a bench. He looked down over a serene expanse of flowers and trees to the noisy road below it. He shut his eyes, appalled by the contrast, as he had never been before.

Yesterday, he had been to see the doctor, who visited the institution every day at eleven, to ask if he could not do anything about his neck. The doctor, who was young, with plump, pink hands and a strange sideways glance, had said: 'Well, Sir Laurence, you've had the X-rays which have shown nothing seriously amiss, just the degeneration common at your age. You have had four weeks of physiotherapy. I am afraid that all that's left is taking the painkillers. Since you turned down my suggestion of wearing a collar.'

'No, that I won't do. I refuse to go round looking like a dog.' He bit his lower lip, scowling. 'So you can do nothing more for me?'

The doctor shook his head. 'That's about the score.' He looked up and gave a nervous smile. 'I'm afraid you've just got to live with it.'

'When I was young, doctors were always telling me that I'd grow out of it. Now they constantly tell me that I'll just have to live with it. Growing old's no fun.'

'Well, I'm sure it has its compensations.'

'Such as?'

'Oh, I don't know.' Again he gave his nervous laugh. 'Having a free travel pass for one thing.'

Now, going over the conversation, Laurence thought: This crazy obsession with Marilyn is really like an illness. I'll have to live with – and die with – it. Just as I'll have to live with – and die with – this bloody pain in my neck. Then the disconcerting thought came to him: But do I really want to be cured? The last time that he had seen Marilyn, more than three weeks ago, she had spoken of those of her patients who were, as she put it, in love with their illnesses and so were determined not to be separated from them. A young AIDS patient, who refused to follow the ferocious regimen of thirty pills per day prescribed to him; an old woman who went on smoking even though her emphysema was so acute that she became breathless merely when she walked down the corridor from her bedroom to the lavatory; a sufferer from skin cancer, who spent every holiday on some foreign beach tanning his muscular body: all regarded their illnesses as capricious, demanding lovers, to whom they could not even attempt to say goodbye, whatever the eventually lethal cruelties that they inflicted.

Was that, Laurence asked himself, how he felt about his obsession with Marilyn?

For a while, hands clasped over his stomach and eyes half-closed, he brooded on it. Then he was aroused by a voice calling: 'Bart! Bart! I say, Bart!' Mervyn was hurrying over to the bench. 'I'm in luck – seeing you like this. I've run out of stamps and I must catch the post. You couldn't spare me a stamp, could you, old chap?'

Chapter XIV

Amazingly, Andy's novel had been accepted. Even more amazingly his recently acquired agent had managed to extract an advance of a hundred thousand pounds. When, less than two months before, Carmen had brought Marilyn the news that the agent had decided to take him on, she had been euphoric. Now, with this far more exciting news, she seemed merely to be dazed, repeating over and over 'Dr Carter, I cannot believe it.'

'I suppose you'll now want to leave us,' Marilyn said, forgetting that, for all her sweetness, ardour and impetuousness, the Spanish girl was essentially level-headed and shrewd.

'Oh, no, Dr Carter! We wish to buy flat, we wish to have baby. I have waited so long for flat and for baby. One hundred thousand is not so much money, not for such things.'

Marilyn nodded approvingly. In similar circumstances, she would have thrown up her job and to hell with it. 'You're a sensible girl.'

'Andy is so happy!'

'I'm sure he is. He has every reason to be.'

A few days later, Carmen asked Marilyn if she would come to a celebratory party on the following Saturday. Andy's closest friend was the owner of a restaurant out west beyond Shepherd's Bush, and he would provide all the food. Andy would buy the drinks.

'Well, yes, I'd love to come. I've always wanted to meet Andy – and I want to meet him even more now that he's about to become a famous author. But there's a problem, I'm afraid.'

'Your friend?' Carmen promptly asked.

Marilyn was taken aback. How did Carmen know about Mehmet? Presumably, if she knew about him, then everyone at the surgery must do so. She herself rarely took part in the gossip constantly circulating there; but she knew that, surprisingly, her partner Jack did. It must be he who had been the source of the news. He had once called at the house on a Saturday afternoon, to make one of his fussy interventions about a patient whom she had seen on his behalf; and there, on the steps just behind him, Mehmet had all at once appeared. Inevitably, she had had to introduce them to each other. Probably he had later talked to the oldest of the three receptionists, a member, like Laurence in the past, of his bridge club, and she in turn must have talked to the others.

'Well, yes, I have a friend coming to stay for the weekend. I can hardly leave him.'

'Bring him, Dr Carter!'

'Well, I'm not sure whether . . .'

'Please! Bring him! No problem. Everyone is friendly. He will enjoy.'

'All right. Thank you.'

At lunch that day, before Mehmet's arrival, Audrey was taciturn, almost sullen. Then suddenly she said, in an oddly stilted way: 'I wonder if I might ask something of you, Marilyn.'

'Yes. What is it?'

'It's about the shower. You know that he – he has now taken to using it.' Audrey could rarely bring herself to utter Mehmet's name.

Marilyn already sensed trouble. 'Yes,' she said. 'But only for a few minutes each day. Just for a shower, nothing else.'

'Well, it's not always only for a shower. Not last Wednesday evening. He had the shower after you both had . . .' Her voice trailed away. 'But he also . . .' She shrugged one shoulder, hesitating how to go on. She had never found it easy to talk about bodily functions. 'Well, it's not all that pleasant to find one's loo choked up with lavatory paper. And – other things.'

'Oh, I'm sorry. I'll have to have a word with him about it.'

'Perhaps I'm becoming a fussy old maid. But there it is. I do like to have things *clean* around me. Particularly such intimate things,' she added.

'Yes, of course.' So far Marilyn had been placatory, but she could not keep it up. After a brief silence, she said: 'Actually Mehmet – like most Muslims – is fanatical about cleanliness. He's always washing. If the loo is clogged with paper that may be because he's used not to sitting on a loo seat but to squatting. Muslims squat – well, many of them. So he might feel it dirty to sit on a seat without first covering it with paper.'

'Perhaps you should buy him one those ghastly chenille cover things. To put his mind at rest.'

Marilyn was taken aback by the acidity of the tone. It was rare for Audrey to speak like that. 'Perhaps I should. But meanwhile – please bear with him.'

'And please tell him to take more care.'

Marilyn decided to tell him nothing.

The restaurant, called The Rake's Progress, was a long, narrow, brightly lit shed, with hefty, bare pine tables and chairs to match, and a bar, followed by a kitchen, at its farthest end. Andy and Carmen were seated at a table, just in front of the bar, which had been set out for eight. There was a carafe of white wine at one end and a carafe of red at the other. Carmen jumped to her feet, her full, shiny purple skirt swirling around her, and ran to Marilyn to embrace her. 'Dr Carter! I am so happy, happy!' The happiness was genuine. Then, before Marilyn could introduce Mehmet, she swung round to him. 'I remember!' She put out a hand to shake his. 'You remember me? Carmen?'

'Of course.'

Marilyn thought: How self-composed he is, how dignified. In his charcoal-grey suit – the only suit that he possessed, she imagined – his beautifully laundered white shirt, subdued blue-and-grey tie, and shiny moccasins, anyone might mistake him for a wealthy foreign businessman. He smiled, then bowed to Carmen.

Impulsively, Carmen raised her hand, seamed from housework, its short-cut nails unvarnished, up to his forehead and touched it. 'No scar! Wonderful! Dr Carter is the best!'

Andy was standing stiffly behind her. With his square head, its sandy hair cropped close to the skull, his square body on short sturdy legs, and his large, thick-fingered hands, he gave an immediate impression of strength and vitality. He might, in his combats and sneakers, have been mistaken for an army physical training instructor. It was therefore a surprise when he spoke, in a pernickety, high-pitched voice that might have been that of one of Laurence's former colleagues at the Foreign Office.

'Good evening, Marilyn. I've heard so much about you. You have a real fan in Carmen.' He turned. 'And this is Mehmet, I take it. Glad you could make it, Mehmet.' He shook Mehmet's hand, but had not shaken Marilyn's. 'Sit yourselves down. Have a drink. The others are certain to be late.'

'This is wonderful news we're celebrating,' Marilyn said, when he had handed each of them a glass of wine.

'Yes. The most I'd ever hoped for was a thousand, not a hundred thousand. That's the luck of the draw, I suppose.'

'Well, merit must have had a lot to do with it. What's the title?'

'*The Knacker's Yard*. It's, well, autobiographical, I suppose. My father was – is – a butcher. Well, in the meat trade. In the vacations I used to work for him. In the book, there's this character – a character not all that different from me. He has this long, up-and-down affair. And then – then he kills'- he gave a little smile – 'butchers – his girlfriend. Which is appropriate, I suppose, seeing that he's a butcher.'

Marilyn laughed. 'I hope the killing isn't also autobiographical.'

He stared at her, unsure whether she was joking or not. Then he laughed and shook his head vigorously: 'Oh, no, no, heavens no!'

At that moment the owner of the restaurant thrust aside an intervening curtain and appeared from the kitchen with a bowl of cashew nuts and another of olives. Having set down the bowls, he stooped and put one arm round Carmen's shoulders and another around Andy's, as though they were all three posing for a photograph. 'This is Brian,' Andy said. 'Brian Raikes.' So that, Marilyn realized, was why the restaurant was called The Rake's Progress. 'He runs – and owns – this place. My best – and oldest – friend. We went to school together.'

Brian raised a hand. 'Hi!'

'Business doesn't look so good tonight,' Andy said.

'Oh, give it a chance. You're too early. Didn't you know that? It's not fashionable to arrive so early these days. It's barely eight o'clock.'

Andy's agent, Sarah, a blonde, middle-aged woman with a large, sagging bosom and wide hips, in a skirt reaching almost to the ground, was the next to arrive, accompanied by a much younger, rangy, twitchy man, introduced by her as 'my partner, Val'. Val eventually revealed that he was a sound-recordist for the BBC.

'Isn't it absolutely super about Andy's book?' Sarah said to Mehmet when, introductions over, she had sat down next to him.

'It is wonderful.' He was withdrawn, yet polite. Marilyn again felt proud of him. What on earth did Audrey have against someone both so willing and so able to fit in with others?

'I wish I could earn that sort of money,' Val said in his husky, almost inaudible voice. 'Perhaps I ought to have become a novelist.'

'It is not something one *becomes*, sweetie. One does not *become* a novelist in the way that one becomes a doctor, or a civil servant, or – or a literary agent. Does one?' Sarah turned to Andy.

Val gave a nervous smile. 'Sorry' he muttered, at the same time as Andy said: 'One certainly does not. The, er, profession chooses one – not vice versa.'

'Like marriages, writers are made in heaven. Or, at least, all my writers are,' Sarah added with a laugh. She turned to Mehmet. 'What do you do, Mehmet?' She had the professional's knack of remembering other people's names and using them.

Marilyn wondered whether he would reply that he was doing nothing because he was not allowed to do anything. But with a smile and no hesitation at all, he said: 'I am student.'

'And what are you studying?'

'English.'

'Well, I must say you're English is very good.'

'Thank you.'

By an extraordinary coincidence, the final guest turned out to be Gilbert Strawson, a cousin of Ed's mother. With him was his tiny, pretty, giggly Thai wife. Of Gilbert, Marilyn remembered that Laurence had once remarked: 'When I first met Gilbert the Filbert he was called the Golden Boy of English letters. But I fear that with the passing of the years it has become more and more apparent that the gold was merely brass.' At Marilyn's last encounter with him, he had been working as literary editor of one of the quality Sundays, she could not remember which. He also wrote finely crafted, highly knowledgeable reviews, the intention of which often struck her as being not so much to give a fair assessment of the book under consideration as to establish his own intellectual and moral superiority to the author. Marilyn had, from the first, taken against him; but she acknowledged that she had had no reason to do so, since he had never been anything other than amiable to her. In the past, she had always shared his own view that he was remarkably handsome, but now the combination of a beaky nose, old age and alopecia had made him look like a moulting rooster.

Soon, Brian, assisted by a girl who looked to be no more than fourteen or fifteen, and a waiter who, when persistently questioned by Sarah, finally admitted reluctantly that he came from Romania – might he, too, be an illegal, Marilyn wondered – had started to bring on an unremarkable first course of smoked mackerel with wedges of lime.

'Well, Marilyn, it's certainly a pleasure to see you after so long,' Gilbert turned to say to her, smoothing his napkin over his thighs. 'Wasn't the last time at poor old Edward's funeral?'

'Yes, that's right.' But Marilyn could remember virtually nothing of the occasion, other than that, throughout the ceremony out at Putney Vale Crematorium and later at an increasingly raucous gathering in the huge, L-shaped sitting-room of Laurence's house, she had felt an extraordinary chill even on that day of heatwave, so that from time to time she had had to control her teeth from chattering. Since she hated to talk about Ed – unlike some of her bereaved friends who would talk endlessly of dead husbands, wives, children, siblings, parents – she now abruptly swerved away from the subject to ask: 'How do you and Andy know each other?'

'Yes, it must seem rather strange. Different generations, different backgrounds. He won a Christmas short-story competition – no, I'm wrong, he didn't win it, he was runner-up – which, for my sins, I'd organized for the paper. There was a party when the stories were eventually collected in a book, and he – he came over and made himself known to me. The attractive little Carmen wasn't with him. After that, well, he seemed to want to keep up, and I eventually pushed some reviewing his way. He's rather a good reviewer. Surprisingly perhaps.'

'It's wonderful news about his book.'

'Yes, isn't it? I had the same sort of luck when I was just down from Cambridge. Not, I mean, an advance of anything like that size. But my, er, apprentice novel was generally, well, yes, acclaimed. But fame is so capricious. After that, I'm afraid it was downhill all the way.' He stretched across the table to grab another slice of bread. Despite his elegant slimness, he had always been greedy, Marilyn remembered.

For a while he munched at the bread in silence. Then, suddenly, he dropped what was left of it on to the table and put his hands over his face.

First surprised and then concerned, Marilyn stared at him. 'Are you all right?' she eventually asked.

'As all right as I'm ever likely to be.' He lowered his hands, turned his head, and smiled at her. 'I was – overcome.'

'Overcome?'

'Weary. I'm so weary of this ghastly world.' He sighed. 'And so weary of my ghastly self.'

Marilyn, not knowing what to say, gazed down the table. At its far end, Mehmet was sitting between Sarah and Gilbert's Thai wife. Both women were laughing, as he told them something, inaudible to Marilyn. Then Sarah's voice could be heard: 'Oh, you are wicked!' Whatever wicked thing he had said, it had clearly delighted her.

'Who is that?' Gilbert asked in a hostile voice.

'Oh, that's Sarah. I can't remember her surname. Andy's agent.'

'Oh, of course I know Sarah. I've known her for years. One of the sharpest brains in the business. I wish she'd been my agent in those dear, dead days beyond recall. No, I mean the young man.'

'Oh, that's a friend of mine. Mehmet Ahmeti.'

'Of yours? H'm.' Gilbert looked over at Mehmet again, then looked down at his plate, and gave a little smirk. 'He seems to be a great success with the ladies.'

'You're not possessive of your wife, are you?'

'Oh, good lord, no! I'm always delighted when she hits it off with someone at a party. It means that I have no qualms about flirting with someone like you. She's my third, you know,' he abruptly volunteered.

'Oh, I thought the total was two.'

'Sometimes I wish it had been! It's such an expense to have had so many wives. I managed to squeeze some money out of the Royal Literary Fund to have these' – he tapped his front teeth – 'crowned, but I doubt if they would look favourably on a request for a grant to help towards alimony.'

When the child waitress had removed the plates of their main course, the Romanian brought in a vast chocolate cake, which he set down in the centre of the table. There was a bubble of sweat on the end of his long nose. Marilyn feared for a moment that it would fall on to the cake. 'Where are the candles?' Gilbert's wife squeaked, to be rebuked by him: 'Don't be silly, darling. This is not Andy's birthday. We're celebrating something far more important.'

She put a hand to her mouth, and giggled in embarrassment. 'Sorry, sorry! I forgot, I forgot!'

Gilbert looked at Marilyn, as though to say 'Look what a silly woman I've married,' and gave a groan.

Brian slipped through the curtain and approached the table with a tray. On it were eight champagne glasses. A moment later the Romanian appeared with two bottles of champagne.

'Compliments of one of the guests,' Brian said.

When Gilbert cried out 'The Widow, the Widow!', Marilyn assumed that he was the benefactor. But then, to her amazement, Brian put a hand on Mehmet's shoulder. 'Here is the

generous man!' He patted the shoulder. When had Mehmet
ordered the champagne? Marilyn wondered. Then she recollected that, during the meal, he had suddenly slipped away, to
go the lavatory she had supposed. Champagne was certainly
not cheap and this particular champagne less cheap than most.
How was he proposing to pay for it? She could only assume
out of some of the five twenty-pound notes that she had left on
the dressing table in 'Laurence's room'. For a moment she
seethed with indignation. He did not even know Andy; and, in
any case, if anyone treated them to champagne, it should be
Andy himself, with that advance of his, or Sarah, who had so
skilfully negotiated it and who had no doubt already taken her
generous cut. Typical of Mehmet to want to make that sort of
splash. Now Carmen would certainly talk about it at the surgery and in no time at all everyone would be believing that Dr
Carter was having an affair with a rich foreigner, perhaps even
a member of the Albanian mafia. But then she thought: How
touching. No Englishman would show that sort of impetuous
generosity. She smiled across at him and, smiling back affec-
tionately, he raised his glass. Then he had to raise his glass
again, as Gilbert called out 'Let's drink to the success of our
golden boy!' Since Andy was clearly over forty, to call him a
boy struck Marilyn as odd. It was even odder that Gilbert
should use the same phrase that, years before, had been used
of himself.

Andy was calling out: 'Brian! Brian! Come and join us for a
glass of bubbly.'

'Well, since the place is so empty . . .' It was now past ten, so
it was clear that the emptiness had nothing to do with the hour,
as he had previously suggested.

'Come and sit beside Carmen!'

'Nothing would have delighted me more. But I've so often
sat beside Carmen and I'm going to have lots and lots of oppor-
tunities to do so in the future. So – I'm going to sit beside that
attractive bird over there.' He had picked up a glass, and now
pointed it, wine slopping out from it, at Marilyn.

'No offence taken! No offence!' Andy was swiftly becoming
drunk.

Brian pulled up a chair from another table and placed it so close to Marilyn's that she could feel his knee against hers. He had an attractive but far from handsome face, with thick black eyebrows and long black eyelashes, a bunched, red mouth, that gave the impression of constantly pouting, and high, gleaming cheekbones. He leaned across the table so that now his arm was also in contact with her shoulder. She could smell kitchen-fat and sweat.

'Andy told me you're a quack.'

'Oh, I hope not. I'm a doctor. Or I like to think that I am.'

'And you're frightfully literary?'

'No, not at all. But I'm one of those people essential to the existence of every writer. I'm a reader.'

'I'm afraid I seldom read. And certainly not novels. It's all I can do to read a recipe in Delia Smith or Elizabeth David. I shan't be reading Andy's novel, even if it becomes a best-seller.'

'Have you told him that?'

'I don't have to tell him. He knows. I did history at Warwick. But that was no good to me. I didn't want to teach, and what else can you do with a third in history? So I went into the catering trade. But tell me – tell me about being a doctor.'

Soon he was asking her about his headaches. His doctor – who was really far too old to be any bloody good – had told him that they were migraines, but didn't one have visual disturbances, that sort of thing, with migraines? He did wonder if the headaches might not be associated with the amount of chocolate that he ate. He was really a chocoholic, always had been. But in that case the headaches must be migraines, mustn't they, since everyone knew that the most common trigger . . .

On social occasions Marilyn had endured innumerable conversations like this. Jack had once told her that, as soon as anyone started such a conversation with him, he would say firmly 'Why don't you come and see me at my surgery? Then we can really get to the bottom of things. But I must warn you that, since you're not on my list, I'll have to charge you.' Whether he did in fact say this, she doubted. He had an innate courtesy, which concealed his essential coldness from those who did not know him.

As Brian droned on and on, Marilyn nodded, smiled, and from to time interjected something. Then, all at once, she became aware that Mehmet was glaring at her from the other end of the table, his chair pushed far back, as though he wished to disassociate himself from the rest of the company. His face was rigid and starkly glistening in its whiteness.

Suddenly he jumped up, pushing the chair back even farther, with such violence that it would have toppled over if Sarah had not quickly put out a hand to catch it. 'Marilyn!' he called down the table. 'I think we go. Late.'

'In a moment.'

'No, now. *Now!*'

Fearing a scene, she got to her feet and reached under the table for her bag. She turned to Brian. 'I'm sorry we can't continue this conversation. But Mehmet has a train to catch.'

She knew that neither Brian nor any of the others believed this. She felt humiliated and furious.

Calmly, with extreme formality, Mehmet said goodnight to everyone in turn, shaking hands, bowing. Then he turned away abruptly and strode towards the door. Marilyn hurried after him.

'Hey!' They were by the door now, and Brian was behind them. He held out a plate, with a folded piece of paper on it. 'Don't forget this!' He grinned.

Before Mehmet could do anything, Marilyn snatched up the bill for the champagne. She glanced at it, then fumbled for some money in her purse.

'I will do,' Mehmet said angrily.

She paid no attention.

'Thanks. I'll bring you your change in a jiffy.' Brian went off. Marilyn sat down at a table by the door but Mehmet did not join her. He gave the door a violent push and marched out into the street, where he at once lit a cigarette.

Eventually, having received her change from the Romanian waiter, Marilyn joined him there. Without a word to each other, they both made futile attempts to flag down a taxi. Few passed, and all were full.

'This is a bad area for taxis,' Marilyn said. 'Too poor.'

'Fuck, fuck, fuck!' Mehmet shouted, startling an elderly, male passerby under a vast, sideways tipped golfing umbrella. He flung his half-consumed cigarette into the gutter.

Finally they caught a taxi. Mehmet opened the door for her and then, as she was entering, gave her a rough push, so that she all but toppled on to the floor. He jumped in after her, pulled back the glass, and gave the driver the address.

'What the hell are you doing?'

'What the hell you doing?' he countered. 'I order champagne, you pay. You think, because I am Albanian, I cannot pay. You racist, very racist.'

'Oh, don't be so idiotic! I paid because I didn't want you to use the money I gave you for your expenses for the week. In any case, you didn't have to order that champagne. You weren't celebrating anything, you were meeting Andy for the first time.'

'You do not understand.'

'No, I don't understand.' She leaned forward and pulled across the glass between the driver and themselves.

'Albanian way,' he said. 'You do not understand Albanian way.' Then he swung round to face her. A hand grasped her arm, so hard that she almost cried out. His mouth was distorted, one side pulled upwards, like a snarling dog's, and his eyes were half-closed. 'What you say to that man?'

'What man?'

'Owner of restaurant.'

'He was telling me all about his headaches.'

'*Headaches!*'

'Yes, headaches. He suffers from headaches. So he thought he'd have a free consultation with me.'

He gripped her arm again. 'No, no. I understand well, very well. He try make love to you.'

'Are you crazy? Let go of my arm. *Let go!*' Reluctantly he released her. He raised a hand to his mouth and bit on a knuckle. 'I watch you. Watch you all time. You think I no watch, but Mehmet watch, watch.'

'This is too silly.' Suddenly her voice was calm. She turned her head aside and looked out of the window. They were now in Kensington High Street. Thank God, they would soon be home.

Again he bit the knuckle. Then he demanded: 'Why he call you bird?'

'It was a joke. No man calls a woman of my age a bird. He was joking.'

'But bird mean prostitute.'

'It certainly does not. If it did, every girl in London would be a prostitute.'

'You lie.'

'I am certainly not lying. Now stop this nonsense. Stop it at once.' She might have been speaking to her dead daughter Carol in one of her difficult moods.

'No, no!' he protested as, first to leave the taxi, she opened her bag to pay the driver. Oh, well, she might as well leave him to it. She snapped her bag shut and ran up the steps, unlocked the door and slipped into the house, leaving the door wide open behind her. Without even taking off her overcoat, she hurried into the sitting-room, grabbed a glass, and poured herself out a stiff shot of vodka.

As she was raising the glass to her lips, he was suddenly behind her. He put out a hand, covered hers with it and then prised away the glass. 'No. Not good.' He set the glass down. She turned on him in fury. Then, all at once, he was laughing. 'Come on. Leave it. Later. Upstairs. *Upstairs!*'

The whole scene in the taxi might never have taken place.

Later, they lay, silent, sweaty and half-asleep, in each other's arms, without bothering about the bedclothes, which had tumbled to the floor. Marilyn stirred herself, raised her head on an elbow, and then with a forefinger gently traced the line first of one of his eyebrows and then the other. Next, she ran the forefinger down his nose to his upper lip.

'I think that was the best,' she said. It had certainly been the most violent. She knew that next day there would be bruises on her shoulders and arms.

He opened his eyes and smiled up at her. He nodded. Then he sat up in the bed and, leaning back against the headboard, folded his arms over his chest. 'Marilyn, I have idea.'

'Yes.'

'Listen to me. Idea, good idea, best idea. We marry.' It was a statement, not a question.

'*Marry!*' She was taken aback, even – she had to admit it – appalled. Was he being serious? She decided to assume that he was joking. 'Oh, no, one marriage was more than enough for me.' When she had said that, she at once felt a pang of guilt for being so disloyal to Ed. So far from marriage to him having been more than enough, it had been far, far too little. 'I don't want another marriage.'

'But I want to marry you. Very much.' Yes, he was being serious, totally serious.

She shook her head, then put a hand to his cock, her cheek up to his. 'No. Things are so wonderful as they are. Perfect. Let's leave them like that.'

She sensed an immediate change in his mood. He pulled away from her, to reach down for the bedclothes and jerk them angrily over his own naked body but not hers. 'Why you no wish to marry?'

'Well, what would be the point?'

'People are in love, they marry. Is that strange?'

'No. Not at all. But . . . well, we have our separate lives.' Then she thought: Yes, I have my separate life but what sort of life does he have? 'If we saw too much of each other . . .'

'When people in love with each other, they wish together all the time,' he countered.

'And often – sometimes – that's a mistake. One of the best things about my marriage was that my husband so often had to go away for his work. Absence makes the heart grow fonder – that's what we say. And it's true. I found that I loved him so much more when he came back after weeks or even months abroad.'

'You always thinking about husband.'

He was right, but how did he know it? Once again, she was surprised and disconcerted by his powers of intuition. 'No, not always. Often I'm thinking of you.'

He made a scoffing sound at the back of his nose. Then he said: 'It is because I am Albanian.'

'What is because you are an Albanian?'

'That you do not wish to marry. Yes, you are racist. All English are racist.'

'Oh, do stop that racist nonsense!'

He nodded. 'It is true. Also – you bored me.'

She knew what he wanted to say: He bored her. To some extent that was true, she had to admit it. With him, she suffered those trashy films, full of natural disasters and violence, that he so much loved. With him, she was unable to share whole areas of her life. He would never read Andy's book, and so they would never be able to discuss it together; and when, excitedly, she had once begun to talk to him about the production of Handel's *Semele* to which Laurence had taken her, he had clearly had no idea who Handel was. She often said that she liked people who were intelligent but unintellectual, and Mehmet was certainly both those things. But between them there was an incompatibility so radical that to imagine that they could marry and share their lives was nonsense.

She sighed.

He got off the bed and reached for a towel. Winding it around him, he said: 'Tell me about this husband.'

She shook her head. 'What's the point?'

'Tell me!' he repeatedly angrily. 'I think you love him more, much more than me.'

She realized that he was one of those people who can be jealous even of the dead. 'He's dead. Don't you understand? *Dead.*'

'How he die?'

'I don't want to talk about it.'

'How?'

She said nothing.

For a while he glared down at her. Then he said 'I take shower' and left the room. It was past two. She hoped that he would not wake Audrey and so provoke yet another complaint. She put one of the pillows on top of another, and smelled that odour – of hair-oil, some sort of aftershave lotion and healthy sweat – that she could always now identify, with a dizzying pleasure, as his. *How he die?* No, she could not bear to speak of it to anyone, not even to him. But she could not stop thinking of it. Still damply sticky from their lovemaking, she thought of it now.

They have quarrelled, as they rarely quarrel, over something trivial. They have just sat out and eaten lunch in the Piazza Repubblica and he has suggested that, for her pudding, she should have what appears on the menu as *zuppa inglese*. 'But I don't want a soup, and certainly not a Brown Windsor or something like that. Don't be so idiotic!' But he insists: 'I want you to try it,' and gives the order to the portly waiter, hurrying, red-faced, from table to table. Marilyn realizes now that a *zuppa inglese* cannot be a soup, but she does not let on, since she does not want to spoil the joke for Carol. The waiter brings what looks like a trifle smothered in too much cream, and Marilyn acts out amazement. Carol screams with laughter, putting her hands to her cheeks, so that an elderly French couple at the next table look over with disapproval. As she dips her spoon into the cream, Marilyn feels a tremendous, serene happiness. She and Ed have had so few holidays in recent years, and this one has been perfect. Laurence had wanted to come too, and after she had decided that she hadn't the heart to tell him that that was out of the question, Ed, with uncharacteristic brutality did so – 'We've been looking on it as a second honeymoon.' Did couples take their child with them on their honeymoons, Laurence, deeply wounded and furious not with Marilyn but with his son, wanted to ask. But he did not do so.

They collect up their belongings, but Ed, who is always forgetting things, forgets the guidebook and has to race back for it. Their hired car has acquired a ticket in their absence and Ed promptly tears it up, not realizing that eventually Marilyn, long back in England, will be pursued by the car-hire firm for the fine. He throws the pieces to the wind, before opening the door by the driving seat.

'No, darling. Let me drive. You drank most of that bottle and you had those Stregas afterwards.'

'I'm not drunk, you know.'

'No. But you might be breathalysed. Let me drive.'

'Oh, very well. Then I'll have a zizz beside Carol.' He is a good driver and he thinks Marilyn a bad one. When she offered to take over from him on the exhausting drive from Genoa to Florence, he refused: 'It tires me far more to sit watching you drive than to drive myself.' He leans over to Carol and puts an arm round her shoulder. Marilyn knows that the nine-year-old girl has reached an age when she hates to be touched, even by her mother. There is a look of apprehension and distaste on her face but she manages not to jerk away.

'We'd better make for the autostrada,' Ed says. He yawns. The wine and the Stregas have made him feel muzzy.

'Oh, no! I thought we'd agreed on those sideroads. I loathe autostradas, with their unending billboards. One hardly gets a glimpse of the countryside.'

'What hour do you think we'll get to Rome?'

'It's not *that* far.'

Marilyn gets her own way. But not before the argument has degenerated into a squabble. Ed tells her 'You always have to do what you want,' and she retaliates 'It's what we agreed. But you never stick to an agreement.' Suddenly, in the middle of it all, Carol screams 'Oh, do shut up, shut up!' Ed then tells Carol that he won't put up with that sort of thing. Now they are driving down a narrow, pot-holed road, with dry, beige, humped hills on either side, virtually no other traffic, and no sign of even a house or a village. Marilyn always imagined that the whole of this area would be one of white houses gleaming out of the vivid green of chestnuts and elms or the subdued grey of olives. There is something sinister about this landscape, as though she had inadvertently strayed from one time zone into another and had arrived, without at first realizing it, into a world that had suffered a nuclear holocaust. She looks over her shoulder and sees that both Carol and Ed are asleep. His arm is still around her shoulder; their faces look strangely shiny and pale. She begins to hum to herself, to keep her spirits up. The tune she hums is 'Volare'. One rarely hears it in England now, but she has already heard it three times in Italy – once in a roadside trattoria, once as a background to the din in a supermarket, and once just now from a loudspeaker outside a leather shop near the Piazza Repubblica.

The road has now ceased its serpentine wriggling, it unspools straight ahead of her. Far away, through a heat-haze, she can see an articulated lorry. Then, as it approaches, she can make out that the driver is wearing dark glasses and a bright-red cap. She hears the hooting, but who is hooting whom she is not sure. The hooting is extraordinarily loud, like the vastly magnified braying of a donkey. From around the lorry, she sees the low-slung Alfa Romeo jerking out into her path and then rushing towards her. She wrenches at the wheel. She turns it to the right, not to the left, because that is the only way that she herself is going to survive.

Marilyn had so often gone over it all both in her mind, as she had done now, or in conversation with Audrey and Vicky. Repeatedly the two women told her, as did others – the Italian nurses and the doctor, the Italian police officer, Laurence who had at once flown out to bury his son and granddaughter, but more importantly, to be beside the woman with whom he was already besotted – that she could not possibly blame herself, it had been an instinctive not a rational choice, it was what every-one would have done in the circumstances. But she did blame herself. Even now, as she awaited Mehmet's return from his shower, she blamed herself.

'What is this?' He was in a fury as, towel draped around him at the waist, he strode into the room. He thrust a sheet of paper out at her. When she took it, it was damp to the touch. It was a pale-blue sheet of the kind that Audrey used for writing the letters that took up so much of her leisure time. On it she had written:

TO THOSE WHOM IT MAY CONCERN
PLEASE LEAVE THIS PLACE AS YOU WOULD LIKE TO FIND IT
THAT MEANS *CLEAN*
DO NOT, REPEAT DO NOT, SQUAT ON THE LAVATORY SEAT
IN CIVILIZED COUNTRIES IT IS USUAL TO SIT THERE
THANK YOU

Beneath this, Audrey had signed her name: Audrey Carter.

It was ludicrous and yet also appalling. How could someone like Audrey, so sweet-natured, tolerant and (as so many people so often said) *good*, have brought herself to write something so disgusting?

Marilyn shook her head. 'I don't understand.' It was only a statement of the truth.

'Who is this woman?'

'What do you mean? You know who she is. My sister-in-law. The sister of my – my dead husband. What can I say? I don't know what's come over her. I'm sorry.'

'Is house hers?'

'Partly.'

'Why you share house with her?'

'Because it's always worked out well like that. And we're – we've always been good friends. After the death of my husband – and my daughter – she was extremely kind to me. She – saved me.'

'Saved you? What you mean?'

She could not bring herself to tell him about those terrible months after That. She remained silent.

'If she write again same thing – I kill her!'

'Oh, don't be silly. It's not all that important. Just don't use that bathroom. Use only mine.'

'But I want shower,' he retorted stubbornly.

'Yes, I know. It's a nuisance. But I want to avoid all this trouble. I'll buy you a shower attachment. Tomorrow. Promise.'

'I like proper shower. Not attachment. After sex, shower. Shower,' he repeated more loudly. He was like an obstinate child, she thought – like Carol at her most difficult.

'Yes, I'm sorry. But there it is. The pair of you don't seem able to agree like civilized people.'

'So Albanians not civilized! I say before, you racist, very racist.'

She put a hand to her forehead. 'Oh, please, Mehmet! It must be almost three o'clock. I have to work tomorrow. Early. Do let me get some sleep.'

'I no understand,' he muttered, as he left the room.

Despite Marilyn's prohibition, Mehmet would from time to time use the basement bathroom. A week, two weeks would pass and he would never go near it; and then, suddenly, after he had left her bedroom ostensibly to go to the upstairs bathroom, she would hear him descend the stairs. Clearly his twin objectives were to annoy Audrey and to defy Marilyn.

On one such occasion she asked him: 'Have you forgotten what I told you?' and he then pretended not to understand, frowning in feigned bewilderment and asking 'What you mean?' When she told him what she meant, he again feigned bewilderment: 'You make mistake, Marilyn. I use bathroom upstairs, your bathroom.'

On another such occasion, she even jumped out of bed, on hearing him descend, and called out after him: 'No, no! Mehmet! Use my bathroom. *Mine!*' He turned nonchalantly at the landing. 'I go get *Evening Standard*. I want see football.' He was lying, of course, but she had no heart to pursue the matter.

Mehmet had left late on the Sunday, saying that early the next morning he had to be at King's Cross for an interview for a job in a pub. Marilyn and Audrey had breakfast together.

From both the stiff way that Audrey moved about the kitchen, fetching more toast from the toaster and more coffee from the percolator, and from her refusal to enter into any conversation other than with a clipped 'Yes', 'No' or 'Oh, really?', Marilyn knew, from the experiences of the months since Mehmet had entered their lives, that a storm was imminent.

Finally, having refilled their cups with coffee for the third time, Audrey said: 'You know, Marilyn, I wish that you could somehow control that rent boy of yours.'

Marilyn was at first stunned by the crudity of it. As she later said to Vicky, when telling her of the incident, Audrey was the last person whom one would expect to talk like that. Then Marilyn felt anger surge up within her, with such violence that she gulped for air. Later, she thought: Now I know what it really means when one says that someone has taken one's breath away. '*What* did you say?'

Coolly, looking into Marilyn's glaring eyes, Audrey repeated it.

'Oh. I see. Well, what precisely is it that my *rent boy* - as you so elegantly put it – has done to need my control?'

'This morning he left an extremely offensive message on my bathroom mirror.' She rose. 'Come and see it!' She beckoned. 'Come! *Come!*'

Marilyn sighed, put down her napkin, and also rose. She followed Audrey down the narrow basement corridor to the bathroom.

'Look!'

Marilyn looked. On the mirror, Mehmet had used what had presumably been one of her own lipsticks – Audrey never used any make-up other than powder – to scrawl, in what might have been mistaken for the handwriting of a young child: WHY NO FUCK ORF! FUCK ORF! BITCH!

How could two adults behave like this? Marilyn put hands to her temples. She groaned audibly. 'Oh, I don't know. I just don't know.'

'If you must have that rent boy in the house, then surely –'

'Do *not* use that term! I will not have that term! Mehmet is *not* a rent boy.'

'You'd have fooled me,' Audrey replied with cool malevolence.

'He doesn't work because the Home Office in its wisdom doesn't allow him to work. So, inevitably, I have to help him. That doesn't make him into a rent boy. A rent boy, in case you didn't know, is a prostitute. Many men support their partners, some women support theirs. That doesn't mean that the partners are prostitutes.'

'Oh, I see,' Audrey said with heavy sarcasm. 'Please forgive me. Thank you for enlightening me.'

'I'll have another word with him.'

'No amount of words will make any difference. Not with that one.'

'Now, if you'll stop wasting any more of my time, I must get off to work.'

Marilyn strode to the stairs and then, as though she were escaping from a fire or flood in the basement, raced up them.

Chapter XV

It had been a boring dinner, the six of them, all men, seated round an oval table in one corner of the sparsely occupied, cavernous dining-room. There had been some animation as they had argued about the terms of the Taiwan contract but, once they had reached agreement about that, everything became increasingly listless. At one point Neil and Noel were aroused as they spoke about the girls in a Singapore brothel to which they had gone together before the clean-up, but, perhaps because they became embarrassed at Adrian's presence, knowing him to be gay, they soon dropped the subject. Even the food, usually so good in this club that Adrian had often thought of moving to, was poor that night: elaborate in its presentation on vast Rosenheim plates, which in turn rested on shield-like metal platters, but the soup lukewarm, the steak tough, the salsify overcooked, the *bombe surprise* leaking its *surprise* from having clearly been left for too long out of the refrigerator in the heat of the summer evening. Not unpredictably, pleading early starts the following morning, they broke up prematurely.

'Have you got your car with you?' Noel asked in the courtyard, his car keys at the ready.

Adrian shook his head. 'Being serviced.'

'What's wrong with that BMW of yours? It's always being serviced. Anyway, let me give you a lift.'

'But I'm not on your route.'

'Never mind. I can go out of my way. Laura won't be home yet. She was going to the National Theatre with a girlfriend and having dinner afterwards.'

Adrian considered. Why doom himself to another half-hour of being bored by this puffy, red-faced man in the too tight suit, the jacket of which constantly scuffed up over the shoulder blades when he raised his arms? With his sort of income, surely he could afford a decent tailor? Adrian noticed clothes, and spent a lot of money on his own. 'That's awfully kind of you, Noel.' Although none of them cared much for any of the others, they were constantly using each other's first names in order to create an impression of matiness. 'But it's such a lovely evening, I think I'll walk.'

'OK, Adrian. As you like. I wouldn't want to walk on an evening as hot as this. But it's up to you.' Noel sounded vaguely huffy and that worried Adrian. He had to keep on the right side of him, at least for the present, since he was the second most important person in the deal.

'It was good to see you, Noel. And thanks again for the dinner. It was terrific. When we next meet, it must be with me at the East India.'

'I look forward to that, Adrian.'

'That was a useful evening's work, Jack.'

'Take care, Adrian.'

'We must meet soon, Peter.'

'Terrific, Adrian.'

'I'll fax you all those details first thing tomorrow, Pat.'

'Do that, Adrian.'

'All the best to Maureen and the kids, Neil.'

'Sure you don't want that lift, Adrian? I'd be only too happy to oblige.'

The hearty, male voices – the tone and timbre of which he could never quite emulate – at last fell silent and he had got away, to strut down Oxford Street towards his flat, overlooking Hyde Park, just beyond Marble Arch. Christ, this evening was a scorcher. He had been an idiot not to accept Noel's offer. His feet were swollen, so that his slender, supple brogues felt as though they had been custom-made for someone with a shoe-size even smaller than his. The high collar of his blue-and-white shirt felt like a damp bandage round his neck, and he was conscious – that was the worst of wearing a raw silk suit, tailored in Hong Kong, as light as this one – of a dampness spreading under his arms, no doubt soon to be embarrassingly visible.

At Selfridges he paused to look in at a window. He needed a new, larger, more versatile microwave for the Sussex cottage. That one looked reasonably priced. Having examined the microwave and another, cheaper one next to it, he then ruefully inspected his reflection in the glass of the window. He must really try to eat less; at forty-two it was disgusting to look so pear-shaped. He put a hand up to his hair. He had thought that having a No. 2 cut would make the rapidly increasing baldness less obvious, but it had only made it more so. He had better let it grow again.

Silently, someone had slid up and halted beside him, ostensibly also to look at the microwaves. They examined each other's reflections. No, no good at all. Certainly young, certainly presentable; but Adrian had no use for that sort of swish, lanky type. With his dark hair, worn almost to the shoulders, and his dark complexion, pocked here and there with acne, he looked as though he came from the Mediterranean. Rent? Probably. Had he been the right type, Adrian would not have cared if he were rent or not. But, as he would often say, it was no use buying a pig for a poke.

The young man drew out a cigarette packet. 'You couldn't possibly oblige me with a light, could you?' The words came out with a slight lisp, in a vaguely foreign accent.

'Sorry.' Adrian was abrupt. If the type wasn't right, he could never be bothered to be amiable. It was the same when, on his Far East trips, some importunate street vendor approached him. An abrupt, even contemptuous Sorry, then a turning on his heel.

As Adrian moved off, he drew a handkerchief out of his trouser pocket and mopped at his face. He wished that he did not sweat so much. Disgusting! It was hardly a come-on. It was because of the constant sweating in this weather that he had splashed himself with so much Caron Pour Un Homme before setting forth to the club. Later, he had realised that that had been a mistake. The potent smell must have confirmed the others in the conclusion that they had already reached about his sexuality.

For a short while the boy trailed after him; then, like a stray dog, following now one person and then another, he was diverted by an elderly man in shorts and baseball cap worn back to front, an American tourist by the look of him, who was ambling along, a hand to the camera slung round his neck, no doubt in fear that someone would try to snatch it from him.

Adrian had reached Marble Arch. Should he go into the Quebec or not? Most people called it the Elephants' Graveyard, but for him and his friends it had become Jurassic Park, after young, beautiful and amusingly waspish Siegfried, now dying of AIDS, had first called it that. It was Siegfried who had also first called Adrian 'The Queen of the Night'. Adrian had not really liked the nickname, even though he had pretended that it amused him. He had always taken so much care not to look or behave like a queen. Apart from anything else, it was bad for business.

He dithered for a while, walking on as far the Underground station and then – oh, what the hell, on a night like this he would never be able to get to sleep anyway – returning, at a far quicker pace, back to the pub. But having entered it, he at once thought 'What am I doing here?' By now many of the customers were familiar to him and he would toy with the fantasy that, at closing time, they merely dossed down, to resume their drinking and chatter as soon as the bar had once more opened the following day.

He had long since become used to the various types jumbled together here: elderly regulars who, for the most part shabby and forlorn, looked like the sort of people whose sole occupation was to collect supermarket trolleys or to sit on park benches and read the *Sun*; rent boys, in tattered jeans and sneakers, with tattooed arms, muscular shoulders and savagely bitten nails; slim, sleek Indians; Cockneys with drooping jowls and beer bellies; loquacious students from the provinces, eyelids fluttering and mouths pulled into extravagant moues; a few men as well-dressed, prosperous-looking, self-contained

and self-conscious as himself; a number of edgy, ingratiating
tourists, peering around and flitting hither and thither.

'Hello, Adrian. Long time, no see.'

'Hello, Mac.' Adrian raised a hand in perfunctory greeting
and smiled. That was all. There had been a time when, in their
early twenties and occupying desks next to each other in a City
office, he and Mac had become the closest of friends on discovering that a love of Wagner was not the only thing that they had
in common. But now they had parted ways: Mac sinking inexorably downward, until he had ended up in his present job as
assistant in a small travel business south of the river, and
Adrian soaring upwards, to the pinnacle of being boss of his
own thriving software firm.

As he strutted on, Adrian heard Mac say to his companion,
an elderly man with a ferruled stick over one arm and a bristling
yellow-grey moustache, known to everyone as the 'Colonel'
although in fact he was a florist: 'That one's got too big for her
bootees.'

Adrian bought himself a brandy, thrusting his way with an
irritable 'Excuse me, excuse me, please,' through the crowd of
people who impeded sales by taking up positions at the bar.
Then, restlessly, smeared glass in hand, he zigzagged back and
forth on a tour of inspection. A plump, wide-mouthed French
regular, who obstinately pestered him and whom he always
avoided or, if unsuccessful at doing that, rapidly brushed off,
gave him a nervous smile. But he pretended not to see him. A
rent boy with improbably blond hair raised his glass of beer:
'Cheers, Adrian. How's tricks?' Adrian suspected the creature
of having stolen some cufflinks that had mysteriously gone
missing. But it could have been one of the others, selected from
ads in *Gay Times*, who had come to the house at about the same
time. 'Hot,' Adrian said. 'I never like the heat.'

As he roamed, he felt a mounting sexual hunger. Beautiful
Siegfried – 'the Siegfried Idyll' Adrian would call him – had
returned to his family in Dusseldorf, his once remarkable
physique blasted and eroded by that ghastly disease. Self-protective as always, Adrian had lost all wish or will to visit him
there. Better to forget him – until, from time to time, consumed

by guilt, he sent a cheque, a letter or a postcard. But however often he trekked back to some stinking, polluted feeding-place like this one and however ravenously he gorged on the flesh so readily available, that unappeasable hunger for a living ghost continued to gnaw at him. What the hell was he doing here? All at once Adrian succumbed to an overwhelming self-hatred, despair and ennui. But he knew that, if he returned to his immaculate flat, a lateral conversion of the first floors of two spacious houses, so different from the Clapham semi in which he had grown up, that hunger would only sink its teeth yet deeper into his entrails.

Then, suddenly, Adrian saw him. 'I knew at once, a *coup de foudre*,' he would later say. It had been exactly the same with dear, dying Siegfried. Who said that lightning never struck twice? A zigzag of fire and one was blasted and scorched up. The man was leaning, with what looked like a gin and tonic in his hand, against the wall just beside the lavatory. Many of the rent boys stood there, so that they could swiftly follow any potential client through the door, if necessary to lay out their wares. Was he a rent boy? Adrian could not be sure. Rent boys did not usually have that still, self-assured, slightly contemptuous manner. A rent boy would have returned his glance, smiled, even perhaps have moved over to him.

Heart hammering, Adrian went and stood against the wall beside the man.

'Hot,' he said. He put a hand under his collar and wriggled the fingers, then pulled a face and grinned.

The man nodded and smiled.

'Do you often come here?'

The man shrugged. 'Sometimes.' From both his appearance and accent, Adrian guessed him to be a Pole or a Russian. Not his usual type, with those broad shoulders tapering to a narrow waist and those large, strong hands, not at all. But he felt this overwhelming excitement, he did not know why.

They began to talk; but as they did so, the man kept looking away from him, sideways or upwards, as though he was not interested and was merely being polite. Adrian asked him questions about himself but the answers gave little away. Albanian, a student, living in North London. That was about it. Adrian began to wonder if he was straight. Perhaps he had merely strayed into the pub, not knowing the kind that it was, and then had stayed on, either vaguely titillated or too lazy to move over to another.

Eventually Adrian looked at his watch. The lights had dimmed twice. 'Closing time. I could have done with another drink – and so no doubt could you. But it looks as if they've shut up shop.'

The man finished his beer and slowly walked over to a table to set down his glass. Was he now going to move off, out of the pub and out of his life, Adrian wondered with dread. He hurried after him. 'I say . . .' He had heard people – builders whom he had tried to chat up, youths whom he had stopped in a genuine desire to be directed somewhere – imitate that accent of his. It was not the accent he had once possessed; but people like that group in the club earlier that evening assumed that it was, so perfectly had he honed it.

The man turned. He did not seem surprised. 'Yes?'

'Why don't you come back to my place for a drink? Only five minutes walk from here.'

The man considered, pulling down the corners of his mouth, his forehead furrowed. He might have been about to make some momentous decision. 'OK.' Offhand. As though he were doing this stranger a favour.

Out in the street, Adrian said 'I don't know your name.'

The man said nothing.

'I'm Adrian. Adrian,' he repeated. 'What should I call you?'

'Call me – Mehmet.'

It was odd that totally unsuccessful sex could also, paradoxically, be highly successful. At least for him. He was like a climber obsessed with making an ascent that he knew, in his heart, he would never achieve. Back and back the climber went, doggedly renewing the effort. But the night began to fall, the peak moved farther and farther away from him as he strained to get nearer to it. It would be *boring* - yes, actually boring, he from time to time secretly and ashamedly acknowledged to himself – if all that striving eventually came to its end and there he was, on top of the mountain, looking down instead of looking up.

Siegfried was the only person who, amazingly, had ever loved him – though innumerable people had had sex with him, a few out of kindness or pity or because, at the end of a party, they were drunk, but most because they expected some return either at once in cash or later in a favour. He was exasperated and even sometimes tormented by Siegfried's passion for him. Early in the morning, he would be awakened by a whoop, and that naked, sunburned body would leap on to him. 'Oh, Siggy! I want to go on sleeping. Please. *Please!*', he would plead with Siegfried, usually in vain, to get out of his bed, just as so often after Siegfried's departure he would plead, usually also in vain, with men far less attractive and charming to get into it.

There was no protest when, heart thudding, Adrian at last summoned up the courage to move, at a crouch, from his arm-chair to the sofa on which Mehmet was sitting, legs wide apart (was he doing that deliberately?) to reveal his ample crotch. Nor was there any protest when, with the caution of someone trying to pick up a feral cat, Adrian slipped an arm round his shoulders. Tentatively Adrian squeezed a bicep. 'You're very beautiful, you know.'

Mehmet's only response was to raise his glass of gin and tonic and sip reflectively from it.

Emboldened, Adrian shifted uncomfortably and then tried to insert a hand through Mehmet's open-necked shirt. Unfazed, Mehmet took hold of the wrist and gently but firmly removed the hand. But Adrian could see, with joy, that he was getting an erection.

'It's a long, long time since I saw anyone as beautiful as you in that dreadful pub. You were the only beautiful person there. As soon as I saw you, I knew.' He had said the same trite things to so many other men. But this time he meant them.

Mehmet remained impassive.

'Shall we go into the bedroom?'

Silently, still with the erection bulging in his tight jeans, Mehmet got up, put down his glass and took out a cigarette.

'You don't want that now, do you?' Adrian was fussy about passive smoking and had not cared for it when, earlier, Mehmet had lit up.

Mehmet put the unlit cigarette down on the table.

Nervously Adrian chattered away, as they began to take off their clothes – he had just been on a business trip to Japan, he had bought that kimono, that one over there for himself, also a wonderful little gadget, very simple, he would show it to Mehmet later, it crushed garlic without leaving all that gunge choked in it afterwards – but Mehmet might have been deaf, so little reaction did he show as he slowly took off one garment after another and then carefully arranged them over a chair. Everything was spotless, there was no sign of sweat. That embarrassed Adrian, who, because of nervousness, had been sweating even more since their arrival in the flat than in the club and the pub.

Adrian decided that it was the most thrilling body he had ever seen – even more thrilling than Siegfried's before it became etiolated from that ghastly disease. Mehmet lay out on his back on the king-size monogrammed linen sheet, his arms behind his head and his eyes turned up to the ceiling. His face was absolutely still; but for the open eyes, he might have been asleep. The cock was erect.

'He suffered me to do what I wanted – or something of what I wanted,' Adrian later told Igor, the former Russian ballet-dancer who looked after his country cottage for him and who once, briefly and unsuccessfully, had been his lover. But *suffer* wasn't the right word. He didn't suffer him. He was merely indifferent. When Adrian kissed him on the cheek, the fore-head and the chest, he responded with nothing more than a tiny sigh. When, full of trepidation, Adrian attempted to kiss him on the mouth, Mehmet abruptly turned his head aside. 'No.' The monosyllable conveyed no indignation, anger or dis-gust. It merely conveyed: That's it, no more.

But how extraordinary the conclusion had been! 'Do you remember,' Adrian later said to Igor, 'that there was once a best-seller with the title *The Rains Came?*' Of course Igor did not remember. 'Well, that's how it was. A storm, a deluge, a tempest.'

He had to see this man again. But how was he to ensure that? He did not even know if he were a rent boy or not. If he were, then he would only return if he now received a generous payment. But if he were not, he might well be insulted if money were offered, and therefore vanish forever. Often in the past, Adrian had said to a pickup 'Is this a cash transaction? It's better if there's no misunderstanding' – only, since he was so physically unappealing, to be told that it was. But somehow he could not bring himself to say that to Mehmet.

Eventually, while Mehmet was having a shower – what an age he was taking! – Adrian got out the pearl cufflinks, in a small black box, that he had been given by the boss of the Japanese firm with which he had just done business in Kobe. They were real pearls, not artificial ones, the man's pretty, simpering secretary had told him, no doubt on her boss's instruction, when the Japanese had glided out of the room to take a telephone call in private.

Mehmet returned from the shower, his wiry, closely cropped hair and his eyebrows glistening with water. A towel was wrapped round his waist. Adrian went to him and tried to take him in his arms, but Mehmet gently pushed him to one side, as a policeman might push aside an onlooker in order to make way for the passage of some VIP, crossed to the chair and reached for his vest.

Adrian picked up the little black box, went over to Mehmet, and clicked it open. 'For you. A thank-you present.'

Mehmet stared down at the cufflinks, with the same indifference that he had shown during their lovemaking. Then he put out a hand, palm upwards, and Adrian laid the box on it.

'They're real. From Japan. I brought them back from a recent trip.' It was a silly present, he thought. Probably Mehmet never wore the sort of shirt that needed cufflinks. But, of course, he could always flog them if he wanted. They must be valuable, if the girl had been truthful about their being real.

Mehmet put the box into his pocket. 'Thank you.'

The perfunctoriness of it filled Adrian not with annoyance but with excitement. 'I've enjoyed our time together, oh, so much, so much!' As Adrian gazed at Mehmet in adoration, the handsome, sulky face was little more than a blur to him. That was because he had deliberately not put his varifocal glasses back on again. He hated men in glasses and he hated himself in them.

'I go.'

'You're welcome to stay the night. It's so late.'

'No, I go.'

'Then I'll give you the money for a taxi. Please. I insist!' he added, even though Mehmet had made no demur. From his wallet Adrian produced a twenty-pound note. 'I hope that will cover it.' Ridiculous, he thought, of course it will.

'Thank you.'

'Would you like me to ring for a cab?'

Mehmet shook his head. 'No. Thank you. Many cabs in the street.'

At the front door, with its steel shutter and innumerable bolts and locks – he had once been burgled by someone to whom he had recklessly given duplicate keys – Adrian said: 'How do I get in touch with you?'

'Give me telephone number, please. I will ring.'

Adrian went into the sitting-room and got one of his cards from his desk. 'That's me,' he said. 'But it's better to ring me here, before half-past eight in the morning or in the evening, not at the office. This is the number here.' He pointed. Last year there had been some embarrassing calls to the office from someone to whom he had given the brush-off. 'Be sure it's this one you ring. OK?'

Mehmet looked down at the card. Then he read out the name of the firm.

'I think that you are big man?'

'Not all that big. A big fish in a small pond, let us say. No Bill Gates.' Adrian gave a nervous laugh. 'What about your number? Might I have that?'

'Better I ring you.'

'You won't forget? Promise?'

Mehmet merely shook his head. Did that mean that he would not forget or that he would not promise?

'Thank you, Mehmet.' Adrian stood on tiptoe to kiss him goodbye on the cheek. But Mehmet again turned away his head.

For five days Adrian waited for a call. He would delay leaving the flat in the morning, sometimes for so long that he was obliged to take a taxi to his office instead of the Central Line; and in the evening, as soon as he had entered the flat, he would at once race over to the answering machine and switch it on. What an idiot he had been not to pay Mehmet! That was it, of course. He would not have wanted a present of pearl cufflinks and he would not have known where to go to sell them. Or perhaps he was not really gay and had merely acquiesced because he wished to have an experience new to him. That had been the case with a Japanese university student picked up in Ueno Park, who, after some clumsy sex, had told him with demure politeness: 'Thank you, sir. I enjoy. But I think I prefer lady.'

Then at long last, after he had leapt out of his morning bath to rush to the telephone, there was that deep, vibrant voice. 'Adrian?'

'Yes.' He felt as if he were suffocating with joy. 'Oh, I'm so glad you've rung.'

Mehmet might have been fixing an appointment with the dentist. How about that evening? he asked. Adrian had a dinner engagement, with two rich, elderly fag hags with whom he played canasta, but he said Oh, yes, that evening would be fine. Would Mehmet like to go to the East India Club with him? 'It might amuse you,' he said.

Mehmet said that that was OK, but he did not know if he could find his way to the club, since he did not know the West End all that well. Would Adrian please meet him outside the cinema at Piccadilly Circus? Which cinema? It took some time for them to get the cinema identified. Just as he was about to ring off, Adrian shouted down the line 'Oh, by the way, don't forget to wear a tie. They won't let you in without a tie.' The first time that he had invited Siegfried to the club had been terribly embarrassing. Siegfried had turned up dressed far more smartly than any else there; but it was a smartness of another time from theirs and he was wearing no tie. Having rightly said that he couldn't possibly wear the grease-spotted tie offered to him by the porter over an Armani sweater, he had angrily marched out, followed by an embarrassed Adrian, who had then taken him to a small and extremely expensive French restaurant around the corner.

It was a relief to find Mehmet impeccably dressed; and his behaviour was no less impeccable. Dinner over, Adrian wondered how soon he could decently suggest a return to the flat. He felt as if he were, quite literally, bursting for sex. If he did not do something quickly, the explosion would cover the walls around them with semen.

But when he at last made the suggestion, Mehmet shook his head. 'Sorry. Tonight I must get home not late.'

'Oh. Is someone expecting you?' Adrian could not resist asking the question. He was insatiably inquisitive about the lives of even the most casual of pickups.

Mehmet nodded.

'Your wife? Or a girlfriend?' It always added to the excitement for him if one or the other existed.

Mehmet merely shook his head. No wife, no girlfriend? He was being maddeningly non-committal.

'Oh, dear. This is disappointing. *Most* disappointing. I'd so much hoped . . .'

On the steps of the club Mehmet said: 'Sorry, Adrian. I forget money. Can you – can you lend me?'

'Of course!' But a cat's paw of annoyance briefly raked through him. He was generous when he wanted something or someone. But, as he often said, he didn't like to chuck money about and he hated to be taken for a ride. 'Will that be enough?' Again it was a twenty-pound note.

'Thank you.' Mehmet stuffed the note into the breast-pocket of his charcoal-grey jacket.

Adrian had expected that together they would walk down the steps and hail the taxi. But Mehmet was racing off, as though late for an appointment.

'Ring me!' Adrian shouted after him. 'Ring me soon!'

Two weekends later, Adrian drove Mehmet down to what he called the cottage, though in fact it was a former Georgian rectory with a lot of clumsy Victorian and Edwardian additions and improvements. Mehmet was delighted with the BMW, from time to time stroking the mahogany dashboard in front of him, as one might a dog or cat; and, as they progressed up the long, serpentine drive, the gravel crunching under the wheels, he at once remarked on the size of the 'cottage' and the grounds – 'Big, big, big.'

Igor could be tricky with guests like Mehmet, either snapping at them or ignoring them all together. 'Don't worry about him,' Adrian would say. 'He's really terribly sweet but he suffers from this insecurity.' The two of them had met when, a refugee from the Soviet Union, Igor was dancing with a small, often insolvent ballet company that spent most of its time on tour. Adrian, because he was in love with him, would often tell him that it was a disgrace that he was not snapped up by the Royal Ballet, the Festival Ballet or the Rambert. But Igor, being slight and narrow-shouldered, had difficulties with lifts, and in any case his sort of graceful, winsome dancing was already out of fashion for men. A fall on an uneven stage in Avignon during a British Council tour resulted in a broken ankle and the end of a career that, in any case, he had never seemed really either to want or to enjoy. Adrian had urged him to take up choreography or teaching, but Igor had preferred to retire to the 'cottage', where he lovingly tended Adrian's growing accumulation of largely *art nouveau* objects and less lovingly (he had a passion for hacking and hewing) the woodland garden. He and Adrian had long since ceased to be lovers, Igor having now opted for life of chastity; but they had been through so much together for so long that the bond between them was tough.

Fortunately, instead of instantly taking against Mehmet, as Adrian had been gloomily fearing, Igor fell for him at a first glance. As the car drew up at the front door, he happened to be coming round the house carrying a pail of grain for the chickens. He was wearing wellingtons, a worn green Barbour jacket, and soiled jeans, rubbed thin at the knees. A red and green scarf was twisted round his head, pirate-wise, and from it a long white-and-grey ponytail descended down his back. Two front teeth were missing. Adrian, who was irritated by their absence, had more than once offered to pay for a bridge. But Igor could no longer be bothered with appearances.

Igor put down the pail and stared at Mehmet as he got out of the car.

Adrian knew at once that everything was going to be all right. 'Mehmet, this is Igor. Igor – I told you about Mehmet. Mehmet is from Albania.'

Igor insisted on carrying Mehmet's smart and obviously new or nearly new holdall up to the guest-room next to the room occupied by Adrian. Mehmet went to the window and looked out on to the tennis court, mown the previous day by Igor, and the trees beyond it. Side by side, the other two watched him, bemused with admiration for the muscular line of his shoulders, the tilt of his neck and the swell of his buttocks. 'Beautiful!' Mehmet finally exhaled to the view beyond the open window. Apart from the comment about the size of the house, it was the first time that Adrian had known him to express any enthusiasm about anything. It was a wonderful moment.

Throughout the visit Igor was at his best, whereas, on other such visits, he had so often been at his worst. He was totally self-effacing, never attempting to come with them on their walks through the grounds or to the village, never joining them before the television set, hardly taking part in the conversations, saying that, Oh, no, he was too busy with weeding the raspberry cage to accompany them to Brighton. But when they needed something, he seemed miraculously to intuit it and was always on hand. Paradoxically, behaviour so angelic irritated Adrian and made him feel uneasy, whereas Igor's often diabolical behaviour to other of Adrian's 'treeks' (as the Russian would refer to them) had always been reassuring, perhaps because expected.

Adrian had feared that he might, over such a long period, find Mehmet boring and even difficult. But, to his surprise, this guest, unlike many others, was never anything other than amusing and amusable. He appeared to enjoy their visit to the Pavilion at Brighton. Although he was totally devoid of any knowledge of architecture or art, he had the intelligence to ask the right questions and to make the right comments. He had never played tennis before but, rushing about the court (high up above, and unseen by the two players, Igor was standing at an attic window and watching intently), he managed to get in an astonishing amount of returns and even soon learned how to produce an adequate serve.

On the Saturday night, the two of them watched television on the sofa side by side, with Mehmet passively suffering the arm that had been thrown round his shoulder and the hand that from time to time brushed against his cheek or felt his biceps. Later, Adrian padded into Mehmet's next-door bedroom in silk pyjamas and Japanese kimono. Because he had taken off his glasses, his small green eyes were screwed up, so that they looked even smaller. Mehmet was sitting up in bed, his chest bare, glancing with puzzled distaste at the illustrations in an ancient copy of *Boyz*, left on the bedside table by some previous guest.

Saying nothing, Adrian clambered into the bed and gave him a hug. There was no response other than a sigh and a turning over of a page. But when, greatly daring, Adrian lowered his hand, the erection was there. 'Oh, God!' Adrian groaned, with a combination of amazement and delight. There was the same refusal to accept a kiss on the mouth, the head jerked aside, and the same reluctance to accept a kiss anywhere else; there was the same impression that he was indifferently going through a routine. But on this occasion, having demanded a condom – Adrian tweaked one out of the drawer of the bedside table and then agitatedly fumbled to open it until Mehmet took it from him with an irritable frown – Mehmet fucked him with cool ferocity, an arm round his neck, so that, at the delirious climax, Adrian thought that this heaving, grunting animal would throttle him, and almost wished that he would.

After it was all over, Adrian wanted to stay there beside him. But Mehmet said firmly: 'Please, Adrian' and gave him a little push. 'Now I sleep. Too much walk, too much tennis, too much Brighton.' He laughed. 'Too much drink. Too much eat. Too much fuck.'

As Adrian was padding out of the room, he was astonished to hear Mehmet's feet thud behind him and then to feel his arms encircling him. 'Thank you, Adrian. You make me good time.' At that Adrian felt Mehmet's lips briefly on the nape of his neck. Amazing! He turned, preparatory to taking him in his arms. But Mehmet was already returning to the bed.

Adrian gazed down at him in unbounded gratitude. 'Thanks, Mehmet. That was – that was really terrific.' He was thanking him as much for that perfunctory kiss as for the violent fucking. 'Thanks.'

Mehmet waved a hand and reached down for the copy of *Boyz*, which had fallen to the floor.

'How did you sleep?'

'Beautiful. It is so quiet, quiet here. Only birds. I sleep, sleep, sleep. Not like London.'

'And Igor brought you some early morning tea?'

'Yes. Why you tell him do that? He not servant, your friend, no?'

The two of them were at the breakfast table. Having set out everything for them, Igor had disappeared, saying that he must get back to that weeding.

'Oh, he likes doing that. I didn't tell him. He – he likes to look after people. Truly. It's not a job for him. It's a pleasure.'

'He your boyfriend?'

'Oh, no! Once. *Once.* Ages ago. Now – we're friends.'

'Partners?'

'In a sense. Yes. We're close.'

'He good man, I think.'

Adrian had never once felt jealous of Igor. He did now. 'Yes, very good. He makes domestic life so easy for me. The only problem is that he hates London and stays in the flat only once in a blue moon. He – he has this love for the country.'

'Good.' Mehmet nodded.

After breakfast, Mehmet wandered off, without saying anything, into the garden. The *Sunday Telegraph* books and review section trailing from one hand, Adrian watched him through the open French windows of the sitting-room. Mehmet plonked himself down on to a plastic chair, fake rustic in design, by the tennis-court and began to smoke a cigarette. Each time that he exhaled smoke, he tipped up his head and, in the still, summer air, blew out smoke ring after smoke ring, each perfect in shape and each disintegrating with extraordinary slowness. For some reason, Adrian found the bare white throat against the dark-blue of his open-neck shirt amazingly erotic and he began to get a hard-on.

Chucking the cigarette, only half-smoked, into a clump of rhododendrons, Mehmet got up and moved off, whistling some jaunty little tune which Adrian could not recognize, round the house and so out of sight. Was he seeking out Igor? Again Adrian felt that momentary pang of jealousy. Then he told himself: Ridiculous! Who would want anything with him?

Eventually Mehmet returned to the tennis-court and, when he saw Adrian beckoning to him, walked up to the open french windows.

'You so lucky,' he said. 'My home Albania so small. Flat. Mother, brother, three sisters, four room. Top of house.'

'Yes, I am lucky.' Adrian suddenly experienced a sweet, yearning sorrow for this man who was so much worse off than he was and who was stranded all alone in a foreign country. 'Come, sit down.'

Mehmet hesitated. 'I wish smoke.'

'Well, smoke then! No problem. You can smoke here.'

Mehmet shook his head. 'No cigarette. Cigarette finished.'

Adrian jumped to his feet. 'I think I have some cigarettes somewhere. A guest left some on the dining-room table only last weekend. Igor found them too late, by then he'd gone. Let me have a look.' He returned a short while later, with a half-smoked box of multicoloured cigarettes. He opened it and held it out to Mehmet.

'What this?' Mehmet looked at the cigarettes in disgust, wrinkling his nose.

Adrian tipped the box up towards himself, to see what was written on it. He squinted down, head tilted to one side. 'They're called Cocktail Cigarettes. They're more expensive than other ones,' he added, thinking that that might reconcile Mehmet to them. 'Apart from their colour, they're no different from any others.'

Grudgingly, Mehmet took one and lit it. He drew on it deeply and then slowly shook his head. 'Different. Not good.' But he continued to smoke it.

On the Sunday morning Igor announced that he was off to the little Roman Catholic church. It was more than two miles away but he preferred to walk than to borrow Adrian's BMW – which he was always nervous of handling – or to get atop his ancient bicycle, bought off their cleaner when she had acquired a car, and therefore without a bar.

'Maybe I go too,' Mehmet said.

'Oh, no!' Adrian was affronted.' Why should you want to do that? You're not a Christian are you?'

Mehmet laughed. 'I am nothing. But – Christian church – maybe interesting.'

'No, no. Let's have another game of tennis. I want to improve that serve of yours.'

When Mehmet had been taking a shower after their last game, Adrian had gone into his room and, with beating heart, had raised the sweat-saturated cotton shirt that he had lent him, and had deliriously sniffed at it again and again.

Mehmet hesitated and then, to Adrian's vast relief, said 'OK.'

'See you,' Igor said forlornly, leaving the room.

Neither of them answered.

All that afternoon, having cleared up the lunch, Igor began to prepare for the evening dinner. As always on a Sunday, there would be guests. Adrian was surprised when Mehmet said to him: 'Maybe I help him? He has so much to do.' 'Oh, no, no!' he answered. 'He much prefers to be left to himself. I'd give him a hand myself if I felt that he really wanted one. But he doesn't – ever. What you have to understand about him is that he's a loner.'

Mehmet considered that. 'Maybe I am loner too.'

'I don't think so. You're far too sociable.' But Adrian thought that the claim was probably true. There was something secret and inviolable about Mehmet; he gave nothing essential away – not his heart, not his past, not even his address or telephone number.

There were five guests: two couples, each composed of a middle-aged man and a young one, and an elderly man by himself, an Egyptian art dealer on a visit to England on business, who had had an introduction to Adrian from a mutual American acquaintance. The Egyptian had arrived in a large hired Mercedes, driven by a man in uniform and peaked cap, because, so he confided to the company, he had lost his licence 'through being silly once too often' and so could not risk driving himself. Everyone was clearly taken with Mehmet, who, without being asked, constantly jumped up to help Adrian with the champagne or to hand round the canapés prepared by Igor. When Mehmet wanted to smoke yet another cigarette, Adrian noticed that he went out through the french windows to do so. Before, he had puffed away even when Adrian was seated no more than a yard or so away from him. Twice the art dealer, who was not a smoker, joined Mehmet in the late evening sunshine. Adrian listened for what they were saying to each other, but he could catch nothing, so noisily were the others chattering away and laughing around him.

Igor did not sit down to dinner with them, but was a constant presence, bringing in or taking away plates, filling up glasses, even picking up a fallen napkin. Neither he nor Adrian was aware that these guests – and other guests – would refer to him among themselves as 'the dumb waiter'. Sometimes someone, with a transitory feeling of guilt, would turn round as he held out a dish and ask him: 'How are the hens laying, Igor?' or 'What sort of apples are you likely to have this year?' and he would then answer politely but briefly in that heavy accent which, after almost twenty years with Adrian, he had still not managed to modify, let alone lose.

Over both dinner and the coffee and liqueurs that followed, there was a lot of gossip about mutual friends in the neighbourhood and a lot of argument about plays, operas and concerts. Adrian feared that all this would bore Mehmet, but he seemed perfectly contented, though playing so little part. From time to time one of them would explain to him 'Harold Pinter writes plays, some people think them works of genius, others a total con,' or 'Britten was gay, you know, homosexual, and that opera of his was the closest that he ever got to coming out in his work.' Mehmet would nod and smile; but Adrian could only guess how much of this he was taking in and how much of it interested him.

Night had by now fallen, and Mehmet yet again went out through the french windows for a cigarette. A little later, the art dealer, who was called Harry, despite his nationality, and who wore a slim gold Longines watch and a number of obtrusive rings, wandered out too. Mehmet had already walked out over the tennis lawn and seated himself on one of the plastic chairs on the farther side of it. His chin was resting on his hand, so that his cigarette glowed close to his cheek.

Adrian reached out for his glasses, abandoned on the table before him, and twisted one earpiece over an ear and then the other. He squinted out. Harry was now also crossing the lawn. He went over to a corner of the garden to fetch another chair for himself and then set it down close to Mehmet's. Mehmet held out the box of cocktail cigarettes. To Adrian's amazement, Harry took one, although he had earlier said that he never smoked.

At that point one of the young men, who worked in the menswear department of Harrods, said: 'Oh, Adrian, have you heard the latest story about Al Fayed? It was going all round the shop,' and Adrian was forced to pay attention to him instead of to the two out beyond the tennis-court.

When he did look again, he realized that both of them had disappeared. He hesitated. He must not make it too obvious, the others must not know. Then he said: 'Is that that stray tom again? He's far too interested in the hens. I'd better have a look,' and hurried out through the french windows. No such tom existed.

In no time at all, having rounded the house, he saw the two shapes beside the raspberry cage. They were so close that it was difficult to differentiate between them, and they were swaying first back and forth and then from side to side. No, they were not having sex or even preparing to have sex. As, feet silent on the long grass, Adrian drew closer, he realized that Harry was trying to put his arms round Mehmet and that Mehmet was pushing him away. Both of them were laughing, Mehmet clearly in no way upset by the advance and Harry in no way upset at having it rejected.

'Oh, so here you both are!'

On other occasions, when friends had similarly made passes at his lovers, Adrian had always been furious, though subsequently forgiving. 'Where friends of friends are concerned, I have the equivalent of an incest taboo – I'm just not interested,' he would loftily tell people, forgetting that more than once he had used his greater wealth to prise away the friend of a friend. But now, to his amazement, he felt no fury at all. That someone invited to his house merely because of an introduction from an acquaintance should have at once blatantly attempted to appropriate his lover, was like being handed a document that authenticated an only just acquired work of art as a masterpiece.

'Yes, we are here,' Harry replied, totally unfazed. He scratched one eyebrow with the long, lacquered nail of a forefinger. 'I was asking your charming friend when is the best time to visit Albania. I only wish that he could come as my guide.'

'I'm sure you'll have no difficulty in attaching one to yourself as soon as you get there. If I may say so, my dear, I can see that you have a remarkable knack for striking up immediate friendships. You must be one of those fortunate people to whom, for reasons no one can fathom, other people at once get stuck like flies to flypaper.'

There was no ill-feeling in the banter. Harry merely pulled a face and then gave a squeal of laughter, hand to mouth.

Later that evening everyone but Adrian and Mehmet danced frenetically. The young man who worked in Harrods had previously been smoking a joint with another of the young men. Now, suddenly leaping to his feet, he decided to do a striptease, to raucous cheers and jeers and cries of 'Come on, get it all off!' When he was totally naked, he sashayed over to Adrian, turned his back, bent over, and waggled his ample bottom at him.

Mehmet, next to Adrian, jerked his head aside in disgust.

Adrian said dryly: 'You're the first person I've ever seen dancing cheek to cheek with himself.'

Harry left first. At precisely ten-thirty the same Mercedes, with the elderly uniformed driver, appeared for him. It was such a long journey back to London, he explained to Adrian, who was helping him on with the pale-brown cashmere jacket that he had taken off because of the heat, and the next morning he had to see someone at Sotherby's 'bright and early – I must be both those things.' At the door, he suddenly turned. 'Oh, I've forgotten something!' Adrian assumed that he was referring to a hat or stick, but he went on: 'I must give your charming friend my card.'

'I doubt if he is likely to buy any *objet* from you,' Adrian said acidly. 'But I'll call him.'

To Adrian's chagrin, Mehmet took the proffered card with obvious pleasure. He then stared down at it, smiling.

'My showrooms and my house are in Cairo. I also have a small flat in Luxor for the winter. Please – come and stay whenever you wish.'

'Thank you.' Mehmet nodded, smiled.

'I promise you a good time. Come. Do come.'

The cheek of it! Adrian's lips were thinned as he once again opened the front door. He did not accompany his visitor out of the house but watched him, door still open, as though he feared that he might slip round to the back and purloin something.

Harry turned before clambering into the Mercedes. He raised a hand and waved: '*Au revoir!*' he called in a French accent as faultless as his English one. '*A bientôt!*'

Without any response, Adrian slammed the door shut. Then he turned to Mehmet, who was standing behind him: '*Well!* The sauce of it!'

Mehmet merely grinned.

When, almost two hours later, Adrian had shut the door on the last of the guests, he moved over to Mehmet with a beam and outstretched arms. Behind him, tray at the ready, Igor was already creeping into the sitting-room, to collect the used glasses.

'I was really proud of you!'

Mehmet was puzzled. 'Proud of me?'

'Yes, you were terrific.'

Then he heard a discreet clink of glasses and swung round. 'Oh, Igor! Look, sweet, why don't you leave that till tomorrow?'

Igor shook his head, his ponytail swinging. 'You know I never like to leave things.'

'I help you,' Mehmet volunteered, to Adrian's amazement.

'Oh, no, no.' Adrian, for so long desperate for his increasingly drunken guests to leave, was now ravenous for sex. 'Igor likes to be left on his own. Don't you, love?'

Igor said nothing, as he began to empty one ashtray into another.

Upstairs, Mehmet went straight to his room. Adrian followed him, put his arms around his waist, and gave a sharp squeeze.

Mehmet moved away. 'I sleep,' he said. 'Tired.'

'Oh, but couldn't we . . .? You don't have to *do* anything,' he rushed on. 'Just let me . . . Oh, please, sweetheart.'

Mehmet shook his head. 'Tired.'

'Oh, well . . .' Adrian drew a deep sigh. 'That's disappointing, really disappointing.' Mehmet having turned away, Adrian stared at his back intently, as though he might somehow be able to will him to change his mind. 'Oh, never mind. There's always another day – or another night. So – goodnight, sweetie.'

Mehmet pulled back sheet and blanket. 'Goodnight.'

Adrian went to his own room and threw himself, still dressed, on to his bed. Well, there was nothing else for it, he would have to wank off. God, what a dreary way to end an evening!

Igor opened the gate for the car and then stood by it like a soldier, erect, hands to the seams of his ancient, soiled flannels, eyes straight ahead, spine rigid. Suddenly Adrian felt a sadness for him, his career over, no prospects ahead of him, no chance or even wish of finding a lover; but he knew that Igor did not feel any sadness for himself. He had opted for this life of solitary caretaking, gardening and minding of animals. Once he had had a Welsh collie and had clearly loved her; but when that dog was run over by a carelessly driven school bus, he had shown no desire to get another.

The day was another scorcher and so, for the drive back to London, Adrian was wearing shorts. He took a hand off the wheel and repeatedly ran it over his own bare thigh. It gave him a buzz; it was almost as though the warm flesh were not his but

Mehmet's, now suddenly responsive to his touch instead of indifferent to it. He began to feel a growing excitation.

Mehmet had been sitting back with eyes closed. Adrian was not sure whether he was asleep or not. But then he sat up, opened his eyes, and said: 'Adrian, I wish ask something. Important. Very important.'

Here we go, thought Adrian, removing his hand from his thigh and gripping the wheel. Money!

'Yes?' he said cautiously. 'Ask away. Mummy's listening.'

'Adrian, I tell you something about myself. I am illegal here.'

'*Illegal!*' Adrian was alarmed. 'What d'you mean?'

Mehmet explained. He had come illegally into the country, he had no work permit and, because of the lack of a work permit, it was very difficult to get any work. 'But I want work, want very much.'

'Yes, I see.' But he did not really see. How was he expected to help?

'I need passport.'

'But what has happened to your own passport?'

In his halting English, Mehmet explained that he had arrived in England on a false passport. It had belonged to an Algerian with French nationality, about his own age and not unlike him in looks, whom he had met in a bar in Paris and who had then become a friend. He had had to give the Algerian money for the passport and he had had to promise to destroy the passport as soon as he had passed through immigration – 'otherwise maybe I make trouble, big trouble for him, if passport found.'

Where was all this tending? 'Yes, I see,' Adrian said again. 'But what exactly – what can I do?'

Mehmet went on to explain that he had a landlord who knew someone who was employed in the passport office. This man in the passport office – already, with a feeling of dread, Adrian knew what was coming – could provide Mehmet with a passport from some EU country. But, of course, he wanted money for that service. 'I have no money. But you – you are my friend.'

Adrian frowned and tapped one hand on the wheel, as though he were beating out some rhythm audible only to himself. Then he said: 'How much money does he want?'

'Two thousand.' Mehmet glanced sideways at Adrian. Then he said: 'Sorry, Adrian. But it is terrible for me – living illegal, no work, no National Health, nothing.'

'Two thousand!' Adrian whistled. 'That's a hell of a lot of money.' Only the previous month, he had spent more than that amount on having a conservatory built, but that was different, that was really an investment for the time when he decided to sell the house, as he had sold other houses, always at a profit. But then the thought came to him, arresting and beguiling: Wasn't Mehmet also an investment?

'If I found illegal, I get deported. Then we not together,' Mehmet said.

Again Adrian beat out the rhythm on the wheel. 'Oh, God!' There was a silence. Then, having reached a decision, he said: 'Oh, very well. But are you sure this man can deliver the goods?'

'Landlord say he is OK, very OK. Old friend.'

'Well, I haven't got the money on me, of course. And I can't give you a cheque. For obvious reasons.' It had suddenly struck him, like a blow to the solar plexus, that what he was about to do was highly illegal. 'You must never breathe a word of this to anyone. Understand? Not a word, not a single word. *Silence!*' He put a forefinger to his lips.

Mehmet nodded. 'OK. No problem, Adrian. You worry too much.'

'Of course I worry,' Adrian retorted peevishly. 'I could go to gaol.'

There was a silence. Then Mehmet looked over to Adrian and said: 'When you give this money?'

This importunity began to rile Adrian. 'Well, not today. I'm far too busy. I have three important meetings one after the other. And then I promised to visit an old friend in hospital.' This last was a fiction. In fact, he had to go to one of his canasta sessions with the fag hags.

'Tomorrow?'

'Possibly. Give me your number and I'll ring you. Just as soon as I've got the money from the bank.'

'I ring you tomorrow. What time?'

'I don't know what time. No, I'll ring you. That'll be best. I don't know where I'll be tomorrow – it's another day of rush. So I'll ring you.'

'But I think it better –'

It was a contest of wills. Adrian, who would never have got where he had but for his persistence, was persistent now. He wanted that telephone number, he was going to have that telephone number. Or else . . .

'No. If you want the money tomorrow, then let me ring you.' He opened the glove compartment and took out the pad and the biro that he kept there for the addresses and telephone numbers of hitch-hikers. He handed both to Mehmet, who took them reluctantly. 'Write your number there.'

With extreme slowness, Mehmet wrote it. 'I hope that right. I do not remember well.' He pushed pad and biro back into the glove compartment. 'You promise?'

'I promise. When you know me better, you'll realize that, if I say I'll do something, I always do it.'

As they reached Vauxhall, there was suddenly a cloudburst. The leaden sky cracked open and the rain sluiced down. Now, Adrian thought, he would be able to find out where Mehmet lived, in addition to having his telephone number. 'God, what a downpour! You've got no mac or umbrella, have you? And I haven't got a spare. I'd better drive you home.'

'No, no. Thank you. You have many, many business. Leave me by Underground, please. No problem.'

'Oh, no. I can take you home. I can't let you out in this.'

They had stopped at a traffic light, just by the entrance to Westminster Station. Then, all at once, Mehmet was opening the door. 'I go, I go! Station near here.' He leaned across Adrian and snatched his bag off the back seat. Shouting 'Goodbye, thank you!', he leapt out of the car and disappeared down into the station.

Chapter XVI

Pipe in mouth, Sylvia's husband Paul put his bald head round the door. 'Hello, Meg! I didn't realize you were here.' Of course the stuck-up bugger realized. He must have known what Sylvia was up to when she took the car that morning. Sylvia told him everything. 'How are things?'

'She saw a new man today,' Sylvia answered for her. 'Very young, like a precocious schoolboy. But he seemed to know his stuff. The older ones have the experience of course, that stands to reason, but the younger ones know far more about all the latest advances. He's put her on to a new drug – Betaferon, I think that's what it's called.'

'Splendid, splendid! Well, let's hope it does the trick.' Never ill himself, Paul hated to hear of the illnesses of others. It was as though he feared that even to hear the word 'cancer' 'arthritis' or 'Parkinson's' could infect him. 'Well, if you'll excuse me, Meg, I must get back to struggling with our tax returns. All this self-assessment seems to be designed to cause one the maximum torture. See you!' At that he was gone. Meg knew that he would not join them for lunch. On the excuse that she did not want to interrupt his work, Sylvia would carry a tray to him.

'I can't think why he won't employ an accountant. I suppose that, now that he's retired, he's glad of something to occupy him.'

Meg thought: I wish I had the money to need an accountant to keep an eye on it for me. 'He's lucky,' she said, in a tone of grudging admiration. 'He doesn't look his sixty-two years, does he? I've never known him to have a day's illness.'

Sylvia quickly put out a hand to touch the wood of the table beside her. 'It's in the genes,' she said. 'All his family live to be a hundred – or thereabouts.'

'Pity our genes weren't better.'

'Oh, I don't know. I have my aches and pains but I've never had a really serious illness, have I? And you didn't have one until this wretched thing hit you.'

Sylvia attempted to put an arm round Meg's waist to support her when they moved into the dining-room, where she had laid out the M & S sandwiches and pots of yogurt for their lunch. But Meg said sharply: 'I'm OK, OK.' It was odd: she never minded Mehmet helping her, but she hated it when Sylvia did.

'You sit yourself down and I'll just take Paul up his tray. He'd have liked to join us, but once he gets his teeth into something . . .' Meg knew that she was lying; he wouldn't in the least have liked to join them. Sylvia vanished into the next-door kitchen, where she placed two cartons, one containing a chicken curry and another pilau rice, into the microwave for Paul. 'Would you like apple juice or orange juice?' she called out, having switched on the microwave and opened the refrigerator.

'To be frank with you, dear, neither. What I need is a stiff vodka.'

'Oh, do you really think . . .? I can't help feeling that you ought to cut down on the drinking.' Sylvia appeared in the doorway between kitchen and dining-room, a carton of orange juice in one hand. 'It can't be any help, not in your condition.'

'You make it sound as if I was an alcoholic. I don't drink as Dad used to drink. Come on, Sylvia! Why not pour me a shot?'

With a sigh, Sylvia did as she had been asked. But she made the vodka a tiny one, before splashing in some tonic, followed by three ice cubes.

Soon, the two women were munching their sandwiches. By the time that she was on her second drink, Meg's cheekbones were flushed and her eyes had lost the dull, dead look that they had acquired in the course of an interminable wait at the hospital. Sylvia leaned forward to ask the question that she invariably asked at each of their meetings.

'Tell me, dear. I meant to ask you. What's the rent position?'

'The rent position? Well, it's where it always was.'

'You mean – he still hasn't paid you?'

Meg bit into her sandwich. Then, mouth bulging, she shook her head. She chewed, swallowed. 'He pays in dribs and drabs. But the problem is, the weeks go by and, instead of catching up, he falls more and more behind.'

'I really think you should give him the push.' Sylvia had repeatedly given this advice. 'I mean, it's not as if you could afford to be a philanthropist.' She saw a look of vague bewilderment on her sister's face. 'You're not a charity,' she said. 'Things are hard enough for you as it is, trying to make ends meet, without your losing money on him.'

'I couldn't do without him.'

'Yes, you always say that. But with more help from the Social Security people I'm sure you could.'

Meg shook her head. 'He's like a nurse to me. That Fiona's got a good heart and we get on fine. But she's always in a hurry – the kids, that husband of hers always coming or going, mostly going, the other people she visits. Without Mehmet . . .'

Sylvia pursed her lips and sighed. They were constantly having this conversation. It got them nowhere. 'Well, it's your own business,' she said.

'Then why do you keep shoving your nose into it?' Meg wanted to ask. But she was feeling too tired for any unpleasantness.

It was good to be home again, even if, with the window open, there was that thump-thump-thump, like a magnified heartbeat, from the hi-fi of the flat on the first floor across the yard, and, with the window shut, one could hardly breathe in this heatwave. She envied Sylvia the quiet and coolness of Highgate. Even when they were children, Sylvia had always expected the best and had always managed to get it. She would never be the one to be struck down with something like MS.

Oh, fuck! She had forgotten to ask Mehmet to buy her her five Lucky Dips. She had stacked the five pound coins on the kitchen table to remind her to do so, but somehow, in the rush of getting ready for the hospital – clean knickers, just in case, a dress that Fiona had clumsily ironed, since she now had so much difficulty in handling the iron herself – they had failed to do so. The night before she had had a dream that she had won the lottery and she and Mehmet had gone away on a cruise, eventually to find, to her joy and his chagrin, that the purser was none other than her Eric. She often dreamed of winning the lottery and even more often of Eric, but this was the first time that she had dreamed of the two together. Could that have some special meaning – an omen?

Soon she fell asleep, her head lolling sideways in the chair, so that her tight, reddish-brown curls fell across her forehead, and her mouth was agape. This time she did not dream.

Mehmet's return roused her. Always, when he returned after she had been on a visit to the hospital, the first thing that he would say after greeting her was to ask how she had got on. But this time, without any preliminary, he announced: 'Good news, Mamma! Very good news!' She could see that he was bursting with joy.

She rubbed at an eye with the back of a hand. Her hands worried her now, they were not merely getting more and more useless but they looked so ugly in their swollen limpness. 'What news?'

'Wait, wait, wait!' He had been carrying a carrier bag when he had entered and now, stooping down to it, he produced a bottle of champagne. 'The Widow,' he said. Meg had no idea what he was talking about but, when he held the bottle aloft over his head, she knew from the cork that it must contain champagne or at least one of those fizzy wines that always gave her an acid stomach.

'What's that for?'

'My good news.' In the same rush he fetched down two tumblers and then got some ice from the refrigerator. Immediately after that the cork of the bottle popped and shot across the room. 'Oh, mind Mr Teddy!' Meg cried out in alarm for the pale-blue teddy bear seated on the mantelpiece. Then, grinning, Mehmet was splashing the champagne over the ice.

'Would you mind telling me what all this is about?'

He handed her a glass and then raised his. 'Mamma, I have money. I have rent.'

'What you talking about? What money? Where'd it come from?'

'Last weekend – you remember? – I visit cousin. In Kensington.' He was always off to visit that cousin in Kensington at the weekends. For that reason she had come to dread Saturday and Sunday, spent disconsolately without either his company or his help.

Meg nodded. She had never been able to discover what precisely this cousin did, but clearly – from Mehmet's accounts of going with him to expensive restaurants, to theatres and, most recently, to his place in the country – he was well-heeled.

'I speak to him of no work, problem with rent. All these things.' He sipped, with shining eyes, from the glass. He was exultant. 'He very kind man, son of mother's brother. Good man. Suddenly he say: "Mehmet, I help you." And he give me money, lot money. Just like that!'

'Oh, Mehmet, how wonderful. I am glad!' Meg clapped her hands together. 'I knew that sooner or later you'd have a stroke of luck. You so much deserve it, my darling, and you've waited so long.' She had also waited so long for her rent, but she did not think of that.

He pulled out his wallet and she could see that it was stuffed with notes. When he took them out and began to count what he owed her, she realized, with amazement, that these were not ten or twenty but fifty pound ones. It was seldom that she saw such notes and she had never handled one.

He pushed the notes that he had counted towards her. 'I think that right.'

She drew back. 'Oh, it looks far too much.'

He laughed indulgently. 'I owe you extra. For lateness. So – more there.'

'Oh, but I don't want any interest. Not from you.'

He nodded. 'Take it all.' When she still refused to take the notes from his hand, he laid them down on the table beside her.

'Oh, but I . . . I hope you're not depriving yourself.'

'All, all for you.'

'Well, I'm sure . . . I'm sure I'm very grateful. I don't know what to say . . .' She realized that if she was not careful if she was going to make an idiot of herself and burst into tears.

'Say nothing, Mamma.'

'I'm so happy. For you, I mean. For me too but for you mostly.'

'I am also happy. For both of us.'

Chapter XVII

It was an unusually trying day at the shop.

An overdressed, middle-aged woman, with dangling earrings and a number of chunky rings on her fingers and even on one thumb, had come in with a skirt that she had bought from one of Audrey's colleagues the previous day. Having edged past another customer who had been standing there before her, she had told Audrey peremptorily in what sounded like a French accent: 'Please! Take a look here! Look!' With a forefinger she indicated the hem of the skirt. 'There is a stain here, please. Oil, I think. I cannot buy a skirt with a stain.'

'May I just finish serving this customer? I'll be with you in a moment.'

The woman waited, shifting from one leg to another and from time to time scowling and heaving a sigh.

'Yes?'

'I do not buy such a skirt. How can I wear such a skirt? I thought that all goods in Oxfam shops are cleaned before sale. This is impossible.'

Her colleagues often told Audrey that she was too kind. One, exasperated, had on one occasion even told her that she was feeble. She hated rows, she even hated arguments. It was less bruising to give in. So, after a brief exchange with the woman, she handed over the seven pounds paid for the skirt and returned it to the rail from which it had come.

'You're not putting it straight back, are you?' the woman demanded. 'It ought to be cleaned.'

Audrey made no response.

A little later the elderly book thief, to whom the other workers would now refer as 'your friend' when talking about him to Audrey, tottered in on his stick and uttered his formal 'Good day, madam.' On this occasion he had a soiled dressing over an eye and a loose bandage round his neck. At once he went over to the shelf of paperbacks at the rear of the shop, while Audrey squinted up at the mirror over the changing-room to watch him. Sure enough, she saw him, as so often in the past, slip a paperback into the pocket of the overcoat that reached almost to his ankles. If the woman with the skirt had not been so exasperating, she would once more have let the matter go. But on this occasion, as he was about to leave the shop, she walked swiftly round the counter to bar his way.

'Excuse me.'

The one uncovered eye was bloodshot, as he turned it up to her. 'Yes?' He gave no impression whatever of anything being amiss. She might have been a stranger accosting him in the street to ask for directions.

'I think you may have taken a book without paying for it.'

He frowned in what anyone but Audrey would have taken to be a genuine bewilderment. 'A book? Me?'

'Yes, I saw you, I'm afraid. In that mirror.' She pointed. 'It's not the first time, you know.'

At this moment another customer, whom Audrey recognized as the surgery cleaner Mrs Flynn, limped into the shop. 'Hello, Miss Carter. How are you?'

Since she could not say: 'I'm just dealing with a thief,' Audrey contented herself with 'Not too bad, thank you, Mrs Flynn.' Then, from habit, she added: 'And you?'

Mrs Flynn began to complain about her feet and the new chiropodist at that NHS place, who had only made them worse. The old man, his way still barred, waited without any sign of agitation or even impatience. At long last, Mrs Flynn moved on to inspect the rack on which the returned skirt was now dangling.

In a low voice, Audrey told the man: 'If you give me back the book, we'll say no more about it.'

'I don't know what you mean. I haven't any book.'

'I'm afraid you have.'

'This is ridiculous.' Even now he showed no emotion; his voice was quiet and flat. 'Please let me pass.'

'Not until you give me back that book.'

Suddenly, without any warning, he put up a hand, grabbed her shoulder and pushed her aside, with such violence that she all but fell over. Then he was out of the door and hurrying down the street. She went out in pursuit; but seeing him jump aboard a 28 bus, which happened to have just drawn up at the stop a few feet away, she gave up with a sigh.

'What was all that about?' Mrs Flynn asked.

'He comes in here and pinches books.'

'You should report him.'

'Oh, he's so old and pathetic.'

'It's the old ones that are often the worst. There was a programme about it on the telly only the other night. Some are real professionals.'

When she arrived home, exhausted and upset, Audrey thought, I need some of Marilyn's medicine, and went over to the drinks cupboard and helped herself to half a glass of her vodka. Now, she thought, she too had become a petty thief. She kept no drinks of her own down in the basement, other than a bottle of sherry for Laurence's rare visits. She carried the glass of vodka down with her, along with *The Times*.

She had already completed half of the crossword when she heard Marilyn above.

'Is that you, Marilyn?' she called up.

'Yep. I'm done in, absolutely done in. Perhaps a bath will revive me.' A silence followed. Audrey decided that Marilyn was now also pouring herself some vodka. Then: 'I totally forgot to tell you that I'd be going out this evening. Sorry.'

'That's all right. I haven't embarked on any cooking yet.'

Audrey wondered whether Marilyn was going out with the rent boy. Probably. Otherwise she was usually more specific – 'I'm going out to the theatre', 'I'm going to a meeting', 'I'm going out with Vicky.' But Thursday wasn't usually one of the rent boy's evenings. It was always Wednesdays and of course the weekends that Marilyn kept for him – though, oddly, he had not turned up last weekend, making Audrey hope that perhaps he and Marilyn were now breaking up.

Marilyn went upstairs and Audrey continued with the crossword. Then the bell rang, not once but in that imperious fashion, peel on peel, with which the rent boy always announced himself. Let Marilyn answer it. Eventually, after another ring, Marilyn did answer, trotting down the stairs in what, Audrey surmised, would be merely a towel or a dressing gown. Audrey strained to catch the ensuing conversation. Since all doors were open because of the heat, it was easy to do so.

'Marilyn! I thought maybe you out. No answer for so long.'

'I was having a bath. As you can see. I got so sticky. It's terribly hot, isn't it? Come in, come in! Get yourself a drink. I'll be with you in a sec.'

'I come up. Why not?'

A laugh. 'Why not? Yes. You can talk to me while I'm dressing.'

'I bring present for you.'

'No, no! You must stop bringing me these presents. Every time you come you bring me one. Please! Stop!'

'Special present. Here. Look.'

There was a silence, then a squeal of pleasure from Marilyn. 'Oh, but Mehmet . . . No, no, no!'

'From Harvey Nichols. You remember? I go there with you when you buy tights. And you then see this . . .'

'Yes, yes, I wanted it so much. And it was far, far too expensive. Fancy you going all the way to Harvey Nicks . . . But this is wrong, terribly wrong.'

Now they were mounting the stairs. Arm in arm, Audrey was sure. Her shoulders would be bare, one hand holding the towel up around her, and then the towel would slip and she would clutch at it. Or it would fall down and he would stoop to pick it up for her. Or he would himself hold the towel around her. There were all sorts of variations and all of them disgusted her.

But what had he given her that had caused her so much consternation and delight? Marilyn would never tell her, because she now never spoke about the rent boy.

Now they were coming down the stairs again, trying to decide, as they so often tried to decide, which restaurant they would go to. Of course, Audrey was thinking, she would pay for the meal, poor thing; but then, amazingly, the rent boy was saying: 'I wish to take you to Clarke's. Someone say Clarke's very good.'

'Oh, but that's far too expensive. Let's go to somewhere like the Café Rouge or the Café Flo.'

'No. I take you to Clarke's.'

'But how can you afford all this? First that wonderful, wonderful present, now Clarke's. Where did you get the money?'

'You remember my cousin – I have cousin with flat near Marble Arch. Remember? I speak of him. I visit him at weekend – weekend I cannot come to you – and he, he give me present . . .'

The rest was lost to Audrey. They had left the hall and the front door clicked behind them.

What was this 'wonderful, wonderful' present? And who was this cousin who had suddenly, on a whim it seemed, shown the rent boy generosity? Audrey, hunched over in her chair and arms crossed over her stomach, as though she were suffering a gnawing colic, brooded on it. Then she jumped to her feet and hurried upstairs.

Marilyn's room was in its usual state of disorder – as though, in Laurence's words, all twelve decisive battles of the world had been fought in it. Absentmindedly, as her eyes darted hither and thither, Marilyn picked up a shoe from the middle of the floor and placed it beside its fellow under the dressing table. She reached for the soggy towel draped across the bed, preparatory to taking it to the bathroom. Then she dropped it, when she glimpsed what was lying over the back of a chair. It was a voluminous, pale grey shawl, with long tassels that looked like the tails of innumerable Persian cats. She went over to it, picked it up, feeling its extraordinary softness and then its extraordinary suppleness, as though of a living thing, and finally held it against her cheek. It must be cashmere, she thought at first, only to realise that, no, it wasn't cashmere but pashmina.

It must have cost a bomb. How much could he have paid for it? That sum of money given to him by his cousin must have been considerable. Unless of course – the thought whirred at her like a javelin – he had stolen it. Or got it in some other way. As a rent boy? People said that rent boys could earn huge sums of money. Yes, that must be it. He must have sold himself to some wealthy woman or even man to get a shawl like that. She didn't believe that that cousin existed.

Having replaced the shawl, making sure that it lay over the chair exactly as it had been lying when she had first set eyes on it – Marilyn, she knew, was extremely observant – she went out on to the landing. She hesitated. Then disgusted with herself but unable to resist the impulse, she opened the door to the room next to it. Once again she sniffed in those combined odours of Caron Pour Un Homme, healthy sweat and cigarette smoke. Why did he never open the window?

Mehmet had now increasingly come to regard this room as his and no longer Laurence's. From weekend to weekend he would leave in it a set of pyjamas, shaving things, washing things, clean shirts and underclothes and even CD disks of Albanian music. He must have taken off that elegant dark blue silk blouson of his because of the heat. It was hanging there, beside his cotton dressing gown, on the door.

Swiftly she walked over to it and began to go through the pockets. A used handkerchief. She stuffed that back. A few coins. Two keys on a silver heart-shaped ring, with the initial M engraved on it in Gothic script. A present from Marilyn? If so, he must have chosen it, since Marilyn would have balked at anything so vulgar. Two cinema ticket stubs. Some pocket matches with 'The Town House' printed on them. A condom. She scrunched it between her fingers and then, with a fleeting moue of distaste, returned it to the blouson. This was odd: a flat, rectangular box of cigarettes which, when she raised its lid, showed cigarettes in a number of different, garish colours. Cocktail Cigarettes, the box told her. She had not seen a box of cigarettes like that since her Oxford days. She was used to seeing used packets of Superking Lights left on the sitting-room or kitchen table, or on the table by his bed.

Last, she came on the envelope. It was from Salonika and it was addressed to him 'c/o Towling', followed by an address. She had always had a remarkably good memory and so, without any conscious effort, she memorized the address now. Towling. She had never before heard that name. It sounded strange – as though the person who had written it had inadvertently omitted an 'e'. She looked inside the envelope but she already knew, from the flimsy feel of it, that there was nothing inside. There were two telephone numbers written on its back, and some figures, jotted down untidily here and there in small columns for addition.

She had so often felt that, in making his visits, he was violating the house and even, in some subtle, horrible way, herself. Now she had violated him. But that thought gave her no satisfaction. It even made her feel vaguely nauseated.

Two days later Laurence was, as he put it, having a day in town, with visits to 'my foot chappy', Trumper to have his hair cut, and the London Library to pick up some books. Dutifully, Audrey had offered to chauffeur him.

With a grimace he climbed into the car. His neck, he told her, was being an absolute bugger. It was clear to her that, in consequence of the neck, he was in one of his moods. 'I've always hated this poky little car,' he complained with real venom. 'Why on earth did you buy it? Too low, no leg room, so bloody noisy.' Then he began to tell her fretfully that she was taking the wrong route, she had absolutely no sense of direction, it would have been so much quicker to have avoided Putney High Street.

However, by the time that he had completed his errands, his mood, like the previously ominous sky, was sunnier. 'Now I'm going to take you out to lunch. There's a Turkish restaurant I'm eager to try. It's mentioned in the *Good Food Guide*. Would you mind awfully driving me there?'

'Of course not. Where is it?'

When he told her, Audrey stopped the car and said that she would have to look in her *A-Z*. She had never been to that part of London. Having consulted the map, she realized that the restaurant was only three or four streets from that address that she had found in one of the ransacked pockets of the rent boy's blouson.

'Found it?'

'Yes.'

'Good girl.'

'It's an awfully long way. But never mind.'

The meal was so good that, by its close, every trace of Laurence's peevishness had vanished. Over their small cups of coffee, a bitter sludge, he even began to suggest that they might take a Hellenic cruise together – 'We don't have to listen to all those old farts telling us things we know already. We can cut the lectures.' He was going to sell off that Queen Anne escritoire, he announced, it was far too big for that wretched little sitting-room of his, and he might as well blue the proceeds on the cruise. Audrey was touched and delighted. He had only once asked her to share a holiday, and that was merely because he had wanted her to drive him around the Highlands.

When they returned to the car, Laurence's face was flushed and his walk unsteady from having drunk the whole of a bottle of wine, with the exception of a half glass drunk by Audrey. 'Whoops!' He put out a hand to the car as he all but tottered over.

'Before I drive you back to Wimbledon, there's something I want to do. If you don't mind.'

'What's that?'

'I want to see a house. Near here. Three or four streets away.' All through lunch an obsessive curiosity had been gnawing at her. She was like a zoologist determined to inspect the habitat of a rare animal.

'A house? What house? You're not thinking of moving are you? You couldn't possibly move into a neighbourhood like this. I can tell you, I'd never visit you here, not even for that restaurant.'

'It's where *he* lives.'

'He?' By now Laurence was used to the way, both conspiratorial and venomous, with which Audrey spoke the monosyllable. 'Oh, you mean the rent boy?' Laurence often brooded on the rent boy. He would like to see him for himself – in order, in effect, to sum up the competition. But there was more to it than that. He felt an odd, awkward, strangling bond with him. At

Audrey's mention of it, he too was now instantly infected with the urge to see the rent boy's lair.

It took some time to find the street, with Laurence irritably telling Audrey 'No, no, we've been up here once already' and Audrey yet again consulting the *A-Z*. Once more he remarked that she had never had any sense of direction, just like her mother. 'How the other half lives,' Laurence grunted in distaste at one moment, as they passed a black man in oil-stained shorts and vest, who was dismantling a car at one side of a narrow street, while two grubby, solemn children, presumably his, stood watching him.

Finally they entered a canyon of high, narrow, grey houses. 'This seems to be it,' Audrey said. She experienced a mounting excitement as she screwed up her eyes and peered for the number. One house was boarded up and looked as if it was in imminent danger of collapsing. Another house, with five brightly-dressed young people, two white and three black, sunning themselves on its steps, looked as if squatters were in occupation. Eventually, they came on a square, concrete block of flats. 'Yes, this seems to be it.'

Laurence felt an agonizing spasm in his neck as he turned to look out of the window beside him. 'The way the other half lives,' he muttered again. He peered at the street sign ahead. 'Devine Street. More Devilish Street. And Number Four. Did you know that in Japan the number four is unlucky – meaning death?'

The door of the block, raised above the street, opened at that moment and they saw a middle-aged woman with a stick in one hand and a plastic bag containing rubbish, standing on the threshold. Then slowly, crabwise, she descended the steps, gritting her teeth as she lifted one leg as though it were some terribly heavy object, not part of herself, and then lifted the other. Her face was crumpled with the effort. Audrey felt an impulse to rush out of the car to help her.

Half way down the steep steps, the woman halted, steadied herself, and then hurled the bag away from her down towards the pavement. She turned and, laboriously heaving herself upwards, a swollen hand to the rail, began her ascent.

'How can people live like that?' Laurence asked. 'Was she drunk?'

'I wonder which is his flat?' Audrey peered up at the sheer, grimy front of the block and Laurence peered up with her.

Then she put her hand to the ignition key and turned it.

Back in the flat, Meg raised the net curtain and looked out of the front window of her sitting-room at the disappearing car. What did those two Nosy Parkers want, staring like that?

Chapter XVIII

It was a bloody nuisance. An emergency over a delayed microchip order forced Adrian to cancel his Friday meeting with Mehmet, when he was feeling at his horniest, and instead to fly off to Seoul.

Once there, he had had to endure a number of unsatisfactory meetings with the bosses of the Korean firm concerned, who at wearisome length either recounted to him every detail of the current slump in the economy of their country, of which he was already fully aware, or told him about the reasons for a strike in the largest of their factories, of which he had known nothing.

In addition to these mental irritations, there was also soon a physical one. After a disgusting meal of tough beef and a kind of putrefying cabbage which his hosts had proudly told him was a Korean national dish and went by the name of *kimchi*, he had decided that he really had to cheer himself up. That meant only one thing. Having been seen back to the hotel by all six of his hosts in a black stretch-limousine, he at once went up to his bedroom, brushed his teeth and sprayed some deodorant under his arms, and then slipped out again. The breast-pocket of his white tropical suit, down the front of which, unaccustomed to chopsticks, he had managed to dribble a scarlet and therefore highly conspicuous sauce, contained one of his visiting cards, on the back of which he had scrawled the name of a bar found in the *Spartacus International Gay Guide*.

Most of the people in the bar turned out to be white; one of them, a stout American in a rainbow-coloured shirt and huge, rectangular dark glasses, was black. Eventually, after Adrian had rejected a constantly smiling Korean with a squint and a pencil-line moustache reminiscent of some Thirties film star, a tattooed bruiser with a shaven head and an almost flat nose lumbered up. He was a far from attractive proposition, and he would not budge from his ludicrous price of a hundred dollars. But, having decided that it was too late and he was too tired to hang around any longer, Adrian finally went off with him.

At first Adrian was dubious about taking someone so inappropriate back to a five-star hotel, and he therefore asked if it might not be wiser to go somewhere else; but the man said that he knew that hotel, it was fine, he had often been there, his brother worked in the nightclub as a bouncer, there was a back entrance and a service lift. The sex was perfunctory and rough, and it was only by thinking of Mehmet that Adrian was able to achieve a perfunctory orgasm. The man then demanded a tip in addition to the agreed payment. Weakly, Adrian added this to the sum. A total balls-up, he bitterly decided, like the microchip deal. But at least after it he was able to sleep.

In contrast, two nights later, prior to his early departure for London, he was not able to sleep at all. This was because of an insane itching in his crotch. He scratched away at it for a time and then, having reluctantly heaved himself out of bed, went into the bathroom. He had already guessed what was amiss; and an examination, with the aid of the torch that he always took with him on foreign journeys for fear of a sudden blackout, at once confirmed his diagnosis. Oh, God! He might have known that that brute wasn't clean. If only a condom had been invented to protect one from crabs! No pharmacy would be open now, and he was leaving too early on the following morning to find one open then. With mounting self-disgust, he fetched down the disposable razor and a tiny tube of shaving-cream provided by the hotel – his own razor was an electric one – and, tongue between teeth, began gingerly to shave himself.

Despite this, all through the flight his crotch went on itching, so that, looking surreptitiously at the man seated next to him to ensure that he was either immersed in his book or asleep, he from time to time inserted a hand into his trousers to scratch at the increasingly raw flesh. What sort of explanation was he to produce for Mehmet? The thought came to him that perhaps it would be better to forgo sex altogether, in order to give the pubic hair time to grow. But he could not bear to wait. He wanted once again to see that pale, muscular body on the stiff, linen sheet, and then to feel that arm almost throttling him from behind, until he all but fainted from a mind-blowing combination of pain and ecstasy.

After much agonizing, Adrian had prepared his excuse. 'I shaved off my bush because I was sweating so much in that heat,' he told Mehmet, as he swiftly pulled off his Y-fronts and hopped into the bed in the flat.

Mehmet showed no surprise. 'Many Muslims shave down that place. I often shave so in Albania. Cleaner.' That was all. The relief of it added to the fervour of Adrian's love-making. But Mehmet's was cool, even though in conversation he had been surprisingly friendly.

Instead of taking Mehmet out to dinner, on this occasion Adrian cooked him scrambled eggs and bacon. 'My friends say that my scrambled eggs are the best they've ever tasted. I hope you'll take the same view.'

Having irritably reminded Adrian that he never ate bacon and demanded that the eggs be transferred to another plate, Mehmet ate stolidly. Having finished, he wiped this plate with a hunk of bread and then popped the bread into his mouth. But he offered no view whatever on the quality of the scrambling.

'Oh, I know what I meant to ask you.' Adrian had just peeled a banana and was holding it in his hand. 'Is it all right about the passport?'

Mehmet helped himself to a banana from the bowl between them. 'I meet him two day ago. I give him money. Now we wait!'

'*What*!' Adrian almost choked on the piece of banana he was swallowing. 'You gave him all that money without getting the passport?'

'Passport take time. Maybe two weeks, three weeks. Man say he must have money first. He pay other man.'

'Are you crazy?'

'Who crazy? You call me crazy?'

Adrian quailed before Mehmet's sudden anger, and at once adopted a conciliatory tone for what he next asked: 'But don't you think – don't you think that it might have been better if you'd just given him an advance?'

'Advance?'

'Well, say five hundred pounds. Instead of that two thousand. I mean – he might just pocket the money and do nothing.'

'He friend of landlord.'

'Yes, but what sort of friend? How long have you known your landlord? And how long has the landlord known his friend?'

'This banana not ripe. Who buy this banana for you? Igor?' Mehmet seemed to be far more concerned about the unripeness of the banana than about the money.

Adrian put his head in his hands. 'You've really got me worried.'

'No worry. No problem. Passport come.'

The passport did not come. Repeatedly, at each of their subsequent meetings, Adrian asked about it, to receive the same answers each time: He must be patient, it was impossible to hurry things along, Mehmet's landlord was honest, the landlord's friend was honest, why was Adrian so upset?

Adrian confided in Igor – reluctantly but he could not think of anyone else in whom to confide – when next he spent a weekend in the country. Mehmet had once again excused himself from coming to the 'cottage', on the old grounds that he must spend the weekend with his cousin. 'I just hope that nothing's gone wrong. The poor lamb's so trusting. He just has no conception how crooked the most respectable-seeming people can be in this country. Two grand is a lot of money – even for me.'

Igor was holding the end of his greyish ponytail in one of his long, narrow hands, their nails caked with soil. Now he put it into his mouth and chewed on it reflectively. It was a habit that Adrian loathed. 'I hope he's not taking you for a ride.'

'What do you mean?'

Igor shrugged and turned his head sideways to gaze out of the window. There was a vague smile on his face that filled Adrian with irritation.

'Oh, there's no fear of that. Mehmet is totally honest – one hundred per cent.' But doubt, an insidiously wriggling worm, was already entering his mind. People were always telling him how shrewd he was (behind his back, this became a cunning bastard). Could he have lost his shrewdness?

'When he tells you he has the passport, ask to see it.'

Ten days later, when Adrian yet again asked 'Is there any news on the passport front?', Mehmet produced none of the usual answers but instead looked glum, shook his head, sighed and then said: 'Sorry, Adrian. Bad news. I have passport but passport no good.'

'What do you mean?'

'Landlord's friend meet me in pub. He give me envelope, say passport inside. Not to open in pub. Home, I open, see passport, French passport, look fine, my photograph, everything. Beautiful. I am happy, happy. Think, now job, now no more illegal. But I show passport to landlord. Landlord look careful. Then landlord say, Mehmet, passport no good.'

Adrian, who had been listening with first relief and then joy, was now aghast at the last words.

'No good?'

'Date on passport 1988.' Adrian was staring at Mehmet in horrified incredulity. 'One – nine – eight – eight,' Mehmet went on, as though to someone deaf or mentally deficient. 'Passport too old. Out of date. No good.'

'But your landlord – isn't he going to speak to his friend?'

'I ask him.' Mehmet shrugged. 'But . . . he say, difficult.'

'What's difficult about it?'

'His friend big man in Home Office.'

'Well, that's all the more reason to speak to him. He's sold us a pup!'

'Please?'

Suddenly Adrian's face was suffused with scarlet, his small eyes popped. He had a way of suddenly losing his temper. On the last night of his visit to Seoul, he had done so with his Korean hosts, inflicting on them such a loss of face that, contrary to custom, not one of them had appeared to see him off at the airport. 'This is fuckin' awful!' he shouted, his accent reverting to what once it had been. 'I'm not goin' to stand for this. You just tell that mate of yours to tell his mate that if we don't either have a proper passport or our money back, we'll go to the police.'

Mehmet put out a hand, as though physically to restrain him. 'No, Adrian. No, no! Not good. No police.'

'Why the hell not?'

'Not good for you. Not good for me. Illegal to give money for passport. No matter passport no good, illegal. Police come, Mehmet become deported. Police come, big trouble for Adrian.'

Adrian fell silent. He had had big trouble with the police once before. He did not wish to have big trouble again. 'H'm. Yes.' Then he wailed: 'Oh, fucking hell!'

Igor had been singing while pushing the vacuum cleaner back and forth in the bedroom. Adrian was changing his shirt and tie before going out to a business dinner. The noise of the cleaner irritated him more and more, until eventually he shouted: 'Oh, for Christ's sake turn that off! I'll be finished in a sec.'

Igor turned off the cleaner and then, humming now instead of singing, flopped down on Adrian's vast bed. 'OK! A little pause!' He sat up, bounced up and down, and then turned over on to his stomach and crossed his legs in the air. Something in his manner, sprightly, mischievous, even flirtatious, as he had not been for years, disturbed Adrian. What had got into him?

'It's so worrying. I can't think what to make of it. You know how I hate to be taken for a ride.'

'Yes, I know, Adrian.' The stick legs still swung back and forth. 'But over the years you've been taken for a ride by so many people.'

'Such as?'

'Oh, what's the point!' Suddenly serious, Igor rolled over again and raised himself on an elbow. 'There's one thing you must do. As soon as Mehmet arrives tomorrow.'

'Yes?' Adrian struggled into his clean shirt, scrupulously ironed by Igor. Oh, shit! He had put on so much weight over the last weeks that a button popped.

'You must ask to see this passport – this passport with the wrong date.'

'Why?'

'Because perhaps – just perhaps – it doesn't exist. Just as the friend of the landlord may perhaps not exist,' he added.

'Oh, what nonsense!'

But Adrian was beginning to feel queasy.

Adrian at once recognized the calm, deep, strong, voice on the telephone as that of Siegfried's widowed mother. He had never met her, but he had often spoken to her when she had rung Siegfried during that period, paradisal it now seemed in retrospect, when the two of them had been together.

A secondary schoolteacher of English, she spoke the language well. 'Mr Martin – I am afraid I have bad news.' Adrian at once knew what she had to say. He braced himself, as for the jab of a needle at the dentist. 'My Siegfried passed away this morning. So peaceful. He had said he was tired, he had gone to sleep, and then . . . just like that.' *My Siegfried.* Adrian resented that. Siegfried had been his as much as – or even more than – hers.

'Oh. Oh, I'm so sorry.' Adrian had never been wholly sure whether she had ever grasped the nature of the relationship between her beautiful, wayward, idle son and this Englishman whom she knew only as a voice at the other end of a telephone line. Siegfried always maintained that she hadn't, but that was difficult to believe.

'He suffered so much. Perhaps – perhaps it is better this way.'

Self-protectively, Adrian did not want to hear any more of the details; but, no doubt because she found it consolatory to go over them yet again, she proceeded to give them to him. It was soon clear that before that quiet drifting into harbour, the voyage had been ghastly.

Eventually, Adrian wanted to shout down the telephone 'I don't want to have all those horrors to remember, I have enough already!'. But of course he could not do that. In mounting panic more than in grief, he made his occasional interjections of horror or sympathy. From the calm exactitude with which she produced each detail in turn – the uncontrollable diarrhoea, the blotches on the skin, the fungus in the mouth, the mental confusions – she might have been a doctor or nurse describing a patient's long dying.

At the conclusion, she asked the question that he had been dreading: Would he be coming to the funeral, which would be held on the Tuesday after next? 'Just a small affair, that was how he wished it, family, a few friends, close friends like you.'

'When did you say it was going to be?' He had taken in the date, but he wanted time to think of some excuse.

'Tuesday twelfth. In the afternoon. You could stay here, if you wish. I'd be happy for that.'

'Oh, lord! I so much wanted to come. But . . . That's the date of our annual general meeting. I simply must be there.'

'Oh. I am sorry. He would have wanted you.'

He guessed, even though the calm, deep, strong tone of voice had scarcely altered that, with an intuition similar to her son's, she had seen through the deception. In an effort to make amends, he said: 'Of course I want to send some flowers.'

'No flowers. But thank you very much. That was his wish. He said no flowers but a donation to some AIDS charity. Only if people so wanted, of course.'

'Well, then I'll do that, of course I will. I'll send a cheque at once.'

'That is kind of you . . . Oh, there is one other matter, Mr Martin.'

'Yes?'

'Your letters. My Siegfried kept all your letters. Shortly before – before it happened, he gave them to me. In an envelope. Sealed. Of course I have not read them. He told me to send them to you. I thought that I could give them to you at the funeral, but since you are not coming – cannot come – I will post them to you. Registered mail, of course.'

'Oh, thank you. There's no hurry. But, yes, I'd like to have them.' In fact, he did not in least want to have them, redolent of those bitter-sweet years of quarrels, partings, reconciliations, jealousies, meannesses and, yes, in spite of all those things, a love that had less and less depended on their never wholly satisfactory sex and that, despite or because of that, had grown stronger and stronger, until that hideous illness had begun to eat away at its roots.

When he had restored the receiver to its cradle, Adrian stood looking down at it. Self-protective, as always, he thought. You could not bear to suffer with him, even briefly and at second-hand, on that terrible Calvary of his. You cannot even bear to buy a plane ticket, which will cost you no more than a dinner party at your club, and suffer for an hour or so in a church and by a graveside.

But I am suffering, I am suffering – here, now!

At that he went over to the sofa and, like a distraught child, threw himself on to it, sobbing and beating with his fists at a cushion, as tears gushed out of his eyes and began to blur his glasses. Pull yourself together. You knew that this was coming. Inevitable. You said your real goodbye to him a long time ago.

Finally, he did manage to pull himself together. He got off the sofa, removed the glasses and wiped them on a handkerchief. Then he pressed the handkerchief against eyeballs that, from his brief explosion of grief, felt as raw as his throat. No, he would not read the letters. He would put them through the shredder at his office, shredding to no more than jumbled tatters all that he and Siegfried had shared. But first he must write that cheque. Did the London Lighthouse still exist? No, better than that, he would send the cheque to the Kobler Wing of Chelsea and Westminster Hospital. He wrote five hundred pounds and then tore up that cheque and began to write a new one. This time he wrote two hundred pounds.

Oh, Lord! Mehmet would be here in less than half-an-hour. He pushed the cheque into a drawer. He would write the accompanying letter and post it tomorrow. Now he must get out of his sticky shirt and suffocating tie into something cooler.

'How are you?' Mehmet asked, in that tone that made it clear that he did not really care a damn how Adrian was.

'OK. I suppose.' Anyone more sensitive or more concerned about Adrian's well-being would have known that he was far from OK. His voice was as colourless as his face; his eyes were red at the rims and his cheekbones were glistening as though still damp from the violent tears of an hour ago. 'The truth is I have a bad headache.' He had been so much looking forward to sex with Mehmet, and now had no desire for it. He thought in wry self-castigation: 'I'm making the excuse of every wife resisting the excessive demands – as it used to be put – of her husband. Except that in this case the husband is so far from making any sort of demands that he is totally indifferent.'

Over dinner at Kensington Place – Mehmet's favourite restaurant, since he was always excitedly spotting people whom he had seen on television or in the *Sun* – Adrian found that the effort of sustaining even the most banal of conversations was almost beyond him. He felt as if had just finished a day-long walk or had just stepped off a plane after a journey tourist class all the way from New Zealand. But Mehmet, eating with gusto, noticed nothing.

From time to time, Adrian examined him surreptitiously. The white poplin shirt looked new and so did the tie that, when Mehmet turned his head to ask the waiter for something, showed a Nino Ricci label. Adrian had never before seen that suit, with its wide lapels and pinched-in waist, rather vulgar he thought and clearly off-the-peg, but expensive nonetheless. Briefly he was transfixed by first a shaft of jealousy (has he found another lover?) and then, even more painful, by one of suspicion. Could that two grand have been spent not on the passport that had turned out to be dud, but, in part at least, on this resplendent wardrobe?

As they left the restaurant, Adrian put a hand to his forehead in a theatrical gesture and said: 'This head is killing me. I really think I'll have to get home to two aspirins and a lie-down.'

He had expected some sign of disappointment and some word of protest from Mehmet; but instead there was merely a shrug of the shoulders and 'OK. I go home.' Once again Adrian wondered whether there might not be someone else. There might even be a woman.

'I tell you what. Why don't we drop into the Elephants' Graveyard for a nightcap?' When Mehmet pulled a face at that, Adrian said: 'A sentimental journey.' Mehmet then frowned in puzzlement. 'Have you forgotten that that's where first we met?' Adrian reminded him sharply. Really he had no desire to go back to the place but, having been in a hurry to get rid of

Mehmet in order to luxuriate in his grief and guilt over Siegfried's death, he now wished to delay their parting, certain that Mehmet was about to meet someone else and determined to stop him.

When they were seated in a corner of the pub, Mehmet looked around him and said: 'Terrible place. These are rubbish people. I hate them.'

Adrian had often felt the same. But now he was riled. 'How can you say that? You know nothing about any of them.'

'I know what they are.'

When Mehmet went off to the lavatory, Adrian suddenly remembered the question that Igor had told him to put. At the time, he had said crossly 'Oh, I can't possibly ask him that'; but now he wanted to do so. For the first time, instead of being exhilarated by Mehmet's presence, he felt irritated, even resentful.

Mehmet was followed out by the man whom the regulars called 'The Colonel'. The Colonel said something and Mehmet laughed and patted him on a shoulder. Adrian wondered briefly if it was the Colonel who had paid for the new clothes; but that seemed unlikely, since he was so notorious for cadging drinks that even the barmen joked about it.

'Mehmet – I was wondering, my dear.' He sucked in his breath and then exhaled it heavily – something he always did when he was, as now, nervous.

'Yes?'

'That passport.'

'Passport?'

Surely he must know what he was talking about? It was ludicrous to pretend otherwise.

'The one from that creature in the Home Office. The dud one. Do you think I might see it?'

'Why you want see it?'

Adrian could already foresee trouble. But he pushed on. 'I'd like just to check on that date – that 1988. Perhaps you and your friend have got it wrong.'

'How we get date wrong? What you mean?'

'Well – perhaps you misread it. I'd – I'd like to check.'

Suddenly Mehmet's face was contorted with rage. 'You no believe me?'

'It is not a question of believing or not. I just wonder whether perhaps . . .' He looked beseechingly at Mehmet. 'I'd like to check,' he repeated.

'What this check?' Mehmet had so much raised his voice that drinkers all around were staring at them. Someone tittered. A voice fluted 'What a tantrum!' 'What you mean?' Mehmet demanded. 'No, you no check! You mind own bloody business!'

More drinkers, farther away from them, were now also staring.

Adrian's temper flared skyward. 'It *is* my business. Two grand is my business. It bloody well is my business.'

'I give you back your money. I get work permit, I get work, I give you back money. You bad man.'

'What do you mean? What are you talking about? Bad man! After all I've done for you. You've been damned lucky. And you've taken me for a ride. Your landlord never offered to help you, and his friend in the Home Office never existed. There was no passport. Yes, you've taken me for a ride.'

Adrian now rose to his feet, heart thumping, preparatory to quitting the pub. There were familiar faces among the onlookers. Some knew his name, some even knew his business. In the weeks ahead everyone would be gossiping about this all too public row.

Mehmet leapt to his feet. For a terrifying moment, Adrian thought that he was about to assault him. 'What this ride? You mean ride to flat to have sex with you? You mean ride to country to have sex? You horrible man. Pig!' Adrian had travelled in the Muslim world on business; he knew the insulting force of the word. 'Do you think I enjoy sex with you? Yes? You think I like sex with pig? You fat, you bald, you ugly, ugly, ugly. You sweat, sweat, sweat, and all time smell.'

Adrian could now hear the titters rising all around him, interspersed with the Colonel's booming laughter. He wished that Mehmet were not so much taller than he was. To answer him, he had to tilt back his head, and that made him feel so much more ineffectual. In an attempt at withering dignity, he said: 'I rather think you'll regret speaking to me like that. Yes, I rather think you will. I'll pay you out for this. This isn't the last of the matter. Not by a long chalk. You ought to realize how vulnerable you are. Yes. You ought to take more care.'

That seemed to have gone home. 'What you mean?'

'Wait and see. Just wait and see. I'm going to see that you get your comeuppance. I'm going to punish you for this. Just wait!'

Chapter XIX

Drat that bird! What did it think it was doing, at this hour of the night or morning? It was still so dark that, from her bed, her dressing gown, thrown over the chair, looked as if it were the menacing shape of someone lolling there.

Meg decided that the bird must be a nightingale, and so, along with her exasperation, there were also feelings of marvel and self-congratulation. Fancy a nightingale singing out there in what passed for the garden of this house – the grass waist-high after heavy rain followed by a weekend of scorchers, and the rusty or mouldering detritus of urban living dotted every-where about it. In fact, the bird was a thrush – as Eric, who, as a young boy wandering the Rainham marshes, had first become interested in birds, would have been able to tell her.

She lay on her side, hand under cheek, and listened. The song, bubbling up effortlessly and then abruptly stanched, only to bubble up again, soon ceased to exasperate her and instead began to fill her with a placid, not unpleasant melan-choly. The little fellow was singing his heart out for her alone, she thought. Everyone else was probably asleep. Certainly Mehmet was, snoring away as a ground-bass to the thrush's coloratura.

Eventually, she got up and, with the aid of her stick, tottered down the corridor to the lavatory. No water came when she tried to flush the bowl. That bloody ballcock must again be stuck. She would have to ask Mehmet to get up on the steplad-der and see to it for her. During the remission, she would have got up herself, but now it would be all that her life was worth to try that caper.

Back in her bedroom, she lifted a corner of the curtain and, craning her neck, saw that the dawn was already breaking. A few pink scratches were darkening to red across the sky; the canyon of the street stretched a greenish grey below it. Occasional trucks were already thundering past on their way northwards. It would be another scorcher, she could feel it already.

She went over to her wardrobe and from the back of it, hidden under a pile of shoes most of them now never worn, pulled out a Safeway's plastic bag. It was there that she kept her stash. A few weeks before she had read a piece in the *Mail* - or was it the *Standard*? - about doctors calling for pot to be legalized for sufferers from MS. She had shown the article to Mehmet that same evening, when he had returned from one of his mysterious errands, and he had said 'Why no give it try, Mamma?'

'The idea of it! It's illegal. And where would I get it? I can't see those specialists prescribing it for me, not if it's illegal, not on your life!'

'Mehmet find some.' He had smiled and patted her hand.

Two days later, he had triumphantly produced it for her. She had been grateful to him, of course, for the trouble and the risk, but she had also been dubious. 'Oh, I don't know if it's really such a good idea.' But he had insisted, rolling her a joint, and then showing her how to inhale it – 'No hurry, Mamma! Slow, slow, slow!' Ten minutes of the joint had been miraculous, at once allaying those terrible puppet-on-a-string spasms and gently untying the knots in her legs, arms and hands. 'When Mamma near end of this, tell Mehmet. No problem.'

From time to time, she would still ask him if he was sure that it was all right for her to smoke the stuff, and he would then laugh and tell her that almost everyone in the country at some time or other had smoked it. Young people constantly did. Now she sat down on the chair by the window, the stash on the table before here, and laboriously – 'these might be fish fingers for all the use they are to me these days', she had complained to Sylvia, holding up her hands, at their last meeting – rolled the joint. Then, no less clumsily, she lit it with the throw-away lighter that Mehmet had found on the top of a 19 bus and had given to her. She inhaled deeply, as he had shown her how to do. The bird was still singing, the sky (she had tugged the curtains fully back) was awash with a pearly light. She felt an extraordinary, wide, vacant peace within her. Again she inhaled.

Her eyes were closed and she was – as she later told Sylvia, though of course she did not mention the reefer to her – 'miles and miles away, in another world' when she heard the sound of a vehicle drawing up outside the house, of its doors opening and slamming, and then of people hurrying up the steps. A woman's voice said: 'OK, Jack. Be with you in a mo,' and a man's 'I almost forgot the file.' Then the bell rang, not once but a number of times.

She staggered to her feet and, head twisted sideways, peered out of the already open window. She could just see the three figures, two male and one female. One of the men, so young-looking that he might have been a schoolboy, and the woman, red-faced and buxom, were in police uniform; the other man, who was stooped and balding, with cavernous cheeks above a neat pepper-and-salt goatee, was in plain clothes, a file tucked under his arm. Meg knew at once what they were about.

Frantically, she stubbed out the pinched end of the reefer in an ashtray and then hurried, ashtray in hand and all but falling over more than once, into the lavatory, where she tried to flush the contents down the bowl. Oh, bugger it! Of course that ball-cock thing was stuck! She hurried back into the bedroom and threw the stash back into the cupboard. Then she stooped and, with a huge effort, buried it under some shoes. The bell to the front door went on ringing and ringing. She felt sick with terror. What would they do to her?

Mehmet, bleary-eyed and wearing only Y-fronts, appeared rubbing with a knuckle at a corner of his mouth. 'Who ring, ring, ring?' he demanded angrily.

'Police,' she whispered, though there was no possibility that they could hear her. '*Police*! They must have come about – you know . . .' She pointed to the cupboard.

'Police! What police doing here?' He was aghast.

'Well, it's obvious. What are we going to do? I couldn't get the joint to go down the toilet. That bloody ballcock!'

'*Police!*' he repeated. His face was now a greenish colour and there was panic, such as she had never seen before, in his widely-staring eyes. He hurried over to the farther window. She thought for a moment that he was going to jump through it. Then, like a trapped animal, he crossed to the other window and peered out, neck craning, as she had done. She at once joined him beside it.

'Someone has let them in!' she cried out. Later she discovered that the person who had done so was the neighbour to whom she referred as Lady Muck.

Now there was repeated ringing at the door of the flat, followed by hammering on it with a fist and shouts of 'Police! Police! Open up, please! Open the door, please.'

'What are we going to do?'

Mehmet said nothing. He was standing in the corner farthest from the bedroom door, his hands clasped in front of him and his head leaning back, eyes half closed.

'I'd better open.'

'No. No!' He opened his eyes wide now, as though waking from a nightmare.

Then she heard a harsh, loud male voice: 'If you don't open this door, we'll have to break it down.'

'All right, all right!' Meg called. 'I'm coming.' Suddenly, she did not know how, she had acquired a totally unexpected calm and strength. She went out into the hall of the flat, not in the least staggering as she had done previously on her way to the bathroom, and walked unerringly down it. She stooped, with none of the usual feeling that she was in imminent danger of toppling over, and drew back a bolt. She straightened, then once more stooped and drew back the other. Then she unlocked the door and pulled it open. 'What's all this? What's going on?'

At that moment, to her horror, she became aware that the door to the flat opposite hers was open and that the black faces of Blossom, her husband and her husband's mother, were crowded round it. Immediately after that she also became aware that a number of people were crushed together on the stairs behind her, some in dressing gowns, some merely in pyjamas or nightdresses, and the porter, Mr Bagley, in a rain-coat buttoned up to his chin, his legs bare beneath it. Conspic-uous both because of her height and because she was standing on the topmost step of all, was Lady Muck in a pale pink kimono, her hair in curlers.

'Sorry to disturb you, madam.' It was the middle-aged, bald-ing man, in plain clothes, who spoke. 'We have reason to believe that a Mr Mehmet' – he raised the piece of paper that he was holding in one hand and squinted down at it – 'Mehmet Ahmeti is living here. Is that right?'

She thought of lying but then decided that that would be no use. There were all those people, the three in the flat opposite, the others crowding the stairs, to contradict her. She nodded. 'What do you want with him?' But she knew that it could only be for supplying drugs. Would they also arrest her as a user?

'We wish to talk about something with him. Is he in resi-dence at the present?'

'I – I can't be sure. I went to bed early, and I was asleep when you started all that ringing and banging.' If Mehmet had decided to jump out of the window into the garden, she wanted to give him all the time possible to make his getaway.

'Perhaps you would be good enough to look, madam. Or we can look for ourselves, if you prefer it.'

Meg almost asked whether they had a search warrant. But she did not wish to antagonize them, and so, instead, she called, 'Mehmet! Mehmet! The police are here. They want to see you.'

Mehmet appeared, still in only his Y-fronts. His lips were pulled back oddly from his teeth, so that his upper gums were visible. 'You wish me?'

'Yes, Mr' – again the man in plain clothes looked down at the file – 'Mr Ahmeti. I am from the Home Office. Immigration. We have received information that leads us to believe that you are resident in this country illegally. I am afraid that I must ask you to accompany us to Hornsea Police Station for further questioning.'

Meg felt a momentary relief for herself – so they were not here about the pot after all. Then she was overwhelmed with dread for Mehmet.

After his previous agitation, he became suddenly calm. 'I get dressed first? You allow?' Meg thought it an odd question: they would hardly take him away in his Y-fronts.

'Of course, sir.'

The policeman followed him.

Meg turned to the policewoman. She had not in the least taken to the Home Office official, but the policewoman looked kind in a motherly sort of way.

'What's going to happen to him?'

The policewoman looked over to the man, clearly feeling that it was not for her to attempt an answer.

'We have to establish all the facts.' The man peered down at the file half open in his hand, as though to refresh his memory.

'And then he can come home?'

'That all depends.' Again the man peered at the file, stroking his beard with the hand not holding it.

Meg suddenly felt a bile-like anger rise up in her throat and explode in her mouth. 'I do think it most inconsiderate to arrive at this hour on a Sunday of all days.'

The man smiled, still stroking his beard. 'There is a reason for that. On a weekday morning, unless it's very early, so many people are at work.'

Mehmet at last appeared with the boy policeman behind him. Meg noticed that he was wearing the suit that he had bought only a few weeks ago, and with it a formal shirt and tie. The poor dear was going to get awfully hot in all those clothes, but she supposed that he wanted to make a good impression.

'Mamma, I wish you do something for me. OK?' After his early terror, he now seemed to be totally in control both of himself and of the situation.

'Yes, of course, love. What is it?'

'Please telephone this lady.' He handed her a piece of paper. 'She friend of mine, good friend. Important lady. Doctor. She have many important friends. Tell her what happen. Tell her everything. OK?'

Meg nodded, panicky and bewildered. Who was this important lady? He had never before mentioned her.

Mehmet went on: 'Tell her Mehmet needs lawyer, best lawyer. Now. Tell her send lawyer, quick, quick, to Hornsea Police Station. Understand. Hornsea Police Station. Urgent. OK?'

Again Meg nodded. Then she followed the four of them out from the flat and to the front door. The policewoman walked first, followed by Mehmet, and the two men brought up the rear. Mehmet's head was lowered and there was a raw-looking flush on the nape of his neck. Thank God all those inquisitive faces had gone. Suddenly a snatch of song, heard repeatedly on the telly, came into Meg's mind – *Neighbours, everybody needs neighbours* . . . Well, she certainly didn't need neighbours like those.

Meg so much dreaded speaking to the unknown woman – if only Sylvia were on hand to do it for her – that she first went over to the sitting-room cupboard and took out the vodka bottle. Without bothering with a glass, she tipped up the bottle and gulped at it, and then gulped again. She sighed. That was better.

She listened as the telephone rang on and on. Since it was a Sunday and still not seven o'clock, this did not surprise her. Patiently she waited. Then at last someone answered. 'Yes. Hello.' It was a woman's voice and it suggested that she had just woken up.

'Is that Dr Carter, please?'

'No, I'm afraid it isn't. If you're a patient, I'll give you the emergency number.'

'Well, it *is* an emergency. But not that kind. I mean, I'm not a patient.'

'I really don't know if at this hour . . . It's not yet eight, you know.'

'I must speak to her. I really must.'

'Well, hang on then and I'll see.'

Meg hung on, until the standing made her feel so unsteady that she carried the telephone over to a chair.

'Yes?'

This must be the important lady. Meg gripped the receiver tightly as she prepared to deal with her. 'Is that Dr Carter?'

'Yes. That's right.'

'Oh, Dr Carter, something terrible's happened! But first I'd better explain who I am. I'm the landlady, I mean Mehmet's landlady. You know who I mean?'

'His landlady? What's happened to him? What is it?' Anxiety made the voice sound harsh, even hectoring.

'The – the police took him off this morning. They arrived and just took him off.'

'But was he with you? I thought he was . . . He told me he had to spend the weekend with some cousin over here on a visit.'

'I don't know anything about that, I'm afraid. He comes and goes and I never ask any questions. But he was certainly here – in my flat – this morning. I don't know what time he got home, though – seeing that I decided to have an early bed.'

'Oh. How odd! He told me he couldn't see me because he had to be with this cousin of his over the whole weekend.' There was a brief silence. 'Anyway – why on earth did the police take him off?'

Meg proceeded to tell her. Nerves made her muddled and even, from time to time, incoherent, so that, increasingly impatient, Marilyn kept interrupting her. The interruptions made Meg even more muddled.

'So he wants me to find him a lawyer?' Marilyn said at the end.

'That's right. A first-rate lawyer, he said.'

'It'll not be easy to find any sort of lawyer before breakfast on a Sunday morning. My family solicitors are in Colchester. I really don't know who to approach. I suppose I'd better look in the *Yellow Pages*. An immigration lawyer, that's what we need.' Marilyn was thinking aloud to herself, rather than conversing with Meg.

'Will you be going there?'

'Going where?'

'To the police station.'

'Well, yes, I suppose I must. Yes, yes, I will. But first I'll have to get hold of a lawyer. I'd better ring off now. Anyway, thank you so much for getting in touch with me.'

The telephone went dead. Meg felt suddenly excluded from the drama in which Mehmet was starring, and that filled her with a sense of abandonment and dread. Should she herself go down to the police station? She hesitated, tapping with her fingers on the telephone receiver. Then she decided that she must. She began looking in the drawer below the telephone table for the card of a minicab firm that had recently been pushed through the door. When she had decided to keep it, she had thought: One never knows when that might not come in handy. It had come in handy more quickly than she had expected.

Chapter XX

The *Yellow Pages* open before her and her mobile phone in her hand, Marilyn sat sideways on her bed and began to ring number after number. She had hurried up to her bedroom to do the ringing, because she did not want Audrey to hear her. Sometimes no one answered, as some telephone in Borough High Street, the Strand or Tottenham Court Road trilled on and on, making her envisage an empty office awaiting the contract cleaners who would soon arrive to get it into order for Monday. Sometimes a recorded voice would instruct her to ring another, emergency number. When she did that, it was only to be told that the duty lawyer wished that he or she could help her but unfortunately that was out of the question, there were already far too many cases on hand that day. Finally, by then in a state of panicky desperation, she got a man, old she guessed from his voice, who said that he would get along to the police station as soon as he could.

Having foregone her usual morning bath and instead merely splashed cold water on to her face, she hurriedly dressed and then raced down the stairs to the kitchen to snatch some breakfast. She had just taken her first sip of scalding coffee, when Audrey appeared. She, too, was already dressed, but she had clearly not had time to brush or even comb her hair, which stuck up in a grotesque, iron-grey quiff.

'What was all that about?'

Marilyn felt a reluctance to respond. She sipped again at the coffee and then said: 'I have to dash out. Something's come up.' She hoped that Audrey would assume that what had come up was an emergency over a patient.

Audrey pulled back the chair opposite Marilyn's and asked: 'What's the problem?'

'The chief problem in this house is that there's no privacy.'

Audrey stared at her, pained, eyes blinking. Then she said: 'Would you like me to drive you – to wherever you have to go?'

'No, thank you. There's no need for you to turn out.' The last thing, Marilyn thought unfairly, was to have Audrey gloating over the disaster that had overtaken Mehmet.

'I'd be happy to help.'

Marilyn shook her head. 'I can get a taxi. At this hour, it won't be difficult.' She now felt guilty for her initial response.

'Don't forget it's a Sunday. Shall I ring for you, while you finish your breakfast?'

'Well, if you would do that . . . Please.'

The whole of London seemed to be spookily empty as the taxi sped northwards. 'Another scorcher,' the driver turned round to say. 'Yes, another scorcher,' Marilyn responded. She was still feeling guilty about the way in which she had spoken to Audrey.

At the police station, everyone seemed to be in a process of either coming on duty or going off it, so that Marilyn had a dizzying, dislocating sense of hurry and confusion all around her. She was asked to wait in a room with some other people, and then taken to another room and told to wait there alone. An officer came in, asked her two or three questions, and said 'I'm afraid I'll have to refer you to a colleague.' The colleague came in and said 'I'll be with you in a moment, Dr Carter,' and vanished never to return. Eventually she wandered out of the room and, having found herself back at the reception desk, asked if the lawyer had arrived. The young girl on duty told her, obviously irritated but in a controlled voice, that just as soon as Mr Hargreaves arrived of course she would be informed, and meanwhile would she please return to the waiting-room?

With an exasperated sigh, Marilyn did as she was told. Soon after, the girl receptionist ushered in a large, middle-aged woman, whose ample body was supported by two sticks. She was snorting with the effort of propelling herself forward, and her nose and forehead were glistening with sweat. She must once have been extremely pretty, Marilyn thought.

'Would you like to sit here?' Marilyn jumped up from her chair by the door.

'Oh, that's all right, love. Thank you. I can sit down over there.' With more snorting the woman staggered across the room. Then, with a sigh that was almost a groan, she lowered herself on to a long, padded bench under the window. 'It's going to be a real scorcher,' she said.

The two women sat in silence, studiously avoiding each other's gaze. Marilyn wondered what the woman was doing at the police station at such an early hour.

Then the woman spoke, in a blurred, breathy voice: 'You wouldn't happen to be Dr Carter, would you?'

'Yes. Yes, I am.'

'Well, I'm Mrs Towling. Mehmet's landlady.'

'Oh, I'd no idea!'

'I'm afraid the poor soul's in real trouble.' She put up an arm and wiped her damp forehead with the back of it. 'I was wondering if it was you. I couldn't be sure. Did you manage to get him a lawyer?'

'Yes. I hope so. But he hasn't turned up yet.'

At that moment the receptionist put her head round the door to ask Meg if she would like some tea or coffee. Meg said that some tea would be lovely. As an apparent afterthought, the girl then turned to Marilyn: 'How about you, Dr Carter?' Marilyn also asked for tea – no milk, no sugar.

Eventually, the lawyer arrived. He was a tiny man, carrying a bulging briefcase, and he seemed to know all the people at the station by their Christian names. One might have expected him to be lethargic and irritable so early in the morning, but he bustled everywhere, smiling, joking, laughing. He constantly addressed Meg and Marilyn collectively as 'ladies' and more than once assured them 'We'll get all this sorted out in a jiffy.' After a while he disappeared and the jiffy prolonged itself. A heavy, dark-skinned, ill-shaven man and a woman in a sari were shown into the room, and then an elderly, well-dressed woman in a beret, whose heavy mascara had run from what Marilyn assumed to have been crying.

At last the lawyer reappeared. 'I must just get some particulars from you, Mrs Towling. About dates and so forth.'

'I'm no good at dates,' Meg said forlornly. 'But if I can be of any help . . .'

After he had jotted down what Meg had told him of Mehmet's tenancy, she asked: 'Can't we see him?'

'No, I'm afraid not. Not until his interview is over.'

'And when will that be?' Marilyn asked.

'Who can say? Soon, I hope.'

At that he got up, said 'I'll be back with you in a jiffy, ladies,' and again vanished.

The interrogation at last over, they sat round one of the three tables in a nearby café. The other two tables, still covered with used crockery and cutlery, were unoccupied. In addition to their cups of cappuccino, there was an opened packet of petit beurre biscuits in front of Meg. She had explained 'I never had time for a bite, I was in such a rush to get to the station. Trouble of any kind always gives me an appetite.' One of her legs was stuck out ahead of her, so that the lawyer was obliged to sit sideways. But, still in the jolliest of moods, he clearly did not mind.

Everything at the immigration department was in a total state of confusion, he informed them with glee. A move to other premises was in process of taking place, a new computer system had been installed and was still not functioning, and there was a rumour – could you believe it? – that rats had been devouring files. One of his clients had been waiting in limbo for a decision for more than five years. Then he looked at his watch, jumped up, grabbed his briefcase and said that he must dash back to the station to deal with another case.

Marilyn followed him to the door and said in a low voice; 'You'll let me know what I owe you in due course, won't you? You've got my address?'

'Oh, we'll see about all that later. With luck, he should be eligible for legal aid.'

Back at the table, Meg was telling Mehmet in a crooning, consolatory voice, like a mother to a child: 'Poor love! You've really had a terrible experience. I don't envy you. Now you must just try to relax. Relax!'

Marilyn sat down. 'Well, at least you're free.'

Mehmet nodded. Then he demanded: 'Marilyn, why you get such lawyer?'

Marilyn was taken aback. 'What's wrong with him?'

'He seemed a nice chap to me,' Meg put in.

'You no understand?' He spoke angrily, as though, out of stupidity or carelessness, Marilyn had mishandled everything. 'He friendly with everyone there. He friend of police. No good.'

Hungry and exhausted, Marilyn lost her temper: 'I'm pretty sure it's because he's on such good terms with the police that they didn't lock you up. Can't you see that?'

But she realized from his sulky expression and the way in which, having glared at her for a few moments, he then swung his body away from her to gaze out through the door, left open because of the heat, that she had failed to convince him.

'Tell us exactly what happened, Mehmet,' Meg urged.

He shook his head. 'Many questions. Many stupid questions.' Then, with sudden viciousness, he demanded: 'Who tell them about me? Who say I am illegal? How they know address?'

Meg recoiled. 'Oh, love, you don't think I'd – '

He waved his hand in a dismissive gesture. 'Not you! Not you!'

Marilyn wondered whether he meant her. How could he imagine such a thing?

Then he said darkly: 'I think I know.' He frowned, brooding. Then he nodded, as though to tell himself, Yes, you're right. 'Bastard.' He nodded again. 'I kill that bastard.'

'Who are you talking about, love?'

'Never mind. Bastard!' He spat out the last word. 'I kill him!'

When they left, Marilyn insisted on giving Meg and Mehmet a lift back to the flat in the taxi that would eventually take her home. Clearly distracted, Mehmet made no attempt to help Meg, so that it was Marilyn who supported her along the uneven pavement to the car and eventually half-lifted her into it. This was not, she suddenly realized with amazement, the professional consideration, devoid of any true feeling, that she showed to patients in similar circumstances. Already she felt mysteriously and reluctantly drawn to this woman, met for the first time, with her flushed, sweaty face, her clumsy hands, dragging feet and air of indomitable sweetness and cheerfulness.

When Marilyn had helped her out of the taxi at the block of flats, Meg said: 'Would you like to come in for something – a cup of Nes or something stronger if you like?'

Marilyn refused out of an uncharacteristic mixture of shyness and awkwardness and later regretted having done so. She would liked to have seen where Mehmet had been living during all the months that she had known him. She was also eager to discover why he had never invited her there and had dismissed all her suggestions of a visit. 'Shall I help you up the steps?'

'Oh, no, dear. You're in a hurry, I'm sure. Mehmet will help me. He's always very good about helping me. Don't worry.'

As her taxi drove off, Marilyn looked back and saw Mehmet laboriously supporting Meg, one arm around her, as she heaved herself up from step to step. There was a devastating pathos about it, and for a moment she had the disconcerting illusion that the deep canyon of the street was darkening as her mood darkened. Then the taxi moved out into the glare beyond. The taxi driver turned.

'Another scorcher,' he said.

On the damp sheet, the room illuminated only by the failing evening light slanting through the window, Marilyn and Mehmet lay out on their backs, side by side but separate, gazing at the ceiling. Like two effigies on a medieval tomb, Marilyn thought – except that two effigies on a tomb would not be naked. Sweat trickled down between her breasts and, acrid to the taste, along the line of her cheek to one corner of her mouth. There was a fan but she had forgotten to switch it on, and now she felt too nerveless to get up and do so. Their love-making had been energetic but heartless, in the manner of two actors who, on a matinee at the close of a long run, shamelessly over-act in an attempt to conceal that their familiarity with the scene that they are playing has finally resulted in a total indifference to it.

Marilyn at last put the question that she had been longing to put, ever since her meeting with Meg two days before. 'Mehmet, why did you never allow me to meet Mrs Towling? She struck me as so sweet.'

He made no reply.

'Mehmet! Did she tell you you couldn't have any visitors?'

He shook his head. 'I am illegal.'

'Yes, I know. But what had that to do with it?'

He spoke up to the shadowy ceiling. 'It is better if no one knows about illegal. I never tell address. No one knows Mehmet's address. Only you. But better you not visit address.'

'Why have you never trusted me?' It was the question that she had often put to herself, exasperated and hurt by his refusal to reveal anything of importance about himself, however much she questioned him.

'Illegal trust no one.'

'But *me, me*! I'm your lover. Surely you can trust me. It was so humiliating and, yes, cruel when you told me never to telephone you, only to write.'

He said nothing. His face was expressionless. She put out a hand and took his hand in hers. She squeezed, squeezed again.

'You haven't even told me who you think reported you.'

He pulled his hand out of her grip. 'Bad man. Very bad man. He tell bad things about me. Home Office man say to me in police station, we receive information, information you are rent boy.'

'Rent boy!' Marilyn felt as if her burning, sweating body had suddenly been plunged into icy water. There was one person who repeatedly used that term when referring to him. But, however strong her hatred of him, surely Audrey would never do anything so vicious as to inform on him? Then a voice within her answered that question: 'Why not? Hatred drives people to do things one would never have imagined them to be capable of doing.'

'I am not rent boy!' He spat out the words with fury, as though it were she who had made that imputation. 'Never rent boy! Rent boy prostitute. I no prostitute. I kill that man! I kill him! I promise you! Kill!'

Terror gripped her heart. She believed that, if at that moment Mehmet's betrayer entered the room, he would be perfectly capable of leaping off the bed and strangling him – or her.

'No, no, darling! You mustn't talk like that. Don't be silly. The police have all sorts of ways of finding things out. That man probably had nothing to do with it.'

He turned to her, propping himself up on an elbow and leaning over her. There was saliva glistening at the corners of his mouth. His eyes seemed to be covered with a gauzy film. 'No, no. This man talk, I know he talk. I tell you, man from Home Office say, We have received information.'

'Information! Did he really say that?' Once again she thought: Could it have been Audrey?

He turned away from her and swung his legs off the bed. Then, naked, he was standing over her. Suddenly, despite the arid sex that they had just had, she wanted to pull him back on top of her. 'Marilyn – one thing. I must ask you. I tell you before. Please, please get me other lawyer. Good lawyer.'

'But that man *is* a good lawyer. He handled your case so well. Yesterday I spoke to him on the phone and he said that we must start to lodge an appeal against your deportation. We only have a few weeks. We must do it at once.'

'I tell you, Marilyn! Why you no understand? I no want this man. I want other lawyer. Good lawyer. This man friend of the police. I tell you, I see him, hear him.'

'All right. As you wish. I'll find someone else. But it's not necessary, I tell you, it's not necessary.'

She turned away and buried her face in the pillow.

Then suddenly, miraculously, just as she had wanted, he was on top of her. 'Marilyn, Marilyn, do what I want!' She could feel his lips on her shoulder and then a hand at her breast.

'Yes, yes, I'll do what you want.'

She knew that she would always do what he wanted.

The next morning, Marilyn rang Laurence.

There was joy in his voice when he first heard her speak. 'Marilyn! It's terrific to hear you. Why do you now never come to see me when Audrey comes? Don't tell me you've been too busy.'

'Well, yes, I have been – preoccupied. In fact, that's why I'm calling.'

'Oh. I was hoping you were calling to ask how I was. I've not been at all well. That pain in my neck, it's become much worse these last few days. I find it hard to sleep. Didn't Audrey tell you? I sometimes think she takes nothing in. Her Rwandans are one thing but her poor old Dad . . .'

'Yes, she did tell me. I meant to telephone. Oh, I'm so sorry. Poor Laurence. Why not try some physiotherapy? I know of a wonderful man. I often send patients to him privately.' As soon as she had said that, she recollected that she had made that same suggestion at their last meeting and he had then told her that he had already tried physiotherapy and that it had only made things worse.

'No good. I was in agony after it, sheer agony. So to what precisely do I owe this call?' All at once the voice had a bitter edge to it.

'Well, I really need some legal advice – about finding a solicitor. And I remembered that you had a friend at the College – Sir Thomas Something or Other – who used to be the head of some famous firm of solicitors. He was friendly to me when you introduced us and so I thought – '

'Too late, my dear.' He said it with satisfaction.

'Too late?' She thought at first that he was referring to the fact that she was ringing at almost eleven o'clock in the evening.

'He's popped his clogs. *Finito*. About ten days ago. He was found in that gazebo at the bottom of the garden. Apparently he'd been there for at least twenty-four hours and no one had missed him. Heart attack, instantaneous. He had always been lucky. He was lucky to get that knighthood, he was lucky to die like that.'

'Oh, I'm sorry.'

'He wasn't really a *friend* of mine,' he said, as though to excuse himself for the heartlessness of his narration. 'Just another person whose company it was impossible to avoid in this place. Anyway – what was it you wanted his advice about?'

Marilyn was reluctant to tell him, but it was difficult to know how to avoid doing so. 'I need a solicitor who's an expert on immigration. For a friend of mine.'

'A friend of yours? Would I be right in guessing that the friend is your Albanian?'

Marilyn realized that Audrey must have already relayed to him the news of Mehmet's arrest and of the subsequent threat of deportation. 'Yes, that's right. We need some legal advice and I don't know where to turn.'

'I wish I could help you. But, sadly – or perhaps happily – I have never been in need of that sort of advice myself. Will you be very offended if an old man, with a lot of experience of the world, himself tries to advise you?'

Marilyn laughed, but it was a laugh without amusement. 'It was the advice of a lawyer that I wanted.'

'Well, for that I do not qualify of course. But nonetheless – since I'm so fond of you – and should hate to see you hurt . . . Well, here goes. Drop it, Marilyn. Or, rather, drop him. I know that, after all that had happened to you, you needed someone of that – that kind. Of course. But from all I've heard – you've never let me meet him – I wonder if someone of that – that kind is precisely what is best for you. I'm sure it would not be hard for someone as attractive and intelligent as yourself to find – '

Marilyn cut in: 'Thank you, Laurence. But I'm not seeking advice on finding another lover. I'm merely seeking advice on how to find a lawyer. Goodbye, Laurence. Goodbye.'

Her cheeks flaming and her heart beating furiously, she put down the receiver.

The next day, by a fortunate coincidence, a long-time patient of hers, a retired judge, brought in his wife, who was in the first stages of Alzheimer's, to see her at the surgery. When on his own, he always flirted with Marilyn in a gallantly old-fashioned, harmless way. Yes, he said, he knew of someone, she had been a neighbour of theirs before moving out to Putney, who might be just the person. She specialized in immigration problems, nothing else. Tough, pretty formidable, he went on. Not the sort of person with whom he saw exactly eye to eye on many subjects, and Marilyn might well find the same. But she was certainly a bonny fighter, and if anyone could swing things in the right direction, then she could. She was called Monica Wright. She was a Swede who had first come to England when she had married an Englishman much older than herself. The marriage had soon ended but she had stayed on. He had always wondered if the marriage might not have been one of convenience.

Marilyn and Mehmet had to wait more than two weeks for an appointment with this woman. Mehmet repeatedly showed his exasperation at the delay – 'Why you get lawyer like this?' 'Why we wait?', 'Why no find other lawyer?' – until Marilyn lost her temper and told him 'Oh, shut up! Shut up! This is one of the best lawyers there is. You didn't like that old man, so that's why we've got her.' 'Why you angry?' he then asked in an aggrieved voice.

The office on the top two floors of a dilapidated Georgian house in Bloomsbury was totally unexpected. When she had spoken to Mrs Wright, Marilyn had imagined her sitting behind a vast, modern desk, a computer and two or three telephones before her and a wall-to-ceiling plateglass window behind. There would be a lift and a waiting-room with copies of *Country Life*, *The Burlington* and *Vogue* on a low, highly polished table. The reality was totally different. Having climbed up a narrow, uncarpeted, creaking staircase in semi-darkness, they reached a room marked 'Reception', in which a bosomy girl, her hair dyed a lurid orange and a diamond stud glittering in a nostril, looked up from writing in a large ledger to ask abruptly: 'Yes?' Behind her, an older woman in trousers and a man's shirt, the sleeves rolled up above the elbows, was perched, her back to them, on a stepladder, reaching for some files. A cloth donkey with only one eye sat on a beautiful period chimney piece beside postcard views and a large notice that read

THE LAW IS AN ASS
AND SO IS THE HOME OFFICE.

The girl was clearly in a hurry. Monica was not yet back from court, she told them. Would they mind waiting a little? She pointed to the landing, where there were three chairs and a square table with a pile of out-of-date newspapers on it.

'Why we wait?' Mehmet asked, as he seated himself.

'Because she's not here.'

'Why no here?'

'Because she's been held up in court.'

It was like talking to a child, she thought. But one had to make allowances. He had been in a state of nerves all day, barely eating anything and smoking cigarette after cigarette. He took out yet another cigarette now. She touched his arm and pointed to the NO SMOKING sign above him. He pulled an exasperated face, made as if to push the cigarette back into its packet and then jumped to his feet. 'I go to street. Call me if she come.'

'Oh, Mehmet, do wait,' she shouted after him. But it was useless.

A young man, smelling strongly of garlic, eventually sat down beside her. He leaned forward in his chair, hands clasped, with a tense, moody expression on his face. Then he pulled some amber worry beads out of a pocket and began to play with them. Marilyn guessed him to be Turkish. From time to time he whistled tonelessly or, ceasing to click the beads, bit savagely at a thumbnail.

Mehmet eventually returned. He and the man stared at each other but said nothing. Mehmet tapped his foot rhythmically against one leg of the table. The sound maddened Marilyn and with difficulty she restrained herself from telling him to stop. He picked up a copy of the *Guardian*, days old, glanced at it, and then threw it down in disgust. The man reached for it, glanced at it, and then also threw it down. 'Where this person?' Mehmet asked. Marilyn made no answer.

Finally there was the sound of someone running up the stairs, and a plain, middle-aged woman in large glasses, a brief-case in her hand, appeared, breathless, on the landing. Paying no attention to the three people sitting there, she continued her rapid ascent, feet clattering in their low-heeled brogues, to the floor above.

At long last, Marilyn and Mehmet were seated opposite to her. The window, with its view over chimney-tops, was unaccountably shut, and so, despite the playing of a fan, its whirr from time to time interrupted by a grinding noise, the attic room was uncomfortably stuffy.

'Now let's see.' Mrs Wright's accent gave no indication of her Scandinavian origins. She pulled a notepad towards her. 'Do call me Monica by the way.' That was something that Marilyn was never able to bring herself to do. 'Now you're' – she pulled a large, red appointments book towards her – 'Mr – Mr Mehmet

Ahmeti, aren't you?' She looked up at him and he nodded. 'And you're Dr Carter.' She smiled at them both for the first time, but the smile was businesslike, lacking in any warmth. 'I have the copy of your original interrogation at the police station from Mr Hargreaves. I looked at it hurriedly while on my way to the court. If I may ask – why did you decide not to continue with him?'

'We wish best lawyer,' Mehmet said.

'Well, that's certainly flattering to me,' she responded dryly. 'But Mr Hargreaves is a first-class lawyer. He knows all the tricks in the business. I learned a lot of them from him. Anyway . . .' She opened an envelope, took out several sheets of paper stapled to each other, and began to turn them over.

'You are Albanian?'

'That's right. My family live in Kosovo.'

'But you entered this country on a false passport.' Mehmet said nothing, merely staring at her. 'Yes?'

When Mehmet was still silent, Marilyn said: 'He bought a passport off a Moroccan in Paris. A French passport. The Moroccan had French nationality.'

'I think it might be better if you allowed my client to answer the questions for himself.'

'Sorry.'

The questioning continued, with Marilyn taking no part and Mehmet answering more and more sulkily.

Then Mrs Wright said: 'Right! I seem to have most of the background details now. The next thing is to see what grounds we have for asking for residence and work permits. You're not married of course?'

'No. We're not married.' Forgetting the earlier reproof, it was Marilyn who answered.

'But you're partners?'

'We are lovers. We've been lovers for, oh, five, six months.'

'Living together?'

'He stays with me over the weekends. Saturday and often Sunday night. Sometimes during the week he also stays overnight.'

'So it's not really a full-time living together?' Neither of them answered. 'Am I right?'

Marilyn felt that she had to excuse herself, not merely to the lawyer but yet again to Mehmet. 'My work keeps me so busy. I felt that I – didn't have time to see him through the week. Too distracting. And I share the house, it's only half mine. With my sister-in-law.'

'Well, I'm afraid . . . in that case . . . I don't really think there's any point in going up that avenue.' She turned to Mehmet. 'I presume that you left Kosovo in the first place because of the political situation?'

He considered for a moment, then nodded vigorously. 'Yes, yes! Political situation very bad. Serbs, Albanians, Muslim fundamentalists. All make trouble, big trouble.'

'Were you ever threatened with violence?'

Again he considered for a moment. 'Many time. Many, many time. Family also threatened.'

At the end, Mrs Wright had already begun to tidy up the papers before her as, without looking up, she told them: 'Well, I'm not entirely hopeful. I'm sorry. We must see. The problem is that Kosovo is no longer considered all that unsafe, not now . . . If you were married – or even if the pair of you had been merely cohabiting . . . But' – she shrugged – 'there it is. We must do the best we can with the tools available to us. Our best course is to ask for political asylum, though as I say, with the change in the situation in Kosovo . . .'

Out in the street, Mehmet at once turned on Marilyn. 'If you marry me – no problem!'

Once again she felt guilt raking savagely through her. Taking his arm, she said: 'Yes, I know. I'm sorry. I can't tell you how sorry I am. But there it is. It's too late now. You heard her say that. If I were to marry you now, it would make no difference. They would see it as a marriage of convenience.'

'I ask you, ask you many time. You say, you love me, always say, love me, love me. But you no wish marry me.'

'Oh, please, Mehmet! Don't go on about it. Let's forget it!'

'How I forget such a thing!'

As they waited, month after month, for the decision from the Home Office Marilyn would often think to herself, in a paraphrase of Dickens, a favourite of hers, *It's the worst of times, it's the best of times.*

The worst of the worst of times were those occasions when, often without any prior warning, his anxiety and frustration ignited to produce an electrical storm, which then indiscriminately devastated everything around them, herself at the centre. Typical was the incident when they were waiting for a bus after the Royal Tournament. She had not enjoyed the performance; but, because he so clearly had done so, leaning forward in his seat, an expression of eager attention and sometimes even wonder on his face, she had felt not in the least restless or bored, as she would have done with anyone else. Trailing slowly out of the exhibition centre, the crowds thick around them, she had linked her arm in his. 'That was lovely,' she had said. What had been lovely had been to watch his pleasure.

The bus was long in coming.

'We're going to have a fight to get on.'

'Why no take taxi?' It was a question which Mehmet, who did not pay for the taxis, often asked. Ed used to laugh at her for her parsimony over taxis. Mehmet got angry over it.

She gave her usual answer: 'Why waste money? We're not in a hurry.'

Suddenly his face darkened. 'People say efficient country. No efficient! Terrible!'

At that she knew already that a storm was imminent. Perhaps, if she managed some diversion, it might still pass over their heads? 'I thought those dogs terrific. The best thing really.'

'Everything inefficient here. Wait, wait, wait. We wait for bus. I wait for my suit, sent to cleaner, two, three days ago, still not ready. We wait for bloody Home Office.' His voice was growing in volume. At any moment people would start to stare at them, as she knew only too well from previous such experiences, in shops, in restaurants or on public transport. If only that bus would come!

'You no hear from lawyer woman?'

'You know I haven't. Of course I'd have told you if I had.'

'Why no ring her?'

'There'd be no point,' she told him wearily, as she had told him so often before when he had put the same question. 'The last time I rang to ask for news, she told me it was useless to do so. She couldn't hurry things along, there was this huge backlog of cases, and we just had to be patient.'

'Patient!' It was something that he was incapable of being.

'Yes, patient. Though I know that's difficult.'

'Why you get me that lawyer?'

'That patient of mine – that retired judge – told me she was one of the best. Later I heard the same from someone I met who works for the Citizens' Advice Bureau.'

'Why you get woman?'

'What's wrong with a woman?'

He pulled a contemptuous face. All that he had so far said she had heard repeatedly before; but now he started on something new. 'This judge – patient of yours. Why you no ask him to speak to someone?'

'How do you mean?'

'Sure he know someone in Home Office. Or maybe minister in government. Why you no speak to him?'

'Well, firstly, he's not a friend, only a patient, as I've told you.' She tried to control her exasperation. 'And secondly – and more importantly – that's not how things work in England. They may work like that in Albania but not in England. If one tries to pull strings, one only hangs oneself.'

'You always think Albania bad, England good.'

She wanted to ask 'If Albania is not bad and England not good, why are you asking for political asylum?' But she remained silent.

A moment later the crowd surged forward as the bus appeared at the bottom of the road. Somehow, Marilyn and Mehmet were carried along in its slipstream and were sucked on board.

'You racist,' he muttered, pressed up against her, his face close to hers. Then in a louder voice, he went on 'That why you no marry me. You think Muslim man no good husband. That why I no can live in house, come only one night, two night.'

The embarrassment of it was excruciating. The people packed all around them could not possibly fail to hear. 'Let's talk about this later.' But to tell him that was as useless as to look up at the sky and say to a storm: 'Why don't you move on?'

His accusations continued, fiercer and fiercer and louder and louder, until the bus had reached their destination and they had struggled off it. Then, suddenly relaxed and smiling, he linked his arm in hers and asked: 'You know what I wish now?'

'No.' Her voice was stony. 'A drink?'

He shook his head.

'Something to eat?'

Again he shook his head. Then he whispered in her ear.

'Oh, but Mehmet, it's so late. And I've to get to the surgery so early tomorrow.'

'Please!'

After each of these devastating storms, there was always this iridescent rainbow.

His obsession with 'that bastard' never abated. Some of the worst of the worst times centred on him. More than once she would be roused by Mehmet's voice, late at night, on the extension telephone in the room next to hers. On the first occasion, she listened intently and heard 'You shit! Shit! Shit!' Then he must have put the receiver down, since silence followed. On the second occasion, similarly woken, she jumped out of bed and ran into the room. But already the call had ended. 'What are you doing? Who are you telephoning at this hour?' 'My business.' 'Were you telephoning that man?' 'My business.' He turned away from her and clambered back into his bed. On the third occasion, she heard his 'Bastard! Bastard!' as she entered the room. 'Will you stop doing that! If you must do it, do it somewhere else. He can have the call traced to this house. That's the last thing I need.' He glared at her. 'You think only of self.' 'Well, I have to. You don't think of me.'

Infuriatingly, in answer to Marilyn's increasingly exasperated probings, he would refuse ever to divulge anything whatever about the 'bastard'. It was, she often thought, like clawing at a locked metal box. Where did he live? How had Mehmet met him? What was his profession? Why should he have wanted to harm Mehmet? To all such questions Mehmet would either say nothing, merely shrugging his shoulders, or he would respond irritably: 'Please. No talk! I no wish talk about that bastard.'

Had it really been this man who had denounced Mehmet? Or could it – as she constantly suspected, only to repudiate the idea – have been Audrey? Audrey might well have thought that she was taking steps to get rid of Mehmet, not because of her hatred of him, but for Marilyn's good. She was, after all, a person who was dedicated to the good of others, and such people could be dangerous.

Audrey was now even more careful that she and Mehmet should never run into each other. Once, when Marilyn had been delayed at the surgery and Mehmet had arrived, punctual as always, on a weekday visit, his repeated ringing of the bell had failed to be answered. Audrey was in her front room in the basement, filing her nails. She knew who it was. But she went on with her filing.

At the weekends she totally disappeared from sight. For each meal, she would scrupulously lay a single setting at the kitchen table. The setting was for Marilyn, not for the interloper.

But if the worst of the worst times often occurred, so, even more often, did the best of the best of them. When Marilyn told Vicky that Mehmet was 'the most wonderful companion when the mood is right,' it was the truth. He could be surprisingly funny, despite his faltering English; he could be tenderly helpful, as on the occasion when, during Audrey's absence on a trip to Paris with Laurence, he had nursed her through a virulent bout of flu; and, of course, he was, as she also confided to Vicky, a terrific lover – 'the best I've ever had.'

Over the weeks and then months of waiting for the Home Office decision, Marilyn began to introduce him to her friends. They not merely accepted him, they clearly liked him. With a trace of patronage but also with affection, some of these friends would tell her, 'He fits in so well.' Some of the women among them would also tell her: 'Oh I do envy you. I wish I had a lover like that.'

But for how long would she have this lover? His anxiety began to infect her, so that it was with increasing difficulty that she restrained herself from ringing up the lawyer yet again with the futile question 'Have you heard anything?' She was, she thought, like a patient who waits to hear whether a leg must be amputated or not. But the patient hears soon enough. For her, the wait had now extended for more than seven months.

Eventually the news arrived, with the arrival of spring. The news had been long delayed; the spring was abruptly premature.

Marilyn was in her consulting room, between patients, when her telephone rang. It was Carmen to tell her that a Mrs Wright was on the line – not a patient, she added, she would not say what she wanted. In her imagination Marilyn had so often prepared for this moment. By now she had convinced herself that, with the support not merely of the statement that she herself had provided but also of the letters in which three experts, one Albanian and two English, set out the still grim political situation in that corner of Europe, Mehmet would be granted his asylum. But now, even as she waited for Carmen to transfer the call, she realized her folly. The decision had gone against him.

'I must tell you that it's not the verdict I expected. His case seemed so strong – particularly after those recent killings. What can I say? But there's the possibility of an appeal, if you'd like to go on with it.'

'Oh, yes, of course. Yes!'

'We can't get legal aid for an appeal. And we'd have to have a barrister. That could all be pretty costly. What do you feel about that?'

'Oh, please, go ahead, whatever it costs.'

Mehmet accepted the news with a quiet fatalism, instead of with the despair and recrimination that Marilyn had dreaded. When Marilyn told him 'The fight's not over, we still have the appeal,' he gave her a melancholy smile and shook his head. He seemed already to be convinced of the uselessness of proceeding any further. She wanted to shout at him: 'What's the matter with you? Are you just going to give in?' He had fought so tenaciously in the past; now all the fight in him had drained away.

In the court he was apathetic, sitting, head bowed, hands clasped and face expressionless, as the two barristers droned away. When questioned, he was not merely halting, vague and often self-contradictory but, even more disastrous, he gave the impression of not really caring what the outcome might be. The verdict again went against him. He had ten days to leave

the country. Marilyn now had a large overdraft, incurred for
nothing.

During those ten days, there were no recriminations, as
so often in the past. He was always calm, sometimes even
cheerful.

'What will you do?' Marilyn repeatedly put the question. To
it, there was a silent, desperate corollary: 'What will I do?' She
could not bear to think of life stretching ahead, arid and joyless,
without him. His departure, she thought, would be as devastating as Ed's death, and it would leave her with the same
gnawing guilt.

Mehmet would shrug in answer to her question and tell her
that he would manage, he could always manage, he would find
some way of coming back. Was he thinking of another false
passport and another period as an illegal? She longed for that
and yet saw the folly of it. From time to time, she would assure
him that, just as soon as it was feasible, she would make a visit
to wherever he was.

On their last night together, they had dinner alone at a
Tunisian restaurant, his favourite, beyond Shepherd's Bush,
and then, since his departure was so early the following morning, at once went to bed. She wanted to make love but, when
she put her arms around him and her head on his chest, he
merely lay there stroking her hair slowly and rhythmically, as
one might a dog's or a cat's.

'How do I get in touch with you?' She had asked the question
before and had received no satisfactory answer.

'I tell you – tell you many times. I will telephone. I arrive, I
telephone.'

She felt weighed down with the dread of losing him forever.
'But can't you give me some contact number?'

He shook his head.

'Or an address.'

'I tell you – I have no address. When I arrive, I find address,
then I telephone.'

'But your family . . .' He did not answer. 'Surely you'll go to
see your family?'

'Maybe.'

'Then I could send a letter care of them.'

'No. Maybe letter get lost.'

She gave up.

'As soon as you're settled I want to travel out to see you. Wherever it is, however dangerous, however much it costs,.'

'We see.'

'No, no, we don't see. I've made up my mind. That's certain.'

Again, he made no answer.

Eventually, with a sigh, he got slowly off the bed and stooped to kiss her, not on the mouth but on the forehead. She put out her arms to draw him down towards her but he jerked away. Then he stared down at her and she saw, with a mixture of sadness and joy, that his mouth was oddly contorted – she had seen patients look like that in the aftermath of a stroke – and that there was a tear glittering in one corner of his eye. The tear looked like a fragment of glass embedded there. 'Oh, Mehmet! Spend the night with me. Sleep with me this last time!'

He shook his head. 'I snore.'

'Oh, that doesn't matter. Don't be silly! If I don't sleep, I don't sleep. Let's be together this last night. Let's!'

He raised a hand in silent valediction. Then he slipped out of the room.

For two days after Mehmet's departure, Marilyn had hardly eaten anything. Her mouth felt dry and tasted unpleasantly bitter, as though a residue of the experiences of the past days still lingered there. Mechanically she smiled, mechanically she palpated or sounded her patients, mechanically she added this or that to their records on the computer and wrote out prescriptions for them.

On the second day, as she hurried out of the surgery, Carmen ran out after her into the street. It was raining and Marilyn had put up her umbrella. Carmen was only in a flowered cotton dress and sandals.

'Dr Carter! Dr Carter! You OK?' Breathless, Carmen caught up with her. The dress was sticking to her shoulders and her thighs.

'You're getting drenched!' Marilyn cried out. 'Come under my umbrella.'

Carmen made no attempt to do that. 'You OK?' she repeated.

'Yes, thank you, I'm fine. Fine.'

'I wonder. I think – maybe . . . You seem – something wrong . . . You are sure?'

'Yes, of course I'm sure! I'm just tired, that's all. Sick of seeing patients,' she added.

'Fine.' Carmen said it with her head tilted to one side, and after that she pulled a little face. She did not believe Marilyn, she felt rebuffed.

'Thank you, Carmen!' Marilyn called out after her as she hurried, at a near run, back to the surgery.

Carmen did not look back but Marilyn knew that she had heard her.

Marilyn's first question on being greeted by Audrey was, as always, 'Any calls?' During the past two days she had never once asked 'Any call from Mehmet?' or even 'Any call from the rent boy?', but Audrey knew that that was what she meant.

Audrey shook her head. 'Only one from Father. He seemed to be worried about you. He asked how you were bearing up. He said that, if you wanted a change, then perhaps you'd allow him to treat you to a weekend break.'

Marilyn shook her head. 'That's kind of him. But I'm far too busy at the surgery.'

'Surely not at the weekend.' Having said that, Audrey flushed, aware of her tactlessness. Marilyn's weekends had always been Mehmet's. Now they belonged to no one but herself.

Having sat down to Audrey's moussaka – Audrey had prepared it, knowing that it was a favourite of hers – Marilyn took two mouthfuls and then pushed it aside. 'I'm sorry. I have no appetite. I don't know what's the matter with me.' But she knew only too well.

Audrey stared at her. Then she said: 'It may be difficult to telephone from Kosovo. From all reports, things are still bad there.'

Marilyn ignored the remark. She sipped from the full glass of vodka before her, then tipped it up and drank almost a quarter. Audrey let out a little gasp. 'Don't look at me like that,' Marilyn suddenly rapped out.

Audrey jumped to her feet, her napkin slithering off her to the ground. She stared at Marilyn, despite the prohibition. Her face expressed all the anguish that Marilyn herself felt but could not express. Then she hurried round the table. She rested one hand on Marilyn's shoulder and with the other, greatly daring, eventually touched her hair. 'Poor Marilyn!' It was what she used to say, touching her hair exactly like this, in the terrible aftermath of Ed's and Carol's deaths. 'I'm sorry.' Then she lowered her head, put her cheek against Marilyn's and burst into tears. 'I'm sorry, sorry. Will you ever forgive me?'

Marilyn jerked away from her. Then, stonily, her eyes fixed on the middle distance, she produced a single, devastating monosyllable: 'No.'

Chapter XXI

On the first occasion that Adrian put out his hand in the darkness, groped for the telephone receiver on the bedside table, knocking over a glass of water as he did so, and then heard that rasping 'Bastard! Bastard!', it was as though he had been punched in the face.

'What do you want? What the hell is this?' He was shamefully conscious of the tremor in his voice.

'You bastard!'

There was a click and silence. He replaced the receiver and at once became conscious of the drip-drip-drip of the spilled water off the table on to the floor. Oh, hell! He groped again, this time for the bedside lamp, and switched it on. Then he pulled a handkerchief out from under the pillows and began to mop ineffectually at the table top. His heart was thudding and he felt a constriction, as of an elastic band, around his forehead.

He lay back and stared up at the ceiling. In the past weeks he had often thought of Mehmet, wishing that he had not precipitated that last scene between them, that those brutal words had never been delivered, and that things were again as they once had once been. But now that this contact had been made, the situation had clearly become even more hopeless than before.

He got out of bed and padded down the corridor to the sitting-room. It was there that he kept what he called 'my little machine', to record the numbers of incoming telephone calls. But on this occasion, all that it had recorded was 'Number Withheld.' He returned to his bed and, though the night was muggy, pulled the blanket up under his chin. He began to shiver uncontrollably and gritted his teeth in order to stop himself from doing so.

The calls continued, sometimes in the daytime but more often in the early hours. Usually they consisted merely of that reiterated 'Bastard! Bastard! Bastard!', but sometimes other things, no less insulting were shouted down the line – 'Fucking queen!', 'You bad shit!', 'Stupid cunt!'. Appalled, terrified, he would nonetheless continue to listen to the end. 'Why don't you put the phone down at once?' Igor asked repeatedly. Igor also told him that he ought to report the calls; the telephone people would soon put a stop to them and, if they couldn't, they could always change the number. Adrian replied that, oh, no, he couldn't do that, he didn't want the scandal. 'But it'll all be confidential,' Igor protested. What Igor did not realize was that, in his heart of hearts, Adrian did not want the calls to end. They were the only contact that he had with Mehmet, and that contact, however alarming and disgusting, was better than none.

Frustrated by the way in which Mehmet, merely shouting abuse and then banging down the receiver, paid no attention whatever to what he himself said in extenuation or protest, Adrian rang back three times, using the number that he had once, with so much difficulty, extracted. The first of these calls, after two o'clock in the morning, was answered by a sleepy woman's voice, in which there was a tremor of incipient alarm. 'Yes, yes. Who is it?'

'Is Mehmet there?'

'Mehmet?'

'Mehmet Ahmeti.' Had he got the wrong number? Mehmet always spoke of a landlord, not a landlady.

'No, no, love. He's away. He usually goes away at the weekends. He's at his cousin's but I'm afraid I've no idea where his cousin lives. Do you want to leave a message for him?' But by then Adrian was ringing off.

On the second occasion, not long after ten, the woman summoned Mehmet.

'Yes. Who there?' The tone was fierce.

'Oh, look, Mehmet, can't we just meet to talk things over? I'd so much like to see you. I'm terribly sorry for –'

'Fuck off!'

On the third and last occasion, one afternoon, the woman said 'Wait a mo,' and a long silence followed. Eventually, in frustration, Adrian shouted down the line: 'Hello! Hello! *Hello!*' Again he waited.

Then at long last the woman spoke. 'I thought he was in his room but he doesn't seem to be there. He must have gone out.'

Adrian did not believe her. Unless she lived in a mansion, it would not have taken her so long to discover whether Mehmet were in or out. Probably she had been arguing with him, in an effort to persuade him to take the call.

From time to time, Adrian would drop in at the Elephants' Graveyard, since that was where he and Mehmet had first met. He rarely bought a drink but instead walked rapidly from one end of the upper room to the other, turning his head from side to side. He would then do the same in the basement one. 'Hello, Adrian' some friend or acquaintance would greet him, or 'Hi, there!', some rent boy whose services he had used in the past; and he would then give a perfunctory acknowledgement, often no more than a nod or a brief smile, and hurry on.

There was an elderly Irish barman who, despite his lugubrious looks, had always been friendly, on one occasion even coquettish, to him. Finding the bar almost empty on a Monday afternoon – Adrian had looked in after a business meeting in Park Lane – he ordered a double brandy and then leaned across the counter to ask: 'Have you ever come across an Albanian called Mehmet here?'

The barman thought for a while, his tattooed arms folded, and then said: 'A lot of foreigners come here. It's not often I get to learn their names. Is he a regular?'

'I think so. I don't know.'

'What's he look like?'

Adrian attempted to describe him. He wanted to say 'He's probably the most handsome man to have ever come into this place,' but instead he told the barman that he was good-looking, dark, tall, well-built, pale skin, black hair, in his late twenties. As he produced each adjective, he realized that to the barman he must seem an absolute idiot.

'Sorry. I don't think I can be of any help. Has he stood you up then?'

Adrian gave a twitchy smile. 'In a sense – yes.'

Eventually the calls ceased. At first, as night succeeded night without one, Adrian felt relief. But then he found himself lying awake, waiting for the telephone to emit that trill which seemed to pierce through the bedclothes and then through his body.

Finally, many weeks later, the call came.

'Adrian?'

'Yes?'

'Me. Mehmet.' As if he didn't know. 'I sorry. Sorry about past. Sorry about calls. Sorry I make big trouble for you. I don't know – I crazy. You are best friend I have in England and I quarrel with you. Crazy! Crazy! I think of you often, Adrian. We have so much good time together – flat, country, parties, cinema, theatre, restaurant. I think I am crazy. Sorry, Adrian, sorry.'

First relief and then joy fizzed through Adrian.

'Oh, don't keep apologizing. I was also to blame. I said – and did – unforgivable things. I didn't realize how important you were to me. Irreplaceable. I've been so unhappy about everything that happened – and about not seeing you.' Over and over he had rehearsed this declaration while thinking of Mehmet in the most improbable places – at board meetings, during a performance of *La Bohème*, at the dentist, at Trumper. He had never thought that he would have a chance actually to say it.

'You not still angry with me?'

'No, of course not. No. I just want to see you.'

'Difficult.'

'Why difficult?'

'You know.' He laughed, indulgently it seemed to Adrian, certainly with no derision. 'But no mind. We forget past. Begin again. Yes? Friends, not enemy.'

'Oh, yes, yes! Why should there be any difficulty? I can meet you any time, any time you wish.'

'You come all way to Egypt?'

'You're in Egypt?' Adrian was astounded.

'Sure. I call from Egypt. Luxor.'

'Oh, I hadn't realized . . .'

'Oh, Adrian, why you pretend?' The tone of his voice had become suddenly acrid. Then, with the former sweetness, he continued: 'Never mind. All in past. Home Office make long, long delay. Then – very quick. Never mind. Never mind! Adrian, I want see you. Why you no come holiday in Luxor? I show you Luxor. Beautiful. Many tombs. You know Luxor?'

'I've never been there, no. I once went to Cairo on business. And once to Alexandria.' Adrian was thinking. It was crazy, he could not once again go through all that he had gone through with Mehmet. But Christ, even if it was the last thing he did, he must once again see him and have sex with him. He hesitated. 'I'd love to see Luxor – perhaps even take a Nile cruise. We could take it together. You could be my guide and interpreter. As a matter of fact, I was going to send one of my people out to Cairo in a month or two. But I could go myself instead. Yes, I could do that. Why not? Business with pleasure.'

'When you come?'

Oh, he sounded so eager! Adrian, alone in the bedroom, the receiver to his ear, smiled beatifically. 'As soon as I can make all the arrangements. How do I get in touch with you?'

'Better I call you. Now I live with friend but tomorrow, next day must move. I call you. This time, this day, next week. Yes?'

Reluctantly, eager to hasten this whole process of re-entering what he now saw as a paradise lost, Adrian said: 'All right then. Ring me in seven days. At this time, here, not at the cottage. I'll have made all the arrangements by then. I hope.'

'Good.'

'Oh, Mehmet, I feel so happy. Why did we have that hideous quarrel? It was so bloody stupid of us.'

But Mehmet was already saying: 'Goodbye, Adrian. I ring next week. OK?'

Then the phone went dead.

It was much later that Adrian asked himself why Mehmet should be in Luxor of all places. Then he remembered: *Now I live with friend* ... Who was this friend? Harry! It must be Harry! That nasty little Egyptian queen, with the bad breath ... He was overcome with disgust and jealousy.

Why did arrangements with Mehmet always have to be so complicated? He refused to come out to the airport to meet Adrian, he refused to meet him at the Winter Palace Hotel, where Mike, his travel agent friend, had booked him a room for five days. Instead he told Adrian to meet him at eight o'clock in the morning in the car park of the Hilton Hotel. He would come there in a car that he had managed to borrow.

'Couldn't you come to the Winter Palace?'

'No. Better Hilton.'

'I'd so much like to have dinner with you after my arrival.'

'No. Better you sleep early. Then ready for sightseeing. We start early because later very hot. Hilton car park. Eight. OK?'

'But why the Hilton?'

There was no answer, only again that 'OK?'

'OK.' It was useless to argue.

Although exhausted from two days of business discussions and lavish hospitality in Cairo, Adrian hardly slept that night of his arrival in Luxor. But as he lay awake, the air-conditioning humming in his ears, he felt none of the customary anxiety or frustration of insomnia. For once anticipation was not merely without any restlessness but was even pleasurable.

It was only a few minutes after five when he left his bed. I feel terrific, he thought. He hummed to himself as he shaved with the utmost care. Then he had a long soak in a foam bath, courtesy of the hotel, got into his freshly laundered open-necked shirt and his beige, raw silk suit, and surveyed himself in the full-length mirror in the bathroom. Even Savile Row tailoring could not disguise how hippy and paunchy he was getting; but in general he was pleased with himself. He went down to breakfast, which, amazingly, because of the parties of tourists setting off for the other side of the Nile before the day heated up, was served from six o'clock.

The taxi drive from the one hotel to the other was unexpectedly speedy, through streets almost wholly devoid of traffic. In consequence, he had twenty minutes to spare before the rendezvous. He wandered through the garden of the Hilton – an elderly, emaciated gardener, raking a lawn, looked up and said 'Good morning, sir' as he passed him – and down to the river. A boat was moored at a jetty and three men, two old and one young, were between them carrying a huge, rusty cooking range on to it. The young man was stripped to the waist. The brown skin seemed to glow with the morning light reflected off the milky, sluggish water. After the three of them had deposited the range and were returning for their next load, the man looked at Adrian, seated on a bench, and gave him a smile of what could only have been encouragement. At any other time, Adrian would have wondered how to carry this casual encounter to fruition. But now he was totally uninterested, and so, without even a smile, he turned his head away. He looked at his watch. There were only twelve more minutes to wait but, unable to do so in patience here on the bench, with the heavily-scented garden behind him and the wide, passive river before him, he jumped up and returned to the car park.

At its far end there was a small, dilapidated Fiat and seated at its wheel a man in dark glasses, with a beard and a straw hat pulled down low over his forehead. Was it . . .? Adrian approached, trying to appear insouciant in case the man was not Mehmet. Then the man turned, faced him, and smiled.

'Mehmet!' Adrian cried it out in joy. He held out both his hands.

Mehmet clambered out of the car. He was wearing a short-sleeved, white shirt, khaki shorts and the Reebok trainers that Adrian had bought him when they had gone on a visit to Bath. He smiled. Then he walked forward, took Adrian's hands, and leaned forward to kiss him first on one cheek and then on the other. His lips felt oddly cold on a morning already so warm; but that only added to Adrian's excitement. 'Oh, it's wonderful, wonderful, to see you!' He looked down at Mehmet's muscular, hairy legs, spellbound. Then he looked up again. 'But why the beard?'

'You no like?'

'I don't know. I'm not sure. I'll have to get used to it. It makes you look older. Beards are really only for men with receding chins. Oh, you look terrific. I can see that Egypt agrees with you.'

Mehmet opened the door of the car. He bowed, in mock deference. 'Please.'

Adrian hesitated. He had to ask the question: 'Whose car is this?'

'Friend's.'

'Yes, but what friend's.'

'Friend's. Just friend's.' Mehmet smiled, head on one side.

Adrian gave up. He knew that he would never get the confirmation that the friend was Harry.

'Where are we going?'

'Across river. To see tombs. Everyone come Luxor to see tombs.'

'Of course!' Adrian felt a huge excitement and joy. Forgetting Harry, he clambered into the car and Mehmet then walked round it and got in beside him. The two men looked at each other and smiled. Then Mehmet leaned forward and turned on the ignition.

'What a beautiful day!' Adrian said.

Mehmet nodded. 'All days in Luxor beautiful.'

Adrian was happy with the silence that followed. He felt wholly relaxed and at peace, with no feeling that he should be making conversation. He gazed out of the window beside him at the paddy fields, at the men thrashing overburdened donkeys to get them to move faster, at the women striding out erect under huge loads, at the children with matted hair and bare feet. 'So this is your new home,' he eventually said.

Mehmet said nothing.

'Are you working?'

Mehmet merely shrugged, staring at the potholed road ahead of them.

Eventually they had crossed the river and were following behind a number of tourist buses, their fumes thick and acrid. Adrian fastidiously took a clean handkerchief out from the breast pocket of his jacket and held it to his nose. 'No Clean Air Act here, I can see.' He always spoke to Mehmet as though to someone whose first language was English. 'I hope I'm not going to have an asthma attack.' But then he reminded himself that he was too happy to suffer one. It was only when he was anxious or miserable that he did.

The buses stopped but Mehmet drove on. 'Where are they all going?' Adrian asked, as he peered back at a party of Japanese in sun hats.

'Tombs of Kings. We come back. Now too many people. I show you other tomb. No people. Found one, two year ago. Beautiful. I show you.'

They were driving up into the blue-grey hills. The engine gave a premonitory cough, followed by another, louder one, and for a moment Adrian thought that they were about to have a breakdown; but then it picked up again, its chugging rhythm resumed. He looked down at Mehmet's bare thigh. He had a tremendous craving to touch it, just to touch it, but Mehmet hated any physical contact other than when they exchanged those two formal kisses at first meeting or parting, or when they were having their brief, brutal sex. Adrian could no longer resist. He put his hand down on the thigh, first tentatively, then firmly. He began to move it upwards, feeling himself suddenly harden in his trousers. There was no responding hardening when, at long last, inch by inch, his hand reached its destination. But, amazingly, Mehmet suffered it to stay there, as never in the past.

The car chugged up a side road and, where there was a dark, gaping wound in the hillside on the right, it came to a halt. 'Tomb,' Mehmet said. He pointed. Then he began to get out of the car and Adrian did likewise. He wondered, embarrassed, if Mehmet would notice his erection.

It was a steep climb up to the black rent in the hillside and the sun was now blazing down. Adrian grew breathless, he could feel the sweat under his arms, along his backbone and on his forehead. Suddenly he noticed that Mehmet was carrying a plastic bag and, as the bag swung round from his hand, that the bag was a Harvey Nichols one. Fancy carrying a plastic bag from Harvey Nicks on a hillside in Luxor! He must have brought it from England. There was something touching about that.

He paused to gasp for breath. Yes, despite his happiness, those fumes had brought on his asthma. He pointed: 'What have you got in there?'

'Water. Torch. Camera. We take photograph in tomb with flash.'

They trudged on. Then the entrance to the tomb gaped before them and Mehmet, again with that ironic bow, signalled to Adrian to go in first.

It was wonderfully cool. It was also, to eyes used to the sunshine outside, impenetrably dark.

'I can't see anything. Are there some steps? I don't want to fall.'

'Wait a moment. I get torch.'

Adrian turned. Mehmet was stooping, a hand extended to reach into the bag at his feet. Then he straightened up.

Against the brilliant light outside, his body was only a black silhouette. Adrian moved towards him. What would be more wonderful than to have sex with him here, now, in this ancient hole in the hillside far away from Luxor and London?

'Oh, Mehmet!'

Something flashed high above the black silhouette, glittering and blinding, like a flash of lightning.

It was the final *coup de foudre*.

Chapter XXII

Laurence sat at his desk, elbows on it and chin cupped in palms. He shivered. It was getting chilly in the mornings, it was time that they put on that central heating. Ruminatively, eyes watering, he stared out into the garden, where the autumn leaves glinted like shards of rusty metal through a slowly dissipating mist. Oh, blast that girl! Suddenly he saw that, in jeans, an overlarge shapeless sweater and wellington boots, one of the gardeners was on a ladder hacking away at a branch of a camellia. He lumbered to his feet, preparatory to rushing out to shout to her to stop. But then he thought, Oh, what the hell, and slumped back into the chair.

He stretched out an arm and drew towards himself a sheet of writing paper. On it was embossed the address of the Brompton Square house that, so many years ago now, he had reluctantly sold to a journalist on some rag or other. He picked up his pen, put a line through the address, and below added the date. He began to write:

My dear Marilyn

I have felt for a long time that I must write you this letter but I do not really know how to do so. I have produced so many versions of it over the past weeks, and all have ended up in the waste-paper basket. It is partly a confession of the terrible wrong that I did to you and partly a plea to you to find it in your heart to forgive me.

You will no doubt be astonished to hear that it was I who, in a moment of madness, shopped your friend Mehmet to the

immigration people. When I did so, I had genuinely duped myself
into thinking that that was what was best for you. You were the
person to whom I felt closest in an increasingly lonely life, and I
did not want that man to go on exploiting you. But now I realize
that my motives were far more complex. I was – yes, I see it now,
I have to acknowledge it – jealous of him because you gave him so
much and gave me so little. It was when Audrey drove me past
the house where he lived that the idea first came to me. At the
time, it seemed so right. Now it seems so horribly wrong.

On the few occasions when we now meet, I can see how desperately unhappy you are. It is like a replay of the ghastly aftermath
of the accident. And this time you do not have Audrey at hand to
console you, since I have been the cause of the terrible rift
between you. I only wish that I could offer some consolation. Perhaps this letter will help. I so much hope so. Perhaps it will also
help me, relieving me of a devastating burden of guilt. A selfish
thought but then, as you will know by now, I am a selfish man . . .

At that point he broke off. He stared down at what he had
written, his face contorted like a child's on the verge of crying.
He could not cope with this insatiable longing and this unre-
lenting hatred of himself. But something, an even stronger
hatred of Mehmet or a ferocious pride or perhaps both of them
together, prevented him from going on with his confession. He
snatched at the sheet and began to tear it up.

As he turned his head sharply to jettison the fragments of
paper into the waste-paper basket beside him, he felt an ago-
nising pain down his neck and then across his right shoulder
and into his arm.

Then the pain was battering, frenzied blow on blow, in his
chest.

Chapter XXIII

On her way back from Laurence's funeral, Marilyn called in at the Patels to see how their son, whom they called Johnny, was getting on. The previous year he had contracted malaria when the family had returned to India for a holiday, and now he still suffered episodes of fever.

His eyes had bruise-like shadows under them as he stared up at her with what struck her as fatalistic resignation. He was shivering uncontrollably and she could see that his pyjama jacket and the pillowcase behind him were both damp with sweat. A sweetish odour, as of honey, hung around him. Her diabetic patients often smelled the same.

She put a hand to his forehead. The skin seemed strangely loose, as though it had been crumpled, on someone so young. 'Are you feeling better today?'

He nodded without conviction.

'He won't eat,' his mother said. 'I've tried everything, all his favourite dishes.'

'Never mind. Just get him to drink lots of juice or water. The appetite will return.'

Marilyn picked up the game of Nintendo lying on the bed, beside a stamp album. If she had ever known that Audrey had given the album to him, she had forgotten. 'What about this?'

'He doesn't seem to be interested.' Mrs Patel's upper lip trembled. 'I am at my wit's end,' she added and abruptly turned away.

Outside the room, Marilyn said: 'If the temperature hasn't fallen tomorrow, I think he'd better go back to the hospital.'

'But he hates leaving home. You know that.' She spoke with despairing anger.

'It probably won't be necessary. I expect that the fever will just burn itself out, as it's done before. This is the one of the few malaria cases I've ever had to treat, but the usual thing is that, over the years, the attacks come less and less often. The body builds up a defence, you see. Then eventually the fever burns itself out.'

Mrs Patel was staring at her in bewilderment. She might have been talking gibberish.

On the doorstep, next to the entrance to the shop, Mrs Patel asked: 'How is Miss Carter getting on?'

'Oh, fine. I haven't seen her for a while, I've been so busy,' Marilyn lied. She shrank from speaking of the funeral, at which Mervyn had given a skilful address, by turns laudatory and humorous, and at which she and Audrey had hardly spoken to each other. On leaving the subsequent reception at the college, the two women had then gone their separate ways, without even a goodbye. 'But, yes, I think all's going well with her.'

'We miss her, all of us miss her. She's such a lovely lady.'

As always now when she returned to the house, Marilyn was at once repelled by its silence and emptiness. She might have been some stranger, house agent's particulars in hand, entering to view premises long unoccupied. Audrey no longer called up from the stairs 'Is that you, Marilyn?' That had always vaguely irritated her – after all, who else could it be? – but now its absence only added to her feeling of eerie dislocation.

She peered into the letter box, wondering if the second post might not have brought something from him. She envisaged it: an airmail envelope, torn at one edge, addressed to her in his childish scrawl, with a number of large, garish stamps plastered all over it. But there was nothing there but a flier about pizza delivery from a newly opened restaurant, a reminder (FINAL NOTICE) about an unpaid electricity bill, and a card from Vicky, who was on holiday for a week with her husband and brood of daughters in Cornwall.

How untidy everything had become! I'm a slut, she told herself, as she gathered up a used coffee cup from the previous evening and a full waste-paper basket from the previous day, preparatory to taking them downstairs. In the past, the kitchen table would already have been laid for supper – for herself and Audrey if Mehmet were not coming, for herself alone if he were. This evening, she opened the door to Audrey's room, as she often now did, and smelled the damp. Basement rooms often smelled like that, if no one lived in them and the central heating was off. Perhaps she should switch it on, extravagant though that would be. Now that she had that overdraft because of those iniquitously high fees paid out to the lawyers, and Audrey was no longer sharing the expenses of the household, she had to be careful.

'I think it better if I move out,' Audrey had said, after more than a week had passed during which they had barely spoken to each other.

'Oh, I don't think that necessary. What's done can't be undone.'

'Yes. Exactly. That's why I think I'd better move out.'

'If you really want that.'

'Yes. Yes, I do.'

Soon after that Audrey had moved into what Laurence called 'a hateful little cubby hole in darkest Fulham.' She had also moved from the Oxfam shop in Kensington to one nearer the cubbyhole. 'How is she?' Marilyn had asked Laurence on what was to prove her last visit to him, two days before his death, and he had replied 'Oh, she's aged, she's aged. But haven't we all?' Marilyn knew that she herself had certainly aged. She had acquired a slight stoop, the backs of her hands were wrinkled, and there was now a faint cobweb of lines under eyes that had become both larger and lustreless.

She took two eggs out of the fridge, preparatory to making an omelette. Audrey's omelettes had always been so feathery. Somehow she herself could never acquire the knack. But the idea of eating nauseated her and she left the eggs lying out on the kitchen table. 'What's the matter with you?' Jack had said to her only the day before. 'You've got so thin. Would you like me to check things out?' 'No, thank you, Jack. I'm perfectly all right. I want to lose weight. I'm on a diet.' He shook his head and gave her a rueful smile. He did not believe her. No doubt he had heard gossip about Mehmet's disappearance.

As she stared ruefully down into the sink, with its unwashed pans, cheese-grater and cafetière, the thought suddenly came to her: She would go and see Meg. It was far too long since she had done so; and, though they never spoke of Mehmet other than to ask each other if they had had any news from him and to speculate about what he might be doing, Marilyn now inexplicably found in her presence the same kind of consolation that she had once found in Audrey's. Perhaps, in each case, the consolation of goodness? Except that, in the end, Audrey's goodness had turned to wickedness.

In the almost empty Underground carriage, she read the slogan opposite 'It's good to talk.' But she could not talk, not even to the people – Carmen, Vicky, Jack, Laurence – who clearly wanted to talk to her, in an attempt to rouse someone once so vivacious from her dull, drooping apathy. *Eventually it will burn itself out.* Would this infection that she had contracted from an unexpected patient in her surgery late one autumn evening just a little short of a year ago ever burn itself out? In despair, she often thought: 'No, I have to live with it and die with it.'

Lost in reverie she almost missed her stop. She rushed to the doors and just managed to slip through them as they were closing. Well, there's some advantage in getting so thin, she thought.

Outside the station she decided to buy Meg some flowers. She was about to opt for some chrysanthemums, but then she thought, remembering the flowers at Ed's and Carol's and now Laurence's funeral, no, chrysanthemums smell of death, and opted for white roses. Although she kept reminding herself that she must economize, it was not in her nature to do so and she spent far too much on far too many of the pinched, waxen blooms.

It was she who had persuaded this charity to take in Meg even though, as the director had pointed out, 'Dalston is really far outside our catchment area.' Two of her patients were also resident there, and one had recently died there. The building was a square, purpose-built, red-brick one, set back from the squat, semi-detached houses, each wearing a gable like a witch's hat, on either side of it. Once the home had occupied a large Edwardian house left to the charity by a benefactor, but it had been far too uneconomic to run and had eventually been sold for conversion into luxury flats. The new building consisted of three floors of tiny bed-sitting rooms, each with its even tinier bathroom and lavatory. The doors to the rooms were wide, giving wheelchair access, and everywhere there were the latest gadgets to help the disabled. Meg would often say wistfully that she missed her flat, and then, visibly shaking off that regret, would remark on how well they looked after her, how much easier it was to move around, and how happily she got on with the other inhabitants.

'Oh, you're in bed!'

'Yes, I began the day feeling rather ropey. It's this weather, I shouldn't wonder. There was a real nip in the air when I opened the lav window, and you can feel the damp even here in this room. I ought to make more of an effort, but there's not the same reason to do so, now that all my needs are being looked after. It's not like it was in the flat.'

Marilyn was holding out the roses.

'Are those for me?'

'Of course.'

'I've never received a bunch as large as that in my whole life. Oh, you are kind.'

'I'll put them in water in the washbasin, shall I? I'll put them in a vase for you before I go.'

'Oh, Micky can do that.' Marilyn did not know if Micky was a man or a woman.

Having deposited the flowers, Marilyn sat down in the wheelchair by the bed. That was the most comfortable place in the room, apart from the armchair. She had always, she could not have said why, been reluctant to take the armchair, even when Meg was, as now, lying in bed. Somehow, she thought of that chair as Meg's, so that to sit in it was, in some subtle way, to usurp it.

'Yes, it's been one of my bad days,' Meg said. 'But in general, you know I really believe I am about to have another of those remission things. My speaking is so much better, everyone tells me that, and it's a long time since I've had that puppet-on-a-string feeling. My eyes are better too – none of that blurring, so that I have no problem with my *Mail*.'

Would she herself ever have a remission, Marilyn was thinking, as she said: 'Oh, but that's wonderful, wonderful.'

'Maybe one day soon I'll be able to move back into a flat of my own.'

'Yes, let's hope so.'

'Oh, but I'm forgetting! One thing else has really cheered me. Can you believe it? At last!' With difficulty she raised a leaden arm and pointed. 'Take a look over there!'

Marilyn looked. On the mantelpiece, between a pale-blue teddy bear and a cut-glass ashtray, a picture postcard had been propped. Without looking at it, Marilyn knew at once from whom it had come.

'Take a look at it!'

Reluctantly, Marilyn got out of the chair and walked across.

She looked first at the picture, which showed the yawning entrance to a tomb – 'Luxor, Valley of the Queens' she read – against a garish orange sunset. Then she turned the card over to look at the postmark. She assumed that the postmark would be Egypt, but it was Dubai. Dubai? What on earth was he doing in Dubai?

The card had been forwarded, presumably by Mr Bagley, from the Dalston block of flats. The message was scrawled in his usual childish capital letters.

HI! GREETINGS TO MAMMA FROM HER SUN. HOPE ALL WELL. ALL FINE WITH ME. LOVE. MEHMET.

'There's no address,' Marilyn said, the card still in her hand. She looked at it again. There was a terrible pathos about that SUN. Brooding on it later on the train home, the words had come unbidden into her mind *O sole mio* . . . 'He doesn't say what he's doing. Or why he's in Dubai or why he was in Egypt. Nothing.'

'Well, at least he's written,' Meg said, thinking, as she so often did, of Eric, who never wrote. 'And he says he's fine.'

Marilyn replaced the card, taking a long time, tongue between teeth, to balance it just right between the pale-blue teddy bear and the vase.

'Haven't you heard from him too?' Meg asked.

'No.'

'Well, I expect you will. Posts are so bad from those countries. Where is this Dubai? Do you think that he has any friends there?'

'Probably. Yes. Oh, yes.'